TO CHINA

WITH LOVE

THE CASE OF THE SYMPATHIC MARTYR

BY MICHAEL CARRIER

"Problem solving Sugar Island style—
smart, decisive, resolute"

A number of very wonderful people helped me prepare this book for publication. Each of them contributed significantly.

Thank you Evie, Charity, Andy, Steve, George, Gay, John, EmaLee, and all the members of Grand Valley Artists, Grand Rapids, MI.

TO CHINA

WITH LOVE

THE CASE OF THE SYMPATHIC MARTYR

BY

MICHAEL CARRIER

GREENWICH VILLAGE INK

An imprint of Alistair Rapids Publishing
Grand Rapids, MI

TO CHINA WITH LOVE

Published 2022 by Greenwich Village Ink, an imprint of Alistair Rapids Publishing, Grand Rapids, MI.

Visit the *JACK* website at http:/www.greenwichvillageink.com

For upcoming books by the same author visit www.greenwichvillageink.com.

Author can be emailed at mike.jon.carrier@gmail.com.

ISBN: 978-1-936092-12-3 (trade pbk)
Printed in the United States of America

Library of Congress Cataloging-in-Publication Data

Carrier, Michael.
JACK and the New York Death Mask / by Michael Carrier. 1st ed.
ISBN: 978-1-936092-12-3 (trade pbk. : alk. paper)
1. Political Intrigue 2. Novel 3.Assassination 4. Plot 5. New York.

What people are saying about earlier Jack Handler books

"Just finished 'Murder on Sugar Island' and can't wait to get the next in the series! Unfortunately, with the holidays it took me awhile to get to reading. But, l must say, the first time l sat down with it l read over half the book!! Love Jack and Kate, and of course Red and Buddy! Hope Santa brings me several more! Please don't stop writing!!! Happy Holidays!" —Susan M

"I want to let you know that I really enjoyed your book 'Murder on Sugar Island.' So much so that I have just received 'Superior Peril' and 'Superior Intrigue' in today's mail. I read 'Murder on Sugar Island' in 4 days. I enjoy the shorter chapters, allowing me to pick up and put the book down for short, quick reads in between chores. I'm anxious to start the next one. Thanks so much for introducing me to Jack, Kate and Red." —Patti from Escanaba

"I work midnights. I recently started 'Murder on Sugar Island.' ... Twenty four chapters in and I didn't want to put it down to sleep. ... Enjoying it very much. You have a remarkable knack for writing." —Marla S

"Well, my husband took my book before I could even read it! He loved it! I just started it and also love it. He just started book two and wants to know how to get the rest! Thank you so much for taking the time to talk to us!!" — Anastasia K

"My wife and I met you in Valparaiso, IN., at the Shipshewana on the Road event. I purchased 'Murder on Sugar Island' for her and you signed it. However, I read it before she had a chance and have since purchased 'Superior Peril' from Amazon. … I'm not a reader but I can't put it down!!!!" —Jake K

"I stumbled upon your book at the Frankenmuth Shipshewana vendor show. I just had the opportunity to read it, and absolutely loved it. Could not put it down. … I will be looking for more of your books to read." —Joan T

Top Shelf Murder Mystery—Riveting. Being a Murder-Mystery "JUNKIE" this book is definitely a keeper … can't put it down … read it again type of book … and it is very precise to the lifestyles in Upper Michigan. Very well researched. I am a resident of this area. His attention to detail is great. I have to rate this book in the same class or better than authors Michael Connelly, James Patterson, and Steve Hamilton. — Shelldrakeshores

Move over, Patterson, I now have a new favorite author. Jack Handler and his daughter make a great tag team, great intrigue, and diversions. I have a cabin on Sugar Island and enjoyed the references to the locations. I met the author at Joey's (the real live Joey) coffee shop up on the hill, great writer, good stuff. I don't usually finish a book in the course of a week, but read this one in two sittings so it definitely had my attention. I am looking forward to the next installment. Bravo. — Northland Press

I enjoyed this book very much. It was very entertaining, and the story unfolded in a believable manner. Jack Handler is a like-able character. But you would not like to be on his wrong side. Handler made that very clear in *Jack and the New York Death Mask*. This book (Murder on Sugar Island) was the first book in the Getting to Know Jack series that I read. After I read *Death Mask*, I discovered just how tough Jack Handler really was." —

Deborah M

I thoroughly enjoyed this book. I could not turn the pages fast enough. I am not sure it was plausible but I love the characters. I highly recommend this book and look forward to reading more by Michael Carrier. — Amazon Reader

An intense thrill ride!! — Mario

Michael Carrier has knocked it out of the park. — John

Left on the edge of my seat after the last book, I could not wait for the next chapter to unfold and Michael Carrier did not disappoint! I truly feel I know his characters better with each novel and I especially like the can-do/will-do attitude of Jack. Keep up the fine work, Michael, and may your pen never run dry! — SW

The Handlers are at it again, with the action starting on Sugar Island, I am really starting to enjoy the way the father/daughter and now Red are working through the mind of Michael Carrier. The entire family, plus a few more are becoming the reason for the new sheriff's increased body count and antacid intake. The twists and turns we have come to expect are all there and then some. I'm looking for the next installment already. — Northland Press

Finally, there is a new author who will challenge the likes of Michael Connelly and David Baldacci. — Island Books

If you like James Patterson and Michael Connelly, you'll love Michael Carrier. Carrier has proven that he can hang with the best of them. It has all of the great, edge-of-your-seat action and suspense that you'd expect in a good thriller, and it kept me guessing to the very end. Fantastic read with an awesome detective duo—I couldn't put it down! — Katie

Don't read Carrier at the beach or you are sure to get sunburned. I did. I loved the characters. It was so descriptive you feel like you know everyone. Lots of action—always something happening. I love the surprise twists. All my friends are reading it now because I wouldn't talk to them until I finished it so they knew it was good. Carrier is my new favorite author! — Sue

Thoroughly enjoyed this read—kept me turning page after page! Good character development and captivating plot. Had theories but couldn't quite solve the mystery without reading to the end. Highly recommended for readers of all ages. — Terry

Here are the Amazon links to all my Jack Handler books:

Jack and the New York Death Mask: http://amzn.to/MVpAEd

Murder on Sugar Island: http://amzn.to/1u66DBG

Superior Peril: http://amzn.to/LAQnEU

Superior Intrigue: http://amzn.to/1jvjNSi

Sugar Island Girl Missing in Paris: http://amzn.to/1g5c66e

Wealthy Street Murders: http://amzn.to/1mb6NQy

Murders in Strangmoor Bog: http://amzn.to/1osAjJ8

Ghosts of Cherry Street: http://amzn.to/1PvWfJd

Assault on Sugar Island: http://amzn.to/2n3vcyL

Dogfight: http://amzn.to/2F7OkoM

Murder at Whitefish Point: http://amzn.to/2CxlAmC

Superior Shoal: https://amzn.to/2pbM89v

From Deadwood to Deep State: https://amzn.to/330eElx

Sault: https://amzn.to/3gq21Dj

To China with Love:

To China with Love

Chapter 1 —

O utside, and directly to the right of the entry door to the diver's lock-out chamber (AKA the *wet room*), hung a waterproof monitor. And on it Henry, Jack's good friend and sizable right-hand man, impatiently watched Jack make his way toward the tether cable connection point via video captured by a fixed-angle video camera located near the nose of the mini-sub. But, just like the case earlier with Agent One, as Jack approached the point of attachment, his image fell out of range of the camera, and so his activity disappeared from the monitor.

The "point of attachment" refers to the place at which a sinking South Korean fishing boat had been cabled to the mini-sub Jack and his SEAL team were using for their covert mission. The UOES3 Button 5.60 mini-sub selected for this operation was, at that time, headed against its will toward the bottom of the Yellow Sea under the tow of the ill-fated fishing boat.

Less than an hour earlier, one of the SEALs on board with Jack had attached a cable from the South Korean vessel so that the mini-sub could be secretly pulled out of the vicinity of the communist neighbor to the north. Those responsible for planning the mission thought it best if the mini-sub refrained from running any unnecessary mechanical equipment that might be detected by North Korean or Chinese patrols.

Unfortunately, even though they were now well south of the 38th parallel, a tenacious North Korean patrol boat had followed them across that imaginary line and sent the fishing boat toward the bottom by ramming it.

Henry took another look at his watch, and then anxiously addressed Agent Two.

"I'm getting impatient here," he said. "Jack's been outta range for too long. I'm gonna need some gear. Can you fix me up? And in a hurry? I'm concerned about Jack!"

"Yes, I can," Agent Two said. "But you know what Jack said as well as I do. He told the both of us that if anything happened to him while he was out there, we should give it thirty minutes, no more, and then cut him loose. By that time he'd figured we would be at the bottom, and that would take all the tension off the tether. So, if we were still alive at that point, we should be able to simply unhitch the cable. And then, if at all possible, just get the hell out of the area as fast as we could. You heard him too. And, he also demanded that if, for any reason, someone had to go back out, it should be a SEAL, not you. He was very adamant about that. He gave you strict orders not to leave this sub. And he was, and still is, the boss. I think it's very clear that it is my job to handle this from here. Not yours—especially if it means venturing outside this SDV."

By SDV, Agent Two was making reference to SEAL Delivery Vehicle, which was the technical term designating the mini-sub that they were using for this mission.

Agent Two had also watched Jack disappear, but from a different screen.

"Listen to me!" Henry growled. "Jack said that I should be the one to pull him back in, if something goes wrong. So, just shut the hell up and help me get ready."

"Have you ever done anything like this before?" the agent asked.

"Of course!" Henry barked at him. "I've dived a lot. So don't waste any more of my time. Get that shit ready for me! And do it now!"

Agent Two knew that Henry was lying about everything. He had heard Jack say that "under no circumstance should Henry ever leave the sub, and that if anyone, besides me, needs to go outside the sub, it ought to be a SEAL."

And Jack had even told Agent Two privately that Henry had never before even thought of donning diving equipment, and that Henry was totally lacking in the type of experience necessary to attempt such an undertaking.

Nevertheless, even though Agent Two was positive that Henry was lying, he knew that the big man was determined to do whatever it might take to save his friend. So, Agent Two accepted the reality of the situation and followed Henry's orders.

However, in Agent Two's mind, the decision to obey Henry's demand wasn't as consequential as it might have seemed on the surface. He just didn't think that any of them would survive to go back home no matter who went out. So, rather than succumb to having a physical confrontation with Henry, he simply proceeded to make ready for his passenger's possible excursion outside the submarine. That preparation included fitting Henry with some very sophisticated rebreather equipment, along with providing him a short verbal "refresher" on how to operate it.

After Agent Two activated the equipment to begin pumping the water out of the wet room, he set about double-checking all of Henry's equipment, particularly making sure the oxygen was functioning properly on the rebreather. As soon as he had finished, he opened the door to the now-empty chamber and directed Henry to step through it.

Before Agent Two could close the door behind him, Henry asked, "You'll fill it up and bring it to pressure?"

"Yup," Agent Two said as he closed the door and began pumping water into the wet room. It was only a long couple of minutes before it was full.

With the pressure in the little chamber now reaching that of the water outside the mini-sub, Henry wrote on the screen beside the door: "Let me know when I can open the hatch. Okay?"

"Yup," Agent Two wrote on the screen outside the door. He then muttered quietly to himself, "This bastard has no idea what he's about to walk into. He's gonna kill himself. But, what the hell. Roger told us before the mission that none of us are likely make it back alive anyway. That's just a simple fact."

The "Roger" Agent Two was alluding to was Secret Service Agent Roger Minsk, Jack's old friend and frequent liaison between Jack and former President Bob Fulbright.

Henry glanced at his watch, but was disappointed to discover that it had now stopped working. *I must have been too rough on it,* he muttered in his mind. *Or maybe it just doesn't like the pressure. Anyway, it's got to have been twenty-five minutes since Jack went out.*

"Am I good to go yet?" he entered on the screen.

"Pressure's up," Agent Two responded. "Check the hatch. Should open just fine. If not, keep at it. It soon will."

Henry adjusted his mask and opened the hatch. He looked around and found where Jack had tied the rope off.

Jack had done that so that they could use the rope to pull him back to safety should he be swept off the fast-sinking mini-sub. Or, so that another team member could use it to pull him back to the sub in the event of injury—incapacitating, or worse.

Sticking his head and shoulders through the opening, Henry quickly executed three firm tugs on the rope. While he and Jack had not beforehand firmly established the three-tug protocol with one another, Henry assumed that Jack would be responsive to that signal given they were both aware that it had been set up for an earlier SEAL dive.

However, Jack did not acknowledge Henry's attempt. He tried it again, but with the same result.

At that point Henry was growing justifiably concerned. So, he carefully eased his large frame further up through the hatch. Now he was standing on the top rung of the egress ladder. Using his shins braced against the frame of the mini-sub, Henry tried the tug signal once again. Still nothing.

Then, realizing that the extra dozen inches did not substantially improve his field of vision, Henry stepped down to the rung below so he could better balance himself. This time he began pulling back on the rope. At first it seemed solidly tied off. But then it appeared to free up a bit. It felt to him like he was dragging a sack of water-soaked flour through the water. But he kept pulling, and the rope continued to coil in his powerful hands.

As he pulled in on the rope, Henry noted that the top of the sunken fishing boat began to come into his view. The descent of the mini-sub then noticeably began to slow, and at the same time Henry noticed that the tension on the tether cable appeared to be loosening.

The pilot of the mini-sub also noticed the change, and so he cut the power and leveled the mini-sub out.

Looks like the fishing boat has reached the bottom! Henry muttered in his mind. *So much for 'Casey Jones' Locker.' Looks like we might not all die today after all. But somebody's got to disconnect that cable so we can get the hell outta here—perhaps it's gonna be my job.*

With his hopes slightly escalating, he ceased reeling in the rope and once again tried the three-tug signal. But disappointment quickly crept back when Jack did not respond. So, Henry repositioned his feet and began pulling on the rope again. This time, however, with their mini-sub virtually stopped in the water, he found that the drag on the rope had lessened considerably. Even so, he still was receiving no positive support for any optimism.

It was then, less than a minute later, the unimaginable happened.

As Henry reeled in the rope, he spotted an object at the end of it. He was in shock, but he kept pulling. After he had managed to pull the rope in another eight to ten feet he was beginning to make out what that object was—it appeared to be the faint outline of a limp human body.

Carefully he maintained the tension on the rope as he slowly stepped up again to the topmost rung to get a better look. And as he rebalanced himself, he focused his eyes on what was emerging at the end of the rope.

Initially, all he could see was what was obviously a human foot.

"Oh my God," he silently mumbled. "Jack's foot! My friend— what has happened to you?"

Most of the corpse was hidden from full view because it was getting hung up on the small railing on the deck of the mini-sub. Henry would periodically lessen the tension, and then try reeling it in again. But he wasn't having much success. At best he was now barely inching the lifeless body along, and then it suddenly slid past the railing and disappeared entirely. Fortunately, Henry had maintained his grip on the rope. And so, while it did slide out of sight, he was still able to stop its fall quite easily. Yet it still remained out of his field of vision.

When he began winding the rope in again, he was able to reel the body in only until it reached the railing. There it became severely hung up once more.

Henry was almost ready to venture outside the mini-sub further in order to achieve a better angle from which to pull, but he was stopped in his tracks when the most unexpected of events took place. It caught him by such surprise that he could barely believe what his eyes were telling him.

Chapter 2 —

While it was less than a week earlier that Jack and Henry for the first time ventured out into North Korean waters aboard the mini-sub, they would both have to acknowledge that actually the first surprise of this whole saga had its beginning a full four months earlier. That was when Henry first learned that his beloved aunt, Aunt Halona, now in her early seventies, wanted to defy the odds and relocate from the warm climate of Arizona, which was the family's historic home, to the harsh weather of Northern Michigan.

While caught totally off guard by her overture, Henry was nevertheless overjoyed at the prospect of having his aunt transplant herself closer to where he lived, so he suggested to her that she "go all the way" and consider moving directly onto Sugar Island. He was shocked when she immediately accepted the invitation, proudly announcing to all her friends and family on her social media platform that "My nephew has invited me to move to where he lives on Sugar Island. That's in Michigan's Upper Peninsula—where it gets very cold. And, I have excitedly accepted his offer."

Henry hurriedly huddled with Jack to discuss possibilities, and Jack offered to provide for her an efficiency apartment right there at the Handler resort. Jack was so pleased that Henry was going to have family nearby that he insisted the lease agreement stipulate "there shall be no charges so long as Halona chooses to reside at the Sugar Island Resort, and remains able to maintain independent living." Jack also made it clear that he would pick up the tab for all the aunt's utilities.

"Why in the world would you do such a thing?" Henry asked. "It's not your job to take care of my aunt. I never expected you to step up like this. And I am certainly not suggesting that you ought to."

Jack just smiled and changed the subject whenever Henry brought it up—and that happened several times. Finally, after a month, Henry just came to accept the favor and not bother to grill Jack further. It was about that same time that Kate finally had occasion to visit them on the island. Henry was quick to take the opportunity to ask her what she thought about his Aunt Halona living for free at the resort.

"Kate," Henry said to her, "I assume that you are aware of the arrangements your dad set up for my Aunt Halona. While it was my idea that she should move to Sugar Island, Jack is the one who insisted that he wanted to personally take care of her rent and utilities. I honestly never saw that coming. That is, I had not expected it. We all know how unpredictably generous your dad can be. Anyway, you do know all about that arrangement, don't you?"

The Kate Henry was talking to was Lt. Kate Handler, Jack's only child from his all-too-short marriage with Greek-American beauty Beth Handler. Soon after Baby Kate appeared on that Chicago scene, the most painful of imaginable tragedies struck the young Handler household—Beth was downed by a bullet intended for Jack.

Now that Kate had progressed to an age greater than that of her mother when she was so unceremoniously struck down, whenever she visited from New York Jack marveled at just how much like her beautiful mother Kate grew year by year. When Jack closed his eyes in Kate's presence he could envision Beth's chestnut-brown hair, with its natural red highlights. Her dark brown eyes, adorned as they were with thick dark lashes, accented her ivory skin tones.

She was five feet eight inches, slender, but very much in shape as she worked out regularly in her New York gym.

Kate's career was as a New York City homicide detective. While she did visit her father and his two foster boys on a frequent basis, the very nature of her position at the big city police department required her to be available virtually all the time. Even though she did not live at the Sugar Island resort, everyone knew that Jack loved his daughter very much, and that he discussed all major matters with her.

"Dad did run his plan past me before he presented it to you," Kate replied. "So, yes, I am aware of the way he set it up with you and your aunt."

"And, you have no problem with it?" Henry asked.

"That's right," Kate replied. "No problem. Not at all. In fact, I agreed with Dad about it, totally. I considered it to be a very good idea. We both thought it would be beneficial for you to have some family around. Everyone needs family. And, this lady, your Aunt Halona. Is that how you say it: *Ha-low-na?* Anyway, Dad saw just how much she meant to you. He called me up right after you told him about her, and he suggested that we invite her to live at the resort.

"And, as it turns out, he really likes the lady. He suggested that we provide a small apartment—one that would not require a lot of upkeep on her part. And, it was his suggestion that neither she nor you should be charged. I thought it was a great idea. What do you think about it? You're in agreement with us—right? You like having her around, I suspect."

"Yes, of course," Henry replied. "She's a great lady. A lot of fun, too. Her friends call her Babs. I really like her. I'm eager to have you two meet. I think you'll get as much of a kick out of her as I do. She's just that sort of woman. I have to admit that it's a little difficult for me to figure out why it is she would leave beautiful Arizona—the sunshine and all—and want to move into this deep freeze."

"Really?" Kate inquired. "I don't think it's that hard to figure out. Did I not hear the talk about her family—some members of her family, at least—hailing from the Marquette area? Right? She's got family roots in the Upper Peninsula. I'm pretty sure I've discussed that with Dad. He seemed to know something about the family history. Blood's a very big draw—especially when you get older. It's always helpful to get to know your people better. And Dad and I both figured that your Aunt Halona could add a fresh dimension to your life. We thought it would be good for you. And, what's good for you would be good for us. Don't you agree? I hope I explained our thinking to you in an acceptable way."

Henry was a genuine Native American. He had been a loyal friend to Jack's family for several years now. He was dark-skinned, with long black hair pulled back into a ponytail. He was powerfully built, with a deep, booming voice which was produced by his broad, 6'3" frame. Unlike Jack, during his years in prison Henry opted to adorn his muscular arms with several traditional tattoos. These included a large eagle and rose on his right bicep, and aces and eights on his left.

"Yeah," Henry said, maintaining a steady smile. "I get what you're saying. I figured that's how Jack was looking at it. But, you're an important part of this whole thing. I wanted to make sure you were aware of what he was doing. And in agreement with it as well. You do know that not only is he not charging her rent but that he's picking up the bill for her utilities, too? You're good with all that as well?"

"Yes, of course," Kate replied. "Like I said, Dad went over everything with me before he presented the offer to you. So, I'm not at all surprised."

Henry was greatly relieved to see that Kate was totally good with the promises Jack had made to him with regard to providing housing and otherwise seeing to the proper care of his little Aunt Halona.

But, it was some time after this discussion with Kate that Henry's whole relationship with his aunt took a major turn into the unknown.

For the next few months after his discussion with Kate, Henry spent virtually all of his free time looking after his aunt—helping her get settled at Jack's resort, familiarizing her with nearby Native American organizations, and introducing her to potential new friends.

During the first few weeks after Henry's Aunt Halona moved into the Handler resort, Jack made every effort to release Henry from all but his most essential of responsibilities around the facility.

"How's it going?" Jack would say to his friend. "I'm referring to your aunt. Aunt Ha-lo-na. Did I pronounce that right? Is that how you say it? Emphasis on the second syllable? Am I saying it right?"

"That's how she says it," Henry replied. "Means wealth, or fortune. As I understand it."

Henry then laughed out loud, "But nothing could be much further from the truth, I'm afraid. Pretty sure she's a long way from rich."

"She makes up for that in other ways," Jack said. "Right? Isn't she just about the sweetest person you've ever met? Can't really say that I know her yet, but that's how she strikes me—just a very nice person. Makes we wonder: are you positive that she is related to you?"

"Yeah, man," Henry agreed with a snicker. "I know what you're getting at. How could that be? Right? But, you hit that nail on the head. Aunt Halona couldn't be any nicer."

Jack was very pleased to see how Henry felt about his *new* family member. He was also glad that he was able to contribute to his friend's delight by making a unit at his resort available to her.

But it was only a short time later then, that Henry's life became very complicated—and Jack's even more so.

Chapter 3 —

O n the Saturday before his unplanned trip to North Korea, Jack received an equally unexpected visit from two old friends from the East Coast—former President Bob Fulbright and Roger Minsk, Head of the Secret Service Detail assigned to protect Allison Fulbright, Bob's estranged wife.

In the hours before his guests arrived, Jack's day was moving along in a manner quite similar to that of most weekend mornings.

He had gotten up early in order to perform his regular Saturday morning ritual: a large frying pan filled with salty bacon, a second frying pan with a full dozen moist, fried-in-butter scrambled eggs, and four full stacks of buttermilk pancakes.

He would always start out the Saturday breakfast ritual by preparing the pancakes, because those he could cover with aluminum foil and slide into the oven on low to keep them soft and warm.

Next, he peeled off a pound and a half of thick bacon slices, and spread them out in an oversized frying pan on low heat. Once about one-third of the pancakes were in the oven, but before he put the eggs on the heat, he would take Buddy, the boys' Golden Retriever which the Handlers had adopted for Red as a puppy from a shelter in Canada, upstairs to wake up the boys.

They were, of course, already awake—the aroma of breakfast cooking had already put an end to their slumber.

"Five minutes," Jack commanded. "Breakfast in five. You can shower after you eat."

Every other morning, except for Saturdays, breakfasts consisted of cooked Quaker Old Fashioned Oatmeal. And that was fine with the boys. But, Saturdays were special. Every other day would start out with a healthy meal. Saturdays were different. It smelled special. And it tasted special. The boys, and Jack, loved Saturday mornings. And so did Buddy, because Jack would always pour just a little of the bacon grease into Buddy's breakfast. That's why Buddy loved Saturdays too.

After he had served notice on the boys, he went back to the kitchen to finish the process. He flipped the last of the pancakes and stacked them on the spatula, opened the oven, lifted the foil, and slid them off on the shortest stack.

He would then add a third of a cup of whole milk to the well-beaten one dozen eggs, and thoroughly stir the milk into the mixture. Next he would slice off a light tablespoon of butter and melt it in a non-stick frying pan. Then, making sure to catch it before the butter could brown, he'd pour the eggs into the pan and turn the gas burner down to a medium-low flame.

Using a different spatula, he frequently separated the eggs on the bottom and brought them to the top. "Nothing much worse than burned scrambled eggs," he often told himself. "At least, nothing *smells* much worse than poorly prepared eggs."

While the protein was cooking, he flipped the bacon over in the pan and checked to see if it was about done. He'd turn the flame up if he felt it necessary, and cover it with a lid. Then he would attend to the scrambling eggs again. Perhaps turning the flame under them down another notch.

As soon as the bacon began to curl up and appear done, he would roll out a triple-thickness of paper towels on a cookie sheet, and lay out the strips of perfectly-fried bacon as straight as possible, and soak up the excess grease with another pad of paper towel applied from the top. He would then tear off a strip of aluminum foil and cover the bacon, and slide the cookie sheet onto the oven rack below the pancakes—turning the heat down a notch as soon as he closed the door. *Good to keep it warm*, he was thinking, *but not good to burn the house down to do it.*

Buddy, who was watching the whole ceremony with a very moist tongue, would suddenly sit up. He would hear the two boys bounding down the steps and heading toward the breakfast table. After a brief stop at the sink to wash their hands, they'd slide their legs under the table and sit down.

Jack would then pop open the oven and remove the four stacks of pancakes and the cookie sheet with the perfectly pre-pared bacon. And then, in the middle of the table, he'd set the deep frying pan with the beautifully prepared, fluffy scrambled eggs—not a single sign of brown or black attaching itself to them.

By then, Buddy would be sitting at attention in the corner.

However, this Saturday was not destined to be like any other Saturday. Just as they had begun to eat, there was a firm knock on the door, followed by the ringing of the doorbell. Jack looked at his watch, and then at the boys. "Go ahead and get started," he told them. "I'll check and see what this is all about."

Jack unclipped his belt holster and removed his Glock 10mm. He left the holster in place, and slid his gun under his belt in the small of his back. As he approached the door he took a quick look at the monitor beside it. A doorbell camera provided him with a wide-angle view of approaching visitors. "What the hell!" he snarled out loud as he quickly unlocked and opened the door.

"Bob! Roger!" Jack said in a tone of unfettered shock. "What the hell is this all about? And so damn early on a Saturday morning. What's up? How early was reveille this morning to get you boys clear up here at this crazy hour?"

Chapter 4 —

D on't know what you're talking about. We were just driving past your house," former President Bob Fulbright quipped. "And Roger caught the drift of that bacon. We couldn't resist it."

"No," Jack said, still in shock. "It's more like you got a body that you need to bury. Right? Or, more like a body that you need me to bury for you. So, spill it. What's going on?"

"Besides the bacon?" Bob asked. "Well, I just had some questions I wanted to run past you, and Roger thought it might be a good idea to take a spin out here and look you in the eye when I do it."

Jack immediately surmised that Bob's use of the first-person pronouns suggested a matter of extreme urgency, spiced with a full tablespoon of something like vinegar.

"Right," Jack said in feigned agreement. "Where'd you guys come from? I didn't hear a chopper landing. You must have driven. Right? Looks like you have a whole entourage out there in my driveway."

"Just us," Bob said. "I didn't bring Allison on this trip. So, it's just the two of us. And, of course, a few Secret Service agents. But they don't mind entertaining themselves. It's their job."

Jack removed a remote from a table by the entry door and triggered "Camera #8," which was the front parking lot camera.

He checked it out carefully and said, "I count three cars, and it looks like probably at least six agents. Do you want to invite them in for breakfast? This morning we're serving pancakes, with bacon and eggs. And I can put a few more on."

"Uncle Bob," Robby blurted out as the three men walked through the breakfast area. His mouth was full of pancakes. "And Uncle Roger. Uncle Jack didn't tell us you were coming. Sit down and have some pancakes with us. We've got plenty. And they're pretty good. Uncle Jack makes the *best* pancakes."

"Hello, boys," Bob said through a broad but sincere smile as he fingered out a select strip of perfectly fried bacon.

"Jack," Bob continued. "Did you notice that your boys did not offer us any eggs? Or bacon? They're willing to share the pancakes, but not the scrambled eggs or the bacon.

"What's the deal here? Guys. You wanting to keep those eggs all to yourselves?"

Red smiled and looked over at Robby.

The two boys had never met one another before Jack entered their lives. Red met Jack when the young man encountered him after Kate had inherited the resort on Sugar Island.

Red was on the run from abusive foster care at the time, and was living in a hut in the woods with his first dog, also a Golden Retriever named Buddy.

Prior to the murder of the resort's previous owner, each night Red would clean out the boats for the resort, and that owner would leave food for Red and his dog.

As it turned out, that former owner just happened to have been Jack's late wife's uncle. So, when the Handlers inherited the resort, they also inherited a fourteen-year-old redheaded boy who seemed to go right along with it.

Robby did not come into the picture until after Red had moved into the resort and became Jack's foster child.

"Uncle Bob," Robby said. "The eggs are all gone, almost, anyway. But we have plenty of pancakes left. And bacon. There is some bacon left, too. If you really want eggs, I'm sure Uncle Jack will make some more. Right, Uncle Jack?"

Jack smiled at Robby but did not respond.

"These fellows are getting bigger every time I see them," Bob said as he messed up Robby's hair. "You must be feeding them too good. We don't need eggs, but I'll take another piece of this bacon. I don't think these two hooligans need it.

"Hey, fellows," Bob continued. "Thanks for the offer. But we had breakfast already. At the airport. But I'm sure Roger here would like to get a cup of Jack's pure black tar java. Got any of that cookin'?"

"Yeah," Jack said. He had already poured out three full cups of his coffee before Bob had even asked. "I've got plenty of coffee. And the boys won't fight you over that.

"Here you go," he said as he set three cups down on a kitchen cupboard near where they were standing. "Now, do you feel like telling me what's on your mind?"

"So," Bob said to Red and Robby, "boys, tell me, which one of you did Kate teach to cook?"

Both Red and Robby smiled and simultaneously pointed at Jack.

"Jack," Bob said. "You never told me about this talent. I never knew you could cook. You shouldn't be keeping secrets like that from us. Roger. Did you know that our mate here could cook like this? That's the sort of info that we need to note—national security, you know."

"Yeah," Roger said as he took a gulp on his coffee. "But I thought that I should be sharing that sort of information only on a need-to-know basis. Pretty sure it's quasi-classified."

"Jack, my friend," Bob said. "Roger told me about your special office, the one you built down in your basement. Don't think I've ever seen it. Suppose you could give me the grand tour of that? Roger says that it's pretty damn cool. I'm thinking about building one like that in my basement. Anything to protect me from the old lady, you know. She keeps showing up at the most inopportune times. I need a secret office like yours."

The "old lady" Bob Fulbright was referring to was his estranged wife, the infamous Allison Fulbright—AKA, Jack's nemesis, and Roger's other boss.

Jack had read the situation perfectly. He knew that Bob and Roger were at his door early on a Saturday morning only because something very important was on their mind. And that "something" was the reason they were there unannounced and seeking a secret meeting.

"Boys," Jack said to Red and Robby. "I want to show Bob and Roger my office. When you fellows are finished eating, rinse your dishes off and stick them in the dishwasher. Feed Buddy. And drizzle a little of this bacon grease over his food. Then take him out and give him a chance to run it off. And, then, after that, what do you boys have in mind? Any plans?"

Red looked over at Robby and raised his eyebrows.

"Yeah, Uncle Jack," Robby said. "We thought we would run over and visit Henry's aunt. He always sees her in the mornings, and he doesn't think that he can make it today. He told us yester-day."

"Okay," Jack said. "See you by lunch time?"

"Sure," Robby said. "Is it alright if we drive the white Tahoe? Henry said he'd put some supplies in the Tahoe. For his aunt."

"Yeah," Jack said. "I suppose. It's got gas, so it's good to go."

"Did I hear that right?" Bob said. "How old are these boys, anyway? Fourteen? I think they're fourteen. They got driver's licenses?"

"Bob, my friend," Jack said with a smile. "This is Sugar Island. You're not in Manhattan or DC—you're at my house on Sugar Island. When you got off that ferry, you left all those rules and regulations in your rearview mirror. Besides, either one of these boys is a better driver than any of us are. So don't you worry about it."

"See what I told you, Bob," Roger said as the three of them headed down the steps to Jack's secret inner sanctum. "Laws don't mean much on Sugar Island. But, he's got a point. I've heard stories about those boys, and their driving prowess. Pretty impressive, I'd say."

Jack did not respond to the comment.

Both Bob and Roger could be heard chuckling until they disappeared behind a heavy steel, soundproofed door on the lower level. Red looked over at Robby and flashed a dry smile. The boys knew that they were being toyed with. But they didn't care—after all, they were going to have the opportunity to run around in a four-wheel-drive Tahoe with mud tires. *What could be better?* they were thinking.

"This is pretty good coffee, Jack," Roger said. "Suppose you could put on another pot down here? What we need to discuss might take a while, and we both got off to a very early start."

"You bet," Jack said as he turned on the tap. He didn't say another word until black coffee was dripping from the brewing basket into the pot.

"Okay," he said, turning to face his two friends. Both Bob and Roger were seated on a large charcoal leather couch. He then joined the assembly by sitting across from them in a matching leather chair.

The large basement lounge was tastefully put together with wide, slate-colored wooden slats on the floor. To add the element of comfort Jack had covered the area where they sat with a hefty rug constructed of contrasting thick white and gray fibers.

In the center of the sitting area he'd placed a steel and glass coffee table.

On the walls of the lounge he had hung several huge photographs depicting the wildlife to be found on Sugar Island. These included professionally shot images of a black bear with cubs, several deer, a bull moose and even a timber wolf. Jack was not about to ignore the fishermen among his friends and neighbors, so he included a triptych of a scene shot out in the Great Lakes. It depicted Henry bringing in a 150-pound lake sturgeon. Red was actually the photographer who shot this treasured three-piece in Kodachrome.

Throughout the entire lounge were filled bookcases and displays of various pieces of Jack's personal memorabilia. Out of sight, but secretly accessible from this large room, were Jack's power generator, emergency oxygen supply, and a huge walk-in safe containing a plethora of his specialized collection of guns and ammo. Of course, all was protected by a sophisticated security alarm system.

"Time for you boys to lay it out. Say exactly what's on your mind," Jack said to them, focusing on their eyes through a resolute stare of his own.

But no one was smiling anymore.

"As you've already guessed, I'm sure," Bob said, "We've got a problem. A large problem. Much more serious than just disposing of a body, I'm afraid. And we wanted to run some ideas past you and see what you think about them."

Jack feigned a smile and said, "Are you sure I poured you the appropriate beverage for this conversation? I do have some very nice twenty-year-old *Pappy Van Winkle's Family Reserve Kentucky Straight Bourbon Whiskey*. Would that suit the situation better?"

"I know you do," Bob chuckled. "I'm the guy who bought it for you. Right? I gave you two or three bottles of it for Christmas. A few years ago now. I'm shocked you've still got any of it left."

"I've got two left—unopened," Jack said. "And probably half of another."

"How was it? Was it good?" Bob asked.

"It was great. As good as it gets. Henry and I broke it open this past fall, after he rescued the boys in Lake Huron."

"That's what I wanted to hear," Bob said. "Glad you enjoyed it. But, I think some of this coffee is perfect for what I've got to say today—at least for right now. We might need a little drink later. I'm not driving today. But, maybe you should save that twenty-year-old liquid gold for a celebration. What I've got to tell you is anything but a celebration, I'm afraid. … Is that brew ready yet?

I'm talking about that tar you call coffee."

"Give me your cup," Roger said. "I'll pour you some."

"Well," Jack finally said as he squared himself to face Bob and leaned forward. "You plan to keep me in the dark all day, or are you going to spill the beans? About what you two assholes have in mind. Just what the hell's the nature of this big problem that you're so worked up about?"

"I would assume that you're pretty much up to speed on this Covid-19 virus," Bob said. "Would you agree with that assessment, Jack? Am I right about that? You've got a handle as to what that shit's all about?"

"I'm not so sure that I would make that claim. I watch the news, like everybody else. But I don't have any inside track on it. And we all know you can't trust what you hear on the news."

"You still talk to your friends in DC," Bob said. "I know you do, because every once in a while someone will ask me how you're doing. And they'll have their little story about something that they did with you—sometimes it'll be about a recent project that the two of you worked on. So, I know I'm not your only friend in the capital. I have a sneaking suspicion that you might know more about this situation that you're letting on right now."

"Why don't you just tell me what it is that I already know, or maybe what you think I should know? Just spill it. Tell me what's going on, and why you're here. What the hell is it, anyway, that you want me to help you with?"

"First, tell me if there could be any microphones, or listening devices of any type, anything like that down here," Bob said. "How about cell phones? Ours we left in the vehicle. How about you? Is your cell phone on you at this time?"

"I figured you'd be going there," Jack said. "I left mine upstairs. And I do not have this room bugged in any way. Except for a couple cameras. But there are no mics. We are as safe right now as we could be—at least in that respect. Now, tell me what's got you so worked up about this Covid-19 virus."

"Have you heard anything about China's involvement with the virus?" Bob asked.

"I know that some leaders are not at all happy with China," Jack replied. "I've heard them blame China for being careless with the virus. And disingenuous about its being contagious. And that's why it was allowed to spread around the world so quickly. Is that what you're getting at?"

"In part," Bob said, after a lengthy pause. "But it's a much bigger deal than just that. What do you know about its origin? Where and how Covid-19 got started—do you have any theories about that?"

"Can't say that I have any definitive info about it. Except for the fact that it started in Wuhan, China, and spread from there. And that this all got started around Christmas 2019."

"What, specifically, do you know about that place called the 'Wuhan Virology Lab'?" Bob asked.

"Only what I've seen on the news. I can assure you, I don't know much. How about you? I'm sure you've been well briefed."

"Well, here's what I can tell you," Bob said. "Some of it is verifiable, and some of it not so much. At least at this time. But, for the sake of this conversation, assume everything I tell you is demonstrably accurate—one hundred percent. You will understand why I am saying this before we head back up the stairs. And you will see why it's imperative that you agree to accept it as fact. If we're going to be able to work together with regard to it."

"Now you're beginning to make a little sense out of this surprise visit," Jack said. "You've got something you want me to do for you. This is not typically the way I like to do things. But, please keep talking."

"For this discussion," Bob said, "let's assume that this Covid-19 virus is a product of the Wuhan Virology Lab, and that it was developed by research technicians and scientists as part of the Chinese Communist Party's program for the development of biological weapons. Would that surprise you?"

"Is that what they're saying, or is that what your guys are saying?"

"Both," Bob declared, adjusting his uncomfortable position on the couch. "We have recently—very recently—intercepted some exceedingly alarming news. And it should scare the shit right out of you. You might already be aware of—"

"Bob, Roger," Jack interrupted. "Just hold on for a minute. Correct me if I'm wrong here, but I'd be willing to bet this whole resort that you two gentlemen did not just stop in to see me and to eat my bacon. You boys are my friends. Have been for a very long time. I trust you, and you trust me. So, let's cut through some of this bullshit and just tell me why you're here. You've got something pretty important that you need me to do for you. Is that not right? Yes or no?"

"Jack—"

"Yes or no, dammit!?"

"Yes," Bob said. "Of course. We have a job for you. But that's not unusual. There's not a day goes by when we could not use your help in some capacity. Not in the past twenty-five, thirty years. There's always room for your kind of help. But, this is different. This time—it's very different."

"Okay," Jack said. "What, exactly, makes this time so different? Just spit it out—tell me. Why the hell are you at my door in the first place, on a Saturday morning? Why not just ring me up on a secure channel? Just what is this big mysterious deal you keep bringing up?"

Neither Bob nor Roger opened his mouth.

"Spit it out! Or I want my damn coffee back."

"Let me tell him," Roger said. "He and I have worked together out in the field dozens of times. He knows how I think, and I know him. Just let me explain what this is all about. Okay, Bob? Jump in if you need to. But just let me explain it. Okay?"

"Go for it, Roger," Bob said. "I just don't want you to be doing any arm twisting, or minimizing. You got to lay it out straight. I'll let you do all the talking. Jack just needs to point me in the direction of that very expensive Pappy Van Winkle's Family Reserve Kentucky Straight Bourbon Whiskey that I bought him. I'm just having a change of heart. About having a drink, that is. So, it's gonna come down to this. If you boys don't drink with me, you'll have to watch. Because I'm sure as hell gonna tip one of these bottles—right now, this morning."

For effect, Bob had made it a point to slowly enunciate each syllable of the liquor's long name.

"And where are your glasses, Jack?" he asked, squinting his eyes to scour the bar. "Drinking glasses, that is. Hell, I might need your reading glasses, too. I want to try some of that Pappy's to see if it's as good as it's supposed to be. As I remember it being. Never mind. I see 'em from here."

With that Bob promptly stood up and walked toward the bar.

"I'll pour you boys a glass too," he said on his way. "You're going to need it as much as I do. I can promise you that."

The bar was completely filled with fine wines and hard liquors. Just as Bob reached for the doorless cupboard where he had spotted the glasses, he recalled that it was Jack's penchant to keep his liquor glasses in the deep cold. So, that's where Bob went first. He popped open the cupboard-mounted freezer and removed three glasses for them to use.

Jack was very surprised, perhaps even alarmed, by the fact that Bob would be hitting the bar on a Saturday morning.

"All right, Roger," Jack said. "Lay it out for me. Don't use big words. Make it as simple and direct as you can."

"Bob and I have talked about this at length," Roger replied. "We're both convinced that we've got a real national emergency. And you, me, and Henry, are the only men in the country that he and I both trust enough to accomplish what has to be done. It's just that simple."

"Sounds pretty ominous to me," Jack said. "Maybe you should lay it out for me, instead of just skirting around the problem. Whaddya say?"

Chapter 5 —

R oger listened intently to what Jack was asking of him, but he still didn't offer up a full explanation of the major problem he and Bob saw as being on the horizon, so Jack followed up: "Foreign or domestic?"

"Foreign."

"Friendly or otherwise? I suppose if you boys consider it a national emergency, then it wouldn't be very friendly. Am I right?"

"North Korea."

"Damn," Jack groaned as he sat up straighter. "I guess that'd be just about as 'otherwise' as it could get. What would we be doing in North Korea? I think that's about the only hostile nation I've never visited. And why would any American need to set foot north of the 38th? What could that accomplish that a few cruise missiles couldn't do from five hundred miles offshore?"

"That was my reaction when Bob approached me," Roger said through an affected smile.

"No," Jack said. "I'm quite serious. No member of that whole Kim clan ever listens to a thing a US President has ever said. And every word that leaves his lips is a lie. Kim Jong-un is the worst of the whole lot. He's not even as reliable as Putin. What's the point in even trying to talk to him?"

Roger glanced over at Bob, and did not answer Jack's question.

It was obvious to Jack that Roger was hoping to have Bob jump into the conversation.

Bob smiled, but said nothing for a long several seconds.

"You wouldn't be talking to him," Bob finally said as he handed Jack and Roger a glass of whiskey. "Nor would you be handing him a glass of this Pappy Van Winkle's Family Reserve Kentucky Straight Bourbon. Nope, while you will be doing a lot of shit over there, talking to the chubby little bastard won't be one of them. But, you won't be blowing him up, either. At least, not if you stick to the plan."

"What, then, is this all about?" Jack asked. "Why do we need to go over there? And what could that possibly have to do with the virus—that Covid-19? You started out alluding to the virus. What does it have to do with North Korea?"

"Several things are going on at the same time, Jack," Roger said. "And they're all somehow related."

"And all bad, I presume," Jack said.

"You could say that," Roger replied. "We really cannot tell you too much more unless you're willing to accept the mission. It would be info that could be difficult for you to deny under oath, should the shit hit the fan, as we fear it might."

"What kind of fool do you think I am?" Jack retorted. "I wouldn't even buy a lawn mower without a test drive. I need to know what I'm getting into, and what—at least in general terms—exactly what the nature of the mission would be. Why is it so damn critical? And how is it related to Covid-19? And why all this dumb-ass secrecy? And why wouldn't I accept the mission? Have I ever run away from any job you asked me to do? What's the big deal with this?"

"For starters, Jack," Roger said. "If you accept this mission, odds are very good that you won't make it home. Not alive or dead. It's that simple. Think of it like this, is Kate ready to raise your boys?"

Jack smiled broadly and leaned back in his chair. "Bob," he said. "Sit down there and look me in the eye."

And then Jack just waited.

After Bob had sat down, Jack continued.

"Explain to me, my friend, why would you come to my house and tell me that I was going to have to die for my country? What could possibly be that important? You always work up a sound extraction strategy. Right?"

"Jack," Bob said. "I labored for—"

"There you go again! Damn you! Just spill it! What do you think happens if I don't say I'll do it? Let's just keep it simple."

"All my experts are telling me that it will be war. Estimates are that, at a minimum, ten million Americans will likely die, and we will virtually go away as a major player on the big stage. That's what's going to happen, if it remains on its current course. Worse yet, that just might even be the case if you do go. No guarantees. But, if you don't, our fate is settled. Roger and I are both quite certain about that. There are several very intricate aspects about this mission, any one of which is well beyond the abilities of anyone else we might look to. At least that's how we're viewing it. If we are even going to see some level of success, we think you are the only man who could pull it off. I really can't get into any more detail at this time, if you even think you might decide against."

"What's this business about Henry?" Jack asked. "You suggested that I get Henry involved. Is that what you're thinking? And you, Roger, even suggested that yourself."

"Henry is your call, entirely," Roger said. "I know you and I totally trust him. And he trusts us. He's a known commodity. We realize that you're going to need help. We've arranged for a SEAL team to aid you. But you're going to need someone like Henry as well.

"But, as for me," Roger continued, "I would really like to join you. Still might. But you and I know that I have not recovered well from one of our last adventures. I'm still carrying two slugs, and have not healed as well as I'd hoped. As far as Henry—he is the best, and I know you read him very well. Like I said, it's your call—Henry, or me at fifty percent, at best. Now, I also know that money isn't the big question with you. But, there is a hefty insurance policy that goes with this: ten million each. That would put your boys through college, and then some. And, if Henry goes, if something happened to him, his family would be taken care of. This is just something for you guys to consider."

"You're confident with the numbers you gave me," Jack said, after a long moment of silence. "That millions of Americans would die—you're pretty sure that would be about right? Now, I get it— that you can't give me the details involved, unless I agree in advance to do it. But, once I know all the details, are you convinced that I will see the urgency as clearly as you two do?"

"You will," Roger said without hesitation.

"I agree," Bob said. "You will see the importance, and the urgency."

"Well," Jack said slowly, "I suppose we all knew that it would eventually come to this—it was inevitable. It's just the nature of this business. Yeah. I'll give it a shot.

"I can't speak for Henry. If it was just for me, I'd pass on even suggesting it to Henry. He's got some new responsibilities. Not sure how much you may have heard, but Henry has brought his aunt, Aunt Halona, to live on Sugar Island. But, I've never met a man more competent, or trustworthy, or shit-ass tough, than that sonofabitch. We've been through a lot together."

"Yeah," Roger said. "He took a round in his back just a few months ago. In Bay City. Rescuing Buddy. How's he doing? I'd really feel better if he went along with you. Do you think that he might be up to something like this, at this time? He knows how you think, and he's just plain good at this stuff."

"He did get lucky—when he got shot. It was a full metal-jacketed 10mm. Through and through. He lost some blood, but no significant muscle or bone damage. Are you in any way making this out to be more difficult than it is? Physically, Henry is probably at nearly a hundred percent. Why don't you tell me a little bit more about it, so I know better what the demand will be on him? And why you think it's so damn important. And what the hell it has to do with Covid-19."

"Then I can assume you're in?" Bob asked. "Regardless of Henry's status?"

"I'm in," Jack replied. "Can't speak for Henry, at this point, but I think he'll want to do it. Whether or not I let him leave his aunt alone is another matter. Tell me more about the mission."

"As I started to explain," Bob said, "two days ago we intercepted a communiqué between the Chinese Communist Party, and the major leader of the Deep State right here in the US. Can you imagine that?"

"The leader of our Deep State!" Jack said. "Wouldn't that be

Allison Fulbright? Your wife, Bob? And your boss, Roger? Isn't that who Allison is in this whole equation? Your regular job is to protect her. Right? And you're saying that her role is that of an international threat?"

Both Bob and Roger reluctantly nodded in agreement.

"That would be correct," Bob said. "One and the same."

"Okay," Jack said. "What made that communication so problematic?"

"First of all," Bob explained. "The communiqué substantiated something we strongly suspected, but could not definitively confirm. That is, that Covid-19 was created in the Wuhan Virology Lab as part of the highly-secretive Chinese Communist biological warfare program. While it is true that the original virus did have as its host the horseshoe bat, it was not until it was reworked in the Wuhan lab, through "gain of function" manipulations, that it was engineered to the point that it was fully weaponized. Fundamentally, it was altered so that it could be readily transmitted between humans—not just bats. And not only was it made highly communicable, but it was also tweaked so that it ferociously attacked those who contracted it—particularly the elderly."

"I've been reading up on that," Jack said. "But didn't we already suspect their involvement? In fact, I thought that there was little doubt that the Chinese Communist Party intentionally unleashed that Covid-19 on the world. They lied about it not being transmittable between humans, when they definitely knew that it was. And then they encouraged travel from Wuhan to points all over the world. I thought we already knew that they did that to spread the disease. Was there ever any doubt? So, that begs the question: why is it such an urgent matter at this time?"

"You're right," Bob said, "we've been pretty much convinced about their participation for some time. But it's where they're going with it from here that creates the utmost urgency. That communiqué indicated that in just a matter of a few days from now—single digits—they are releasing a second virus: they call it Covid-22. It is much more dangerous than their first engineered coronavirus—Covid-19. This new virus, without the proper preventative, is virtually always fatal. And our scientists believe it will be at least equally contagious."

"You've got to be shitting me!" Jack barked.

"No, I'm not," Bob countered. "If what they say is correct, that's what's headed our way."

"How are they going to deal with it?" Jack asked. "How are they going to avoid it? The Chinese—how do they survive it? What is this preventative you talk about?"

"There is a prophylaxis," Bob said. "It's not a vaccine. It must be taken in advance. But, in ninety-five percent of the cases, it will prevent those who take the medication from contracting the fatal symptoms of the Covid-22 virus. This prophylaxis is not even a patented compound. There are no records that we can locate as to what goes into it, or how it works.

"The word is that nearly one hundred thousand doses of this medication were distributed to members of the Deep State here in the US. We did manage to get our hands on a few hundred of them from the Israelis. The Israeli army was kind enough to pass them along to us. Just like in the case with Covid-19, their covert operatives in Iran found themselves in possession of several hundred thousand—they were meant to be used by important people in Iran."

"What did you mean by your comment?" Jack asked. "That the Israelis managed to get hold of the preventative prophylaxis just as they did for Covid-19? I didn't know that there was an official means to prevent Covid-19. Not until we had the vaccine."

"Sure there was," Roger said. "Again, we got our hands on several million of the Covid-19 tablets, which was nothing more than HCQ—hydroxychloroquine. That was thanks to the Israelis. When the Chinese Communist Party spread Covid-19 abroad, they tried to protect some of their allies—just like they're doing with the new virus. Israel is pretty amazing in this. They have quite a number of embedded NOCs, agents operating with non-official-cover, in the Middle East, particularly among groups that they consider to be threats—such as Iran. Well, just like that time, the Chinese recently sent to Iran a large number—millions—of doses of an antiviral compound."

"You mean that stuff actually works?" Jack asked. "Hydroxy-chloroquine?"

"All I can say definitively is that the Israeli army preemptively provided the treatment to members of their military, and they were at times able to hold the weekly death due to infection down to double digits. And that's pretty much how the Chinese outside of Wuhan avoided getting sick as well. They distributed their treatment to all of the Party members in Beijing. In fact, the only area of the country that suffered significantly from it was Wuhan. And that was by design."

"By design!" Jack repeated. "How's that work? Who the hell designs suffering and death for thousands of their own people?"

"Bob," Roger said, "I would like to interject a thought here. Jack has agreed to do the job. I know him very well. So do you.

Once he buys in, he won't back out. Right? You know that. Right?"

"Jack's as good as they get," Bob replied. "And more responsible than any other contractor that I've done business with. So, Roger, what's your point here?"

"I suggest that we owe it to him," Roger said, "to fill him in on the whole story—even the back story. The more he knows—even the material that's totally classified—the more he knows, the better the job he can do. So, I suggest that we take the time to level with him. And to answer any questions that he might have. Can we agree on that?"

"Sure," Bob said. "You take over. I'm going to help myself to another shot of that bourbon. Damn, that's good. I'm sure happy I bought it for you in the first place. Good move on my part."

"Okay, Jack," Roger said. "This is going to take a few minutes. But it's all information that you should have. It is, of course, for your ears only. That means that it is not to be shared with another human being—not even Henry."

"Let's have it," Jack invited.

"Covid-19, as we've already said, was altered in the Wuhan lab. It was part of an intense gain-of-function effort carried out by Chinese Communist scientists. As we said, they started out with a virus sometimes found in bats—horseshoe bats—which are indigenous to an area some distance away. Once it was developed, it was tested to see if it could be transmitted to humans, and then from one human to another. Once it was altered to meet those requirements, it was deemed 'ready to use.'

"The Chinese Communists were greatly angered by the way the previous POTUS handled their leaders with regard to trade and sanctions. They were furious about it. So, they decided that they would like to take America down a peg or two, or more. And the only way they felt they could do this without full-scale nuclear war was by using a weaponized virus, which is exactly what Covid-19 turned out to be."

"You're not messin' with me, are you?" Jack asked. "That whole virus thing was an act of war?"

"I'm afraid so," Bob said. "Are you familiar with a book entitled *Unrestricted Warfare?*"

"Never heard of it."

"It was written by the Chinese Communist Party as a solution to the challenge they believed was posed by America. Basically, the CCP intend to take over the world, and this book outlines how they plan to do it. They did not believe that they were in a position to defeat America using standard weapons and practices, so they developed another method. Translated into English it is, 'Unrestricted Warfare.' Included in that sort of methodology is the use of numerous forms of unconventional methods of war, including those involving biological weapons—germ warfare. In that book, it is deemed a totally legitimate form of combat for the CCP to engage in."

"I am aware that they intend to replace us, economically, within the next decade or so," Jack said, "but I had not heard how they planned to do it. And you're suggesting that the Covid-19 is a bioweapon. Is that right?"

"Absolutely," Roger said. "There can be no doubt about that."

"Is that why the Chinese Communists encouraged worldwide travel for a month and a half after the outbreak in Wuhan?" Jack asked. "I thought at the time that act was beyond curious."

"That's exactly right," Roger said. "It was carefully planned out—strategized. We suspected something was up when this was all going on, but they kept denying that there was a problem. It was, of course, the Chinese New Year. There were over a billion world travelers moving freely throughout the Wuhan area. People were flying in from all over the world, but none were allowed to fly between Wuhan and other parts of China. That looked very suspicious to our intelligence at the time. And that's why POTUS instituted the travel ban with China. However, the virus was already taking root in Europe."

"Do you have proof of that?" Jack asked.

"Well," Bob said, after taking a long drink of his bourbon, "with these latest communications between the CCP and the US Deep State—the secret communiqué in particular—we now know a whole hell of a lot more than we did. It has been catalogued by the CIA as CCP TOP SECRET 2021—997. This document, which is now commonly referred to as *Doc997*, has gone a long way toward confirming many of our suspicions.

"One of the very interesting revelations it provided is a greater understanding of the whole Covid-19 attack. They indicated in that message that they had produced over two billion doses of hydroxychloroquine before they released the virus on their own people. They distributed them throughout their whole country. Except, as I said earlier, except for the Hubei Province—that would include the Wuhan area. They sent a lot of it to Russia, the Democratic People's Republic of Korea, and to Iran. And, we assume that they made it available to all of their secret agents throughout the world. But that was about it. And, as I've said before, Israel somehow managed to steal some of what they sent to Iran. They, the Israelis, analyzed it and determined it to be largely composed of HCQ, combined with what appeared to be something akin to Remdesivir."

"Then," Jack said, "What's this shit about it not working on victims? Isn't that what the FDA came up with? That it didn't work?"

"That was partly a political decision, and partly a financial one," Bob said. "First of all, once the Deep State saw the value of getting involved in the pandemic business, they worked with the establishment to stage a fake FDA test of the HCQ by using it on an elderly group of Covid-19 patients who were already so severely infected with the virus that there was virtually no way to save them. Suffice it to say, the CCP treatment protected all the residents of Beijing, Moscow, the elite of Iran, and, to a degree, the Israeli military. It does work best as a prophylaxis. It's a fact that once Covid-19 has totally penetrated a person's cells, it can be very hard to get it out without serious damage. Taken early, it greatly minimizes symptoms."

"Hang on!" Jack blurted out. "You said there were financial and political benefits to be gained in this pandemic. How can anyone make money with it, and why in hell would Deep State operatives in the US sabotage the health and well-being of their own country?"

"Financially," Roger replied, "there is nothing to be gained if people used the HCQ/Remdesivir compound to protect themselves. HCQ has been around forever, it's mass produced in India, China, and elsewhere. And it's cheap. There was no money to be made by Big Pharma with HCQ. Unless, of course, some a very enterprising members of Big Pharma print up some new labels and stick them on repackaged bottles of HCQ. That would be worth millions. That's all speculation.

"However, millions of dollars would be chump change to what they'd hope to gain. What they were all shooting for were the exclusive marketing rights for the distribution of bona fide vaccines. Whichever Big Pharma players were able to patent and produce such products would make that entity secure for generations to come. That was the business end of that whole Covid-19 fiasco.

"But, like I said, there are political aspects to it as well," Roger continued. "Deep State has its own slate of candidates, up and down the line—Democrats, Republicans and Independents. They believed that their best chance of gaining ground at the polls would be to force the whole country to shut down. If they're successful at wrecking the US economy, they believe that their candidates would benefit.

"Because of perceived potential political gains, Deep State has pretty much bought into this new Chinese Communist plot to bring America down. That's what this second stage is all about—bringing America down."

"A second coronavirus?" Jack asked. "That's what you're suggesting—right?"

"That's what we're being led to believe," Bob said. "If this second communiqué— *Doc997*—is for real. And, we have no reason at this point to doubt it. If it is accurate, in just a matter of days Covid-22 will be released in Boston, New York, Chicago, Detroit, New Orleans and Los Angeles. All on the same day! But, it has apparently not yet been disseminated in this country—not yet, anyway. According to Doc997, it's to be hand-delivered from a university professor. One who is in the US right now. But, that's all the info we have on him, or her. ... We're quite confident that individual is currently in the States."

"Holy shit!" Jack said. "And there's nothing that we can take to protect ourselves from this really bad bug?"

"They apparently have a preventative for it," Roger said. "It works with the new virus much like their hydroxychloroquine compound worked to prevent death from Covid-19. But, unlike with Covid-19 and existing medications, no effective prophylaxis currently exists in the market. At least there is nothing in the market that's accessible to us that will work for this Covid-22. That's what we've been led to believe. They had to develop the prophylaxis from scratch. And, like I said before, they did not obtain a patent for the new treatment, because to do so would require that the formula be recorded. Believe me, we've been searching the databanks. We've found nothing recorded. Anywhere."

"And it's pretty deadly?" Jack asked.

"Like nothing we've ever seen before," Bob said, after hesitating for an inordinate length of time. "Incubation time is two days—much less than the earlier strain. And, you're dead in five. Highly contagious. And I do mean *highly*. According to their hype, it's easier to catch this Covid-22 than it was its predecessor."

"Okay," Jack said. "I'm getting this. But I can't see how I can stop it. If it's already somewhere in the US right now, what can I do in North Korea? *North Korea*—of all places?"

"It's as convoluted as all hell, Jack," Bob explained. "But, you are right—there's nothing you or anyone can do to actually stop this thing—not directly. And not without starting a world war. If we launched every missile we have in our arsenal. If we blew up every city in China, they would still be able to unleash that damn virus, and kill a few million. And maybe a hell of a lot more than a few million.

"So, we're going to take a page out of Sun Tzu's classic—*The Art of War*. Hell, it's more than that. We're adding a chapter fourteen to that fifth-century-BC treatise on how to fight a war. And you're the warrior we've selected to wage it. You, Henry—if he's willing, and available—along with a couple SEAL fighters tossed in."

Jack sat back in his seat and laughed out loud. "Who did you get to draw up these battle plans?" he asked. "Some West Point freshman dropout? I'm really eager to find out what you have in mind for me. Seriously? Half a dozen of us, and a few Glock tens, and we're somehow going to whip the world's largest standing army. Is that the gist of what you're suggesting?"

Both Bob and Roger posed with less than sincere smiles at Jack's comment, but they weren't laughing.

"Here's the plan Bob and I came up with," Roger said, after having given Jack's comments time to sink in. "And I doubt that you will even fire a weapon on the whole mission—none of you. Ahhh. Let me take that back. I know you better than that. I'm sure that you will wreak more than your share of havoc on the poor Chinese, and probably the North Korean army as well. They will be glad to see you leave, if they even know you're there. But, if our plans were to go perfectly, none of you will be forced to un-holster a weapon—of any sort, or caliber."

"Go on," Jack said. "Tell me more."

"We will go into this in greater detail before you leave. But, for now, we'll just cover the basics. And let them soak in."

Jack said nothing as he stood and walked over to put on another pot of coffee.

Over the next hour Bob and Roger laid their plan out for Jack. They explained how he and Henry, along with two SEAL warriors, would be transported through Korea Bay in a mini-sub and dropped off on the beach near the northern border of North Korea and China. The four of them would then proceed on foot, carrying with them a missile warhead. They would proceed until they met up with a North Koran missile technician. That man was planning to use them, Jack, Henry and the SEALs, to help him and his fiancée defect to the West. In return, they would install Jack's warhead into a missile which was about to be launched.

The only names they had for the man and his bride-to-be were Tarzan and Jane. Tarzan was not only a significantly important member of the Communist Party, he was a prominent member of the North Korean leader's personal family. Important enough that he feared he would be targeted for death should the CCP plan in any way run amuck.

"So, Jack," Roger explained. "Your team will deliver this special warhead that we have prepared for you to the Sohae Satellite Launching Station up north close to the Chinese border. In a few days from now, the Democratic People's Republic of Korea are planning to launch one of their long-range intercontinental ballistic missiles—a Hwasong-21—over Japan and out into the North Pacific. These newer versions of the Hwasong-21 missile allow for some highly secret special features of the rocket while in flight—thanks to technology provided to them by Russia.

"China will have some of their naval fleet in the Yellow Sea, and some in the Sea of Japan. No one will be expecting it, but, with your help, we will have installed in the substituted warhead the necessary hardware and software to allow for the course of the missile to be altered considerably. If all goes as planned, the new course of the missile, instead of taking it over Japan, and then out into the Pacific, will cause it to pass over some of most expensive and sophisticated Chinese naval crafts, including the largest aircraft carrier in the entire Chinese fleet."

"No shit," Jack said. "How does that work?"

Jack was beginning to feel a fresh rush of adrenaline throughout his whole system. He was now eager, if not anxious, to hear the rest.

"It won't be that difficult. When the time comes, we will feed you the coordinates and programming instructions necessary to accomplish our objective. You will have these before you board the SDV—that is, the acronym for the SEAL Delivery Vehicle. The only really tricky part is that you have to be physically quite near the missile itself when you program the coordinates—there are radio signals the warhead must be receiving directly from the missile for this to work. We want to wait as long as possible to provide this info for you as we need to base it on the latest data as to the location of specific elements of the Chinese fleet. This part of the mission is highly sensitive, as I'm sure you can deduce.

"The SDV you'll be using is a newer version of the old standby MK-11. If you know much about these vessels, you'll be pleased to learn that the one we've got for you is a dry mini-sub. That means it will be much more comfortable for your mission than the older wet products such as the original MK-11. You'll be brought up to speed a little further down the line on this part of the mission.

"The USS Jimmy Carter will drop you off in the SDV while south of the 38th parallel. Of course, there are a number of details that we will not be discussing at this time. You will be filled in on those a little later as well. Suffice it to know, once you are in the SDV, and at least until you are back in South Korean waters after the mission has been completed, we will have no radio communication with you whatsoever—too dangerous all the way around.

"We're thinking that their fleet in that theater is most likely going to be somewhat stationary for the launch, so the coordinates we give you later should be fine. And, even if the missile does not score a direct hit, we are including a relatively small explosive device in the dummy warhead, so even a near miss will accomplish our goal."

"And how will that work?" Jack asked. "How will a near miss solve the problem with the new Covid-22?"

"We believe that the best we can hope for," Bob said, "is that in the middle of all the excitement, which this so-called *errant* missile will create, exasperation brought about by the unexpected will force the hand of either the Chinese Communist Party to directly contact their agent, or agents—as there could be more than one here in the States. I'm talking about the ones who are actually holding the virus. And it is thought, or hoped, that this will result in those agents seeking to make contact with their master in Beijing. We are fairly confident that all the vials are at a single location here in the US, probably on some university campus. We also believe that it is likely that all the vials are in the possession of a single person—that *Doc997* communiqué made that substantially clear. That is, if we are interpreting it correctly. We just don't know who that person is, or where he or she is. And, we do not know for certain whether or not there is a backup plan. We're hoping to gain that info as we progress.

"Jack, what's your thinking on this up to this point?"

"Off the top," Jack said, "it just seems to smack of misdirected energy, maybe overkill. Maybe underkill. Dropping a bomb on a two billion dollar boat, just to force someone we don't know to pick up his phone and make a call. Is there not a more direct way to accomplish the same thing?"

"Exactly the point," Roger said. "It will have to seem to somebody on the other side to be way over the top. And that's what we're looking to accomplish. This is asymmetric warfare. Will it work? We don't know. If we had even some concrete data as to who it was over here who was in possession of the virus, we could put pressure on that person. But, if we were wrong, it would be too late—too late for all of us. Imagine for a moment, ten million dying Americans—all at the same time. On average, one hospital patient requires at least two medical professionals—doctors, nurses, aides, etc.—to care for him at any given time. We don't have a spare twenty million medical personnel. And, from what we've been told, those ten million victims will be during the first week alone. Add to that number, every member of the medical staff at every hospital in the country, and you will begin to see the magnitude of the problem."

Jack thought about what they had just told him for nearly a full minute, and then he said, "Do you boys actually see this as working?"

Neither Bob nor Roger spoke immediately. Nor did either of them seek to make eye contact. Finally, Bob tried to explain: "To characterize this mission as a slam-dunk would be a blatant lie—even for James Bond in his prime. In fact, even to suggest that it provides those participating a few opportunities for contingency planning would be a dramatic misstatement. Each individual aspect of it is rigidly inflexible. Plus, the whole mission is fraught with immense danger and difficulty. We know that the risk element is not of concern to you. But the physical rigors involved, with each leg of it, they present a major challenge even for trained SEALs. Pile onto that the fact that you men dare not allow yourselves to be captured. Forget about the pain and agony that would be waged against your mind and body, we—back here in good old DC—will be forced to deny any knowledge of your very existence. That means, if you should become reasonably confident that capture is imminent, you must terminate yourselves, and the other members of the team. That is the only acceptable step to take, at that point. Jack, are you okay with that?"

"Makes sense to me," Jack said. "I would not let myself be captured. I've seen what they're capable of. That's enough for me right there. But, I do get what you're saying—there's not a way an undertaking like this can deal with any loose ends. What about the other men on this mission. Are you going to be having this conversation with them?"

"No," Roger quickly replied. "But you are. This will be your job—or a part of your job. You must make it clear to everyone with you that there can be no escaping alive by surrendering. If any of you are captured or killed, we will deny any knowledge of the mission. If any of you are wounded, and if the injuries are such that you are unable to escape with the wounded, then you must terminate the wounded. Under no circumstance should any one of you be left alive in or near North Korea. Still game to go, Jack?"

"Absolutely. But I'm going to need more information."

"Such as?" Roger asked.

"How about that couple that wants to defect?" Jack asked, "What would we do if one of them is wounded? Same rules apply?"

"Yes," Bob said. "Roger and I have discussed this, and we have decided that if either one of them is killed or seriously wounded, do not be burdened by bringing them back. You will have the means in that SDV to covertly dispose of a body. And if the one who survives wishes to remain with the victim, terminate the one not wounded as well. We can have none of the participants talking to the enemy once this mission is completed—absolutely no one."

"How is success or failure to be determined," Jack asked, "for the mission as a whole? That is, what in your mind constitutes a successful mission?"

"We will regard this mission as a success," Bob answered, "if it creates enough of a stir that the principal terrorist reaches out and tries to communicate with the CCP, to the degree, or in a manner that we are able to detect it, scrutinize it, and act upon it in such a way that we are able to round up the virus that is already in the US. That would make it a success. Now, if you are able to round up the defectors, and make it back to Guam, or Tokyo, then that would be icing on the cake.

"Unfortunately, you guys will not have any idea about success or failure until you land at the selected out-of-the-theater location, and enjoy a shot of good whiskey, along with a fine Cuban cigar, of course. So, you damn well better make it back alive if you hope to find out. We, Roger and I, are not likely to meet you there. But, we may communicate in a secure fashion with you while you are there. At some point down the road, the four of us will meet face to face, and we will debrief you.

"As for the present, perhaps we can spend the night here at your resort, if that's okay. And leave first thing in the morning. Any idea what Henry's going to do? Think he will want to join you?"

"I can't see him passing on it," Jack said. "But, if that's what he chooses to do—pass on it, I mean—then I assume we've got plenty of help with the SEALs. Right?"

"Sixteen men on a SEAL team," Roger said. "Four SEALs on the boat. So, the sixteen would include the backups. We'll need somebody to pilot the boat. A navigator. And two men, besides yourselves, to transport the substitute warhead. So, we'll have plenty of warriors to draw from. We can make further plans on the flight to Tokyo. Nail it all down. Bob will be heading directly back to DC, but I'll be going with you as far as Tokyo—in spite of my physical situation. And I will be the first one to greet you when you get back out—either in person, or otherwise."

"Well, my friends," Jack said, as he stood to his feet. "I've heard enough for now. Let's call it good. I'll need some time to get the boys squared away. Not sure how I'm going to handle that yet. Gotta get hold of Kate. But, I'll be good by morning. We've got some great units available for you fellows. I'll fix you up. What are you going to need? Four units total? We can do that."

Before Roger could respond, the intercom rang: "Jack. Henry here. Saw the limos out front. I called Robby on his cell and he told me that you had company—Bob and Roger. Wondered if you might need me."

"Yeah, Henry, come on down. Bob and Roger didn't want to have cell phones around for security reasons. Turn yours off and leave it up there, and then come down. They are just leaving. You should catch them before they take off. And, yes, I do have something to discuss with you."

Jack then clicked off with Henry and turned to address Bob

and Roger again.

"I've got Henry stopping over. I thought it would be good for him to come down here and say 'Hi' to you fellas. We can discuss the plans for a few and get his take. I'm flying out in the morning?" Jack asked. "Right? Can you stay put for a little longer, and see Henry? Big things are taking place in his life recently—with his aunt moving in and all. My gut tells me that he'd be very unhappy with me if I didn't let him know what's up, and what I'm doing. But it might not be wise to totally count him in just yet. He's very busy looking out for his Aunt Halona these days. He might like a break. And make a little extra money. But, we'll see."

"Right," Roger said. "We'd love to see how our old friend's doing."

Chapter 6 —

J ack immediately headed up to open the door and greet Henry. However, when he swung it open, he found Henry standing about ten feet away from the house. He was talking on his cell. Henry heard Jack open the door, and he looked up at him and signaled with his free hand that he would need a minute to finish the call. Jack acknowledged his request and returned into the house.

A few minutes later Henry did knock on the door.

When Jack opened the door to invite him in, Henry nervously announced, "Jack. I need to see you for a minute first—before I come inside. Can you step out so we can talk? Only take just a minute. But it is important that you know what's going on."

"Sure, Henry," Jack said as he went out and closed the door behind them. "What's up?"

"I just got a call. I've got a problem," Henry said. "Could be a big problem."

"Really?" Jack said, trying to ease his friend's discomfort. "What's up?"

"Aunt Halona is sick—very sick. We thought it was the flu, but the diagnosis just came back—just now, in fact. She tested positive for Covid-19."

"Oh my God!" Jack said. "Are they sure?"

"The doctor had them take a second look at the results. He said it is definite. She's got Covid."

"Is she in the hospital?" Jack asked.

"No," Henry said. "And that's what the doctor is insisting on— that she immediately enter the hospital. And that's what I tell her she has to do. But she refuses to go. Absolutely refuses to go. She has her reasons. So, I'm gonna have to take care of her here."

"Are you sure about that? I've heard that with that damn Covid, patients her age really need constant medical assistance—the kind they can only give them in a proper hospital."

"Trust me," Henry said, "she has her reasons. She'd rather die than go to a hospital."

Everything had been going smoothly—both in Jack's world, and Henry's. But then it happened: Covid-19. Initially it seemed a long distance away. First, it was in China. "Let's keep it there!" Jack was fond of saying during the early days of the outbreak, always followed with, "Fat chance of that. It's only a matter of time."

And he was right. Soon it hit Washington State and California, and then the East Coast.

Before long it had infested most if not all of America's urban areas—especially among the older populations in senior care centers.

For a while it appeared as though Sugar Island might be spared. And then it happened. At first there were only a few. And then some more. Before long, Henry's Aunt Halona got sick.

"Hey, Henry," Jack said in his most reassuring voice, "Let me talk to Bob and Roger for a minute. I'll explain it all to them. But, I don't think you should expose our friends to this Covid shit. So you go inside to the kitchen, and pour yourself a cup of coffee, and I'll excuse both of us with Bob and Roger. No problem. They'll understand. Go ahead and head in. I'll be with you in just a few."

"But," Henry said, "there was something important that you wanted me to talk to them about. Shouldn't we do that first? I can spare a few minutes."

Jack smiled and said, "I just wanted them to see you, so they'd know that I've not been abusing you. And, I thought it'd be nice for the four of us to chew the fat, so to speak. But if your aunt has Covid, it would not be righteous for you to expose them. They'll understand. I'll explain it to 'em. See you upstairs in just a few. You can tell me more about your aunt up there. Okay?"

"Yeah," Henry agreed. "Sure. I'll pour some coffee. See you in a bit. Where are the boys—Bob and Roger? Are they still having breakfast?"

"No," Jack replied. "They're in my office downstairs. I'll be right up."

At that point Henry did go in, while Jack went back to fill Bob and Roger in on Henry's dilemma.

"Look, fellas," Jack said. "We've had a taste of the unexpected show up this morning. As I said before, you can count on me for this job. But it looks like we're gonna need a few of your SEALs, because Henry is having a family emergency."

"No shit!" Roger blurted. "What's up? Is he okay?"

"He's fine, but his aunt, the one I told you about who just moved in here at the resort to be by him, she is not doing so well. And, can you believe it—she's been diagnosed with Covid. Ain't that a crock of shit?"

"You're kidding?" Bob said. "Is it for certain?"

"According to Henry, it's for sure. Got the diagnosis earlier this morning. He thought that she just had a cold, but the test came back positive. It's Covid-19. So, this is what we do. You fellows should book a hotel in the Soo for tonight. If that bug is going around here, you should get as far away from it as possible. I'll plan on flying out of Sawyer in the morning. You'd have me going to Chicago, I'd assume. What time should I be at the airport?"

"Get there as early as possible," Roger confirmed. "We'll have something waiting for you. Earlier the better. We'll take it from there.

"Take this secure cell phone," Roger said, handing Jack a new phone. "It's safe to use until you arrive in Japan. Discard it there, and a different unit will be provided for you in Japan. And do give Henry our best. You can tell him that we'll arrange to have the finest SEAL team in the service work with you on this mission."

"I'm sure you will," Jack said. "You always take care of me."

The three men said their goodbyes, and the two visitors went to their cars.

Jack was disappointed. He had been able to work with Henry on every one of his missions for over two years now, and always with the best of success.

"It is what it is," Jack said to himself as he saw his other two friends off. And then he ventured into the living area to join Henry. "How are we going to deal with Aunt Halona? And how can we talk her into going to a hospital?"

"Not gonna happen, my friend," Henry told him. "She has her reasons. She just will not go."

"Well," Jack said. "Tell me why. I've got coffee, and some time. Please explain to me what she's thinking. I want to hear it."

Jack realized the seriousness of the situation. Henry's Aunt Halona had become the central point in his best friend's life. Jack knew enough about Covid to convince him that without the proper medical care, and given her age, Henry was likely to lose her.

"Are you sure you want me to tell you the whole story?" Henry asked. "She's repeated it to me two times now. Trust me, she has thought it through. She will not go. Should I tell it to you like she did to me?"

Jack did not answer. He just sat down, sipped his black drink, and smiled at his friend.

It was over two full cups of coffee that Henry spelled out the whole saga of why his aunt hated hospitals so badly. Here's how he explained to Jack:

Aunt Halona has always been afraid of hospitals—probably because the only time she had ever visited a medical facility was the night Dakota, her husband, died. He had just purchased a new red Harley Davidson Roadster. For years he had talked about buying a bike. He hadn't owned one since they had started dating, and for the first time in their married life she felt that they could afford to take the plunge.

"I love Harleys," he would tell her. "The only thing I love more than the sound of a Harley coming to life in my driveway is the sweet sound of your voice in the bedroom."

"Those words always made me laugh," she related through a smile and a tear.

"Well," she went on to say, "Dakota always loved motorcycles. He was riding a Harley Sportster when I met him. He called it his 'Ironhead 1000.' I had no idea what that meant, but I'm pretty sure that's what he called it. It was down in Flagstaff, Arizona. He was working at a tourist place just east of Flagstaff. A ghost town named 'Two Guns.' It was just off Route 40. And I was working at a little coffee shop in Flagstaff. He and a friend came in one evening, and I fell in love with him on the spot. He always said I just liked his bike, but it was a lot more than that.

"We dated for a month. Saw each other every night, just about. And when his work ended in Two Guns, he asked me to marry him. I said yes.

"So, he sold old Ironhead, and we moved to Phoenix directly. He had a job lined up there. Without any doubt, those years, right after we got married, they were the best years of my life. I went to work in a restaurant. Rented a tiny apartment right in town. I got pregnant six months after we were married. That was with your cousin Charlene. Named her after Dakota's mother. She was our only child.

"We had ten great years. He got a raise, and was able to save up enough to buy a used Harley.

"And then it happened. He jumped on his bike one morning. Heading into work. It was only a few blocks from our apartment. A car didn't see him, and hit him. I didn't know what was happening. I heard the ambulance, but did not know they were picking up Dakota.

"After just a few minutes, I heard a knock on my door. A policeman asked me if I knew a man named Dakota. I said, 'Yes, that's my husband.' He asked me to sit down, and then he told me. My husband's bike had been hit by a car and he was seriously injured. He offered to drive me to the hospital to see him. I dropped Charlene off with my neighbor across the hall, and went with the policeman to the hospital. Scared me to death. First and last time in a hospital for me.

"I went up to the operating room, and they would not let me in to see him. Said I would have to wait. It was a long time—probably two hours, or more. Seemed like an eternity. And then they wheeled him down the hall to a room. I was still not allowed to go in. Not at first.

"Finally, a doctor came out and told me that Dakota was asking for me. I thought that meant that he was recovering. But, that was not to be. Everyone there knew it—that he wasn't going to make it. Everyone except me. They all could see that he was injured too badly to be saved. Anyway, I walked in the room. My hopes were up. But then our eyes met. I could see that things were bad. He couldn't talk. Couldn't even utter a word, or even move his head. He had this huge hose stuck in his mouth. But we were able to look at each other. I could see how much he loved me. It was written all over his eyes. I swear, our eyes talked that morning. Mine told him how very much I loved him. How important he was to me. His eyes told me the same story. Not a single word was spoken. But words were not needed.

"That's when I realized how really bad it was. I leaned over him and kissed him on the forehead. And when I pulled away, his eyes did not follow me. In fact, they didn't move at all. He was dead. Right there in front of me, my darling Dakota passed away.

"From that day on, I never stepped through the doors of a hospital. Not one single time. And I never will. I've had sickness in my family. I've been very ill myself—pneumonia. My mother had pancreatic cancer. And I dared not visit her. But, she understood. At least, I think she did."

"Well, that's my aunt's story about hospitals. At first she thought that I could take care of her," Henry said, "and that she might just remain in her apartment at the resort. But her doctor insisted that she enter the hospital. Like I said, she would have none of it. 'Then I'll just stay here, and die,' she told me, 'if that's the way it's gotta be, that's fine. I just can't set foot in a hospital. I honestly would rather just die here.'

"So," Henry continued, "that's what I'm gonna have to do. Take care of her here."

They had barely finished that second cup of coffee, when Jack stood to his feet and said, "I do not think that it's a great idea for the lady not to avail herself of the best medical help available. However, I appreciate her resolve. Let me see what I can do. I'll talk to you a little later."

Henry excused himself, and Jack immediately got on the phone to his friends. During the course of the remainder of the morning and early afternoon, Jack virtually turned a portion of the resort into a hospital.

He hired eight nurses to work there full time. He set it up for two of them to work eight-hour day shifts from eight to four, two for evening shifts from four to midnight, and another two nurses to split the night shifts and weekends. Invariably there was to be some overtime, even though they pared the night shift to a single nurse.

But for the most part, the eight nurses would be able to get the job done by working only the assigned hours.

Fortunately, one of Jack's neighbors on Sugar Island was a retired medical doctor who had served in military hospitals. Everyone knew him by his first name and his title—*Dr. Jeff*. He was one of Jack's best friends on the island, and so Jack immediately drafted him to regularly look in on Aunt Halona, and to consider himself to be on call should a medical decision need to be made. Dr. Jeff also volunteered to take care of staffing. If one of Jack's staff were unable to come over, the staff members all knew to clear it with Dr. Jeff.

Needless to say, Henry squirmed more than a little at putting Jack—his boss and his friend—in such a bind. Jack, however, had no problem with it. "I've always wondered," he flippantly offered to Henry, "I've always wondered how I was going to spend all my ill-gotten gains. Just kidding, of course. Both of us most certainly earned every penny we ever got paid. You probably more than me. But the only reason it went into my bank was that I figured I had the better accountants."

Actually, truth be known, it wasn't the accountants that Jack relied on. He just knew he had better tools to hide cash—such as the half interest in that Chicago bar. He had hung on to a part of that bar because he knew it might come in handy if he needed a place to secrete away some funds.

"I'm really thankful that we can support such a worthy cause," Jack continued, making reference to Henry's aunt. "Your Aunt Halona is worth what we're spending. I just hope to God she's able to pull through this thing. From everything I hear, this Covid-19 is a very bad bug—especially if the patient is older. We'll just do our best and see how it goes."

Henry was very grateful for all of Jack's help. Unfortunately, from the moment she was diagnosed, Henry was not allowed to visit her. To compensate, he drove his Ram 2500 truck, with its slide-in camper bolted down in its box, and parked it outside her window just so he could be near her. "I'll spend nights there, and then go home and shower when the first shift of nurses starts in the mornings. I can do this until she gets well. Or … whatever."

The first day was not good at all. In fact, fearing she would not survive the first twenty-four hours, that Saturday afternoon Dr. Jeff, her "treating physician," had a ventilator brought in, and he immediately put her on it.

Henry knew what that meant. Or at least he'd heard what happened in similar cases. People had told him that only one in five victims of Covid-19 ever come off the ventilator alive.

But, there were so many stories about Covid floating around that Henry did not know whether he should buy into that fear, or move ahead as though it were just another one of the rumors. So, that's what he did—he simply opted to get out of Dr. Jeff's way.

Chapter 7 —

C oncerned about the Aunt Halona matter, and Henry's desire to stay onsite to help his aunt, Jack was torn as to how he ought to proceed: should he avoid engaging Henry altogether? *After all,* he reasoned, *my friend Henry most certainly has his hands full just dealing with his sick aunt. Should I at least let Henry know what I'm up to? In the end, if all goes the way Bob suggests it's likely to, this just might be the last time he and I ever speak to one another.*

Jack was also troubled that Roger had not actually provided many details about the mission; only that it would last as few as seven days, as many as ten, or quite possibly even much longer—perhaps forever for some of those engaging. But Jack was aware that all field operatives fully understood that the actual duration of a mission was always an unknown. And, in the case of this particular mission, Jack deduced from his conversation with Bob and Roger that the word unknown was probably too optimistic a term to adequately depict this mission's menacing level of unbridled danger.

Jack played back in his mind the parts of his talk with the two men that related to the various challenges of this undertaking. First, they had made it clear that the mission was one that would take all of the participants totally out of the US, placing them in physical confrontation with both China and North Korea, and that the point of contact between opposing parties in this dispute centered around the testing of a new North Korean missile.

Then Jack recalled that it was Roger who had suggested that he enlist Henry to go with him. Initially, Jack too was all for soliciting Henry's services. But at this point, not only did he oppose pulling Henry away from his sick aunt, he was having second thoughts as to the wisdom of even sharing anything about the mission with his friend.

Jack at first had never even considered looking to anyone besides Henry to be his partner—not until he was blindsided by the severity of Henry's family emergency had he felt the need to look beyond his buddy Henry. Now, with the whole scenario in a flux, and with the timeline narrowing, Jack felt that he should run everything past Roger again. So he called him.

Roger was very cautious as to what he would say even over a secure connection. So, without expressing any details, he explained to Jack that given the strategic importance of this project, they would definitely need the best help out there. And because Roger knew beyond a shadow of a doubt that he, Roger, was at this time physically unable to step up and provide the type of assistance Jack would most certainly require; and, further, since it was seeming more and more likely that Henry would not be available, he would find for Jack the most experienced SEAL team available.

Roger did encourage Jack to not entirely write Henry off—at least not just yet. He suggested that he "tell Henry, in very general terms, what Bob and I have asked you to do. It would be wise for you to keep Henry in the loop. If he has a chance to think on it, he might opt to join you—even given current circumstances. I know he tends to be like that. If he wishes to help you, but suggests that the mission be delayed a week or two, let him know that it cannot be put off—not even one day. But, I definitely believe that Henry at the very least needs to be given a chance to participate. As I understand the situation right now, I do not think that Henry even knows anything about this job. Am I right?"

"I have not yet told him that I am about to accept a job," Jack explained to Roger. "He was altogether too wound up about the condition of his aunt, and what he would need to do to help her. And I get that. He's approaching it exactly as I would expect him to—as I would want him to. I do have to say that if he and you were available, you both would be my first choices. I do recognize the urgency. This mission is operating on a calendar of its own. I understand that it *cannot* be delayed."

"I know the feeling," Roger replied. "You're right on both counts. Henry is a special man, and there is no time to wait. How sure are you that he wouldn't want to do this? It's not like he can do anything to help his aunt right now. Am I right? He's not a doctor."

"That's not the point," Jack said. "He's not under any illusions. He senses that it is his responsibility to watch over his Aunt Halona. And, by God, that's what he says he's going to do—no matter what. I can't fault him for that. Henry is just one hell of a man. Simple as that."

"Don't get me wrong," Roger explained. "I totally get it as well. It's that sort of dedication that makes Henry so damn valuable in the field. Henry is Henry—there's not another man like him. I just wish that things were different. Still, I suggest that you should at least run this mission past him. You know, just a few of the general details we shared with you—nothing specific. He simply deserves to know what's going on. He's earned that. Am I to understand you've told him absolutely nothing about this?"

"Right. We haven't discussed it."

"Don't you agree with me that you should? He's been your right-hand man for quite some time now. I think you should at least let him know what you're up to. Just do so in the most general of terms."

"I hear you," Jack said. "He's stopping over this evening so we can go over some things pertaining to his aunt. At the very least, I'll let him know that I've got a job to do for you boys, and that I might be gone for an extended period of time, so he's prepared."

"Good idea," Roger responded. "You and I can discuss it further in the morning—when you're at the airport. We'll use the secure phone I gave you. And I'll be about setting up your SEAL team from the plane."

As planned, at six o'clock that evening Henry knocked on Jack's door.

"Hey, Jack," he announced as he walked in. "I can't believe how busy you've been today, setting everything up for my aunt. Brother, you were on fire. You got it all squared up in her apartment. It's like a damn hospital over there—nurses and everything. And Doctor Jeff. He's quite the guy, isn't he?"

"That's not the half of it. He's actually the one who set the whole thing up—not me. We really didn't mean to push all that past you, but it had to be done pretty much like he did it. That is, if we're going to take care of her outside a real hospital. And, we didn't have much time to get it all done. That's why we rushed it a bit."

"How're we gonna cover this?" Henry asked. "Auntie is on Medicare. I don't think there's any other insurance, and you know

I don't have any money. How's this gonna work? Send the bills to me, and—"

"Not open for discussion," Jack interrupted.

"But—"

"I mean what I'm saying," Jack retorted. "We're not going there. Not now, not ever. So just drop it!"

Henry considered pressing the matter a bit, but thought better of it.

Jack, while he was hesitant to do so, at that time felt constrained to explain to his friend a little bit about what he was up to. He told Henry that starting in the morning he would have to be gone on an overseas mission, that he might be away for as long as ten days. And possibly even longer. When Jack explained in the most general of terms the sort of job he was about to do—that it involved China and North Korea—Henry said, "Holy SHIT! Roger going with you? Right?"

"Not this time," Jack said. "He's busy on another project right now. And he's not healed up after his last mission with us. He said he'd give me the best SEAL team the Navy's got. He told me that they are all the best there are, but some have a little more experience with this sort of work, and that he would check around and make sure he gets the one that best fits the bill. I trust him to do just that."

"Hell no!" Henry blurted out. "He knows—we all know—that I am that best man. If this job involves those two bad actors Communist China and North Korea, then you can't tell me that it isn't just about as dangerous as it gets. I'm going with you—end of story. I'll have it no other way. You'd do the same for me. You know damn well you would. I'm goin'! And that's the end of that story!

Tell Roger that I'm going with you."

"But what about your aunt?" Jack said. "You've got to be around for her."

"I've done everything I can for her. Hell! You've done everything that can be done. Period. She's going to live or die regardless of where I am. I can't even get in to see her. Can you believe that! Jack, we've already been through too much. You know what I'm talking about. You're there for me. And I'm there for you. That's just the way it is."

"Who's going to take care of my boys?" Jack asked. "Kate's busy with her job. She doesn't even know I'm headed out. I thought that this time around you could stay and see to them, and your aunt. Really, that's how I planned this."

Henry slid his coffee over and spread his huge hands out on the table. "Bullshit! Bullshit! Bullshit!" he said. "That is all a bunch of bullshit. Jack, tell me honestly. Kate's on her way. Isn't she? I know damn well she is. She knows you're headed out. And, who's the one that always has your back when the going gets really shitty? Or better, who would you most want having your back, when all hell breaks loose? Me, right? Isn't that the way it is? Tell the truth?"

Jack didn't have to think about it. He knew Henry very well, and he trusted him completely. So, he did not answer Henry's question. Instead, Jack said, "Henry, that's not the question—"

"The hell it ain't!" Henry retorted. "That's all it's about. Somethin' happens to you over there, who the hell's gonna raise those two boys? You and I both know that I ain't qualified to be their father. The best thing I can do for them is to make sure you make it back in one piece. If you haven't called Kate yet, you gotta call her right now. She's gotta catch the next flight out of New York.

She can pull that off. She's a lieutenant out there. Hell, that has to count for something. Those boys can survive for ten days without us. That's a hell of a lot better than forever without you. You know them better than I do. It won't be a problem. They can check up on my aunt every day. It'll keep them busy, maybe even out of trouble.

"We'll do that job. We'll get back here afterwards. Pick up where we left off. That's the way it's gotta be. It's the way it's always been. Period. End of discussion. We don't make it, then Kate has to jump in and take over with the boys—permanently. You damn well know that's the way it's been ever since I joined up with you. And that's the way it works best. Right? You know I'm right."

Again, Jack did not even look up. After a minute he said, "I do have Kate on the way. Called her earlier. And now, I'll tell Roger that you and I are going to handle this job. You'd better get packed."

Chapter 8 —

It was barely seven o'clock when Jack called Roger to let him know what was up. It sounded to Jack like it was just what Roger had expected to hear all along.

Henry stood next to Jack during the call. He paid great attention to the way Jack laid the case out on the phone, and he seemed entirely satisfied with what he'd heard.

"We've got a lot to get done yet tonight," Henry announced. "We're gonna have to get my camper stocked up for the boys. At least enough to last them until Kate gets here. What're you thinking? She make it yet this week?"

"She hasn't bought her tickets yet," Jack said. "I wasn't sure how I was going to put it to her. She would have been one pissed off little tornado when she learned that you weren't going. She would not have thought much at all about that arrangement. Sometimes I think she has more confidence in you than she does in me. She is planning on heading out, but I'm not clear on the details at this point. Neither is she, either. She's got some preparations to see to, and then she'll be flying in."

Henry did not react to the comment that Jack had not told her that "good old Henry" might not be going with him.

"I will call her right now and see where she's at with all this," Jack said. "If she doesn't make it right away, that's still all cool. The sheriff knows me very well. And, this is Sugar Island. Different set of rules out here. The boys will be fine with or without Kate for the short term. I do need to tell her that the boys will be sleeping in your camper."

"And I'll grab it and bring it around to the door so we can load up," Henry said. "I'll first toss in some of the stuff from my stock—snacks that I know they would like."

After Jack had spelled out for Kate as much as he dared, he walked outside to gather up the boys.

"Hey, fellas," he called over to them. They were shooting baskets with two other boys from the island. "I want you to come in because I need to talk to you."

"Uncle Jack," Robby pleaded. "It's fourteen all. Can't we just finish the game?"

"Play to fifteen, win by one, and then come straight in," Jack said.

"The game's to twenty-one," Robby said. "Have to win by two."

"This time it's to fifteen," Jack said firmly. "Whoever scores the next point, wins. Unless you want to finish it tomorrow."

"Fourteen-fourteen," Jack heard one of the visitors say. "Catch you here tomorrow after supper."

"Before supper," Jack dictated. "You boys will have to finish the game in the afternoon—before supper."

The two boys then followed on Jack's heels as he re-entered the house.

"What's up, Uncle Jack?" Robby asked as he ran a glass of water. Red was staring at Jack through a terribly confused expression. Both of the boys knew that it was most unusual for Jack to so abruptly interrupt one of their totally acceptable activities. They sensed that something noteworthy was about to go down. And, given the situation with Henry's Aunt Halona, they both feared the worst in that regard.

"Is Henry's aunt okay?" Robby asked as he sat down at the table. "Is something happening with her?"

"As far as I know," Jack replied, "her situation has not changed. She is very ill, and the Covid bug is just about as bad as it gets, but that is not the main reason why I called you guys in."

The two boys exchanged glances, but were silent.

"Henry and I are taking a little business trip," Jack explained. "Not sure how long we'll be gone, but it's going to be up to you two men, and Buddy, of course, it'll be your job to keep an eye on Henry's aunt and make sure everything is under control over there. Henry's going to park his camper outside her window, and you boys will basically move out of the house and live there in the camper until we get back. At least, you'll be spending the nights there. During the days you can come back to the house to study, and have meals, and whatever. But, at night, you'll be staying in the camper. Much like you spend the nights in your bedroom. The camper will be your bedroom, and evening snack area."

Red looked over at Robby to get his attention, and he raised his eyebrows.

Robby captured the drift of Red's glance, and asked, "Is Kate coming out?"

"Kate has some business to take care of in New York," Jack answered. "When she winds that up, she'll fly out to the resort. She will cook for you, like she always does when she comes to the island. You boys will have your meals over here, but still spend nights in the camper. Kate will do the shopping as needed—like picking up milk and eggs, and other basics. During the day she might take you with her to help. Just remember, at night there will be no exceptions. You—"

"We will be in Henry's camper at night—*every* night," Robby uncharacteristically interrupted.

"Exactly," Jack responded, not particularly pleased having Robby speak over him.

Wonder where that came from, Jack said to himself. *Didn't feel like blatant impudence, but was not exactly appropriate, either.*

Red picked up on it and flashed a brief glare in Robby's direction. It was sufficient to serve the purpose. Robby zipped his mouth as he picked up a half-full glass salt shaker and pretended to examine it.

"If the condition of Henry's aunt takes a turn—for good or bad, you should just sit on your information until we get back. Not even Kate will be able to get hold of us."

The boys looked at each other. Jack saw their uncertainty and explained, "Think of it like this. When a spacecraft returns to Earth, there is a period of time that it goes entirely silent—communication of any sort just cannot be accomplished. That's—"

"A plasma blackout," Robby interrupted.

"Yes," Jack said. "A plasma blackout. Well, that's just the way this is going to work. Think of this business trip like that."

Red began smiling and nodding his head, and he looked over

at his friend. Robby was again a little embarrassed at having interrupted Jack, but when he caught a glimpse of Red's big grin, his face sprouted a huge smile as well—he knew exactly what Red was thinking.

"Like that 'Stereo-B' spacecraft," Robby said. "We were reading about that. When it flew behind the sun we lost contact with it. That was for nearly two whole years. You and Henry aren't flying behind the sun, are you?"

Jack and Red both chuckled.

"Nothing like that," Jack said. "But it's sort of the same notion. From the moment we leave in the morning, we will not be able to talk to you, to Kate, or to any of our friends. That's just the way it has to be.

"And then, when we get back home, everything will go back to normal. One morning, you'll open the camper door to let Buddy run, and the pleasant fragrance of me burning bacon will attack your senses, and you'll come running. That's exactly how it's going to be.

"But," Jack continued, "in the meantime, it is absolutely critical that you don't even think about trying to call Henry or me, or even anyone else—no matter what. And I mean no matter what. Take up every issue with Kate. That is, when she gets here. Until we get back I will have to put your cell phones away. Just remember, like I said, do not even try to call us for any reason. Even an unanswered call to our numbers could draw unwanted attention to us, and if the wrong people are monitoring them, it could cause harm—to you and to us."

With that last directive issued by Jack both boys began to understand that this was not a typical business trip—such as what would be expected if a representative from a computer firm were flying into New York to sell a product. At the same time they were both thinking the same thing: *Uncle Jack and Henry are not going to be selling or buying anything—they are going to be running around some foreign country, blowing things up and shooting bad people.*

Jack knew before he uttered those words of warning that they would give the boys a pretty clear picture of what he and Henry were going to be up to, but he did not want to mislead them in any way.

Just at that moment Henry walked in the door.

"Hey, fellows," he said, "why don't you give me a hand in moving some of your Uncle Jack's food and snacks over to the camper. He knows what you should be taking over there. Right, Jack?"

"Right," Jack said. "Think of it like this. Whatever you like to eat, say, at ten o'clock at night. Stuff you'd come down to the kitchen to get—that's the food you will want to keep in the camper. Don't overdo it. You can add snacks when you wind up your day. Make sure you have plenty of drinking water. And food for Buddy. When Kate gets here, she can pick up whatever you need, and help you get better organized. The critical thing is this—once you sign off and enter the camper, that should be it for the day. Anything comes up, in that camper, that's where Kate, Dr. Jeff, or any of the nurses—that's where they should be able to find you. Got that?"

Neither of the boys had any problem with their orders.

Once the camper was loaded, Henry drove it over to his aunt's apartment, and backed it up as close to her bedroom window as was possible. That was in order to give the boys a good view into his aunt's sick bed—that is, of course, should the nurses opt to leave the blinds open.

While Henry was doing that, Jack sat the boys down and expressed again his "wishes" with regard to their activities while he was away. The boys nodded their agreement right up to where Jack told them to promise not to drive Henry's truck except in the most "urgent of emergencies." But, as soon as that directive sank in, Red glanced over at Robby with a puzzled expression.

This prompted Robby to ask Jack, "What would you consider an 'urgent emergency' to be? When would it be okay to use the truck?"

Jack stared deeply into their eyes—first Robby's, and then Red's. "You'll know what constitutes an urgent emergency when you see it," he uttered slowly. "There should be no doubt in your mind, and it will be clear as a bell when you explain it to me when I get back. If something should come up, you must log all miles, and be able to justify them. And just know, I will be checking the odometer before I leave. I need you not to play any tricks on me, with anything. My Tahoe keys will be here too—for an emergency. When Kate gets here, make sure you always get her permission before you drive any vehicle."

Both boys understood exactly what he was saying.

Jack went on to tell them that it would be okay with him if, during the day, the boys occupied themselves with activities of their choice, as long as they did not leave the vicinity of the resort, try to make any calls, or fail to get their homework completed to the best of their ability.

"However," Jack said, "we are going to do things a bit differently this time around. I want you each to give me your cell phones."

Red looked over at Robby with a very confused wrinkle of his brow.

"Red and I were wondering what that was all about—losing our phones and all. Why?"

"Can't elaborate," Jack replied. "Just know, as I said before, that I do not want either of you to make any phone calls, or send any texts or go online, period—not until Henry and I get back. Same goes for Kate, when she gets here. Personal phones are going to be off limits for a little while—that is, until you see me when I'm back, and I put your cell phones into your hands."

Henry had walked back into the Handler house and so he heard Jack's words. "That should also go for us too?" he asked. "Right?"

"Yup," Jack replied. "Henry and I will be securing our phones downstairs as well."

Jack then hugged each of the boys and told them, "Just remember this, Henry and I are leaving for a week or so—might be less, or even a little longer. It is important that you remember not to even think about making any calls on anybody's phone. Not until we get back. And not to move Henry's truck—or mine—except in an emergency. Kate will be here shortly—probably tomorrow. You yahoos will be sleeping in Henry's brand new camper, she'll use my unit here at the resort. Any other questions?"

"What if we have a question for Kate?" Robby asked. "How do we ask her?"

"If it can wait until morning, ask her at breakfast. If it's an emergency, one of you can go over and wake her up. But no phone calls!"

Jack read the expressions on the boys' faces. They had questions right then, and he knew that those questions were dealing with the nature of the mission. So, he thought it appropriate to fill them in as much as he could.

"As I said earlier," Jack explained, "the job Henry and I are about to undertake should take about a week to ten days. We are not at liberty to discuss it in detail, except that it will not provide us, you boys included, with the license to use our phones, computers, or any other personal modes of communication, not until we have completed our tasks, and are back on the island.

"When I get back, you'll get your phones back.

"Beyond the lack of communication, this job amounts to little more than a typical day at the office. It's just that I will not be able to talk to you until I get back. That's all. Kate will be totally in charge when she gets here. So take everything that can't wait to her. She'll be on her way here from New York as soon as possible, so then she will be able to handle everything pertaining to the resort.

"Now, I want you boys to do us a big favor. Henry, especially. That's his aunt in that room. We want you guys to be here, to stay nearby, in case you're needed for anything. We don't expect you to sit on your hands out there in the camper all the time, just be ready in case you're needed for something. Like, if one of her caregivers in there needs a hamburger. Or, if she needs help with anything, I want you to be ready to lend a hand. Can we count on you fellows for that?"

Both Red and Robby nodded in the affirmative. "Does that mean that we can drive out and buy lunch for a nurse? Would that be emergency enough that we could log it and you'd be okay with it?"

"Nice try," Jack chuckled. "When Kate gets here, you would

run over and tell her that one of the nurses needs some food, or whatever. And Kate would take care of it. Until Kate arrives, one of you would have to serve as the resident fry cook. But, a food request does not make either of you fellows DoorDash drivers."

The boys looked at each other, clearly disappointed with Jack's words.

"Then, I think we should be all set here," Jack said. "Remember, under no circumstance do I want either of you two to enter the aunt's living quarters. Not until we get back. Then we'll all do something fun together at that time. Okay?"

"Like what?" Robby said. "Like, what kind of fun do you have in mind?"

"You'll see," Jack said.

"Be thinking about it," Henry added. "We're always open to good ideas. See what Kate thinks. She'll be in on it too."

"Any other questions?" Jack asked.

Robby started to open his mouth. But Red, realizing that Robby had already been pushing it with Jack, poked him with an elbow. Robby got the message and shut up.

Jack saw it, and halfheartedly inquired, "No more questions? Then, until Kate gets here, you boys are largely on your own. See you when we see you. Probably next week."

It was obvious to both men that the boys were concerned about what was going on, but everyone was trying to put on a brave face. Jack then sent the boys over to the camper even though they were not ready to turn in.

As Jack and Henry walked off, Henry started to laugh. "You do know why Red elbowed him, don't you?"

"Absolutely," Jack said. "Red did not want any more orders

from Uncle Jack. He was ready for me to shut up. Smart kid!"

"And," Henry said, after the boys were well out of the range of hearing, "The reason for not using a phone. Is that to prevent any sort of monitoring issues?"

"Right. As soon as the shit storm we're causing hits the fan, every phone call in the world is going to be scrutinized for key words, and for locations. Even retroactively. It won't be easy for all of us to block out all contacts, but we'll do the best we can. It might save some lives—namely, our lives. Gotta be done like this."

Henry knew exactly what Jack was getting at.

"Let's get some sleep," Jack said, "Tomorrow's going to be one big-ass day."

With that, Henry headed over to his cottage for the night.

On his way home, Henry's trek took him past his aunt's unit. At first he considered stopping in to see how she was doing, but he immediately thought better of it. *Nothing to be gained by disturbing the caregivers, he reasoned. All I would do is waste some nurse's time and energy. They've already got their hands full. And I might expose Jack and myself to that crazy Covid bug. Not wise—and not necessary.*

He did take a moment to look in the window where his aunt was resting. There was a nurse attending her at the time, and another standing at her right hand.

Henry then walked quietly over to the camper and looked in on the boys through a camper window. They appeared to be playing cards. Buddy looked up at him and wagged his tail, but did not make a sound.

"Time for this old warrior to find a bed," he mumbled to himself. And then he continued on his short walk home.

Henry was right—the boys were playing poker. However, when the two teenagers awoke in the morning, the vision of aces and kings would not be the first one that came to mind, nor the most beguiling.

Chapter 9 —

The first night in Henry's camper proved anything but uneventful for the Red and Robby duo—not so much as it related to the condition of Henry's aunt, as it did to the surprises that unexpectedly confronted them from without.

While it was nearly two in the morning, the boys had just fallen asleep. They were certainly tired enough to make them want to give up on the day, but the fact that they were anxious about having those closest to them about to embark on what they knew would be a very dangerous mission, combined with the discomfort imposed upon them by the unfamiliar, small physical confines of Henry's camper, made anything resembling normal sleep an utter impossibility. But then, it happened.

It started when Buddy woke both boys with his standard alarm of warning—a steady, low-volume growl: "Grrrrrrrrrrr!"

As soon as the first one ended, it was followed by a second, "Grrrrrrr!" the latter a little louder.

The camper was a nice one—constructed around a sturdy welded-aluminum infrastructure, it provided a double bed in a cabover, and a dining area seating cushion that served as a second sleeping area at night. Red took the big bed up top, and Robby slept down below. Buddy, of course, assumed the position of protector, and guarded the camper from a rug by the door.

"Grrrrrr-rufff!"

Buddy was now not only escalating the decibels of his warning, he added a second syllable, and had assumed a more aggressive posture by standing to all fours and raising the hair on his back.

Red sat up in bed so quickly that he bumped his head on the low ceiling.

Robby pounced with both feet to the floor. "That's *very* weird!" he announced.

Neither of the boys was able to quickly obtain his bearings. Robby cracked open the blinds at the bottom of the window and surveyed the surroundings. To the south was the largest building on the complex. It housed the main common area for the resort, along with a small number of hotel-like one-room units. To the north of that building were several of the resort's units, with Jack's residence, and the rest of the structures located in staggered fashion to the north and east. Of course, Henry's Aunt Halona's cottage was directly behind the camper.

Buddy seemed to be barking in the direction of Jack's residence, so that is where Robby was looking.

Red rolled over in bed and began peering out of the small window next to it.

"Did you see that?!" Robby said in a loud whisper. "Over by Uncle Jack's house. Do you see what I'm seeing?"

Red growled in a way that signaled agreement. It was correctly interpreted as such by both Robby and Buddy. Nothing more was said for the next five minutes. The boys both just watched.

Finally, Robby mumbled, "I don't see them anymore. Do you?"

Red replied with his agreement response, just slightly muffled.

"Really," Robby said, turning to look up at his friend. "Where are they?"

Red pulled away from the window so he could make eye contact with his friend. He then threw Robby a curved arm gesture, indicating that he believed the men had left the resort altogether. He then offered up the same signal, but this time using his index finger to arc off in the distance, suggesting across the St. Marys River to the Michigan mainland.

Robby understood that to mean that Red had seen the strange men disappear to the south, into or perhaps across, the St. Marys River, undoubtedly using the same boat that they had arrived in.

Buddy had stopped growling, but was whining in a very eager fashion, nose glued to the crack where the door met the jamb, front paws pouncing up and down.

"What do you suppose that was all about?" Robby asked.

Red shrugged his shoulders and raised his palms signaling that he didn't have a clue.

"Do you think we should wake Uncle Jack up to tell him what we saw?" Robby asked.

Red shook his head emphatically as he wrote on a piece of paper, and then he handed it to Robby and signaled with his finger that Robby should write what he was thinking down on it.

Red always tried to have a pencil and tablet nearby for just this sort of situation. Robby flipped it over to the blank side, located a pencil in the drawer of a little desk, and then he began writing a description of what he had seen. This included a quasi-detailed drawing of the two men as he recalled them. Red did the same once he saw what Robby had begun.

Red placed a book under the tablet and wrote these words: "Uncle Jack. First night, before you left on your business trip, Buddy woke us up growling. He had heard—or smelled—some prowlers outside. I saw two men by our house. They were dressed in black. I think they were wearing night-vision glasses. I did not see a flashlight. After a few minutes they disappeared down toward the river. I think I saw a boat heading across the St. Marys for the mainland. We did not wake you up because we knew you needed your rest. Hope we did the right thing. P.S., It was about 2 A.M."

Red then looked down at Robby and observed that he was still working on his, so he just tore the sheet off the tablet, slid it into the book, and set the book on the shelf at the head of his bed. He then began scrutinizing the horizon in the direction of the river, but he did not spot any additional suspicious activity.

A few minutes later Red checked out his friend again. Robby had now stopped writing and had stood up. Red held out his account for Robby to take. So, the two boys exchanged notes.

This is how Robby described the event: "Uncle Jack. This happened on the night before you and Henry left on your trip. Red and I were asleep. It was about 2. Buddy woke us up. He heard something outside. Red and I both looked out, and this is what I saw. I saw two men sneaking round your house. I think they were wearing dark clothes. Pretty soon they disappeared. Red thinks they headed south toward the St. Marys River. I did not see any flashlights or a boat. Since they left, we did not want to bother you. We will keep our eyes open while you are gone. —Robby."

They each finished reading the note the other boy had written. They looked at each other and shrugged their shoulders. Robby said, "Your note looks about like mine. What do you think, Buddy? Can we go back to sleep now? I'm tired."

Buddy walked over to Robby to get petted.

"Think I should let him have a little run?" Robby asked Red.

Red nodded, and then scooted down so he could slide off the bed. He slipped on his shoes and put a leash on Buddy's collar.

Robby understood what Red was doing. They did not want Buddy to take off into the river chasing the scent. But they both knew that the poor animal was thoroughly stressed out by the episode and would need a little exercise in order to vent. Robby put his shoes on as well, and the three of them stepped outside. But they did not venture toward the main house.

Five minutes later they all returned, and this time successfully retired for the rest of the night.

* * *

7:30 arrived, and all three of them still slept. Finally, at 7:45, Buddy began to whine. Red's eyes popped open, but this time he did not abuse his forehead on the low sleeper ceiling. He leaned forward, bracing himself on his elbows. Buddy sensed his friend stirring, and he looked up at Red and registered a muffled bark, which the awakened fourteen-year-old rightly interpreted as meaning, "C'mon, kid, time to let your best friend out of this stuffy prison."

But Robby beat Red to it. He did not even bother to tie his laces, or snap on a leash. He simply opened the camper door and Buddy launched himself out, landing a front leg first nearly eight feet away. He stopped to get his scent-bearings, and then broke into a frenzied race with his shadow over to where the boys had spotted the men-in-black prowling around earlier.

Both boys hurried over to the main house where Buddy was

now sniffing. Buddy was about his own business, but the boys bus-ied themselves searching the geography adjacent to the building for evidence of whatever it was that went down the night before. Because it had all occurred so late, and while they were so terri-bly tired, it now all seemed like a bad dream. That is, until Buddy walked up to Red and proudly dropped an object for him to take a look at—it was a knife. But not just a common one, like you might find in the kitchen, in the pocket of a teenager, or even in your av-erage hardware store. It had a six-inch fixed black blade with a saw on the back of it, a molded but soft black plastic handle textured for grip, and a thin knotted strap.

Red picked it up and examined it.

Robby, who was standing about twenty feet away, had watched Buddy running up to his friend, and he saw Red pick something up.

"What did he find?" Robby asked, as he walked swiftly over to his friend.

Red carefully handed the knife over to Robby, as a deep look of concern gripped both boys' faces.

"Where'd he find this?" Robby asked.

Red pointed toward the St. Marys River. The boys looked at one another, and began to slowly walk toward the dock. Their con-centration was glued to the ground in search of more evidence.

After about twenty minutes of fruitless searching, Robby broke the silence: "When's Aunt Kate gonna get here? I forgot. Did Uncle Jack tell us?"

Red stopped walking and looked out across the St. Marys. He thought for a moment, and then looked Robby in the eye. Shrug-ging his shoulders he shook his head and flashed his friend an affected grin of uncertainty.

"Yeah," Robby moaned. "Me either. And it don't help much that we can't use our phones."

Red then pointed toward the camper, and then signaled that they should leave the knife there.

"Good thinking," Robby agreed. "I don't feel comfortable walking around carrying something like this."

So, that's what they did. They took it back to the camper and wrapped it in a few paper towels and foil, and then laid it in the middle of the small table.

"Should be safe here," Robby said.

Red nodded in agreement.

But, as so often is the case with Red and Robby, it is always wise to expect the unexpected. They were soon to learn that their adventure was just getting started.

Chapter 10 —

E arlier that morning—before daybreak, while the two boys still slept—Henry had grabbed his travel bag and briskly strode over to Jack's house. The two men then immediately jumped into the resort's all-purpose Tahoe and headed for the Sugar Island Ferry. From there they were to proceed over to Sanderson Field International Airport, where Bob Fulbright had a Gulfstream G650 waiting for them. The short flight would terminate in Chicago, where the two men would catch a B-52 Bob had assigned to fly them nonstop to Japan.

It was while waiting to get off the Sugar Island Ferry that Jack called Roger, on the secure cell of course, to bring him up to speed on Henry's decision. That was, however, pretty much the sum total of what the two of them considered at that time. The only other info that Roger provided was this: Sanderson, Chicago, and Tokyo. Whether or not plans regarding additional planes, trains or automobiles even existed beyond those that were already laid out, they did not discuss.

But this lack of elaboration was inconsequential to Jack. Roger had already explained to him that in every case possible only the information absolutely needed would be provided for them, and that they would be made aware of next steps only as situations dictated. "That way," Roger had told Jack, "should the mission run amuck, and should any of them be captured, there would be only a limited amount of intel that they might be forced to give up."

"It just works better that way," Roger explained.

Roger could see that his two friends, while they were totally committed to the mission, both lacked the level of knowledge necessary for proper preparation. So, when it was confirmed that Jack and Henry had boarded the B-52, he and Bob thought that this would be an opportune time to bring the two men at least somewhat up to speed on awareness of what they were getting into. So they called Jack.

"Not only can this mission provide tremendously valuable information to our military, " Roger told them, "but it is also off the chart with regard to the challenge it will present to those who are willing to accept it. I really don't see any clear path to surviving it," he continued. "Success or failure of the mission itself—I fear this will likely mark the end for some or all of those who dare undertake it. I have spent many mind-numbing hours pondering the prospects for developing a viable plan for a successful extraction. But, I have to confess, I have failed to come up with one; at least, not one with which I am reasonably confident.

"No matter how talented you are, or how well you perform, it seems to Bob and me that it would be highly unlikely that some, if not all of you, even though you may accomplish all or most of what we're looking for, that at least some of you will still not make it home alive. At some point, I have to think that it will get the best of us. No matter who we might send—whether it be any one of the SEALs, or Jack, or his buddy Henry, or, hell, even Jack Ryan himself.

"Nevertheless, we have determined to take the risks, and commit the most valuable of our resources, because of what is at stake. There are some other aspects about this missile, the one China is sending to North Korea at this time, that make it double troublesome. You'll find out more about this as we go along. But, according to the specs delivered to us, it looks as though it will work. We have determined that as long as the targets chosen are clustered to within a thousand kilometers of one another, it can be devastatingly effective in this aspect of its performance.

"How can we defend against that?" Roger then asked rhetorically. "Well, that's one of the things that the Chinese are hoping to learn with this test. There's a lot *I* don't even know about it. We really have no concrete notion of what to expect. But, the Chinese don't know everything about our defense capabilities, either. And, ultimately, that is what this is actually all about—at least from their end. What the CCP has in mind is to monitor our defenses when this missile is launched, they hope to glean some pertinent info regarding how we would prepare to defend against it. Whether we would employ land-based, airborne, or satellite defenses. Or what combination of them.

"Should we shoot this test missile down?" Roger asked, again rhetorically, after having paused for a long moment. "We would not want to. Not unless we felt imminently threatened. But, we would be on high alert. And be following all the necessary protocols right up to taking it out—if that's how we would choose to deal with it. And that is precisely what the Chinese will be looking at. If the missile starts out heading in the direction of some of our assets, our military will have to regard it as a hostile act, a potential attack, and we will be forced to move into a higher state of readiness. That alone could give away our defense posture. At least, the Chinese monitoring stations will be hoping it goes down just like that.

"And so," Roger asked, turning his attention to Bob, "what is it, exactly, that you are hoping our guys can accomplish?"

"I can't get into much detail on that," Bob said. "Not until we are actually in the process of the mission itself. Just know that while everything seems in a flux, we do have a plan. But also keep in mind that our plan does not guarantee any degree of survivability. While it is heavily weighted toward success, it does not offer much in the area of extraction. It just simply cannot—there are too many unknowns. We are still working that part out, and will continue to do so all the way through. We simply do not have a real good handle on just how the North Koreans and the Chinese are going to react, what obstacles they might toss at us, or how quickly. Just don't know some things—many things. Nor are we even able to predict them in any reasonable way. So, we don't have much to say about getting you boys out. Our heart is in that part, but there are no guarantees. And honestly, I'm not going to lie or mislead you, we probably cannot even offer a solid likelihood. At least not at this time."

Roger weighed his friend's words, and then said, "It sounds like these brave men are themselves doing the job of an anti-missile missile. And we all know that those things are never reusable."

"I wouldn't go quite that far," Bob said, a little irritated at the way Roger phrased it. "I promise that we will do our best to bring all the men back. But it's not going to be easy. And I can't even tell you how we might do it. It's just largely an unknown, at this point."

"More than that, I would think," Roger persisted. "Bringing those guys home in one piece is not even a critical factor in determining the mission's success. Doesn't that sound just about right?"

Bob remained silent for an uncomfortably long time. He was thinking.

"You could think of it like that," he finally said. "But, I can assure you, I will not send men out on a dangerous mission until I am confident that I have made my best effort to develop a plan that offers a reasonable chance of survival—regardless of the strategic significance of that mission.

"But, ultimately, you're right. The mission will be deemed successful if the principal goals are achieved. Those goals, as we've explained, will be satisfied if two objectives can be achieved. First of all, if we can pull it off without being required to give anything away regarding our defensive posture. That is, if our defense gurus are not forced to tip their hand. Second, if we can discombobulate the enemy to the point that they permit our security personnel to thwart their efforts to release Covid-22, that monstrous scourge, on Americans. That's what we're after. If we can accomplish those two goals, this mission will be a total success—even if it means losing a few troops. That's just about as blunt and honest as I can be.

"We would like to provide you more details, and we will as we move along, but for right now, that is all we feel appropriate to share with you."

Both Jack and Henry were already familiar with performing under tight security measures, so neither of them had an issue with it.

While the two men did sense that they were still being kept somewhat in the dark about the mission, as their trip progressed they found that by following carefully the conversations they were having with crew members onboard the B-52, and by observing some of the equipment that they were provided with by CIA agents, Jack and Henry were able to figure out some of the more obvious aspects of the mission. Also aiding them in their efforts to ferret out the details were the bits and pieces of information dropped on them by those responsible for the special training they received on the flight.

For instance, upon boarding the B-52 in Chicago, both of them were handed a packet of maps and charts. They were told to study them carefully, and to memorize as much as they could, because every piece of paper contained in that envelope would be collected from them in Tokyo—that they should deplane with nothing on their person aside from the clothes they were wearing when they boarded.

Jack and Henry were quickly able to glean from the notes that the job Bob Fulbright had for them involved being flown into Japan from Chicago, and then from Tokyo to Seoul via Korean Air. On the last leg of the flight they would be posing as American businessmen. From there they would somehow be deposited on the shore of the Yellow Sea at a spot near the Sohae Satellite Launching Station in North Korea—a site located only a few kilometers from the Chinese border. There they would hide out until they had received orders to move inland toward the launch site. The information provided at that time contained only a few sparse details—specifics, they trusted, would be provided later, and then only on that timely "need to know" basis, as had been explained to them earlier.

Again, both Jack and Henry studied the information provided, sparse as it was. Once they had completed two runs through it, Jack suggested that they discuss what they each had gleaned.

"We have to realize that the intention here is to provide us with a basic overview of the mission," Jack offered. "Nothing more."

"Exactly," Henry agreed. "Roger and Bob don't get into a project without precise goals and a well-developed plan to attain them. I don't see any of that here. Any theory as to why that is?"

"For one thing," Jack offered, "Experience tells me that it was done in this way on purpose—this lack of detail is almost certainly intentional. Would have to be."

"I would think so too," Henry replied. "But that's not the way they typically do things. And they know it's not how we like to do things. Anyway, reading between the lines, I'd say that we're gonna get dropped off in *northern* North Korea, and, it'll be from there that we will be making our way over to the missile launch site. And then, we will be doing something to interfere with the success of a soon-to-be-launched missile. If I'm understanding this correctly, and if it follows a similar path as have other recent missile tests, this one is designed to head east-southeast, and pass right over Japan. I suppose that could make a lot of people nervous—like the previous tests did. What do you suppose the deal is with *this* test that makes it so different? Or, do you think it's somehow similar to those they were kicking out of that site a couple years ago? What do you suppose makes this one so damn special?"

"Great question," Jack said. "We'll certainly know more later. But, there was one clue, I suspect, hidden in this statement. I'll read it out loud. It says, 'the principal task is the altering of the missile's guidance system to follow less objectionable paths to its/ their targets.'

"That's particularly interesting, I think, because I was of the opinion that the missiles the North Koreans have been testing do not actually possess much in the way of maneuverability—at least once prepared for launch. Previous tests pretty much had to follow a rigidly pre-programmed route—it practically had to be set at the factory. To have them want us to *alter* the current missile's targets, while it's on the launching pad, that strikes me as very curious—and that is curious in a very significant fashion."

Jack then turned to more squarely face Henry, and he said, "Also, what I think even more intriguing is the use of the plural, as it refers to *paths and targets*—and even uses the plural pronoun. I'm thinking that might suggest that this new rocket—that new version of the Hwasong, while possibly being more maneuverable, it looks like it's able to deliver *multiple* payloads, to *different* targets. That's certainly new for the Koreans."

"Oh hell, Jack," Henry said, after pausing to digest what Jack had just offered, "If you're right, I can see why Washington would be nervous—a large, long-range missile with after-launch maneuverability."

"And multiple warheads," Jack interjected. "The ability to hit more than one target with a single missile launch."

"If that is the case," Henry said, "then Japan and the rest of the world has plenty to worry about. Sounds to me like they stole some of our designs. Do you think?"

"China has sophisticated missile technology," Jack said. "More likely the North Koreans would have been given it to them by their big brother—the CCP. In fact, China is likely to be actually running this entire show. That could be something else that's got DC so worked up. Just like Bob and Roger suggested, China just might be pushing the buttons in order to see what DC is going to do about it. I'm sure we will have our Navy out there in the Pacific monitoring the whole show. We always do in these situations."

"This shit gets pretty complicated, doesn't it?" Henry said as he fidgeted with his seat. "It's like some kinda crazy game."

"And these new seats are not much for comfort," Jack said, "you're either using them as a bed, or you're gonna be sitting straight up.

"And even more interesting," he continued after giving it a little more thought, "You might be right, it just could be that this enhanced programmability that we're suspecting, it just might be that it's the technological advancement itself that's got Washington so worked up. Especially in the hands of the North Koreans."

The flight to Tokyo aboard the B-52 was both swift and high. While they did spend a lot of time talking and studying, they did find some time to close their eyes. And that was fortunate for them, because it stood as the last time they would sleep until after much neighboring geography was turned into an inferno, incinerating hundreds of thousands of men, women and children.

Chapter 11 —

E ven though Jack had given the boys permission to run errands and otherwise keep themselves entertained during the day, they both thought it a good idea to hang around the house until Kate arrived. But, since they did not have any specific idea as to when she would be getting there, they opted not to leave sight of the house—at least until they had a chance to check in with Kate, or until dusk dictated that they resume their post in the camper outside Aunt Halona's sick-bed window.

Initially they determined that it would be helpful to their "investigation" if they could identify the knife Buddy had found. "Aunt Kate will probably know right off what it is," Red scribbled in his notebook for Robby to read. "But it would be nice if we could figure that out before she gets here. I would really like to do a Google search, but Uncle Jack did not want us to go online. So, maybe we can check it out in the library."

The library Red was referencing was the sizable room of books in the basement—not the part of the lower level that Jack designated as private, but down the hall from his secured area. Like Jack's office, the heating and cooling system for the lower level maintained the entire area at a consistent 70 degrees Fahrenheit, and humidity at 35 percent. While his office door was always kept secured, both with a physical lock but also with a well-designed electronic alarm system, the library door was always unlocked, and all security electronics were armed only when the system was programmed upon leaving the house in the "Away" mode. The reason being that Jack wanted the boys to make themselves at home in the library whenever they wanted.

From the time the boys came to live at the resort they had always felt comfortable doing their research online. So, they both found the whole experience of looking in bound books a little disconcerting. When Red first moved in, he knew nothing at all about printed encyclopedias or search engines. In fact, it was Jack that taught him how to use a computer. As far as reading was concerned, at twelve years of age—which was before he had moved into the resort—Red had been tested in school as functioning at the third grade level in reading. It was only after hours of tutoring by Jack and Kate during Red's first year with the Handlers that he learned to read well enough to have the courage even to crack a reference book.

Now, however, at fourteen both boys read at beyond a twelfth-grade level, and they both were proficient on a computer.

When Kate and Jack set up the library, many of their friends and neighbors did not understand why anyone would invest nearly eighty thousand dollars stocking a home library with books geared to the enlightenment of two fourteen-year-old boys. Jack did opt to skip most contemporary fiction, and even non-fiction, in lieu of the possibility of accessing most of it online. However, he did choose to fill the shelves with all manner of classic works in print, as well as an inordinate number of reference works, including a 1971 set of *The Compact Edition of the Oxford English Dictionary Complete Text Reproduced Micrographically.* The boys always liked to tease their Uncle Jack about those books because they always had to have a magnifying glass to use them.

So, the first section of the library the boys went to on this day was to the part that housed the twenty-two volumes of the *World Book Encyclopedia.* They looked for *knives* to start with. Having no luck, they looked up *knife.* Finally they sought out *combat knife,* and from there they finally discovered a knife similar to the one Buddy had found. The one pictured in the book was called a 'navy tactical knife.'

"I think it," Robby said, "the one Buddy found, I think it might be like a Navy SEAL knife. I saw ones like it in military surplus stores. My dad used to take me to surplus stores with him. We'd usually just look around. He liked that kind of stuff. But, I think I remember seeing knives that looked like this being called 'navy tactical knives.' I think the one Buddy found looks just like them. And the pictures in the encyclopedia, that's what they're called in there too."

"Buddy's knife," Red wrote, "it isn't new. Not at all."

"You're right," Robby agreed. "In places the paint is completely worn off. And the handle—the grip—there are deep gouges and scrapes. It looks like it's been well used. And do you remember the junk that was built up at the top of the blade? Where it connected to the handle? The part that protects the hand from sliding onto the blade."

"The bolster," Red wrote. "It's called the bolster. Or quillon, I think."

"Yeah," Robby said. "I guess that's what it's called. I've heard it called the *hand guard*. Anyway, that knife had a bunch of gunk built up there. I think it looked like the owner had skinned a deer with it. Recently. That looked to me like fat and dried blood. It looked like a hunting knife after gutting a deer. You know what I mean? If you don't clean a knife after you use it to gut a deer—it looks like that."

And then Red's eyes flashed. He looked up from the book as though he'd seen a bolt of lightning. He wrote, "I'll be right back. Wait here."

Robby did not wait more than five seconds before he took off after his friend. It was as though he could read Red's mind. *He's goin' over to the camper to get that knife,* he was thinking. *I'd bet on it.*

The boys had wrapped the knife with aluminum foil and left it on the table in the camper because they thought they might get in trouble if they were caught running around with it. Plus, they wanted to show it to Kate when she got there.

Robby was right about Red—and right behind him. That's exactly what Red was in such a hurry to check out. However, Red's jaw dropped when he searched the table where they had left the knife only minutes ago, and it was gone.

The paper towel and foil remained, but the knife was gone!

Just seconds later Robby bolted through the camper door. When he saw Red standing there with the foil in his hands, he looked around for a few seconds, and then asked, "Where's the knife?"

Red held the foil out, tossed it on the table, and then looked Robby in the eye.

Robby did not need a translator to figure out what had just happened.

"Oh my gosh!" Robby moaned. "One of those men-in-black from last night—probably the one who lost it—he must have returned and picked up his knife. That must be what happened, don't you think? How did he know to look in the camper?"

Red did not respond.

How do we explain this to Aunt Kate? Red asked himself. *Man, I sure wish she'd get here?*

Chapter 12 —

I'd forgotten just how involved all this shit is," Jack complained to himself, but somewhat aloud. He was wrestling in the belly of the B-52 with testing out a wetsuit and hooking up the oxygen tanks. "This used to be a simple task. Never gave it a second thought. But now it is anything but automatic, now I have to think each step through, and try to remember what comes next. I must need more practice. That's all I have to say about it."

Henry overheard him and assumed a grin, but he did not respond verbally. He was not used to hearing Jack complain about having to do any menial tasks, so he did not know how serious his boss was about these issues.

I'll just keep my mouth shut, Henry said to himself. *Better safe than sorry. Anyway, Jack looks like he's still wearing his cynical Handler smile.*

While they were lacking details, both men were well aware of the gravity of this mission. It going to push them not only physically beyond anything they had ever experienced before, but also into areas of knowledge and capabilities that they simply did not possess. "Why," they asked themselves a hundred times, "would

Bob and Roger select *us* to perform it? Surely there are real Navy SEALs who could better deal with the rigors that this mission will ultimately demand. Why us?"

* * *

To this point in time, everything had gone as Roger had promised. The flight from Chicago to Tokyo took a little over ten hours, which was pretty much standard for commercial flights. Almost immediately upon landing in Japan, "friends" of Roger, disguised as airport personnel, escorted them aboard a two-hour Korean Air flight to Incheon International in Seoul—again, just as earlier detailed by Roger. At that point, however, things began to change.

Upon deplaning in Incheon, they were hurried over to a private hangar at the airport. It was there that they were encouraged to physically experience more of the specialized equipment that they were about to encounter. While it is true that they had earlier been introduced to written instructions for much of the more sophisticated gear during the ten-hour transpacific flight, this time all the new equipment included brief sessions of additional hands-on tutoring by field-trained instructors.

There they spent over two hours learning many of the intricacies involved with the newer, sophisticated military gear that they would be using.

"Take this rebreathing equipment, for instance," the trainer said. "This device allows you to maneuver underwater without creating any bubbles. That's because the carbon dioxide that the body discharges is captured, filtered, and then recharged with just the perfect amount of oxygen. When operating properly, no bubbles reach the surface of the water, that way hostiles in nearby patrol boats will not be able to detect you below—at least not easily. Pretty *lit*, right?

"Or," the trainer added after taking a closer look at Jack, "maybe *cool* is a better word. This rebreather is simply very cool. Right?"

Henry threw a glance of feigned wonderment. Jack caught it but did not respond.

The remainder of the time was spent in much the same fashion. One piece after another was defined and demonstrated, all in the shortest possible time. Before the trainer would move on he would always ask, "Do you have any questions?" Jack had served in the Marines during a time before the existence of MARSOC (Marine Corps Special Operations Command), so much of what the trainer demonstrated came along well after Jack's years of service. Even so, Jack regularly read up on the latest developments in the type of equipment that was being made available to the various services. While he had not received formal training on the use of the rebreather, he had actually employed the equipment on other missions he had performed for Roger. Those missions, however, occurred before Henry had come to work with him.

The same was true with regard to the use of various underwater munitions—even though much of what the trainer was showing them did not exist when Jack served, through the years he had simply learned how to use the equipment through necessity. And even those devices with which he did not possess any hands-on experience, he was, in almost all cases, well read concerning them.

That was not the case with Henry. Almost everything presented during that two hours of abbreviated training was either totally new to him, or at least nearly so. But, what made Henry valuable to these operations was primarily his dedication to the mission, a sharp mind, and numerous physical gifts. When presented with a difficult task, he always attacked it head on, and he did so with all of his almost superhuman strength and keen mind. Both Bob and Roger knew that when Jack and Henry were faced with an impossible challenge, they always put everything they had into it, and virtually never failed.

After this period of intense training on the new equipment, Roger's assistant re-entered the hangar and announced that the time to depart had arrived. "Leave absolutely everything that you entered with," he said. "I'll repeat that. You must not have anything on your person that might identify you, or pertain to this mission, or even the United States of America for that matter. *Nothing.* Personal belongings—credit cards, driver's licenses, permits of any sort—even your favorite brand of cigarettes, should you smoke. They all must be left behind at this point. I have a large envelope for each of you. You are to place everything you have with you in that envelope, seal it, and leave it with me. That includes wallets, watches, rings, or any other jewelry. From this moment on, you will not need any of that. It will all be returned to you at the end of the mission."

"Excuse me for a second," Jack interrupted. "We each have our own watches. But neither of them is in any way personalized. May we keep them?"

After examining the watches carefully, the assistant handed them back and said, "They're fine. And I assume they fit. You may keep them."

"And put these on," he continued. "I've got a new set of duds for each of you. And, yes, they are in your proper size. Perhaps the style might not suit you, but the clothes will do just fine. The bag they're in has your name on it. Remove your new fatigues, put them on, and then place the clothes you are now wearing in that bag. And then stick your envelope in that bag as well."

Neither Jack nor Henry were much troubled or surprised at the nature of the clothes they were given—they commonly followed that same protocol when engaged in field operations. Jack received a pair of well-worn tan khaki work-style pants, wool socks and a stretch knit hat, work gloves, nondescript Korean-made shirt and underwear, black rubber high-top boots, and a heavy work coat—all also Korean made. Henry's outfit was largely the same, just in a larger size.

Once he had gathered up the two bags, with the envelopes inside them, the agent directed Jack and Roger to a black Kia Telluride that was just pulling into the hangar. The side and rear windows were deeply tinted—to the point that it was difficult even from the inside to see through them. And, when Jack closed the door behind him, it sounded more like a safe door closing than that of a typical eight-passenger SUV. The glass itself appeared to be over an inch thick.

After they were seated and belted, Henry tapped on the glass with his left knuckles, then looked over at Jack and smiled. "I guess this mission has officially begun," he said.

Still, they had no definitive idea as to where they were then headed. Sense of direction alone told them that they were pointed to the southeast. Which did not tell them much, as there were only two possible routes available, given Incheon International is located on an island in the Yellow Sea and is connected to the mainland only by bridges.

Speeding down the lengthy causeway supporting the Incheon-daegyo Expressway, they crossed over the Incheon suspension bridge, and then continued onto the mainland. There they turned south and headed toward a nondescript plot of wooded real estate located just north of Calvary Baptist Church off Seochang-bangsan-ro. Jack tossed a glance of raised-eyebrow wonderment at Henry, who accepted it with a grinning slow shake of the head.

They next blindly proceeded down a dirt trail several hundred feet before they spotted the first line of the next chapter—a Bell 206 helicopter that Roger had warming up for them. After quickly exiting the SUV and taking their seats onboard, it was less than five minutes after their SUV hit that wooded drive before they were airborne and on the way south to the Port of Bushan, one of the largest container ports in the world.

After around forty minutes the chopper set down in another wooded area, this one just east of Kosin University, which was within minutes of the port. Again, Roger had an armored black Kia Telluride waiting for them.

Still, both Jack and Henry remained largely in the dark as to how they would actually be deposited on land in North Korea. That dilemma, however, seemed to solve itself within minutes when their chopper dropped them off near a dock and they were directed onto a waiting thirty-eight-foot South Korean fishing boat.

"Well," Jack said, "I suppose that tells us half the story—or, at least the first pages. Cinch this squid boat, or whatever it turns out to be, won't be transporting us into North Korean waters. So, I suppose we'll just have to wait and see how they pull the next leg off. I'm thinking we will end up on some sort of submarine. But, that's just my thinking."

It was late in the morning by the time Jack and Henry had

settled in on their comfortably large fishing boat.

"I'd say that there's nothing quite like being the last fishing boat in port to shove off," Jack commented. "Especially since this is primarily a shipping port, not one designed for fishing boats. But, no big deal. At least we are on our way out. Just wait until we've finished our dirty work. We're gonna have to exercise a bit more caution as we progress into waters more hostile than these, I would think."

Less than five minutes after they had boarded the boat, dock workers loosened and unhooked the mooring ropes, and off they headed.

* * *

"You have to put one of these underwater uniforms on as well, my friend," Jack said to Henry as he strapped on his air tanks and a mask.

"But what they showed us earlier was one of those fancy-Dan rebreathing setups," Henry said. "That's not what this is."

"Just put it on and stop griping," Jack told him. "This is what they've got for us on this part of the mission. Just assume that they're saving the fancy-Dan shit for later."

And was Jack ever right.

Chapter 13 —

It was late in the afternoon when Kate drove up in her rented white Tahoe. Both boys were eager to see her, so they were sitting on the wrap-around porch playing cards. Buddy lay only a few feet away, with his head resting just above the top step of the main approach. He knew something was up, but was probably not aware that his two best friends were nervously tossing cards down in anticipation of Kate's arrival. All three of them had spotted her vehicle, and they all knew that a strange white Tahoe almost certainly indicated that the new player would be their over-anticipated Aunt Kate.

The logic behind their conclusion was simple. First off, they were expecting Kate—their Uncle Jack had prepared them for her arrival. Plus, they were not expecting any other visitor. Thirdly, whenever Kate visited, she always flew into Chippewa County International Airport, and she always rented a white four-wheel-drive Tahoe. Always.

"Hi, Aunt Kate!" Robby yelled before she had even parked. Both boys and Buddy took off running towards her. And, as was always anticipated, Buddy won.

"Can we help you?" Robby said. "We'll carry your stuff for you. It's in the back—right?"

"Thanks, boys," Kate said with her consistently huge, loving smile. After stepping out of the vehicle and giving each of them a sincere hug, she dropped to a knee and hugged Buddy. His tail was wagging so wildly that it threw his whole body into a dance of greeting as he planted a full-tongue kiss right on her tightly-closed lips.

"I am so happy to see you guys!" she said at least three times. "How long has it been?"

"Christmas," Robby blurted out immediately. "You were here over the holidays—Christmas and New Year's. I remember. You took us snowmobiling."

"You're right!" she said, laughing loudly. "And you wise guys drove into the river! Dad and Henry had to come and pull you out. I remember that part very well."

"That was me," Robby said, blushing just a bit. "Red did better. At least he kept his dry. We had to take mine into the mechanic afterwards. We sure had a lot of fun, didn't we?"

"We always do," Kate said as she messed up Red's hair and winked at Robby. "Right, kiddo?"

Red nodded.

"Yeah," Kate said. "You guys can haul my stuff in. That would be great. You can just stick it all in my bedroom. I'll put it away later. Are you hungry? Or can you wait until dinner time? I had lunch on the way. But I'd be happy to fix you a sandwich if you're hungry now. What'll it be? Now or later?"

"We're all set, I think," Robby said. "Red and I made sandwiches earlier. So we should be good."

"Bet you'll be glad to get back in school," Kate said as the four of them made their way toward the house. "Get all this Covid stuff behind us. At least you have hot lunches in school."

Robby checked out Red before responding. He noted an effort

by his friend to not give much away at this early stage of Kate's visit to Sugar Island, so he simply smiled and nodded slowly, but did not offer a comment.

"So," Kate said as they walked, "what's new with you two? Aside from your extended Covid vacation? Any new girlfriends you need to tell Aunt Kate about?"

She had sensed their reluctance to open up to her, and she thought she might redirect some of their stress by turning the conversation to a topic she was certain they would resist.

"We don't have any girlfriends," Robby quickly threw back at her.

That was exactly the answer Kate expected. And, it was delivered with the precise level of exuberance she anticipated as well. *Okay, now*, she was silently thinking. T*he next topic that comes up will be what these two boys actually wish to talk about.*

They had barely closed the entry door behind them when Robby broke the silence.

"After you've had a chance to rest up a bit," Robby said. "Red and I have some questions to ask you. But, it's okay to settle in first."

"That sounds a little ominous," she replied. "Just set my stuff inside my bedroom while I get a drink of water. I'm not tired, and I'd really like to hear what you have to say. Okay?"

"Yeah," Robby said. "We'll take your clothes and stuff up and come right back down. I'm sure—we're sure—that you're gonna want to hear what we have to say. It is very interesting. At least we think it is."

"Can't wait to hear all about it," Kate replied. "Can I get you something to drink?"

"Water would be good," Robby replied before he checked with Red, who had begun to nod his head in agreement. "Red will have a glass of water too."

"Done," Kate announced, a few decibels above her normal volume. "Then that'll be our plan."

Kate filled Buddy's water bowl first, and then poured three large glasses of ice water from the fridge.

The boys both sat down at the dining room table just as she was setting the waters in front of them.

"What's this doing here?" she asked as she fingered through the "C" volume of World Book. "C, what starts with C that would pique your interest to look up in an encyclopedia, no less? Does Dad know you guys are thinking about getting a cat? Wonder what he thinks about that?"

"We're not going to get a cat," Robby said. "That's not what we were looking up."

"Not cats, you say. Then, tell me, what C word were you after? If not cats. Girls starts with a 'G,' so it can't be that you were looking up girls. Maybe it's 'cute girls' that you were checking out."

"Combat knives," Robby said, almost interrupting her. "We were checking out combat knives."

Kate set her water down and looked at Robby, and then at Red.

"Combat knives," she articulated slowly. "What on earth led you to doing that?"

Red reached over and asked with his eyes if he could slide the book over to show her something.

"Sure," she said, pushing it in his direction. "Show me what you're talking about. Now that you've got me really interested."

As Red began turning pages, Robby said, "last night we had

a visitor. Actually, we had a couple visitors. At least two. I think it was around two o'clock. We'd been sitting in the camper playing cards, and we had just turned in. And Buddy heard something outside. When we looked out, we saw two men over here. Dressed in all black. They were by the house. They were trying to look in the windows, we think. Uncle Jack must have been working downstairs. Or, maybe he'd gone to bed. But, he must not have seen or heard anything.

"We thought about slipping the leash on Buddy, and checking it out. But, by the time we could have done that, those men were long gone. We were afraid to let Buddy run off after them. They headed for the river. We figured they must've had a boat. And, we didn't want to disturb Uncle Jack."

"You sure you saw two of them?" Kate asked. "And they were dressed in black?"

"And looking in the windows here at the house," Robby said. "We sure did."

"Okay," Kate said. "I get that. We'll have to keep our eyes open, I guess. You didn't recognize them, did you? Do you think you could identify them? If we could find them? Or look at some pictures with the sheriff?"

Both boys were slowly shaking their heads.

"No," Robby said. "It was dark, and they were a long way off. I'm sure we would not be able to identify them."

"What I don't get is this," Kate said. "If they were so far away that you aren't able to describe them, or be able to pick them out of a lineup, what could that have to do with combat knives?"

Red then slid the World Book back over in front of Kate, and he pointed to a picture of a black military combat knife. He looked over at Robby as if to encourage his friend to explain.

"Here's what happened," Robby said. "This morning we got up and checked it all out. Uncle Jack and Henry were already gone, of course. Actually, it all seems like a dream now—a bad one. We came over here where we'd seen the men. By the house. We let Buddy off his leash, because he was all eager to investigate everything. Well, just about the first thing that he did was to tear off running down toward the river. We didn't see everywhere he went, but he was gone only a few minutes, and then he came running back with something in his mouth. I didn't see him do it, but Red did. He dropped a combat knife right by Red's feet. It looked just like the one Red's showing you. Almost exactly like that one."

"You're kidding!" Kate stated in genuine surprise. "Get it. The knife. And show it to me. I want to check that baby out."

"We can't," Robby said. "We don't have it anymore."

"Oh, come on," Kate pleaded. "You've lost it? Okay, you boys— stop playing games with me. Go get the knife and show it to me. I really want to see it."

"We didn't lose it. It's just gone. That's the whole thing," Robby explained. "We really don't have it anymore. Truly. We put it in the camper. All wrapped up in aluminum foil, so that no one would cut themselves on it. It was very sharp. And then, when we wanted to take a closer look at it—after we found it in this encyclopedia, it was gone. The foil and paper towel were still on the table, but the knife was gone."

"Oh shit!" she growled. "No! That's just not possible. Pardon my language, but you boys can't be right. Stuff like that just doesn't happen. What is it that you're leaving out?"

Both boys were very disappointed that Kate did not believe

them.

"Honest, Aunt Kate," Robby said. "As far as we know, that's exactly how it happened. As far as we know. We put it there on the table in Henry's camper. And we did not see anyone go over there. We were over here at the house, in the library. It was not until we went in to check out the *fat gunk* I saw on it. And Red wanted to examine it closer. When he—"

"Wait a minute here!" Kate interrupted. "What are you talking about? What's this fat gunk you saw on the knife? Describe that to me."

"You know," Robby said. "Where the blade meets the guard— the guard that keeps your hand from sliding forward onto the sharp part. Right there. It looked like a hunting knife does after you gut a deer. If you don't clean it. You know—some fat and hair get stuck right in there where the guard is. There wasn't any hair or any blood—at least not fresh blood, in there, but it sure did look like fatty, gunky stuff."

"And Red went in the camper to check it out?" Kate inquired.

"Yes," Robby said. "Actually, we both did. I was right behind him. We both ran back to the camper to check it out. And the knife was gone."

"But the foil that you'd wrapped it in," Kate said. "That foil was still there? But no knife. Right? That is what you're saying. Right?"

Red was nodding his head in agreement.

"That's exactly what happened," Robby said. *"Exactly."*

"Well," Kate said. "You two characters haven't lost a step. You're just as exciting as you've always been."

The boys looked at her, and gave her a smile she saw as demonstrating more agitation than joy.

"I'll be right back," she said. "You guys give me just a minute. Don't go away. I'm going to use the girls' room, and then the four of us will retrace this whole episode while it's still fresh on your minds. We've got to see if we can make sense out of it. Okay? It'll only take me a few."

Kate was gone only for a total of about seven minutes.

Red noted that the toilet had not been flushed, but he did not communicate that fact.

But both boys did notice that she was now wearing a jacket, and under it was a very noticeable Glock-sized bulge on her left side. And on her belt was clipped her shield: City of New York Police.

"Let's go take a look," she said. "There's got to be a logical answer to all this. We'll get it figured out. Eventually. Let's go check it out. And then I'll cook you some delicious dinner. How does that sound?"

It was obvious that the boys were in favor of both of Kate's suggestions. She had a reputation for being an excellent cook—so sitting down to one of her creations would definitely be a treat.

But they also wanted to get to the bottom of the combat knife business. And to figure out who these men-in-black might be. Their Aunt Kate, they believed, was the perfect person to succeed on both counts.

"So," Kate said, as they headed over to the camper, "you guys are spending the nights in Henry's camper standing guard over his aunt's place. Is that how it is? And if any of the staff looking out for her, if one of them needs *anything*, you guys are right there to help. Is that about right? I didn't have a chance to discuss much with Dad, but I think that's how he explained it. Is that how you fellows understand it?"

"Yup," Robby replied. "But, Uncle Jack did not want us to go into Aunt Halona's unit for any reason. And, if they needed to talk to us, they should be wearing a mask—the nurses. I guess that's kinda the law. Not sure how that works, but that's how we think we're supposed to be doing it."

"How about the men-in-black?" Kate said with a slight chuckle in her voice. "Do you recall if they were wearing masks? And were they black or surgical? Just kiddin' with you. I want to get another look over there at the camper. Take a little look around."

The boys were pleased that their Aunt Kate could still see the humor in life. That was another one of their very favorite things about her—humor.

Red led the way to the camper, and the other three followed closely. But when Red opened the door, Buddy squeezed in first.

Once all of them were inside, Robby closed and latched the camper door.

"Wow!" Kate exclaimed. "It sure does get a little confined with all of us in here at the same time. You guys are okay with that? Do you have enough room?"

"It's fine," Robby said. "We do alright with it. And Buddy's fine. He likes to get out every once in a while. But I think we're comfortable enough. Right, Red? It works for us okay, I think."

Red nodded in agreement.

"Now," Kate asked. "This is the table where you'd put the knife. Is that right?"

"Yes," Robby said.

"And," Kate continued with her little interrogation, "I suppose that, here in the middle of the table, I'll bet that this is the foil you wrapped the knife with. Is that correct?"

Robby started to pick it up, but Kate stopped him.

"We don't want to touch that again," she said as she slipped on a pair of latex gloves. "I'm sure any prints we might have lifted from the foil are already corrupted, but I might be able to pull something off the knife. We should start adhering to protocol from here on out."

She then tucked the foil into an evidence bag she had in her jacket pocket, and she labeled it.

"Don't mind me," she said through a large Kate Handler smile. "It's just the way we do things. At least, the way *I* do them."

"Okay," she continued, "Right now I'm going to run over to the aunt's unit and see what anyone over there might have seen. You fellows wait here. I'll be back shortly, and then we'll go start some delicious dinner. Keep Buddy here with you, inside the camper. I'll be right back."

The boys were good with that. This had been a very intense half hour, and they were ready for a little break.

Kate excused herself again and walked over to Aunt Halona's unit. She slipped a medical mask on and rang the doorbell.

Almost immediately a nurse came to the door. But, instead of opening it up, she motioned for Kate to wait outside. She took a step backward and pushed the button on the intercom.

"Hello," the nurse said, "How can I help you?"

"I'm Kate Handler—Jack's daughter. Jack's the owner of the resort. And I am a New York City police detective. I have a couple questions I'd like to ask you. It's fine if you wish to wait inside. We can do this over the intercom. Would that be okay?"

"Sure," the nurse said. "So, you're Mr. Handler's daughter. Kate.

We've heard a lot about you. And we know that you're a police officer. What would you like to know?"

"First, how's the aunt doing today? Any changes?"

"No changes, really. She had a peaceful night. And today she seems to be holding her own. But, no marked changes—good or bad. She seems to have stabilized."

"Well, that sounds like good news to me," Kate said. "My next question has to do with activity you might have observed at the boys' camper last night. And earlier today, for that matter. Did you happen to see anyone over there today, by my dad's house, or by the camper, besides the boys?"

"Yes, we did."

"Tell me what you saw."

The nurse's answer caught Kate by surprise. Even though she was a seasoned homicide detective, she was not anticipating the nurse's words.

"About three hours ago," the nurse said, "possibly a little longer. Maybe four hours, two strangers—men we have not seen around here before. They were on foot. Looked like they came in from the direction of the driveway. They came all the way up and were walking around the camper looking in the windows. At first we thought it was the boys, but the men we saw were bigger than the boys. The whole thing was very strange. They were over there for only a few minutes. And then one opened the door and went inside. But only for a minute—at the longest. And then they left the same way they came in. They had a car parked over by where you parked."

"Really," Kate said, again caught off guard. "Then this is what I would like you to do. I would like you, and anyone else who saw these strangers, I want you to log it all, and put your little report in an envelope, write my name on that envelope—that's Kate Handler, and then attach it to the report for your shift. Will you do that for me?"

"Yes," the nurse said. "Absolutely. And, there was one other thing that we thought was really strange."

"What was that?" Kate asked.

"Both of these men-in-black had weapons. They both carried black semi-automatic pistols. I don't know what kind they were, because they all look alike to me. But I do know what a semi-automatic looks like, and that's what they had strapped on their belts. And, they both had knives too. All very strange. Actually, the one had a knife. The other one, he had a knife thing—holster. Or sheath. Is that what you call them? The thing you use to carry a knife?"

"A sheath," Kate said. "You carry a knife strapped to your belt in a sheath. Is that what they had?"

"Yeah," the nurse said. "Exactly. One of them had an empty sheath. He's the one who entered the camper. When he came back out, he was carrying a knife in his hand. And he strapped it into his empty sheath. And then they left."

Kate thought for just a moment, and then said, "Let me guess. The knives they had strapped to their belts—they were black too. Right?"

The nurse in charge was nodding affirmatively.

Chapter 14 —

The fishing boat chosen for the first leg of their journey, which at thirty-eight foot was extraordinarily large for a boat of that type, set out with them aboard from the huge port at Busan. Most South Korean fishing boats were under twenty feet. But, while this one was very lengthy, like the standard fishing vessel it had no onboard comfort facilities.

The ride on that boat out of Busan was virtually uneventful. Jack and Henry were shown to a small, empty storage room down below and there they donned the most basic of shallow-water diving gear and awaited the transfer. They correctly assumed the jaunt aboard the unusually large South Korean commercial fishing vessel would be relatively short, and totally transitional. Even though they had not been briefed regarding the mode of transportation that would be chosen for them, they had discussed it between themselves and concluded that the bulk of the trip to their delivery point would most likely be on board some sort of an American submarine. But, how they were to hook up with such a vessel proved not within their purview—especially given the fact that they were currently leaving port on a pretty basic commercial fishing craft.

What they did not consider at the time was the level of subterfuge necessary to employ in order to hide the fact that the US Navy was in the process of delivering a surprise gift to the North Korean missile program, and that it was using two tried and true civilian warriors to head up the presentation.

Jack and Henry were correct in their supposition that they would eventually be transported to their destination, at least in part, by a US submarine. But, they also knew that both the Chinese and the North Koreans kept a very close eye on all military ships moving in and out of South Korean ports—so they were not certain just how Bob and Roger would be pulling it off.

At that very time Chinese surveillance was keeping a very close eye on the USS Michigan, which was presently docking in Incheon. That nuclear-powered submarine just happened to be one of the largest and most dangerous ships in the world, therefore it garnered a lot of attention. Measuring around 560 feet in length, with its 150 Tomahawk missiles, it brought a lot of firepower into the region—a fact that did not escape notice by the CCP. While logic would dictate that a huge vessel of that type would find the facilities at Busan, the US had it docked at Incheon to draw attention away from what Bob and Roger were up to with their mission out of Busan.

To accomplish their goals, Bob and Roger felt it was necessary to secretly bring another submarine into the arena, while not disturbing the USS Michigan, or attracting the watchful eyes that were monitoring it. To accomplish that, they had to come up with an even more stealthy plan.

This is how they decided to handle it: they would keep the USS Michigan right where it was—docked in plain sight at Incheon.

While at the same time they would bring another large submarine into the area unannounced, but keep it submerged and relatively far offshore.

Already on that sub, the USS Jimmy Carter, was the contingent of Navy SEALs handpicked by Roger to aid Jack and Henry on the mission. It included a total of sixteen SEALs—teams "A" and "B", each comprising of four SEALs, and then two sets of backups for those teams.

Like the USS Michigan, the USS Jimmy Carter was also a very modern nuclear-powered vessel. Commissioned in 2005 as a Seawolf-class sub, it measured over 450 feet. The main reason it was chosen for this mission is that it was already fitted with the necessary apparatus to transport the sort of mini-sub that Jack, Henry, and their SEAL team were going to need.

Ideally, Jack and Henry would have been able to board the sub at the same time as did the SEALs, but the mission had come up so unexpectedly that the simultaneous boarding option became impossible. So, Bob approved a plan proposed to him by the SEALs themselves.

This is how they worked it out: two SEALs would open the hatch in the USS Jimmy Carter, and snag onto a weighted tether dropped from the fishing boat. Once the tether was secured at both ends, Jack and Henry would then follow it down to the open hatch, and so board the sub.

Even though Bob thought the plan to transport Jack and Henry to the USS Jimmy Carter substantially too complicated, he was convinced that to attempt it in any other way was wrought with too many possibilities for failure. Roger was even more concerned about this detail of the plan, and his anxiety about it was one of the principal reasons that Jack and Henry were kept in the dark regarding it until the last minute.

In fact, it was only after hours of late-night deliberation that Roger finally became agreeable to sign off on the elaborate procedures necessary to pull it off. "I can tell you right now," he told Bob, "If Jack were to know in advance about this convoluted aspect of what we are planning for them, he would throw a fit. He does not put up with this type of horseshit. And that's what it amounts to, in my opinion: unmitigated horseshit."

To which Bob replied, "And I don't think much of it either. But what the hell else can we do? We can't openly bring a second big ship into this theater right now—and certainly not dock one. We're between that proverbial *rock and a hard place*. You and I both know that we can't just be parking our big guns together like that—the naval command would not permit it. Look at what happened at Pearl Harbor. Besides, we can use the USS Michigan as subterfuge. They'll be watching that sub while the other one is delivering the goods. After all, this won't be the first time we've had to secretly transfer personnel to a submerged sub. Your problem with it this time is that it involves our friends—*your* civilian friends—men who have never attempted anything like this before. Isn't that right?"

"Sure," Roger replied. "That's undoubtedly a large part of it. But, even though Jack is the most competent and dedicated civilian operative we've ever had, he is not a young man. All this extracurricular activity has to take its toll. This mission is tough enough without this additional shit being dumped on them. But, I don't disagree with what you're trying to accomplish here. I do see your point."

"You just wish that there were an easier way—"

"Not so much that it might be *easier*," Roger interrupted. "It's not the level of difficulty that I object to. It's just that this whole thing is turning out to be more involved than any of us are used to. It's just too damn convoluted. That's it. Convoluted is the right word to describe it."

"I get it," Bob replied. "So, I guess that means you like *convoluted* better than *horseshit*. Is that about right? Then, I'll give you five minutes to come up with a better alternative. I'd be happy to entertain a better plan if you can produce one."

Five minutes passed without a word being uttered.

* * *

Down in the belly of that South Korean fishing boat, final preparations were underway to transfer to the USS Jimmy Carter. Even though both Jack and Henry were more than a little frustrated at the elaborate labyrinth of steps they were being required to execute with this mission, they were determined to do what whatever they had to do. "When Bob finally ties a bow on his end of this project," Jack said, "I want him to believe we did everything possible to make it work. We need to make it no less successful than those missions we've performed before—at least when it came to the level of success as measured by outcome at conclusion."

At first Henry just watched as Jack donned his diving gear.

After Jack was all set to go down, he threw a frown at his friend, as if to say, "What the hell you waiting for?"

Henry picked up on it, and copied the procedure just employed by his friend and boss.

While they did wonder about it, and while Henry did experience moments of self-doubt, once they had successfully tethered down to and disappeared into the bowels of the USS Jimmy Carter, which was waiting for them about five miles out, all insecurities and second guessing evaporated—at least for the time being. Or, perhaps better stated—only for the time being.

Chapter 15 —

T he USS Jimmy Carter was unique in the US Navy on several levels. For starters, it was the only US submarine ever named after a living president. Furthermore, at one and a half times the length of a football field, this submarine displaced 12,139 tons, and possessed a sophisticated power train that ran nearly silent. But, in addition to those superb attributes, the aspect that made the USS Jimmy Carter particularly favorable for this mission was that it already came equipped with a relatively new Dry Deck Shelter resting right on top of it.

A Dry Deck Shelter (DDS) is a specialized chamber used to deploy small numbers of Navy SEALs in their Delivery Vehicles (SDVs).

The typical SDV is a miniature submarine specially engineered to run virtually silent, transport four Navy SEALs (on average) plus their equipment, dive to about one hundred and ninety feet, run between seven and twelve miles per hour, and go up to twelve hours between charges. SDVs are able to run silently because the propeller was turned by an electric motor, and the motor's power source was an efficient array of Lithium-ion batteries.

And this mission was deemed to require every ounce of stealth that the US Military was capable of delivering.

Now, any US submarine can be used to deliver SEALs. And, in general terms, few submarines in the world run as quietly as a Seawolf-class Fast Attack submarine. However, even though it moves about quietly for its size, it is not able to maneuver as close to shore as it would have to in order to place SEALs where they have to go on a mission like this—at least not without being detected, or running aground.

That's why a mini-sub was required to bring the SEALs in close enough to the shore that they could easily swim, or perhaps even walk in.

Another important factor has to do with the Dry Deck Shelter (DDS) mounted on the top of the USS Jimmy Carter. That device allows for the dispatching of a mini-sub without alerting those who might be watching. In general terms, there are two basic types of mini-subs that fall into the SDV category—wet ones, and dry ones. A wet SDV is a mini-sub that, once the SEALs have entered it, is filled with water, thus forcing the SEALs to wear their wetsuits and breathing equipment at all times.

It is viewed as ideal not to have bubbles escape the SDV when SEALs are exiting the vehicles, because bubbles are easy to spot by surface ships. Obviously, if the SDV does not contain air, none can escape. The problem with the wet SDVs is that they are very uncomfortable for the SEALs to spend much time in. The most commonly deployed wet SDV has been the MK-11. Consequently, most often submarines equipped to deploy SDVs, such as the USS Jimmy Carter, were fitted with Dry Deck Shelters large enough to service the smaller SEAL Delivery Vehicles like the MK-11. That's why, for missions such as this one, the Dry Deck Shelter had been enlarged to accommodate the brand new UOES3 (User Operational Evaluation System-3). It was thirty-two feet long—about ten feet longer than the MK-11, and it provided a dry chamber to transport SEALs. And, even more significant for a covert mission such as this, it was equipped with a tiny, one-man fillable wet chamber to accommodate "bubble-less" SEAL deployments.

Plus, it was larger, so it could somewhat comfortably transport four SEALs, and a crew of two. For years engineers have been trying to perfect a compact DCS (Dry Combat Submersible). While the UOES3 might not yet have met all the requirements sought in order to be considered "service-ready," both Jack and Henry, along with the SEALs accompanying them, all were pleased to be using a dry vehicle—especially given the physical distance involved.

On this mission there were to be a total of six men—a Navy pilot (or driver) and his navigator, Jack, Henry, and two highly-trained SEAL divers to help them carry out their physically demanding tasks.

Technically, if called upon, the UOES3 would be able to transport two more human beings—oxygen supply was adequate, and there was room to anchor a couple of people down, albeit without the comfort of physical seats. And that was to be the case on the return, because they were anticipating bringing out of North Korea two refugees—a man and a woman.

But, even on the jaunt out to the missile launch site, they were still packed like sardines in a can. That's because of their special payload—two US-made W-80 nuclear warheads, along with all the additional computers and programmers they would need in order to facilitate making the nuclear devices appropriately operational, and at the same time rendering the North Korean missile seemingly erratic.

The W-80s are specialized devices, with characteristics and features that made them perfect for Bob's purpose in this instance. Not only were they physically small enough so that the men would be able to move them around quite easily, they were very deadly.

While the W-80s were actually compact enough so that Jack could have fit both of them inside the UOES3, SEALs actually placed one of them in a sealed enclosure and attached it to the side of their mini-sub like a torpedo; while the second W-80 they were able to strap down inside the UOES3.

That meant that the mini-sub driver and his navigator had to be particularly careful in maneuvering around fixed objects and natural obstructions such as rocks. Not that bumping up against a boat dock or a rock would cause the device to detonate, but it could easily damage it and make it unusable or even unstable.

Another aspect about the W-80 devices that made them useful to this mission was that they were substantially adjustable. The device's yield could actually be raised from a minimum explosive force of five kilotons of TNT, to as powerful a yield as one hundred and fifty kt (kilotons). That is to say, it could be set to do as little damage as one-third that of "Little Boy," the bomb that destroyed the city of Hiroshima to end WWII, to be as devastating as ten bombs the size of "Little Boy."

For this mission, on Roger's direction, the armorer pre-programmed each of them to explode with a force of five kt., which was the minimum. However, should Roger or Bob have a change of heart, they had sent the digital programmer with Jack so that he would be able to adjust the explosive force upward, should something come up late in the game that would cause it to be deemed necessary. Or, given the desire to do so, the detonator could be deactivated altogether, making the device virtually inert.

As indicated earlier, the W-80 device was relatively small in size. It weighed just under three hundred pounds, and measured about one foot in diameter and three feet in length. Two men could lift it, but it would have been extremely difficult for Jack and Henry to move one very far without help, especially in light of the anticipated environment.

But, there was an additional piece of equipment that was also important to the mission. That was another torpedo-shaped enclosure. It was made in China according to North Korean specifications. It was a little over nine feet in length. And, because it was constructed out of aluminum, it weighed just under one hundred and sixty pounds. That meant that, once a W-80 was installed in the enclosure, the whole "torpedo" weighed about four hundred and sixty pounds. The four men could handily manage it under water, provided they did not have to move it terribly far or expeditiously, and if they had something firm beneath their feet.

However, had they opted to transport the second nuclear device in the same enclosure, it would have been altogether too heavy for them to wrestle with under any circumstances.

So, the plan was to "pilot" the UOES3 as close into shore as possible. On landing, Jack and Henry, along with the two SEAL divers, would carry the enclosure onto land until they'd found the precise spot for pick-up. There they would deposit the heavy enclosure, and then return to the mini-sub to retrieve the second W-80. Once they had both nuclear devices, and the enclosure, hidden at the pick-up spot, they would hunker down and look for their ride.

* * *

Roger had deliberately waited until Jack and Henry had successfully settled in on the USS Jimmy Carter before elaborating on any of the details for the more critical aspects of the mission. But now, after they had been introduced to the SEAL team, and it had become clear to Roger and Bob that Jack and his crew would be able to work together successfully, Roger felt comfortable in spelling out to the men some of the more cogent particulars.

"Because the range of the UOES3 you are about to use is limited," Roger said to them through a secure military communication system, "as is the case with all vessels of the SDV Class, it was deemed appropriate for you to have some help along the way—first by the USS Jimmy Carter nuclear submarine, and then, because it would be much too dangerous to send the huge submarine into North Korean waters, you will be aided on the next leg of the voyage by a North Korean fishing boat, in much the same fashion as you were helped along earlier by the South Korean fishing vessel.

"It was thought that the USS Jimmy Carter could transport your SDV out into the Yellow Sea, but not far enough to attract unwanted attention—that is to say, the big sub will stay well south of the 38th parallel. There, your SDV will be detached from the USS Jimmy Carter.

"At the same time, the USS Jimmy Carter will drop a second power supply—a fresh battery pack. It will be there for you on your return trip, in the event you might need it. After depositing the emergency power unit, the big sub will dive as deep as possible, and proceed back toward the Pacific.

"Your SDV will then dive to its maximum depth—one hundred and ninety feet. Once at that depth, you will carefully move into waters north of the 38th parallel.

"At the time and place stipulated in the instructions given to your crew, you will begin to slide over into North Korean waters, and then slowly head north and east. After an hour, your mini-sub will begin rising toward the surface. And then, at precisely the designated time and location, a friendly, well-compensated North Korean fishing boat will pass over you.

"As I said, this is spelled out in detail in the instructions given to your crew. It will be pretty much the same method of connection as was implemented with the South Korean fishing boat earlier. Using a cable and a hook, one of the SEALs onboard the mini-sub will physically exit the vessel, and will latch your UOES3 onto that cable.

"Once a secure connection has been accomplished, the fishing boat will then tow you to a point nearer your ultimate destination. Without moving in close enough to attract attention, the fishing boat will swing around to return to the fishing lane. Using the slack created by the changing of direction, one of the SEALs will detach the tether cable, all the while the fishing boat will remain in motion.

"After the tow line has been removed from the mini-sub, it will dive to the maximum depth permitted by the shallow waters near shore. And, using its own power, it will pull in as close to land as possible. This is in the immediate proximity of Oma-Do, a small island just a few miles west of the Sohae Satellite Launching Station. Next, your team will exit the vessel and begin moving to land the equipment necessary to carry out the remainder of the mission. This equipment would include the torpedo modules, two additional sets of scuba diving gear for your additional passengers, and whatever else is listed on your preparatory notes.

"Once all the equipment for the mission has been removed from the mini-sub, it will then move back out to a point approximately one thousand feet from land. And there it will wait until the mission has been completed at the launch site."

That was the end of Roger's tutorial. However, once finished with his rather exhaustive briefing, Roger determined that this would be a good point to break off and allow the men a little time to mull the mission over among themselves. So, he concluded with these words: "Well, that'll be it for now. If an emergency should arise, you know how to reach me. Otherwise, I'll touch base with you down the road."

Jack and Henry both understood what Roger was saying. They knew him well, and they recognized his words to mean that from this point on, "there can be no turning back. And I do not think it appropriate for you to ask more questions."

At that point the six men—Jack, Henry, and the four SEALs of Team A—began gearing up. They were all happy that Roger had quit talking. But even beyond that bit of welcome news, they were all very pleased that the mini-sub selected for the mission was a dry one; this was particularly the case with the veteran SEALs, as almost all of their training had been done on the older wet systems. They openly expressed their surprise and pleasure at the nature of the new mini-sub.

Jack was particularly pleased that, as he put it, "The time has finally arrived—the time for less talk and more action."

With that, the six of them were directed to board the mini-sub. As they proceeded out of the Jimmy Carter, each of them was presented with a set of waterproof instructions. Four of them were exactly the same—those were presented one each to Jack, Henry, and SEALs #1 and #2. The pilot and navigator received the same instructions, plus additional pages relating to their respective roles in maneuvering the mini-sub.

Chapter 16 —

B ack on the island, Kate and the boys were sitting at the dining room table digesting the matter that lay before them—the men-in-black. While to say that little else was on Kate's mind while preparing dinner would be an understatement, even though she made every effort to bring herself and the boys around to a mindset conducive to an enjoyable evening meal, the elevated stress level did not escape the teenagers' attention.

Once the boys had closed up and locked the door to the camper for dinner at the house, she inquired of them what they would enjoy the most having her prepare. And, as is typical when discussing food with fourteen-year-old boys, they immediately fixated on their dinner. The boys' eyes met, and Red flashed a big smile. Robby knew what it meant.

"Uncle Jack picked up some nice steaks day before yesterday," Robby announced. "He was going to cook them for us tonight until this mission came up. ... Maybe *you* could cook them? We'll help do it."

"Steaks!" Kate said with a spark of genuine excitement. "I always love a good steak too. Is that what you guys would like?"

"You bet," Robby said. "Uncle Jack was going to cook them on those new black rocks. Did you ever do it like that?"

"You're kidding," she said. "You guys have those rocks to cook on?"

"Uncle Jack thought we would like to do that once in a while. He bought the whole setup. We tried it once with hamburgers. It was great. So he thought it'd be good to try it with real steaks. Could we do that tonight? We think it would be fun to try. And, we will help. I promise."

"Yeah," she said. "You'll have to work with me on it. I've never done it before. Let's give it a shot. I agree—I think it'll be fun. Have you or Dad ever cooked steaks with them before? Or anything besides burgers?"

"No," Robby replied. "We've used them just that once—with those burgers. We were gonna look it up online before we did steaks, but we're not supposed to go on the internet until Uncle Jack gets back. And, like I said, we did try it out with burgers. And they were very good."

"Whoa!" Kate declared. "This is going to be interesting. I want you boys to stick close while we're doing this. In case I need to pick your brains."

Red laughed as he made a noise and assumed a stance mimicking the spraying of a fire extinguisher.

Kate and Robby both laughed.

"Hope it won't come to that," she said. "But I am pretty sure that we're not going to learn how to do this in one of Dad's old cookbooks. Have you guys ever read anything about black rock cooking in a book?"

Red was shaking his head in the negative.

"No," Robby agreed. "I've not read anything about it. How hot are these rocks supposed to be, anyway?" he asked. "I think Uncle Jack said that they should be about seven hundred degrees. But not more than eight hundred. How do we do that? The oven stops at five hundred."

"I have a good friend who has tried this," Kate said. "She told me that she heated them on the top burners on her gas range. You can tell when they're hot enough when a single drop of water boils off in under ten seconds. She also warned me about getting burned. Those rocks have to be extremely hot, and that can be dangerous."

"Uncle Jack has these special tools to handle the rocks," Robby said. "Not sure what he called them, or where he keeps them, but they are kinda like stainless steel pancake turners. He had a special word for them. But I don't know it. And then he's got these ceramic serving dishes, and little steel squares that the steak sets on while you eat it. At least, that's how it was with burgers."

"I think you can put a few drops of olive oil on the rock before you do the steak," Kate added. "And some sea salt."

Red held up an index finger to get attention, and then he acted out cutting the steak in small pieces.

"Right," Kate said. "When you do the steak, I think you first sear each side for a few seconds, to seal in the juices. And then cut the steak in half, leaving half on the hot rock, and the other half off to the side. And then you cut the part you're cooking into bite-size pieces. That way you can cook only what you're going to eat right away. And then, when you've finished eating the pieces you've cooked, you can do the same thing with the other half of the steak. That way you get the whole thing the way you want it. And nothing gets overcooked. At least ideally."

"Uncle Jack likes steak sauce on all his steaks," Robby said, "even his hamburgers. So do Red and me. I know we've got plenty of steak sauce."

"Yeah," Kate agreed. "I know he likes his A-1. Right?"

Both boys nodded in agreement.

All the while Kate was putting the meal together, her mind was racing. *What can those men-in-black be up to?* she wondered. *The nurses both noted that the men they saw were packing semi-autos. And something that looked like navy combat knives—just like the one the boys described. It appears that it was the main house here that they found most interesting. They did enter the camper, but that was only to retrieve lost property. It was by this house that the boys saw them hanging around. So, maybe, I'll get a chance to meet them. Maybe tonight, after the boys head over to the camper, I'll have to take a look at Dad's surveillance system. Might have something interesting there for me. Wonder how sophisticated those characters are? Dad's concern was that the cameras should all be covert. Those jerks probably don't know that they were recorded. It's always best like that, otherwise—*

"Aunt Kate, is it too early to get the steak out?" Robby interrupted her thoughts. "Uncle Jack says it's good to bring steak up to room temperature just before you apply the heat. Think we're ready yet?"

"I would say so," she replied as she opened the refrigerator door to see what her father had purchased. "Oh. Terrific. I see he picked up some ribeyes. They will be great. Even if I mess up a little. Perfect. I'll just set them over here and let them warm up a bit. I hope you boys are hungry. These are going to be good, alright. And he's got all these cheese and butter dips, too. I didn't know Dad liked cheese dips on his steaks."

"We think he bought some of that stuff for you," Robby said. "He told us to package and label what we don't eat—or don't think we're gonna eat right away, and toss it in the freezer. He said he would go through it later. But I think he got some of those dips for you. Red and I have been thinking, Aunt Kate, about tonight. Maybe you'd like to have Buddy stay over here with you for the night. In case you have some unwanted company. What do you think about that? Would you like him to keep you company?"

"That's sweet of you to offer to share Buddy with me," Kate replied. "I just love him, but he needs to be with you boys. That's what he's used to. I'm fine over here. That's how we've always done it. Buddy likes to sleep with you guys."

"Except," Robby said, "we're always over here in our rooms. Buddy is very familiar with this house. He spends the nights downstairs. He sleeps on the rug by the door. Uncle Jack says he's guarding the house. He wouldn't mind spending the night here, where he usually does."

But Kate had other plans. *If those men-in-black return tonight,* she was thinking, *I would rather know it, and be able to spring a little surprise of my own on them, rather than have Buddy scare them away with his bark.*

Chapter 17 —

J ack and the team had reviewed and confirmed every entry on the list of preliminary procedures that had been given to them before exiting the USS Jimmy Carter, the host submarine, and entering SDV. The four SEALs had gone through similar drills innumerable times during their years of training, plus all of the SEALs were veterans of hundreds of related training exercises, as well as dozens of actual missions, many of which involved the use of various SDVs—wet and dry. So, for these procedures, Jack and Henry, for a large part, followed the SEALs' lead.

Upon the men's final preparations before leaving the Jimmy Carter, Roger did take the opportunity to give them a verbal send-off: "Well, boys, had I any reason to think that I could add to your mission, I'd either be suitin' up with you, or staying in communication. But, that's not the case. I know that you're the right men to handle this the way we need it handled. And the time has finally come to let you do it."

And then, taking a lengthy pause to make sure that he had the attention of all the men, he said, "I have no doubt that the six of you are the very best America has to offer. You four SEALs most certainly represent the crème de la crème among American fighting men. And I can personally assure you that these two civilians you've been nice enough to take along on your mission with you,

I can attest that the former president and I have been on missions with both of them. And they are also as good as it gets. Believe me, if I were healthy enough to contribute in a positive fashion, I'd be there with you. Good luck. And Godspeed."

Jack and Henry, like two of the other four warriors, were at that point fully decked out in a sort of military grade scuba gear— highly specialized equipment that neither of the Sugar Islanders had ever seen before. Even though it was designed to be trim and compact, it still would have made for an uncomfortable ride, had they have been forced to wear it for the whole trip.

Jack and Henry were, of course, considerably older than the rest of the team. *If this feels tight now,* Jack said to himself, as he shifted about trying to find the most agreeable position for his aging frame, *I can only imagine how jammed together it's gonna be in the mini-sub. And that UOES3, even though one hundred and twenty inches longer than the old MK-11, it is still gonna be difficult for us to make ourselves fit. It was definitely designed for younger men. And that I ain't.*

But, as his trademark dictated, when faced with irritating circumstances Jack sealed his lips against excessive complaining. This even in spite of the fact that nearly all the comfort devices aboard the submarine were turned off to make it run quieter.

"All for the best," Jack muttered to himself. "And, after all, anything that'll make this little run quieter is okay with me ..."

* * *

It was about three hundred miles north of the island of Jeju, and forty miles off the South Korean mainland, and at a depth of about 190 feet, that the nuclear sub released the mini-sub SDV. After releasing the SDV, the Jimmy Carter virtually reversed course, and headed back south toward the Pacific, while Jack and the men allowed the SDV to remain static at the maximum depth. After the stipulated time, which was approximately one hour, they began moving northward toward their target.

And then at the time Roger had stipulated, which was again about one hour, it ascended to a depth of twenty feet, and then assumed the same speed and direction as that of an approaching North Korean fishing boat.

Once position, speed and direction were established, one of the SEALs slipped out of the hatch and snatched a weighted tether that had been dropped from the fishing boat. After he'd latched on to it, he quickly connected it to the hull of the mini-sub. The pilot of the mini-sub then cut power to save battery, and they proceeded in the direction of their target—the Sohae Satellite Launching Station.

Now, however, they were totally under the power of the North Korean fishing boat. This was the part of the plan that greatly enhanced the mission's possibility of at least a minimum of success.

* * *

After the U-turn that allowed detachment, the USS Jimmy Carter continued on its pre-established southward course that could eventually lead it out into the Pacific, toward the Philippines, and then on to Pearl Harbor for regular maintenance. It did, however, have some more work to do before it moved on.

Almost immediately after releasing the SDV, the big sub dropped to the maximum depth permitted by shallow waters, cut power and rested virtually on the floor. It was there (37.40043, 123.99782), near the point where they parted ways with the SDV, that the USS Jimmy Carter dropped a backup power supply for the SDV. Fortunately, the Yellow Sea is a relatively shallow body of water, so it was not difficult selecting an appropriate nearby spot to leave it.

They did, however, equip the battery package with a floating device and an anchor that would guarantee that it would sink to a level greater than 190 feet, which was the maximum standard operating depth recommended for the SDV.

Since the power supply was to be used only in the event of emergency, it was also there that the USS Jimmy Carter lay in wait until directed to move on, which was roughly almost three full days.

The plan was for Jack's boat to hook up with fishing boats, both for the adventure into North Korean waters, and for the return trip south of the 38th. If something problematic were to happen, and the SDV was to run out of power, hopefully it would be relatively near the 38th, so they could retrieve and employ the fresh battery pack.

Certainly, it would have been handy had it been feasible for the big sub to cross the 38th and dispatch the mini-sub on the North's doorstep, especially since the range and speed of Navy SEAL Delivery Vehicle (SDV) is substantially limited. But, such was not in the cards. The plan developed by Bob and Roger's team, using fishing boats for cover, was the best possible proposal for keeping their presence a secret. And success required secrecy of the first order.

As the mission progressed, nearly all of these "emergency provisions" proved necessary.

Chapter 18 —

Back on the island, Kate was still dealing with the logistics of her first night. She was not anticipating the "adventure" she was faced with upon arriving—the matter of the SEAL-like intruders that had so troubled Red and Robby. Under any normal circumstances she would have enjoyed Buddy's company at her feet when she slept, but she had plans to confront the invaders by surprise, and she thought Buddy might give her plans away.

Some time ago her father had shared with her the existence of numerous secret sensors that he had placed on the property, and she was quite confident that he had not told the boys that those sensors even existed. It was not his intention to monitor outside movement continuously, as the normal night-time stirring of raccoons and other critters of the dark would create too much activity to make monitoring feasible. Rather, his desire was to be made aware of roaming man-sized living creatures, but only when he sensed the existence of a security problem. On this night, Kate was expecting the return of the "men-in-black," and she sought to monitor it.

Therefore, she instructed the two boys to take Buddy with them for the night.

"When you head over to the camper," she told them, "just take Buddy with you. But be sure to latch the camper door. If I need you, I'll pound on it and wake you up."

Even though they had suggested to Kate that Buddy could stay with her for the night, they were relieved when she declined their offer. They were as attached to their four-legged friend as they were to each other. And Buddy felt the same way about them.

"What time did Dad want you to head over there?" Kate asked. "Did he give you a specific time?"

"Just when it got dark," Robby answered, "or when it started to. He wasn't specific. At least, I don't think he was," he added with a glance over at Red. "He just wanted us to get over there around the time it got dark. He was pretty clear about that."

Red was nodding slowly in agreement.

"That's how I recall his instructions for me as well," Kate agreed. "So, that's how we'll do it."

The three of them finished dinner, and the boys helped Kate clean up afterward.

"Absolutely fantastic job with those steaks," Kate said to them. "Can't believe how good they were. When Dad gets back, we're gonna have to make dinner for him and Henry. Show 'em how it's done. What did you think? Wasn't it great?"

"Yeah," Robby replied. "We both thought it was great too. Right, Red?"

Red smiled and nodded his agreement.

"You guys are certainly being helpful tonight," Kate continued to applaud them with her words. "I'm wondering—do you have an ulterior motive? Is something else up?"

Robby threw Red a glance. Red was smiling.

"Well," Robby said. "Maybe. I don't know. We did want to be helpful, and all. But, we thought that maybe, if you had some time tonight, maybe you could show us how to play a new game that Uncle Jack bought for us. It's a board game."

"Really," Kate replied. "What's it called? Is it one we've played before?"

"If you did," Robby said, "it wasn't with us. He just went in town and bought it for this trip. We haven't even had a chance to play it with Uncle Jack or Henry. And we'd like to not look stupid if we play it with our friends. It's becoming a popular game."

"Not look stupid?" Kate repeated very deliberately. "Okay. That sounds like there's some girls you fellows are trying to impress. Is that the case? Sure it is. Who are they? 'Fess up!"

"Not girls," Robby said, his face rapidly turning crimson. "At least, not just girls."

Red found this opportunity to run Buddy a bowl of fresh water.

"The name of the game Uncle Jack bought for us," Robby said, "is called Azul Summer Pavilion. We think it looks like a lot of fun—or could be a lot of fun."

"Did you have your friends come over to play it with you yet?" Kate asked. "Or how did you do it?"

"We couldn't do that," Robby said. "Because of Covid. But we did play an online game called Azee. It's like Azul, we think. It was patterned after the board game. We play Azee with friends from school, and talked about it. That's why Uncle Jack bought Azul for us."

"Yeah," Kate said. "I always like learning something new. Dad probably figured it might keep you guys out of trouble."

She then smiled, looked up and said, "Good luck with that, Dad—wherever you are."

"Sure, we can give it a try. Tell me a little bit about it while you set it up. Can three people play?"

"Sure," Robby said. "Two can play alright. But it's better with three or four, I've heard."

"What's the point?" Kate asked.

"It's all about building and decorating a Portuguese palace," Robby said. "I'll read you what it says here. It says: King Manuel I, when on a visit to the Alhambra palace in Southern Spain, was mesmerized by the stunning beauty of the Moorish decorative tiles. The king, awestruck by the interior beauty of the Alhambra, immediately ordered that his own palace in Portugal be decorated with similar wall tiles. It then becomes a competition to see who can accomplish his strategized goal first. You get points, and stuff."

"And the girls beat you?" Kate asked.

"*Every* time we played," Robby said. "Well, we only played twice. But they won both of them. Easily."

"Maybe it's more a girls' game? Is that the case?"

"No, some of our guy friends—regular guys—they're saying it's a lot of fun. We'd really like to learn to play it well. Can you help?"

"We'll see," Kate said. "But, weren't you telling me that you were playing a little different game with them? That is with the girls, I mean?"

"That was Azee. We can't go online until Uncle Jack gets back. We figured if we could learn to play better with the regular Azul board game, maybe we'd get good."

"Let's give it a go," Kate said. "How long does it take to finish a game? We don't want to start something we can't finish."

"Forty-five minutes. Less than an hour," they said.

"We'll be okay," Kate said. "We can do it here at the house. We have enough time for at least one game."

They did play the game. In fact, they had time for two complete games before the boys had to go to the camper, and she won them both. But, the boys did not seem troubled to be beaten by Kate. She was always good at everything she attempted. So her victory did not come as a surprise.

"That was a lot of fun," she said. "I'm glad you taught me how to play this. Let's just leave it out and we can do it again—maybe tomorrow evening after dinner. We've got to sharpen up your interior decorating skills. But, are you sure you really want to beat the cute girls?"

"We don't really want to beat them," Robby confessed. "We just want to be competitive. Not to look stupid. You know what we're saying. Right?"

"You gonna walk Buddy on your way over to your vacation villa?" Kate asked. "Because, once you close and lock that camper door behind you, I'd like it if you did not go out anymore before I get you for breakfast. Unless there is an emergency—like a camper fire. Or in case one of the nurses needs something. And, if something like that happens, I want one or both of you to come over here immediately and tell me about it. Okay?"

"Sure, Aunt Kate," Robby said as they left. "We'll stay in until morning. Good night."

After she saw them off, she began scrutinizing the outside cameras and motion sensors.

Chapter 19 —

Kate was relieved to discover that six outside cameras were all triggered by motion sensors. None of those particular pieces of equipment required the network. *Dad, in all his wisdom,* Kate was thinking, *had his engineers design two separate and totally independent systems—one that operated online, the other utilized home-run hardwired runs.* Once she had located the main console for the cameras, she tested to see how it worked.

"Let's see," she mumbled to herself, "looks like he's got thirty-six cameras coming into this processor. That's a hell of a lot of cameras, even for my dad. And, I think cameras 12 through 17 are the critical ones that I need to keep my eye on for tonight. Some of this is starting to come back."

Kate was beginning to remember the walk-through her dad had given her back when he first brought the cameras up to operational.

"Seems like he showed me a portable monitor," she was thinking sometimes out loud, "one that we could set to remotely monitor any group of cameras, like these outside units, and the processor would send a short burst of video to the monitor whenever the motion sensor tied to that camera was activated."

Kate was very pleased when she found a 3x5 cheat-sheet card explaining the basic operation of the cameras and remote monitors.

"Damn," she muttered through a sly smile, "All this stuff was state-of-the-art technology back when he had it set up. Now I'm afraid it's a bit antiquated. But, it will all function perfectly fine off-line. And that's what I need for right now."

The little card indicated that the remote monitor would run on battery for two hours if fully charged. "But, for longer operation," she said aloud to herself, "it is twelve volt, so I can plug it into a USB port. … Oops, no. It would have to be something like a vehicle accessory outlet."

She thought for a second, and then recalled that her rental Tahoe did have a cigarette lighter.

That ought to work just fine, she reasoned, as she put on a pot of coffee. *No doubt I'm going to need all of this. Maybe more! Something tells me that these guys are coming back—if not tonight, soon. With Dad still home, I know they didn't get what they came for. And it just seems like I'm gonna have to find a good place to park—at least tonight, and maybe for a few. I just know that I'd better be ready for anything.*

Kate gave the boys enough time to get themselves in a go-to-bed mood, and then she made her move. She ran through her check list:

*   Glock and two spare magazines
*   Adequate Coffee
*   Memorize Camera Locations
*   Camera Monitor

*   Cell Phone (Pre-paid burner for emergency only)
*   Snacks
*   Bottled Water
*   Facial Tissues
*   Good Book
*   MacBook

"There," she said out loud. "I think that ought to do it. But, how am I going to read? Without using interior lights. Need to grab one of Dad's little clamp-on LED flashlights."

Kate then looked around until she found one, and she clipped it onto her "Good Book" for the night.

Once she had thoroughly reviewed her list, she quickly shoved all of her surveillance essentials into two shopping bags, and headed for the Tahoe.

Even though she realized that the odds were the *men-in-black* would not be poking around until well after midnight, she wanted to get settled in well before that time.

As soon as Kate got in she started the engine, checked the fuel level, switched all lights off—both inside and outside the vehicle, and turned the radio on super-low volume.

"Let's see," she mumbled to herself. "How's my view? Am I far enough away so as not to be obvious; yet close enough to see everything I need to see?"

Kate studied it for a few minutes. She learned the camera locations and practiced their controls. She then turned to look behind her.

"I'm a little too obvious here," she said. "Better if I backed up across the drive—between those little pine trees. Fit in better back there, I think."

So, Kate shifted into reverse and squeezed into the more se-
cluded parking slot.

"There," she said after she'd parked, "I shouldn't stand out so
much back here. And I won't have them sneaking in behind me,
either."

She double-checked her lights. She then twisted the interior
light control to the left until the interior went totally black.

"That should do it nicely," she said as though talking to someone else.

"Oh!" Kate said a little too loudly. "I'd better crack these windows, if I'm going to leave the engine running." So, she lowered
both rear windows about an inch, and did the same for the two in
front as well.

She took one more very careful look around.

"Yes, I do believe that ought to do it. Should have brought
night-vision binoculars. Tomorrow. I'll grab a pair for next time.
Now, how about the monitor?"

She broke it out, removed a lighter, and plugged the video
equipment into the empty outlet.

"I should keep this as low as possible," she said. "And tone it
down as far as possible."

After placing the monitor on the seat next to her, and dim-
ming it down until she nearly had to squint her eyes to make anything out, she took one last survey of the inside of the Tahoe, and
then breathed deeply. "That should do the trick," she said.

She looked around to find the best location for her little reading light. She concluded that she might best clamp it onto the
steering wheel. "That way it will be close enough to illuminate the
book, and sufficiently low so as not to be seen from the outside."

With that, she mentally settled in for the night.

For the next two hours she did nothing but read her book, and take an occasional visual survey of her surroundings. The monitor Jack had provided with the system would activate a small LED and a smaller low-volume Sonalert on it, and they were tied into several passive infrared devices that were located throughout the scene captured by the cameras. If a living creature of sufficient size entered its field of view, it would trigger a LED and the alert, notifying the viewer that something was wandering within range.

"Finally," she muttered out loud, "Those two boys have finally turned their lights off. Must be they're in for the night as well. It's just about time."

An hour passed, and then another. She poured her third cup of coffee. Still, she saw nothing going on that was out of the ordinary.

She basically repeated this covert procedure for the first two nights after her arrival. During both of which she neither saw nor heard anything out of the ordinary. She was working it into a regular routine. First she would pack a little carry-me-through-the-night bag of quasi-healthy snack foods, along with a large thermos containing black coffee. While she would change it up a little, for the most part, the elements that made the cut were similar if not identical each of the nights. These included grapes, Lara Bars, pumpkin seeds and a single iced tea.

While it remains a fact that on the third night she did not see or hear anything not to be expected on any given night in the Upper Peninsula of Michigan, that does not mean that nothing was taking place.

What she did not know or suspect was that a pair of eyes were fixed on her each of those nights—even in the darkness. They were locked on her through an AGM Global Vision FoxBat Night Vision 7.4 Scope. She had no idea she was being surveilled, largely because the lookout was being facilitated from across the St. Marys River. And, it was at night.

This third night was to be her last. "If I don't catch these *men-in-black* tonight, I'm done with this," she told herself. As it turned out, even though she was totally unaware of the eyes watching her, just such an event was underway nevertheless.

This time, the third night, one of those nefarious *men-in-black* had again spotted her, and this time he sneaked up behind her Tahoe. He slipped a small rubber hose around the exhaust pipe, and sealed it with duct tape. Before he attached it, he shot nearly a full aerosol can of a non-lethal sleeping agent into the hose, and then tucked the other end of it into the crack of the rear window opposite from where she was sitting. The sleeping agent dulled her senses almost immediately, so she never even noticed that slowly the Tahoe was filling with poisonous carbon monoxide. After a time, she slumped over onto the steering wheel. Had she bumped the horn when she went out, the boys would have heard it immediately, and could have come to her rescue expeditiously—but no such luck came her way on her third night back on Sugar Island.

She was out like a light, and harmless as a dove with a broken wing.

"With that much carbon monoxide pouring into the truck, death should come quickly, and quietly," one of the *men-in-black* said to another. "Should be only minutes before we can move in."

Chapter 20 —

The two boys were sound asleep when the carbon monoxide overtook Kate.

They were following their regular schedule. Right after they had taken Buddy on his goodnight walk, they broke out the deck-of-fifty-two, along with two boxes of plastic poker chips, and one of them would start shuffling.

When it was just the two of them it was always a given that the game they would play would be Texas Hold 'Em. In that game each player is dealt two cards to start with—called the "hole cards." Then five "community cards" are dealt to the center of the table. Betting takes place after each card is revealed.

For the past three days they all had fallen into their routine—Kate hers, and the young ones, their set patterns. The two boys and Buddy would retire to the camper promptly at the given hour (or perhaps the position of the sun), and Kate to her "observation post" in her Tahoe. So far, she had observed nothing out of the ordinary—to the point that she had begun to question the wisdom of hanging out nights in a rental truck.

At the end of the second night, Kate had declared to herself with measured hostility, "One more night. One more night of good sleep wasted, and then I will move back into the house and a real bed. Looks to me like those *men-in-black* are long gone. Or, at least they appear to have given up."

The boys had observed on this third evening that Kate's spirits seemed a bit elevated, but they did not suspect that she was preparing to wind up her surveillance—much less her corporal survival. In fact, they did not even suspect that any such things even existed for her to "wind up."

The two boys both felt that Texas Hold 'Em was the perfect poker game to go to sleep by. That is to say, it did not require a lot of thinking, and certainly did not lead the players to count cards— which, experience had taught them, was all pure exhausting thinking. The Texas Hold 'Em game was simple, and had proven itself to be sleep provoking.

Later, when questioned by detectives, the boys estimated that they played poker until around 10:30, at which time they turned the lights off and went to bed. Both of them indicated that they thought they fell asleep right away—probably by 11:15, they estimated. And Kate's third night was no different. At least not in terms of the set routine.

They fell asleep by 11:30, and never stirred until Buddy started growling and barking lowly, at around 1:15 A.M. The barking woke both of them up.

Detectives, being detectives, added a possible thirty minutes to the fourteen-year-olds' version of the timeline. "I know kids," Det. Townsend had frequently said.

In an effort to loosen the boys' ability to recall all the events of the evening, the Chippewa County detectives—Det. Greggory Townsend and Det. Lestor Conners—asked them to reconstruct, as best they could, everything they had done and said from the time they left Kate in the house, until they found her succumbed to the poisoned air in the Tahoe.

Both Townsend and Conners knew Jack, and they were aware that Red was unable to speak, so they gave Red a pad of paper and a pencil, and asked Robby to describe everything he could remember, and for Red to interject his thoughts into the narrative by writing them down and presenting them to the detectives when he had something to add to or correct in Robby's narrative.

"Understand what we're asking for?" Det. Townsend asked.

Both boys responded in the affirmative.

"Let's see now," Det. Townsend said, "You finished dinner around seven-fifty. Is that correct?"

"Yes," Robby said. "Maybe a bit sooner than that, but around that time."

Red was nodding slowly in agreement.

"Okay, then," Det. Townsend said, "Robby, why don't you take it from there."

"Right," Robby said. "We, Red and I, took Buddy out for his last walk of the night. We walked down by the river. Buddy likes it down there. I'd guess that we were gone a total of twenty minutes. Or so."

Robby looked over at Red, who was again nodding.

"As soon as we got back to the camper, which was probably eight-ten to eight-twenty, Red took a shower. I didn't take one—had one yesterday. And when he got out, we decided to play some poker—Texas Hold 'Em. That's our favorite poker game. Most of the time, at least at night, that's what we play.

"My first hand, I was dealt a 7 of hearts, and a jack of clubs.

Red got, I think, an 8 of spades and a king, red, I think diamonds."

More details than I need, Det. Townsend was thinking. *But, that's alright. Better more than less.*

"You have a good memory," Det. Townsend said to Robby. "Do you remember who won that hand?"

"Red won. He won the first three hands. He was very lucky. But he didn't win much of my money—chips, actually. I didn't bet much because I had really crappy hands. But, I won the fourth hand. Big. I was dealt two queens, and the table turned over another one. I had a high three-of-a-kind. Hard to beat that with only two players playing fair. So I won.

"Red had two pair. So he bet heavy. At that point, I was ahead. But, it didn't take him long to catch up and pass me. I should have bet more when I had the three queens. I just didn't want him to drop out. I still did okay. Up until then. Don't you think?"

"How many hands did you play?" Det. Townsend asked. "In total. Just estimate."

"I don't know," Robby said. "Maybe a dozen, I'd say. They don't take very long. I know you need to figure this out, but do you have any word on Kate's condition? She gonna be okay?"

"I know she's on your mind," Det. Townsend answered. "But, she's in good hands right now. And we need to get to the bottom of this while it's fresh. I need to ask more questions."

Red flashed ten fingers. He then signaled a waffle, and pointed up, and then down.

It took a moment for Robby to figure out what Red was saying, but then he figured out that he was signaling his answer to the detective's question.

"That should be about right," Robby agreed. "We were getting pretty sleepy. And we decided to give it up for the night. We must have played about ten games."

"And you think you might have turned in at about eleven-fifteen?" Det. Townsend asked. "Does that sound right?"

Robby was nodding his head.

Red nodded a little more slowly, and he was again signaling with his hands a "give or take" gesture.

"So," Det. Townsend responded, "eleven-fifteen ought be considered an estimate? Would that be an accurate assessment? Maybe it's off a little? By fifteen minutes, perhaps?"

Both boys nodded affirmatively.

"I'd say so," Robby replied. "It might even have been earlier. We were both getting pretty sleepy around ten-thirty. We don't go to bed by the clock. We go when we're sleepy."

Again, Red nodded slowly in agreement.

"Okay," Det. Townsend said, as he made notes.

"Now," he continued after writing for about a minute. "While you were engaged in your poker game, do you recall anything happening that was out of the ordinary? Did you hear anything? Did your dog—Buddy's his name? Did Buddy bark, or behave as though he had sensed something out of the ordinary? Did anything like that at all happen?"

Red took some notes, and then looked over at Robby. He then slid the tablet over for Robby to see.

Robby took a look at what Red had written and said, "Red thinks I should tell you about Buddy growling. And I think so too. I was going to tell you about that next. Not sure exactly what time it was, but it was right in the middle of a hand—toward the end of the game, though. Buddy suddenly stood up and growled.

He pointed his nose toward the main house. Like he heard some-thing. He sometimes does that if he hears a cat, or a raccoon. Or, a person. Usually, if it's a person, he starts barking. He didn't really bark. Just growled, and sniffed the air. But he didn't bark. Do you think that's when they stuck that hose in Aunt Kate's window? Is that what you think?"

Robby looked over at Red. Both boys were evidencing tears beginning to form.

"We don't know anything for certain," Det. Townsend replied. "If you were piecing this together, given the estimated timeline we've established, what time do you think that would have been?"

Red wrote "11" down with a question mark, and showed it to Robby.

"I would agree with Red. It was not long before we wrapped it up and went to bed. Eleven would be my guess too."

Then Red wrote something else down, and Robby read it.

"Do we know how Aunt Kate's doing?" Robby articulated. "Is she going to be okay?"

"The last word we heard was that she had started breathing on her own," Det. Townsend said. "That's a very good sign. She's still getting some help with that, and she has not fully recovered. She is doing a lot better than she was when we got here. They worked on her extensively before even leaving for the hospital. They wouldn't head out of here until they had her somewhat stabilized. No doubt about it, your Aunt Kate is one very, very lucky young woman. And, she would not still be alive now had you boys not got her out of that Tahoe when you did. Your quick action saved her life. No question about that. Now, I am not saying that she is totally out of the woods. Not yet. But, it does look like she is moving in the right direction. And she has you two young men to thank for—"

"And Buddy," Robby passionately interjected. "Buddy is the one who woke us up. If it all turns out good, if Aunt Kate is okay, in the end, it will be because of *Buddy's* barking. It will be because *Buddy* saved her. Not us."

Tears began to stream down Robby's cheeks as he grabbed Buddy and began to hug him. It became clear to Det. Townsend that he was about to lose control of the interview.

"For sure," Det. Townsend said, doing his best to assure the boys that Kate was going to be just fine. "Your Aunt Kate is receiving the best treatment possible, and I'm sure she is eager to come back to the resort. She knows, and so do we, that the three of you—Buddy included—you were all responsible for saving her life. She is lucky that you responded the way you did, and when you did. We all can see that. Right now, the most important thing we can do, you two boys and me, and Detective Conners here, is to figure out who it was that tried to hurt her. And to make sure this does not happen again—to her, or anyone else. Can you guys help me do that?"

The detective's soothing words were exactly what Robby needed to hear. He grabbed two paper towels from the roll on the camper's table, and heartily blew his nose on them. Then, using the back of his hands, he wiped the tears from his eyes and cheeks.

Red was moved to tears as well, just in a more subdued fashion. Immediately after Robby had rolled off his paper towels, Red did the same.

He had appreciated Det. Townsend's soothing words, but he suspected that the detective was presenting a more positive review of the facts than reality warranted. And so he penciled out a short message for the detective: "When can we see Aunt Kate?"

Det. Townsend read the note and turned to his partner and said, "Detective Conners, would you step out and check on that, please?"

"Absolutely," the partner said as he stood to his feet. "I'll get right on it."

Det. Conners had been silently sitting at the table with them throughout the whole interview. While he had not verbalized much at all after the initial introduction, he had definitely been busy taking notes.

Townsend and Conners liked working together, and they had been at it for nearly a decade. During that time they had developed a method of conducting an interview that had worked very well. Det. Townsend would ask all the questions, while Det. Conners would take extensive notes and attempt to capture nuances. If Conners had something he wanted to hear more about, he would write it down and slide it over to his partner. And then, after the interview was completed, they would sit down together over a cup of coffee and discuss what they might glean from the exchange.

That was their time-proven system for friendly interviews, and that's what this was with the boys—a very friendly fact-finding discussion.

However, when an interview morphed into a more hostile form of interrogation, the two detectives employed a totally different style. But, no need to go there because it was clear to both that this conversation would never turn in that direction.

Det. Townsend was not comfortable proceeding with the interview without his partner present, so he suggested to the boys that they take a little bathroom break and perhaps he would like to have a drink of water.

"Best, Detective Townsend," Robby advised, "if you use the water in the fridge. It's cold, and we filled the pitcher with water from the house. Henry has some bottled water in there too. Take your pick. The water from the faucet here is fine too, he says, but he prefers to drink the water in the fridge. So do we, and I think you should."

"Wonderful," Det. Townsend said, "hand me one, please, before you sit down."

Red was just closing the bathroom door, so he popped open the refrigerator door and grabbed four bottles of water and set them on the tiny table.

"Thanks, son," the detective said. "This is exactly what I need."

Just as Red was sitting down, Det. Conners walked back in the door.

"Well," Det. Townsend said, "What's the latest word on Kate? Good, I hope."

"I talked with Deputy Fisher down at the hospital. He's with Kate right now. He said that she's been receiving oxygen, so he hasn't talked to her much yet. Just making eye contact, nodding—stuff like that. And, she is hooked up to an intravenous of some sort. He wasn't sure right then what they were administering. But, he said the doctors seemed very positive. No ventilator—thank God. Might want to put her in a chamber. I think Fisher called it a hyperbaric chamber. I think that's what he called it. But—"

"Right," Det. Townsend interjected. "That's a pressurized oxygen chamber. It pushes oxygen under pressure into the body so that it brings the patient up to where he, or she, should be, in situations like this. That all does sound good. Just the fact that they've not had to use a ventilator. That means your Aunt Kate is breathing totally on her own. That's very good news. But, she's not ready to talk to you. We'll monitor her condition carefully, and as soon as the doctors say it's okay, we'll run you down there and make sure you get in to see her—Covid or no Covid. One way or another, we'll make sure you see her. Very good news all around, I'd say."

The boys smiled for the first time that day. Robby tore off another paper towel and again blew his nose on it.

"Sorry 'bout that," he apologized through a red face of embarrassment.

"No problem at all," Det. Townsend responded. "We're all just really glad that she's doing well. There is one thing that I think we should do without waiting any longer. We should get hold of Jack and let him know that everything is looking better and that his daughter should be okay. Now, how is it that we can talk to your Uncle Jack?"

"Can't," Robby said, looking over at Red. "Uncle Jack and Henry are working. We're not sure where they are, or what they're doing. They left early in the morning a few days ago. Said that we must not try to call him about anything. And that he'd contact us as soon as he could."

"Really," Det. Townsend said. "That all sounds pretty mysterious. How about emergencies? How did he expect you to deal with something like this? What if his resort burns down? You'd have to call him then. Right?"

"I don't think so," Robby said. "He told us that Aunt Kate would take care of everything while he was gone. And that's what he expects us to do—do what Kate says."

Red nodded in agreement.

"I do know your Uncle Jack pretty well," Det. Townsend continued. "And I am aware that he does go off on jobs for his clients.
Is that what's happening this time?"

Robby looked over at Red.

"We truthfully do not know where he is, or what he's doing.
Aunt Kate is in charge until he gets back. That's all we know for
sure. He told Red and me to sleep in the camper until they get
back. To be ready to help the nurses in case they need us. Or Aunt
Halona, that's Henry's aunt, in case she needs something. She's
pretty sick with that Covid. If the nurses need something in the
night, they can come to the camper and wake us up. When they
open the blinds up at night, we can see right in there and watch
them take care of Henry's aunt. And that's what they do at night—
they open the blinds, and take care of Aunt Halona. They forgot
once, to open the blinds, and Red had to go knock on the glass.
They immediately made it so we could see in. And they apologized. She, Henry's aunt, looks pretty rough, but she doesn't look
like she's getting worse. But we really can't tell much."

"Okay," Det. Townsend said slowly, after taking a moment to
think about what Robby had just said. "I'll have a talk with your
Uncle Jack when he gets back. Don't worry about it. Your Uncle
Jack takes very good care of you boys. I know that. Everyone
knows that. What I'd like to do, right now, is to walk over to Kate's
Tahoe, and have you fellows tell us again everything you can remember—everything that happened last night. Shall we do that
now? Can we?"

Red and Robby were still a little troubled about Det. Townsend's
tone when discussing where their uncle was off to, but they rose to
their feet without a word and headed for the door.

"Now, correct me if I'm wrong," Det. Townsend said. "You boys woke up about one this morning."

Red immediately struck Robby on the arm, and shook his head.

"We heard Buddy growling," Robby said. "Actually, I think I heard him first. It was about one-fifteen, I think—we think."

"Okay, right," Det. Townsend responded. "Buddy woke you up at about one-fifteen."

The detective knew that the boys had said it was 1:15, but he was testing their level of certainty and consistency.

"So," the detective continued, "Buddy growls and barks at around one-fifteen. You boys wake up. What's the first thing you did?"

At that point all four of them, along with Buddy, were walking across the expansive lawn toward the drive where the Tahoe was parked.

"When we heard Buddy bark, we thought something was up. He doesn't do that unless he hears something. And, he has a way of barking so only we will hear it. He wanted to wake us up, but he wasn't trying to scare anyone away. There's a difference in the way he barks. Anyway, we opened the door and just let Buddy run. Usually we keep him on a leash if we think that he's barking at one of the guests, or a worker. But, at one in the morning. No one should be out there."

"So," Robby continued, "Buddy took off this way," he said, pointing toward Kate's Tahoe. "When we went to the camper that night, I think her Tahoe was parked closer—earlier. For some reason, she must have moved it. Not sure what that's all about. But, that's what I think."

Red was nodding in agreement.

"We found a wireless security device in the truck," Det. Townsend said. "It was monitoring some cameras around the property. We think she backed into the spot behind her so it would make her less conspicuous. So, her changing location slightly— that's not a question, or a problem, at this point. What we want to know is what you boys found when you got out here, and what you did. Now don't take that wrong. You boys saved your aunt's life. Whatever you did was right. What we want to hear right now, are any of the details—things you might have overlooked telling us the first time through. We understand that before, when we talked, your only interest was in getting your aunt to medical help. And, all that worked. You did great. Now, what we're interested in is what you might remember that could help us in catching the perps—the one, or the ones, who poked that tube into her window. The idea was to do her harm, and we want to catch them."

"We understand," Robby said. "And we want to help you. When we let Buddy run, I thought he would head for the house. Because that's where the activity was a few nights ago. But he didn't. I don't think he even looked that way. He just bolted out toward the Tahoe. And we ran after him."

"What did he do when he reached Kate's truck?" Det. Townsend asked.

"He ran right to the driver's side and jumped up on the door— with his front paws. Anyway, he sneezed. I think he was looking in. He acted like what was coming out of the window hurt his nose. He whined and jumped backward. And he turned. And barked at us. All four windows were open an inch or so. Like the others still are. So was the window by Aunt Kate. We had to break it to get her out. Aunt Kate was slumped forward, and a little to the right—to *her* right. We could see that we had to get her out of there quickly. And the doors were all locked. So Red grabbed a large stone from over by those bushes, and used it to shatter the window. We knew that it was safety glass, so Red used his elbow to break enough out so that he could reach in and unlock and open the door. Red then grabbed her by the shoulders, tipped her toward us, and we pulled her out on the ground. She did not have her belt on."

"Was she breathing?" Det. Townsend asked.

Red nodded his head, and held up his right hand indicating *a little* with his thumb and index finger.

"What happened next?"

"Red turned the Tahoe off, and he and Buddy stayed with Aunt Kate, while I ran over and used a nurse's phone to call the sheriff's office."

"Why not use your own phone? You have a cell phone. Right?"

"Uncle Jack did not want us using our own phones for anything until he got back to the resort," Robby answered.

"Even for something like this?" Det. Townsend asked.

"That's how Uncle Jack wanted us to handle it. That's what he told us before he took off. Anyway, he locked our phones up when he left the island."

Det. Townsend looked over at his partner with a wrinkled brow, and a question expressed with his affected smile.

"Okay," he said to the boys. "Robby, you ran over to the apartment where Henry's aunt is living. And you woke them up?"

"They weren't asleep," Robby said. "They were awake. They have three crews with Henry's aunt—two on each shift. She's got Covid. And Uncle Jack hired some nurses to take care of her. One of them would have come over to help Kate, but Uncle Jack had told them not to leave the apartment for any reason. We knew what he had told them, so calling for help was the right thing to do."

Det. Conners busied himself writing notes, while Det. Townsend feigned inordinate interest in what he had written. It was obvious to both boys that Det. Townsend was deep in thought. Finally, Det. Conners looked at his partner, slid his notes over for his partner to read, and pointed with his pen to a particular point.

Det. Townsend briefly studied it, and nodded his head. "Did either of you perform mouth-to-mouth exercises?" he asked the boys. "Or apply any other form of resuscitation, to help your aunt breathe?"

Robby said, "I didn't."

Red shook his head, indicating that he had not done anything like that either.

"She seemed to be breathing," Robby said. "I think that means the only important thing for us to do at that point was to call for help. Isn't that right? I asked them on the phone what I should do, and they told me that if the victim was breathing on her own, then to make sure that she be kept warm, stretched out flat on her back, and that nothing should be squeezing on her neck or chest. So, I grabbed the blanket out of the back of the Tahoe and covered her with it. We looked, nothing was squeezing against her neck or chest. So, I think we did all we could."

"Then you boys did everything right. And your aunt is going to be fine because of it."

"She's not really our aunt—not like she's actually related to us. But we love her like an aunt. How long will she have to stay in the hospital?" Robby asked.

Det. Conners shook his head, and said, "They did not have that information for me. If she keeps improving, she should be able to come home quite soon, I would think. But they didn't say when I talked to the deputy."

"That means we're going to have to find someplace for you boys to stay until Kate's well enough to come back to the resort," Det. Townsend added. "We can't have you boys staying here by yourselves. Do you have friends, *adult* friends, where you could stay for a few days?"

Both boys enthusiastically nodded in the affirmative.

"Who would that be?" Det. Townsend asked. "Is this an adult?"

Again, they both nodded.

"That's really great," Det. Townsend replied. "Do they live on the island as well?"

"Yes," Robby replied quickly.

Det. Conners softly kicked his partner until their eyes met. Both men were involved a few years earlier when both Red and Robby had taken off and lived in the woods on their own when the sheriff was investigating Jack Handler. Neither of the veteran lawmen had any doubts about what would happen if they tried to separate the boys and house them off the island. The last time that was tried the boys ran away and found their own housing by breaking and entering vacant cabins and cottages.

The deputies thought about it for a few seconds, and then decided that whatever solution that they might develop, if it involved the boys, but was not developed directly by them, it would immediately fail. And when it failed, it might very well cause more harm than good.

"Then," Det. Townsend said, "this is how we will handle this. You boys make arrangements, call me and let me know what you have in mind, and we will—"

"We don't have phones," Robby interrupted. "But we can get the nurses to give you a call."

"That works," Det. Townsend said, peeling a card from his wallet. "Just let me know who you're staying with, and how we can get hold of them. Do it as soon as possible, too. So it can be included in our report."

Red nodded, and Robby responded quickly with, "Okay, that's what we will do, as soon as we can."

Red and Robby were still wearing the pajama pants and white t-shirts—their typical sleepwear on any given night. They were anxious to put on regular jeans, clean t-shirts and hoodies. So, they ran over to the house and got changed.

Everyone there that day, probably including Buddy, knew beyond a shadow of a doubt that the boys would venture out on their own until Kate was released.

The two detectives excused themselves for a few minutes and they walked about twenty feet to the rear of the Tahoe to talk.

"You know as well as I what's going to happen if we try to remove these boys from the island," Det. Conners said to his partner. "We've been there before. Those are good kids, as teenagers go, but who knows what they'll do if we try to remove them. Let's just wait and see what they can arrange. And be ready to live with whatever the hell they come up with—as long as it sounds even remotely plausible. We'll find something to put in our report, however questionable it might be. How does that sound to you?"

"I just know for damn sure," Det. Townsend responded, "that

I don't want to face off with Jack Handler if we hassle his boys. He will raise living hell with us. I've heard stories about him—what he's capable of, if he thinks you're shittin' with him, or his. I've run into the guy a few times. Can't say that I really know him very well. But he does strike me like a guy you don't want to mess with. Like I said, I've heard stories. I'm not scared of him, or anything like that. But it would be best for all concerned not to rile him up. You know what I'm saying?"

The two men exchanged insincere smiles, and then Robby called over, "Detective Townsend, we think you ought to take a look at what Red just found. We think it could be important."

Chapter 21 —

That tube, the enclosure used to transport one of the W-80s, had to be exactly right. Otherwise, it would doom the whole mission to failure. Here is why the nature of that enclosure was so significant to the project's success:

On November 28, 2017, North Korea launched a Hwasong-21 Intercontinental Ballistic Missile from Pyongsong, which is located just north of the capital, Pyongyang. The missile traveled to a great height—2,800 miles—and then came down in the Sea of Japan. International "Missile Watchers" determined that the test appeared to have been a success, and they estimated that the missile had a potential range of over 8,000 miles—which would have permitted it to have taken out Washington, DC, or any other point in the rest of the United States, had it been properly armed and so aimed.

However, it appeared to the experts that the North Koreans had fitted the rocket with a virtually weightless mock payload, thus making the missile much lighter. The experts further speculated that had an eleven-hundred-pound nuclear weapon actually been installed in the missile, which is what the standard-to-maximum payload for a missile of that type would call for, it would have cut down the range considerably.

This critical analysis did not set well with Chairman Kim. So, he ordered that all future missile tests must include an aluminum enclosure, the exact same size and weight of the nuclear weapon called for by that particular missile, and that it then must be mounted within the missile to simulate an actual warhead.

It was just this sort of aluminum enclosure that Bob had technicians construct for Jack, Henry, and the Navy SEALs to transport in the mini-sub—it was intended to replace Chairman Kim's dummy payload module. Typically, the North Korean dummy warhead would be filled with one hundred and twelve gallons of water mixed with a special glue, an inert compound designed to stiffen into a quasi-solid slime when combined with a few pounds of a special solidifying compound (which was nothing more than borax). The total weight of the cylinder would approximate the weight of the nuclear warhead designed for that missile, and thereby provide more accurate numbers for the test; and, of course, for subsequent propaganda.

This time, however, since the cylinder the US team was providing would already contain two three-hundred-pound W-80s, only twelve gallons of liquid would actually be required. Under any normal conditions, the discrepancy would catch the attention of the military technician attending the process of filling the dummy, but that would not happen this time. Two of the North Korean technicians were working undercover for the CIA. One of them a man named Hong Yun-Chol, and the other a woman, Kim Un-Jong. They had secretly fallen in love on the job, but thought it best not to share their mutual attraction with their supervisors and party leaders.

Instead, only months earlier they had been approached by a group leader based in Pyongyang. He (who must remain anonymous, so will henceforth be referred to by that term: Agent Anonymous) had observed their predicament and confronted them. They expressed to him that they wanted to get married and raise a family, but that they feared bringing children into the North Korean world under the current leadership.

However, Agent Anonymous, on orders from DC, took a chance and offered them a solution. He told them that he worked for American Intelligence, and that if they would aid his efforts on one small project, he could arrange to have them removed from North Korea. He said that he would help them resettle in New York State—such as a rural area in Upstate, or perhaps on Staten Island.

Anonymous further informed them that they would be provided with well-paying jobs in the US, and be given a modest home. That would be modest by US standards, but quite outstanding when compared to anything that would ever be available to them in North Korea.

They were concerned about their identity, and he assured them that they would be officially declared dead, so that there could be no repercussions.

They jumped at the proposition, largely because they both had heard rumors that Yun-Chol had also caught the eye of communist leaders in China and that the Chinese Communist Party was thinking of grooming the young man to step into a leadership role in The Democratic People's Republic of Korea. The couple feared that this extra attention might very well catch the eye of local Communist Party regulars, and possibly result in the execution of both of them—which is a reality that occurs all too often under a communist government, and is considered greatly to be avoided if possible.

The US plan was for Yun-Chol to drive a service truck to meet Jack, Henry and the two SEALs near to where the UOES3 was to make land, and then to help them load the torpedo on the back of the truck, and then to load the second US warhead on the truck with it. After securing the entire package, the four of them would then be driven by Yun-Chol a short distance up the road to a near-by home, and there they would have waiting for them a special-ized recon-style all-terrain tracked vehicle. The team would then place the tube onto the vehicle, and then load the second W-80 into the tube enclosure with the first W-80, and secure it.

At that point, aside from programming, Jack's personal role in the delivery of the nuclear package was supposed to have been completed. Using a remote programming keypad, Jack would per-form the programming required by the addition of the nuclear enclosure.

Once that task was finished, and the enclosure secured to the half-track, Jack would then signal for Yun-Chol to deliver the package to the launch site. Yun-Chol would drive the vehicle west toward the Sohae Satellite Launching Station. The launch site was only about a mile from where the transfer would be made.

Once at the launch site, using a small crane, Yun-Chol would switch the dummy module out with the nuclear enclosure Jack had provided. Then, under Un-Jong's supervision, Yun-Chol and his aides would secure it inside the nose cone of the Hwasong-21 rocket. After completing the mount, Yun-Chol would add the necessary water to bring the weight of the enclosure up to the desired level, and he would connect and secure the umbilical cord to the mother rocket. He would, however, only feign adding all the hardener.

Interesting to note here that this whole process would have been impossible as late as November of 2017, because that was when the North Koreans developed the ability to fuel horizontally. This improved process saved an enormous amount of time a missile was required to spend on the launching pad. Plus, it allowed for attention to be drawn away from switching out the dummy warhead.

It was to be at this point, once Yun-Chol connected the umbilical cord uniting the rocket with the nuclear package, that Jack was to again become responsible for the process, as he would remotely take over programming through using the keypad he had been given by Roger and Bob.

With all the lead up successfully carried out, Jack was ready to jump in with both feet. His first task in this stage of the program was to marry the module he was given to the brains of the Hwasong-21. To do this he simply followed nearly to a 'T' the instructions left him by US agents. This procedure kept the package of nukes integrated with the location of the rocket while in flight, so that the package would be released at the most opportune time for the W-80s to successfully find their individual targets.

Even though the individual W-80 modules had the ability to sprout wings and fly, they were not able to propel themselves whatsoever. That meant that they absolutely had to be released relatively near their proposed targets.

Although it had not occurred to him at the time, Jack now understood why the stiffening agent added to the water within the module would not be the real thing.

Initially, Jack did not believe that he would be given any influence as to what the new targets to be selected might be, nor was he led to believe that he would be able to determine the strength of the blasts. He assumed that those aspects of the programming were not for him addressable. He thought that because the only input that he actually received training for had strictly to do with the successful marriage of rocket to module.

However, when the time came for him to go online with missile, he found that his programmer did have the ability to program a number of various functions, beyond merely uniting the package with the Hwasong-21. For one, the electronic programmer he had been provided appeared to allow him to determine the level of ferocity he might choose for each of the nukes to unleash upon detonation. And, once he discovered that he had this power, it was after only a few moments of consideration that Jack opted to kick the explosive force of each of the bombs up to the max—which was a level far above what was "recommended" by Roger's people. His aggravation about the whole mission pushed him to be as destructive as possible. "What the hell difference does it make," he asked himself, "if it blows up like a firecracker or a stick of dynamite? It's all going to be out in the middle of the ocean anyway."

But, after he had hit "ENTER," instead of shutting the programmer down, he decided to read the next line: "Select the GPS coordinates for target #1." He thought about it for a minute, and then muttered, "Well, I'll be damned! Do you suppose that I might actually be able to select targets? … H-o-l-y s-h-i-t!"

Thinking that just might be the case, he referred to a small GPS Map Finder given to each of them when they originally set out. He located on it the co-ordinates that he thought suitable: 30.82350,111.00373. He entered that GPS on the programmer, and then hit "ENTER." It then told him to "select desired distance above target to detonate." Again, he thought for a moment, entered what he thought appropriate, and hit "Enter."

Almost immediately the programmer asked him to select the coordinates for target #2. He quickly considered his options, checked his Map Finder again, and then entered these coordinates: "30.53920,114.35077." After establishing elevation options, he hit the "ENTER" button.

Once he'd completed the programming on the second GPS, the programmer asked, "Given starting location, may I reverse the order of the coordinates for the two targets selected?"

Jack again thought, *what the hell!* And entered "YES."

A huge smile crept across his face as he again prepared to close down the programmer. "Are you sure you wish to leave programming?" the device asked him.

He was still smiling when he hit "YES."

"Hell yes!" rolled smoothly and quickly off his tongue.

Once his active role in the launch sequence was completed, he and Henry began preparing for their escape. The plan laid out beforehand was for Jack, Henry, and the two SEALs to wait at the house with the truck.

Jack lingered at the site for a little longer. He was obviously deep in thought. That is when he removed a black super-broad chisel-tip marker from his pocket, one he had found and picked up earlier while in the mini-sub, and he wrote a message in English vertically on the torpedo-shaped enclosure. When he had finished, he took a step backward and read the words he had written. He then smiled broadly, and he retraced over the message he'd written to make it more visible, should anyone have occasion to read it. He then considered tossing the marker away, but thought better of it. Instead, he snapped the cover back over the tip and tucked it in his pants pocket.

"I'm done with them," he announced. "You can take it away."

With that comment, the North Korean soon-to-be defector, Yun-Chol, started the engine on the tracked vehicle and headed to the launch site to complete the work.

The mission, to that point, was turning out just as planned.

After completing their final operational steps before launch, instead of taking shelter in the observation room, the couple excused themselves to use the restroom. But, rather than head to the toilet, they both made their way quickly to the tracked vehicle, and drove it all the way to the beach, which was where they'd agreed to rendezvous. Using GPS, they quickly located their target, ditched and hid the tracked vehicle. And, with Jack, Henry and the SEALs leading the way, the six of them beat it over to where the UOES3 had landed to start with.

Even though they knew it would be incredibly tight fitting them all into the mini-sub, the unit itself was designed to accommodate four SEALs and a crew of two. Roger's revised plan was for all eight of them to somehow squeeze onboard. This included the two crew, two SEAL operatives, Jack and Henry, and now, the two North Korean defectors. "It will be uncomfortable, to say the least," Roger had told them while still onboard the USS Jimmy Carter, "but somehow you will make do. For this mission to even have a shot at one hundred percent success, you have to make this part work."

"Well, Henry," Jack said. "You ready to rock and roll?"

"Let's do it," Henry said behind a smile of determination.

And ...

Chapter 22 —

Back on Sugar Island, Detectives Townsend and Conners looked at each other intently before responding to Robby's beckoning articulation, "Detective Townsend, we think you ought to take a look at what Red just found. We think it could be important." However, they did not further waste time in responding.

"Yes, my young friends," Det. Townsend said as he led the way over to where the boys were standing, "what have you got for us?"

It was obvious from the tone of his voice that Det. Townsend was growing weary of having to deal with these two young lads. Even though he and Det. Conners did sympathize with their predicament, what was being forced upon these two veteran detectives was the inconvenience of having to deal with a situational circumstance substantially outside their playbook. Nowhere in their "Detectives' Book of Rules" would they find anything such as was being forced upon them by Jack Handler. They were discovering themselves required to accept rules that could not be found in any policing handbook either of them had ever read, simply because they possessed a healthy fear of what Handler would do to them should he come back and determine that they could have treated his boys with greater respect. It was, however a 'healthy fear,' because they had both heard about situations in which Jack actually became physically hurtful to those with whom he was severely displeased.

"Check it out," Robby said, pointing down by Red's foot. "We think you will want to take a closer look at this, that's why we haven't touched it. If there's any prints on it, they won't be ours."

Det. Townsend at first bent over to get a better view of the object. "What do you think it is?" he asked the boys. "Do you have any ideas as to how it might of got here?"

"None," Robby said. "We play over here a lot. We use the little road—the driveway, to toss a football. We think we would have spotted it before, if it had been here even as late as yesterday afternoon. We think it was probably just dropped here. By accident. We can see that it's a coin. But, do you know what kind of coin it is? Neither of us has ever seen anything like it before."

Det. Townsend dropped to his knees to get a better look.

"Detective," he said to his partner, "hand me an evidence bag, and tweezers. We're gonna want to get this to the lab. Check for fingerprints, and origin—all that regular shit."

It was obvious to the boys that Det. Townsend was not pleased with himself for having released that little piece of profanity in the presence of the boys. It had simply just escaped his lips because of his frustrations. *I'm sure they've heard worse than that come out Jack's mouth a million times,* he was thinking. *It isn't going to kill them, I'm sure.*

The truth is that the boys were not used to hearing their Uncle Jack use much profanity of any sort when he was conversing with them, or around them. Of course, their ears were tickled daily by a substantially more coarse strain of foul language produced by classmates; so, on this day, they had no problem with it. All it actually conveyed to Red and Robby was Det. Townsend's growing level of frustration.

The boys did have two major concerns at that moment. One was that the detectives would quickly get to the bottom of their find, and that the whole case would just melt harmlessly away—at least as far as it involved them. Their second concern was in creating some physical distance between themselves and Det. Townsend. Both boys sensed that the two detectives were growing a little apprehensive as to how properly to deal with them, in that they were being viewed as two fourteen-year-old *children* without a responsible adult to watch over them. And, since they could see that Det. Townsend at least appeared to pretty much run the show, they wanted to establish some physical distance between themselves and him—with appropriate permission, of course.

"Okay, boys," Detective Townsend said, "I want you two to stand in place exactly where you are. Don't move a muscle. Don't walk or sit down. Wait right where you're at. Detective Conners and I should have searched this area thoroughly earlier, and we didn't. That mistake is on us. So do not move until we tell you that you can, or that mistake will be on you, and we will not be very happy. Got that?"

"Yessir," Robby replied. "We will stand right here and not move."

The boys could both recognize Det. Townsend's exasperation level was topping off, and it was now being directed at them. They knew that they were presenting him with a challenge that he did not appreciate. And so, the best thing they could do right then was to obey him to the letter, or they would end up in the county juvenile detention center—or take off and run through the woods. And they did not want either circumstance if at all possible to avoid. Still, both boys so strongly preferred independence to confinement, were it to come to that in this matter, their unspoken rule was to run away before submitting.

Red looked deeply into Robby's eyes, and Robby knew what that look meant. What it told Robby was that if and when the detectives began walking them toward one of their patrol cars, they would bolt.

They both had been through similar situations throughout their earlier life experiences, and they were well practiced at sensing this sort of trouble before it actually presented itself. *Better behave now*, they were thinking, *or it will soon be too late.*

They could not have been more correct. Det. Townsend glanced up until his eyes fell on one of their patrol cars, and he said to his partner, "Why don't you grab that car, swing it around on the drive, and bring it up on the gravel. Park it no more than seventy-five yards up the drive. We've got equipment in the car that we might need. Plus, I want to block that drive off."

Yup, the two boys were both contemplating, *they're thinking about locking us in the back seat of the patrol car.*

They were ready, and their glances at one another clearly communicated their thoughts.

In fact, if the situation appeared to warrant either of them bolting from the scene, that's exactly what would have transpired. If one of them were to be constrained, the other one would not wait around for his friend to break free. No further communication was necessary.

The location they would run to lay about a mile from the resort. To get there required crossing a creek. But, they would not simply jump in and wade across it. They had even practiced their escape several times—and further discussed it frequently. They would run in slightly different directions, covering over a quarter of a mile of rough terrain in and out of the woods, and then hit the stream in virtually the same place (though not likely at the same time).

Once in the water, they would make their way upstream as rapidly as possible, and then, at a location selected earlier, they would emerge on the rocks, and then make their way through a thicket of heavy brush and briars. They had even rehearsed the escape route with Buddy, so that he could maneuver it on his own if need be.

And then, if all went as planned, they would all finally arrive at their secret sanctuary. Red had built it some time ago when forced to hide out from sheriff's detectives who were intent on placing him back in what he regarded as a "totally unacceptable" foster home.

They both agreed that it was not going to happen to either one of them again—at least not if they could possibly do anything to prevent it.

They liked the Handlers, and Henry, so that's where they chose to stay. But both of them agreed that they were not willing to gamble on getting stuck in any foster situation not involving Jack, Henry or Kate. And, truth be told, their concerns at this point were legitimate—Det. Townsend's thoughts were beginning to view their removal from Sugar Island as a legitimate possibility.

"Yessir, Detective Townsend," Robby said. "We promise we will not walk around here anymore. But, we do have a question—

a suggestion."

"Yeah," Detective Townsend responded, looking over at them with just a sliver of perceivable irritation, "what's your question?"

"Both of us just have to go to the bathroom," Robby said. "Could we go up to the camper and use the toilet? And then we could just wait there until you get done. That way we wouldn't get in your way either. Would that be okay? And we could take Buddy with us. I'm sure you don't want him disturbing anything."

As they were standing there, Robby had ahold of Buddy's collar to make sure he did not do anything to corrupt the newfound piece of evidence.

Detective Townsend looked over at his partner. Neither of the detectives expressed any sign of negativity with Robby's request, and so he said, "Yeah, go ahead and run over to the camper. Go straight there, though, one behind the other, and in single file. If you see anything on the way, don't touch it. Just give us a shout and we will check it out. But, when you get to the camper, you should enter it and wait right there. Because, we will have more questions. And, if either of you have any more ideas, just make a note of them. Write 'em down. We'll talk about it after we wind up here. Okay?"

"Thank you," Robby said. "We will wait over there until we hear from you."

As they got out of earshot from the detectives, Robby said to his friend, "I don't really get the feeling that they want to stick us in detention, do you?"

Red was shaking his head to the negative.

"Good," Robby said in a relieved fashion. He always regarded Red's opinion highly.

Chapter 23 —

The rationale employed by the two boys, vis-à-vis the two veteran detectives, for excusing themselves from the scene surrounding Kate's rented Tahoe was in part legitimate—they both were actually seeking to relieve their bladders. However, under any normal circumstances, they would simply have stepped off the drive and found a tree that appeared to be looking for a little human nourishment. But, they had correctly sized up the situation and determined that it would be to their advantage to create a little space between them and the law.

They had barely progressed another hundred feet before Red reached over and touched Robby's swinging left arm. As soon as his eyes shifted to meet Red's, the mute boy began shaking his head slowly, while signaling with his eyes that they should not look back.

"I get it," Robby uttered in a whisper. He then told Buddy to "go to the camper."

That's all it took, and Buddy bolted off toward it in a flash.

The two fourteen-year-olds continued on their hurried trek toward the camper—single file, of course. When they got there, they quickly entered and used the toilet—Robby first, at Red's insistence, and then they sat down at the tiny table and discussed the events of the day.

"What the hell kinda coin was it that we found?" Robby asked. Red was beginning to get used to hearing Robby lace his conversation with a few low-level profanities when no adult was around to hear. "I never saw anything like that before. Did you recognize it?"

Red did not write anything down immediately, he just assumed a dumbfounded expression, lifted both palms up, and slowly shook his head.

After he had a chance to think it over for a minute, he did begin using a pencil. "I saw something like that before. Similar. On Henry's computer. I think it was Chinese. A Chinese coin. This one looked like it had been glued on a shoe, I think. Or boot. And it just fell off. Might not have been same guy who tried to kill Aunt Kate. Might have??"

Red had underlined the word "not" to draw Robby's attention to his questioning the likelihood that the coin might have fallen off the shoe of someone other than the man who tried to kill Kate.

"The side we saw didn't have glue on," Robby said. "At least I didn't see any. And that hole in the middle—what was that all about? We can be sure of one thing, it was not a US coin. Right? We never had anything here. Not that looked like that. Right?"

"Not us," Red wrote. "Maybe glue on other side?? I didn't see any glue in the hole. But, whoever glued it on wouldn't want glue to be showing. Look on other side, maybe?"

"Yeah," Robby replied. "Maybe. I sure would like to get a look at the other side of that coin. The side that we could see looked pretty clean. Like, he might have kept his boots, or shoes, pretty cleaned off. And the coin got polished up a bit when he did it."

"Figures," Red wrote. "Maybe the shoe polishing eventually

broke the glue loose. Possible."

"The side we could see was shiny," Robby added. "That likely means that it hadn't been out in the weather long. Or maybe he sprayed it with some kinda clear coat. Might very well have been dropped by the guy who tried to kill Kate. Be nice to know where the coin was from. If we knew that, we might be able to figure out where that jerk was from. Too bad we can't Google anything. Might be able to find that very coin quickly."

Red sat there silently for a minute, and then started writing feverishly. "Think about it—nobody ever glues coins to boots or onto any clothes. I don't think it was glued on anything. Somebody just lost it. Simple. One side was a little shiny, but so could the other side have been just as shiny. We don't know. Maybe it went through the wash? Could be. All that the shine tells us is that it was not laying in the grass for very long. Let's go to big house, and take a look in an encyclopedia!"

He closed his suggestion with an exclamation point to convey urgency.

Robby's eyes lit up. "We promised to stay in the camper."

"Won't be a problem," Red wrote. "Flush toilets good reason. It works."

"Let's go!" Robby exclaimed as he immediately bolted out of the camper door. Red and Buddy were right behind him, but Red stopped and reached back into the top of the door trim to retrieve a key to the main house. He then closed and latched the camper door.

"Got it?" Robby said with excitement when he realized what Red was up to. "Good. Let's go."

As they unlocked the door and entered the house they noticed that something was askew.

"The alarm's been turned off!" Robby observed. "Somebody's been in the house, and disarmed it. I wonder if Detective Townsend knows about that?"

Red flashed what Robby had come to call "Red's puzzled grin."

Robby considered for a moment just what he thought Red might be conveying.

"Detective Townsend," Robby said to Red as he stood there at the keypad. "Are you thinking that maybe the detectives turned it off—the alarm? That could be. But, I'll be damned if I'm gonna go ask 'em. They're already in a bad mood. That'd just make it worse. Let's quick check the encyclopedia for 'world coins.'"

The boys ran into the library and Robby grabbed the World Book.

At first Red looked over his shoulder, but then impatience carried his eyes back into the stacks. He went immediately to the "Cs," and found nothing of interest. He then went to the abbreviated card catalog Kate had set up when her dad moved in. By cross-referencing he found the title he was looking for: The World Encyclopedia of Coins.

"Could Uncle Jack actually have this book?" he asked himself. "Looks like he just might."

And there it was under the "Ws."

Red slid it off the shelf and headed for a table. On his way he made a noise indistinguishable by most humans. Robby, however, knew it to mean, "Come here, quickly!"

Robby left his encyclopedia on the table and scooted immediately in behind Red and checked out his find over his shoulder.

Red had been turning pages for only a minute before he

slammed his finger down on a picture.

"That's it!" Robby barked. "Right?! Isn't that it? Isn't that what we found? I think it is, don't you? What do you think?"

This time Red exhibited a bit of a grimacing smile, known to Robby as meaning, "Could be, but I'm not too sure."

"They do all look a lot alike to me, too," Robby said. "With that square hole in the middle of it, and all. But, I think all the coins I saw, so far, that have the square hole in the middle. I think they are all from China. Right?"

This time Red was displaying another tight smile, but one totally lacking grimace. The absence of the little scowl rendered it totally indiscernible to Robby. *Guess I'll just have to make my own mind up about it,* he was thinking. *I'm going with Chinese unless Red comes up with a better idea.*

Red continued spinning pages past their noses, and reading the copy as fast as he could. Finally, he slid the book slightly forward, but did not close it. *That,* he concluded, *would be a rude thing to do to my best friend.* But, in his mind, he had finished his research.

"Chinese?" Robby asked as he sat down in the hard oak chair next to Red. "It's a Chinese coin, right?"

Slowly, but in a totally definitive style, Red nodded his head in agreement. He then reached to the center of the table and removed a piece of paper that had been put there for his note taking. And he wrote: "Chinese coin. I'm positive!"

Both boys sat there for a few moments, a look of satisfaction owning their faces. And then, finally, Robby said what neither of them wanted to hear: "But, that does not mean the guy who lost the coin was Chinese? He just might have liked it because it was so different. That's right, too. Isn't it?"

After a few more long seconds had passed, Red began his slow nod of affirmation.

"Then," Robby muttered. "It doesn't really mean a thing, does it? Not a *damn* thing."

Over the past six months or so Red had been acclimating himself to Robby's developing vocabulary of curse words. To date he'd noted his friend's liking for only three: shit, damn and hell. *How long*, Red asked himself, *will he be satisfied with that limitation?*

"Right," Red wrote. "Doesn't prove anything. But, it is still evidence, depending on how it's handled. It could be useful. What seems even stranger is that these guys lost a coin and an expensive combat knife. Almost like leaving a signature on purpose. Came back for knife, but still strange."

Robby knew what Red was thinking, but did not respond or comment.

Det. Townsend did not hear what Robby said, or know what Red was thinking. But he was a first-rate detective, and so he was all about preserving the significance of what the boys had found.

After excusing the boys from the "crime scene," his second reaction was to direct Det. Conners to "exercise caution with the coin, because there might be some prints on it."

And that is exactly what his partner did. But, even though the mysterious coin did serve to distract their immediate attention from the plight of the two boys, their concern for the kids' well-being still nagged at them.

Chapter 24 —

There was a high level of restrained joy gripping the hearts of Jack and his team as they filed back into the UOES3. Fortunately, the SEAL crew had rehearsed the loading procedure in their minds many times in preparation. But, even though the other two passengers had not practiced boarding at all, the fact that they had apparently accomplished all that had been set before them was enough to warrant a sense of elation.

From the moment that all six of them had gathered on the beach before boarding, Jack made it clear, particularly to the North Korean technicians, that until further notice there should be no audible conversation taking place—not to one another, and not to the rest of the crew. He was not so sure that they understood when he whispered his words, but he was quite positive they were able to read his sign language. When he declared his silent proclamation to Yun-Chol and Kim Un-Jong, at the same time he made sure that SEAL Agents One and Two were reminded of his orders which were the same as he had delivered to them at the time they first entered the mini-sub.

Jack even intended his directive requiring total silence to apply to his personal communication between himself and Henry.

Further, no matter how eager he might have been to report their success to Roger and Bob, or how much he would have liked to discuss the mission with the others on the mini-sub, he determined to muzzle his exuberance for the foreseeable. *This mission will not truly be complete,* Jack reasoned, *until the fireworks have successfully been set off, and every participant has reached land in America—safe and undetected. Until that time, we must maintain total silence.*

When he had a few moments free, Jack played back in his mind an earlier meeting the two men had in the belly of the B-52 carrying him and Henry to Japan—the little caucus that took place at onset of the mission. While Roger and Bob were not physically present with Jack and Henry, they were there with them via video. Roger's words of warning to the two warriors were of particular significance to Jack now at this stage of the operation.

Not for one moment during the course of the mission, right up to the point where Jack and Henry found themselves at the present time, did either one of them sense misgivings with regard to the nature and scope of the mission, or how it had been presented to them. In fact, as far as Jack knew, they had completed it successfully—at least to that point.

Furthermore, from Bob's residence in DC, that is exactly how he and Roger viewed the mission as it was going down.

Henry would not have disagreed with Jack's non-verbalized assessment. Even though those aboard the mini-sub had not yet achieved a positive escape, or even been given a very good plan for such, Henry believed that he was detecting a sincere sense of accomplishment emanating from Jack, and that was good enough for him, at least for the time being.

"Later," Henry said to himself, "if we survive this, and when inclination and circumstance permit, I just might seek additional details from Jack about how the 'boss' regarded the work we will have just done. Such as: 'do you think DC believes that the goal was satisfactorily achieved? Was Bob satisfied? If so, was he totally satisfied, or just partially? And how about you, Jack—were you happy about it?' That is, of course, if we survive to ask questions about it."

One thing that Henry could not get out of his mind was Jack's unshakable smile. "Is he actually gloating?" he asked himself. "And, if so, is it somehow justifiable? Or, has Jack just been breathing too much bad air? What's really up with that guy?"

For the next four and a half hours all went much as expected. They had anticipated very crowded conditions, and in that they were not wrong or surprised. After pouring all the warm bodies into the mini-sub, they immediately slipped out into the sea until they had reached the predetermined point where they were to establish connection with a North Korean fishing boat. There they submerged to the maximum, which was a depth of 190 feet. Since the water's depth was at that point was 247 feet, they were comfortable all around. Once they confirmed the coordinates, they cut all power and waited. They were all pleased that they were able to power down for nearly forty minutes before the rendezvous was due to take place.

After thirty-nine minutes, they began to rise slowly toward the surface. At precisely the right time they snagged the weighted rope which was dropped for them from a friendly North Korean fishing boat, attached it to the mini-sub, and off they went in the direction of their next blind date—the northern edge of the Northern Limit Line (usually referred to as the NLL, or the 38th). There they were to be disconnected, and hopefully they would successfully cross it into southern waters under their own power. In other words, it was largely a reversal of the protocol they had followed to get to the launch to start with.

From there they would head in the direction of the waiting USS Jimmy Carter. But instead of hooking up with the big sub immediately, they would be met by another South Korean fishing boat, and be towed out in the deep waters by it. Then, it would eventually be able to hook up to the USS Jimmy Carter once again, and be hitched up to it for the remainder of the operation.

Now that the mission had appeared to have reached the point where all that remained was their secretly passing across the 38th, a simple fact occurred to all directly involved—there actually seemed to be very little that any of them could do at that point to change the outcome. They were, after all, still in the Yellow Sea well north of the NLL, where all maritime geography inside that designated area was basically controlled by the DPRK. And, conversely, waters south of the NLL were free for all to sail in—but they weren't there yet. Further contributing to the passive aspect of their situation, they were not even under their own power. They were being towed beneath a diesel-powered North Korean fishing boat.

So far so good, they were all thinking as they moved along silently beneath the wooden hull of the friendly northern fishing boat.

The thought was that by having their motor off they would accomplish two important things: first, they would conserve power. They understood that their battery would not be sufficient to take them back to the reserve battery waiting for them south of the 38th, much less power them to a safe harbor. So, it was determined that being under tow would allow them to sufficiently conserve power. While it was true that a spare battery pack hidden at the bottom of the Yellow Sea did await them should it be needed, their desire was to not be forced to spend time or energy searching for and hooking up the spare package.

For just a moment Jack had sufficient quiet time to consider bringing Kate and the boys out here to dive. *Certainly we would want to venture out only in waters south of the NLL,* he was thinking. *But, it's just a fact that these waters are unique in the world—-polluted as hell, but unique just the same.*

But, as soon as he allowed serious thought about such a family adventure, the realization soaked in as to just how dangerous this geography was about to become. And so he quickly relieved himself of that exercise. *Shit! I would never bring my family into these waters,* he then thought, *not in a thousand years.*

He quickly realized that his fanciful planning was simply the fruit of his perceived success. He was gloating. And he knew it was too early to gloat.

And then his mind played with the thought that being fastened to the underside of a fishing boat would provide them with another advantage—it would make them virtually invisible to any type of satellite or aerial imaging. Not only would the fishing boat hide them from physical view, but the fact that their motor was turned off eliminated sonic-sensing surveillance devices.

In spite of his efforts to control himself, his confidence was growing by the minute.

Initially, they had hooked up to a North Korean fishing vessel just a few kilometers off the coast. Only the captain of the fishing boat, along with his first assistant, were aware that the mini-sub had tethered itself to their underside—a favor for which the CIA paid them handsomely.

Once they had neared the 38th parallel, one of the SEALs got out of the sub and disconnected the tether. And then the pilots of the sub took it down to the maximum depth allowed for the terrain, while the fishing boat drifted off and continued fishing.

After twenty minutes, the pilots steered the sub south across the 38th, and then powered down again. There they waited for their next ride—that being another larger South Korean fishing vessel.

All seems to be going well, Henry thought. *Once we hook up to the South Korean friendly, we should be home free.*

He took a few moments to reflect. *No doubt about it, this did turn out to be the most challenging mission he had ever attempted. As advertised, I suppose you could say. I still have no way of knowing for certain, but if I'm reading Jack correctly, we did what we set out to do. I'll find out more about that later. And then there are these passengers. This loving North Korean couple. Soon to be husband and wife, Jack says. It'll be interesting to hear their story, if DC even allows us to talk to them in the States. I'll bet they've got a tale to tell.*

It's really not Jack's nature to take a chance like that—bringing two more bodies into such a confined area. I suppose he did the calculations for the oxygen requirements, and I'm sure Roger and Bob have also looked at it. So, it's all probably fine. Anyway, I'm good with it if it saves a couple sympathetic freedom seekers. I'm very good with that.

While Henry was lost in his thoughts, he felt their sub beginning to rise in the water. Must be our ride is here, he reasoned.

He was correct. After a few minutes he observed one of the SEAL team suiting up to go out and do the hook up.

After another twenty minutes or so the diver returned and removed his tanks. He nodded to Henry, indicating with a big smile that everything went well. Soon afterward Henry felt the sub begin to surrender its location to the will of the fishing boat.

"We are on our way to a safe harbor," he said to himself. "All good news yet again."

But his elation did not last very long.

While he was unable to view anything on the video screens, particularly with his fellow passengers all cramped up in a very limited amount of space, he did detect a muffled shock wave outside, and felt a simultaneous quaking within their tiny vessel. He knew something unusual was going on, and that it probably wasn't good. He looked at Jack. The reaction he received in return reflected his concern. An expression of "this should not be happening" had gripped Jack's face.

Almost immediately they both sensed the end of forward movement. And then, after about two minutes, they both figured out what had just transpired. It seemed obvious to them both that the boat above them had become disabled. *Perhaps it was hit by an unfriendly torpedo or missile,* they reasoned.

"Prepare for impact!" Jack barked, breaking the silence. "The fishing boat up top is going down. And it's gonna be headed our way! ... Brace for impact."

Chapter 25 —

Kate had awakened at the War Memorial Hospital in Sault Ste. Marie. She was still so very beautiful even after spending the night in a hospital bed. Sure, she had messy hair and was wearing no makeup, but she still had on the skinny black jeans with a black t-shirt, and her favorite jean jacket was hanging loosely over a nearby chair. Her boots were tucked neatly under that same chair. The first words out of her awakened mouth were, "The boys! Where are the boys? Are they alright?"

It was easy to see that Dep. Fisher, who was still at her side, was greatly relieved that Kate was lucid, and that her mental faculties appeared fully intact.

"Yes," Dep. Fisher replied. "Your two young men are just fine, and they have been asking about you. I'm sure that Detectives Townsend and Conners will be relieved as well to hear that you've come out of this ordeal, and are fine. You are fine, right? Do you have anything specific that you'd like me to pass along to the officers in charge? Or to the boys? I'll call the detectives up and see if they've got questions for you. Do you think you're ready to talk to them—to the detectives? About this case? Could you do that?"

"Yes," she said. "I want to talk to them as well. But, you can assure me that the boys are doing fine. Right? You're absolutely positive about that? Do you know if they saw or heard anyone, or anything out of the ordinary?"

"I've been here with you ever since you got here," Dep. Fisher said. "I was on scene when we found you, but I rode in the ambulance and stayed with you. I did see the boys when they directed the detectives to your vehicle. They are the ones who saved your life—them, and that Golden Retriever. It was actually the dog that alerted the boys to the problem. So, I'd say you've got those boys, and that handsome dog, to thank that you made it through all this. Now, are you somehow related to those boys? I thought I heard them call you their aunt. Are you actually related, or is that just a term of endearment—aunt?"

"Let me get this totally straight," Kate said, sitting up in her bed but not answering the deputy's question, "Both of the boys—Red and Robby, both of them are fine. Is that what I hear you saying?"

"Well," he replied, "I only heard the one talking. But Detective Townsend, he's the one I've been reporting to, he said the boys are both okay, not injured or anything, and that they are asking about you. And when I was on site, they were perfectly fine."

"That's all that matters," she said, as she lay back down. "Now, what was it that you asked me?"

"Those two boys, the ones that found you and called us, are you actually related to them?"

"Yes," Kate said. "I am ... and I'm not. Their names are Red and Robby. They're both fourteen years old, and they are my dad's foster boys. They both come from troubled backgrounds, and they've lived with my dad for a year—or two, actually. They are absolutely wonderful kids. I consider them my little brothers, but they call me 'Aunt Kate.' So, yes, we are truly related. And, they are the ones who saved my life. Isn't that what you said? Buddy and the boys? Right? Buddy is Red's dog, but we all love him. He is a wonderful dog. Friend, actually. Buddy is more like a good friend to all of us. When can I see those guys? Can I leave here now? I'm fine. I really should get back to the house. I don't want them there by themselves."

As soon as she had said that, she wanted to retract it.

Damn it, she was thinking. *They're going to be pulling the boys out of there. Why did I have to say it that way? Damn it! Damn it! Damn it!*

The door in the hyperbaric chamber was already open, so she simply threw her covering off, slid a hospital gown over her t-shirt, adjusted it appropriately, and swung both legs over and out.

"I don't think you're supposed to be getting out of that machine until the doctors okay it," Dep. Fisher said. "Better just hang in until the doc gives his permission."

Kate would have none of it. "I'm a detective myself," she told him. "I'm sure you already know that. I need my boots and my gear. I had a weapon when I got here, or I assume I did. Can you help me get it together? I need to get back to my boys. Will you help me or not? I am not staying here another minute. You gonna help me? I'm not sticking around here. So, just see if you can help me. Okay?"

Dep. Fisher didn't know what to do. He recognized that her determination had kicked in and that she was not about to be dissuaded. He immediately made a call.

"Detective Townsend, Deputy Fisher here. Our female patient, Kate Handler, she's in the process of checking herself out. She's not listening to me. She wants me to get her equipment for her. All of her equipment—including her sidearm. I don't recall seeing her weapon on her person. What do you want me to tell her? I would have to physically restrain her, in order to keep her here. She'd have none of that."

"I would never send a weapon on an unconscious person," Det. Townsend replied. "Of course I removed it, labeled it, and secured it in my trunk as evidence. She's got to know that's standard protocol—even in New York. Keep this in mind—that woman is Jack Handler's daughter. She's a lieutenant in the New York City Police Department. Homicide, I believe. If she is able to get around on her own, and if she chooses, do not, under any circumstance, try to physically restrain her. Her father would have your hide nailed on his barn door. Do not lay a hand on her."

"I get it," Dep. Fisher said. "Shall I take her back out to Sugar Island?"

"Exactly," Det. Townsend said. "You've got a patrol car at your disposal? That's a question."

"Pretty sure we do," Dep. Fisher said. "My partner followed the ambulance down here, and he's in the building. Haven't seen him for a few minutes, but I'm sure he's around. Shall we just bring her with us and come back out?"

"If you're sure she's up to it," Det. Townsend said. "Check with her doctor. But do not try to restrain her under any circumstance."

"Yes, sir."

"On second thought," Det. Townsend said, "do not consult with her doctor on this. If that woman wants to check herself out, as long as she's balancing on her two feet, back her up. Drive her out here, if that's what she wants. Do not raise a fuss with the doctors."

Det. Townsend realized that if the doctor insisted that she remain in bed, he would undoubtedly request that Dep. Fisher restrain her.

"We can't go there," Det. Townsend added.

Just as Dep. Fisher was winding up his conversation with Det. Townsend, Kate walked back in the room housing the hyperbaric chamber, which was where she'd left Dep. Fisher.

Kate's long brown hair was now brushed. She'd tossed aside the hospital gown, and was now wearing her black boots and her denim jacket with the sleeves rolled up. She appeared ready for combat.

"Ready, Deputy?" Kate vociferated in a near bark. She was anticipating objection or at least hesitancy on his part, and so opted for a tone geared to minimize resistance.

"My boss wants me to drive you out to the island, if that's what you want," Dep. Fisher replied. His compliant response surprised her.

"My sidearm?" she said in a less aggressive manner. "Any word on where it is?"

"Detective Townsend—that's my boss. I'm sure he labeled and sealed it as evidence. You can take that up with him when we get there—to the island. You're looking great. Are you good to go? We can leave right now, if you wish. Have you squared it all away with the front desk?"

"I'm checking myself out," she replied. "They're not happy. Didn't exactly get their blessing, but I need to get out there and check up on those boys. So, if you're ready, and willing to drive me, let's hit it. I'm good to go."

By that time Kate's demeanor had returned to that of the genuinely pleasant barometric level she always strove to maintain—a development not wasted on a grateful Dep. Fisher.

As they walked past the front desk, they both made it a point to pick up their stride a bit, and to not make eye contact with anyone. What they missed in the process was the head-turning gaze of a darkly-dressed Chinese gentleman who stood at the admitting desk talking with Kate's attending physician, and the lady in charge at the station.

Kate caught his eye as he talked to the nurse.

Chapter 26 —

E veryone in the mini-sub was already strapped down except for the two North Korean passengers—"Tarzan and Jane," as Jack referred to them. They, too, surmised something untoward was taking place. Tarzan tightly gripped his bride-to-be beneath both of her arms. At the same time, Henry grabbed the man by the upper arm and squeezed tightly.

As the fishing boat sank, just as Jack had predicted, it slid across the sub's bow, tearing a relatively clean fourteen-inch gash through the fiberglass hull. Water began gushing in. One of the two-man SEAL diving team started to disconnect his safety belt, but Jack blurted out loudly, "Leave your belts on! Do not unhook them until the slack in that cable is taken up! We're going to the bottom. Our tow truck is sinking, and it's gonna drag us down with it. We don't know how deep it is right here. So stay the hell right where you are, and leave your belts hooked up until I tell you otherwise. And, Henry—you hang on to Tarzan and Jane. Stay at it until I tell you to release them."

The SEAL did as Jack said. He strapped himself back in and checked his instruments to be sure the front pump had kicked in.

It was only a matter of seconds until the tether lost all slack and the weight of the fishing boat began aggressively taking the mini-sub with it. At first the shock seemed enough to jerk their mini-sub in two. The force of the encounter with the end of the tether cable lifted both of the North Koreans off the blanket they had spread out to rest in. Henry maintained his grip and steadied them back in place. Immediately the sinking boat began pulling the bow of the mini-sub steeply downward.

"Jack! How deep can this tin can go?" Henry shouted.

"Operational depth is sixty meters," Pilot One said. "Crush depth—not sure. I wouldn't want to go below a hundred and ten. We're diving much too fast right now. Can't adequately adjust pressure. We need to cut that damn cable ASAP! Sixty meters in feet is one ninety. Don't think we know crush depth. Lock out for divers is only one hundred twenty feet. We're well past that."

"We have a remote release on that rigging loop, but it isn't working. Must be damaged. Have to release it manually."

As he spoke, one of the divers, the one they referred to as "Agent One," was preparing an attempt to do just that.

Jack, Henry, and the SEALs all knew that to leave the mini-sub under these circumstances would most likely prove fatal for that diver. But not to disconnect the tether straightaway would certainly result in death for all the passengers onboard. Jack and the SEALs all knew that it had to be done—and quickly.

Agent One entered the door to the floodable chamber and began filling it. The only tools he took with him were a small ball-peen hammer, a pair of adjustable pliers, and, of course, his diving gear. He had the tools strapped to his side to free up his hands. The moment the gauge indicated that the pressure in the chamber equaled that outside the sub, Agent One popped the hatch and stuck his head out of the opening. He was immediately taken aback by the speed at which they were descending.

Damn, I hate this, he muttered in his mind. *Never trained for this shit. I have no real idea of what I'm up against here. What tools I might need. None of that.*

He was wearing a camera strapped to his head, so everyone onboard could monitor his progress. It was obvious to those watching that he was not comfortable with his task.

After closing the hatch behind him, he carefully as possible made his way toward the point where the tether cable was attached to sub. *Maybe I'll be able to disconnect it easily,* he was thinking. He knew that he should have checked it out better before setting out, but he did not wish to take the extra time. *I know that I'm dealing with a steel cable and not a rope, but I have no idea as to how I might detach it while taut. … I suppose I'll find that out in short order.*

He did not want to get careless. Were he to lose his grip on the tiny rail that ran almost the entire length of the mini-sub, the force of the swirling water that was generated by the two vessels rushing toward the bottom of the Yellow Sea would sweep him away to his certain death.

Must hang on tightly, he repeated with intensity in his mind.

As he neared the connection point it became clear what he was dealing with. Just as he recalled from when he originally hooked the cable to the mini-sub, it was secured to the mini-sub's hull with a heavy-duty anchor shackle. What he did not remember was that it was so huge, or how the anchor shackle was secured to the cable. As he neared it he saw that it was 1-1/2 inch galvanized steel unit, and that it was secured to the sub by a two-foot length of cable that was added for this mission to facilitate connecting to the cable that would be dropped from the fishing boats.

The only way to disconnect the union was to unscrew the bolt screw-pin shackle at the end of the tether. That was pretty much what he had expected. Except, it was substantially larger than he remembered. *What the hell is this all about?* he asked himself. *That's the size of something you'd use on a locomotive—not a tiny little mini-sub. Way over the top. Pliers are a good idea here. Just might work.*

Damn, I'm really beginning to feel the pressure. He continued to complain to himself after experiencing more difficulty. *Wonder what my depth is.*

He glanced down at his gauge. *Forty meters,* he said to himself. *One hundred and thirty feet. I got to get this thing done. And fast!*

His training told him that it is never good for a diver to pass forty meters in a dive without a pressurized suit. He had done it before, and survived. So he knew he could deal with that pressure for a short time, and then depressurize appropriately. So, he zeroed in on the job at hand and went to work.

He latched the pliers onto the threaded screw-pin and began turning it to the left—once, twice, three times. *Damn,* he said to himself again. *This is slow as shit. Gotta hurry.*

After the tenth quarter turn, the pin slipped out of the threaded arm of the shackle, but not far enough to release the five-eighths-inch cable. The drag force of the struggling mini-sub was putting too much pressure on the pin and would not allow him to slip it out of the loop of the cable.

Agent One aggressively adjusted his grip on the pin, but could not pull it free. He could still turn it to the left, but the pressure being exerted on it by the sinking fishing boat would not allow him to pull the pin the rest of the way out.

Like everyone else on the little sub, Jack's eyes were glued to the agent's every move. Suddenly he snapped off his seatbelt and shouted at the pilots.

"Turn this thing toward the fishing boat!" he bellowed. "And then hit the gas—full speed! Do it now! I don't give a damn how deep we go. We've got to take the pressure off that cable or he won't be able to free it up. Do it now! And don't piss around! Hit the damn throttle, and crank it around!"

Agent Two quickly realized what was happening too, and so he barked at the cockpit, "Steer this thing in the same direction as the fishing boat, and go full speed. Got to take the tension off this cable. Or rope—whatever the hell it is."

It took less than a minute for the cable to grow a little slackened. Via the agent's headcam, everyone could see that the cable was beginning to sag—albeit only a little. The agent continued to hold tightly on to the cable so he would not be swept away by the rushing water. He had reattached his pliers onto the threaded pin and was about to give it one last yank when the unforeseen again occurred.

With the agent's full attention focused on the point at which pliers met the pin, the full-throttled mini-sub slid upwards a little, and then over to the nearby bottom of the sinking fishing boat. Unfortunately, as it did, the agent's unprotected skull smashed into the other vessel's hull, stunning him enough that it not only damaged his headcam, but caused him to release his grasp on the cable. As soon as he let go of it he helplessly lost his balance.

Jack and the others in the mini-sub were aware that they lost the video feed from Agent One's headcam, but they did not see how it happened—they had no idea that the fishing boat had smashed so ferociously into his head.

"Shit!" Jack barked as he broke full-speed toward the wet room. "We've lost the feed. Pump that sonofabitch out so I can go help him get that cable off. Time is critical here. Hurry up and do it! And keep your foot on the gas!"

The pilots did as he ordered. They maintained the speed at full, and continued to steer the mini-sub toward the bottom.

Jack looked around until he found a good-sized hammer. "This is what that sonofabitch needs," he said. "Something to talk tough to that connector."

He strapped the hammer securely to his belt, and then pulled on it to be sure it would not fall out.

"Boss," Henry shouted, as Jack headed toward the wet room. "Let me go," he said. "I see what the problem is. I think I can do it."

"Sit your ass back down," Jack commanded. "This is my mission. I'm in charge. Now, do what I said and buckle your ass back up and keep your eyes open. If I fail to free this mess up, it'll be someone else's turn. But not until then. I'm the one going out this time. You got that?"

"I got it," Henry said.

"Now," Jack said as he was checking to see if all the water had been pumped out of the egress chamber. "When the pressure's back up, I'm gonna open the hatch and go out. I will secure the hatch behind me. I know it's getting pretty deep out there—way beyond standard operational depths. I don't have a camera on, so give me thirty minutes, if you don't hear from me, drain the water out, have another diver suit up, and come out into the wet room. And then refill and pressurize it. If I'm still not pounding on the hatch, open it up and take a look. I will have a rope tied to my ankle. Signal me by sending three short tugs on it. I'll respond with a single tug. If I fail to answer after a couple tries, I'm dead. Pull the rope back and unhook the rope, and you go out. Got that? I do not want you actually leaving the sub unless I'm dead. Whatever you have to do, you should be able to do it from the hatch ladder. Do you understand now what I'm expecting from you?"

"We hear you, Jack," Henry said.

"Pay attention to what you do here," Jack said, addressing Henry and Agent Two as he finished suiting up. "Our survival might, hell, not might, it will hang on how we handle the next thirty minutes. Got that?"

"We'll not let you down," Henry said. "You know you can count on me."

"Yes, I do," Jack said as he prepared to close the wet room door behind him. "I know very well how you and the SEALs always come through under pressure."

Jack made it a point to alternate eye contact with his friend and with Agent Two as he carefully articulated those final words.

Ten seconds after he had secured the door, Henry could hear the room filling with water. And, once the pressure had equalized, he heard the hatch open, and then close. He looked at his watch.

Henry stood straight and cast his glare back on the screen in search for Agent One. Still no luck. So, out of impatience and frustration, he took a long look at the gauges on his rebreather. *I have no idea how all this shit works,* he lamented in his disjointed and racing mind. *I just know if it's not working, or if you use it wrong, it'll kill you, and you won't even feel it happening. It's just shit, bang, sweet dreams—you're dead.*

God, I cannot even imagine what would happen if Jack gets

killed. Or, what if I die here today. Actually, that wouldn't be so bad. Would be better to lose me than him. Hell, I can't begin to imagine what life would be without him. Who would break it to those boys? Jack's their hero. Somehow, someday, I knew this moment would come—sooner or later. It just had to. It's been close before. It's just that this time I'm having time to think about it. And Jack has always known it as well. He knew that eventually it would all catch up to him.

If he were the one standing here where I am, right now, and I was the one out there, maybe getting ready to die—or maybe dead already—he'd be thinking the same things about me. I just wish to hell that Agent One would get that damn cable off and drag his sorry ass back to the sub. And bring Jack with him. What the hell could be so difficult about it? Damn him!

With those spurious thoughts racing through his mind, Henry took another meaningless study of all the gauges on his closed loop rebreather. That's what they were all using on this mission, but Henry did not understand much about it. He had heard that the closed loop system held several advantages over the old single tank open loop hardware. For one, the newer equipment did not produce bubbles. That fact alone provided a very significant plus to a military covert diver, as it made his presence virtually impossible to spot from the surface without the use of some sort of electronic detection device.

Other advantages included the length of a dive possible with the new equipment, and the depth permitted. The rebreather would allow a diver to remain underwater for many hours, and at depths of several hundred feet. Another big difference between a rebreather and the older open loop diving hardware was that the new method shortened and simplified the process of decompressing at the end of a dive.

As Henry understood it, the rebreather "scrubbed" the carbon dioxide that was exhaled by running it through a filter composite that looked a lot like cat litter. With the CO_2 removed, and a little oxygen added, along with some additives that he didn't fully understand or appreciate, what was exhaled could be cleansed and rebreathed—with no bubbles escaping.

Henry did not pretend to have a handle on the new equipment he might be called upon to use, but he was confident that if the diver kept his oxygen on, and didn't start to feel lightheaded, he was most likely using the apparatus in an acceptable fashion. And, if that happened not to be the case, he would not survive the episode. And, most likely, he would not even sense that he was in the process of dying.

For just a few seconds he considered that, if he had to go out, he might just turn his oxygen off, that is, if his best friend was killed on this day. He saw no future in moving forward. He'd read an online article about a Navy officer who accidentally did not turn his oxygen on before he went in. He didn't recognize the fact that he was not getting oxygen, and it killed him. The Navy officer did not know that the human mechanism that creates the desire to breathe is the buildup of CO_2 in the body. The reason he never sensed the need to breathe was that the scrubber was working just fine in its task of removing the CO_2. He just did not realize that he was not getting oxygen. A tragically fatal oversight.

Momentarily, Henry considered that as an acceptable way out. But, then he had a vision of the two boys, and he knew that he must do his best to survive the mission so that he would be able to help raise those two fourteen-year-old young men. He had to stick around, if only for them.

Henry watched Jack make his way toward the tether cable connection point via video captured by a permanently-affixed camera on the small deck of the mini-sub. But, unlike with Agent One, Jack had no headcam—not even to start out with. So, just as was the case earlier with the SEAL diver, as Jack approached the tether's point of attachment, his image fell out of range of the mounted camera, and his activity disappeared from the monitor.

Henry took another look at his watch, and then abruptly addressed Agent Two.

"I'm getting impatient here," Henry said. "Jack's been outta range for too long. I'm gonna need to put on this diving gear. Can you help me get it set up? And in a hurry?!"

"Yes, I could," Agent Two said. "But you know what Jack said as well as I do. He told the both of us that if anything happened to him, while he was out there, give it half an hour, then cut him loose. By that time he'd figured we be at the bottom, so it'd take all the tension off the tether. So, we should be able to simply unhitch the cable—if we're still alive. And then, if at all possible, get the hell out of the area as fast as we can. You heard him too. And he also demanded that if for any reason, someone had to go back out, that it would be a diver. The only divers on this boat are us SEALs, not you. He was very adamant about that. He gave you strict orders not to leave this sub. And he was, he is, the boss. If it requires going out, I think it's very clear that it's my job to handle that from here on. Not yours."

Agent Two had also watched Jack disappear, but from a different screen.

"Listen to me!" Henry growled. "Jack said that I should be the one to pull him back in, if something goes wrong. So, just shut the hell up and help me get ready."

Of course, Agent Two knew that Henry was not trained for such an exercise, but at this point, all logic had escaped the mission's lexicon. So, he prepped him to go out.

As soon as the wet room was pumped out, Henry opened the door and stepped into it.

"Fill it for me and bring it up to pressure," Henry said. "And let me know when I can open the hatch. Okay?"

Agent Two had double-checked all of Henry's equipment, particularly making sure the oxygen was functioning properly on the rebreather. As soon as Henry had stepped through and sealed the door he began filling the lock-out chamber.

It seemed to Henry only a long minute before the little room was nearing full. He took a look at his watch, but it had broken under the pressurized water.

It's got to have been twenty-five minutes since Jack went out, he muttered silently in his mind.

"Am I good to go yet?" he entered on the monitor.

"Pressure's up," Agent Two said. "Check the hatch. Should open just fine. If not, keep at it. It soon will."

Henry adjusted his mask and opened the hatch. He looked around and found where Jack had tied the rope off.

Sticking his body through the opening up to his midsection, Henry tugged firmly on the rope three times. Since Henry and Jack had beforehand firmly established the three-tug protocol with one another, Henry assumed that Jack would have been immediately responsive to that signal were he able to sense it. Jack did not answer.

He tried it again, but with the same result.

Henry then stepped down to the rung below so he could better brace himself—besides, the extra dozen inches did not substantially improve his field of vision. And he began pulling back on the rope. At first it seemed solidly tied off. But then it appeared to free up a bit. It felt to him like he was lugging a sack of soaked flour through the water. But he kept pulling, and the rope continued to coil in his powerful hands.

Looks like picking up speed worked! Henry determined as he observed the SDV slowing. *Maybe we all ain't gonna die today after all!*

With his hopes slightly escalating, Henry ceased reeling the rope in and once more tried the three-tug signal. But disappointment quickly crept back in when again the signal was not returned. He repositioned his feet so he could continue reeling in the rope, but this time he found that the drag on it had lessened considerably. *Why would that be?* he wondered. *Could it be that the fishing boat has reached the bottom?*

But still he was receiving no positive support for any optimism.

In less than a minute, however, the unimaginable happened. As Henry reeled in the rope, he spotted the faint outline of what appeared to be a body at the end of it. He was in shock, but he kept pulling. After he had managed to retrieve another three or four feet he saw something beginning to appear over the side of the mini-sub. Carefully he maintained the tension on the rope as he slowly stepped up the ladder again—this time to the topmost rung. And, as he rebalanced himself, he focused his eyes on what was beginning to emerge at the end of the rope.

Initially all he could see was a human foot, with the rope tied around the ankle.

Oh my God! he silently exclaimed. *Jack! What has happened to you?*

Most of the corpse was hidden from full view because it was getting hung up on the small railing on the deck of the mini-sub. Henry would periodically lessen the tension, and then try reeling in again. But he wasn't having much success. At best he was now barely inching the lifeless body along, and then it suddenly slid along the railing and disappeared entirely. Fortunately, Henry had maintained his grip on the rope. And so, while it did slide out of sight, he was able to stop its fall quite easily.

Still, it remained out of his field of vision.

When he began winding the rope in again, he was able to retrieve the body only until it again reached the railing. There it became severely hung up once more. This time he couldn't budge it.

Henry was almost ready to violate Jack's orders and venture outside the mini-sub further in order to achieve a better angle from which to pull, but he was stopped in his tracks when the most unexpected of events took place. It caught him by such surprise that he could barely believe what his eyes were telling him.

There, right where Jack's body was snagged, a diver appeared.

Holy shit! Henry fretted in silence. *Agent One is alive and well!*

Henry struggled heartily to get a grip on the whole situation, while Agent One freed up Jack's body so that he could reel him into the tiny chamber.

Once Jack had slid over the little railing, Henry made short work of pulling him on up and through the hatch. As gently as he could Henry eased the body to the floor of the chamber.

With Jack's corpse safely inside the sub, Henry climbed back up the ladder to check on Agent One.

He's looking very labored, Henry reckoned. *I'd better get outta the way so he can get inside.*

The wet room was designed to accommodate one person comfortably. Two could squeeze into it. But three—that was definitely a crowd, especially when one of them was lying dead on the floor.

Henry struggled to find some free space to place his feet as the diver arrived.

At first Agent One stuck his head through the hatch to see if there was room. Seeing that Henry had organized the small wet room well enough for him to fit, as long as he remained on the ladder, he turned himself around so that he could slide his feet through the opening. Before he entered the mini-sub, he slipped off his fins and slowly lowered himself by climbing down the ladder using his hands only. When he neared the bottom, he reached up and fastened the roof hatch.

He remained with his feet on the bottom rung, and then signaled the pilot that he should initiate the gradual depressurization of the wet room. And so the process began. At the same time, the pilot began to slowly level out the mini-sub, checking all systems in order to ascertain the extent of any damages that might have occurred during the past forty minutes. If they were able to determine that the vessel was somewhat seaworthy, they would then begin to consider escape options.

Henry assumed that the diver would know how long it should take to depressurize the wet room to a safe level. He had been told in training that they should always depressurize at a relatively slow rate, even though they were using closed loop rebreathers.

They were also told that the mini-sub should not dive to depths greater than 190 feet. Henry was not certain just how far down the sinking fishing boat might have dragged them. So, he just backed off and allowed the diver to take charge. Besides, Henry's heart was heavy beyond measure at the loss of his friend and mentor.

But, it was just as Henry was reaching his conclusion for the short term that the most startling event he could have imagined occurred.

Chapter 27 —

It was a real surprise for both of the boys, but Red was the first to see that Kate was riding in the front passenger seat of the deputy's patrol car as it drove up. The boys had just stepped out from the house to give Buddy a chance to stretch his legs. The patrol car had driven up to within one hundred feet from where they were standing. Red slugged Robby on the upper arm with the back of his right fist, and immediately bolted toward her. Initially, Robby objected to the severity of his friend's seeming aggression, but when he spotted Kate's open-armed greeting, he also took off at full speed.

Buddy, as always, was leading the way.

At the same time, Det. Townsend was knocking on the camper door. "Hey, boys," he nearly shouted, "your Aunt Kate is on her way here."

He had walked over from the Tahoe in order to inform them about Kate's improvement, and her desire to leave the hospital and join them on the island. Of course, the boys had earlier left the camper and sneaked over to the house to do a little research.

The words "your Aunt Kate is doing much better, and she is on her way out" had just escaped Det. Townsend's lips when his eye caught a glimpse of the boys and Buddy bolting toward the deputy's arriving patrol car.

Kate had dropped to her knees to exchange kisses with the

four-legged hero who not only had handily won the race, but had earlier saved her life. And she was still hugging the tail-wagging marvel when Red reached her. He grabbed his favorite woman in the world around the neck and planted a big kiss on the top of her head.

Robby's arrival knocked all three of them to the ground, with Buddy heartily licking them all on their faces.

Tears flowing down her cheeks, Kate rose to her knees enough to throw her arms around both of the boys. The three human members of the Handler clan, remaining on the gravel in front of the patrol car, had at first fought their natural inclination to express emotion. Buddy, however, was right there to happily remove all outward evidence of emotional tranquility. That's when they finally yielded to it and opened the floodgates.

Dep. Fisher, a little embarrassed, looked up at Det. Townsend and began walking toward him.

"Am I ever glad to see you," Det. Townsend said to the deputy. "Actually, I'm most elated about the package you just delivered. My God, am I ever thankful that you were able to bring Jack's daughter out here to watch over those boys."

"Otherwise we'd of had to take them in to child services," Dep. Fisher said. "Would have been a lot of extra paperwork. Right?"

"That's not the half of it," Det. Townsend said. "Not even the half of it. I know enough about these boys. They would have bolted the second they suspected that was what we had in mind. We'd have had to go out looking for them. And then, we'd have had to deal with Jack when he got here. He'd have kicked all our asses by the time this was over. *Literally!* Thanks to you, we just lucked out in a big way. That's all there is to it. You did a good job!"

"How's the investigation goin'?" the deputy asked. "Anything new?"

"I've got forensics on their way to go back over the Tahoe, among other things," Det. Townsend replied. "Prints, primarily. Not optimistic, though. Seems unlikely that they would have worked without gloves. But we will see. And then, that's a rental. It's going to have all sorts of prints on every inch of it. But we have to go through the motions nonetheless. Never know what they might find.

"I just sent Conners over to check out the house. We saw no evidence of intrusion. At least not at first glance. But I really won't know anything definitive until I've talked to him. I suppose it's time to break up that love-fest. Need to ask the lady some questions. See what she can recall."

"What do you want me to do?" Dep. Fisher asked.

"Come with me. You can keep an eye on the boys. I might want you to help us out with them. It might give me an opportunity to question her a little better. Find out what she saw, or can recall."

"Yes, sir," the deputy said.

By the time Townsend and Fisher reached the group, Kate and the boys were on their feet, and all were a little embarrassed at what had just transpired.

"Great to see you doing so well," Det. Townsend said. "Have to say we had some concerns from the last time we saw you. Never know how things like that are going to turn out. Glad to see you've recovered so quickly. How are you feeling now? Some repercussions, I suppose. Think you'd be able to go over some stuff with us? Your boys were just great, but if you're up to it, I'd like to ask you a few questions while it's fresh on your mind. What do you think?

Could you handle it yet?"

"I'm fine," she said. "And I'm absolutely good for it. Nothing more important to me right now than getting to the bottom of this. But, I'm not so sure anything is 'fresh on my mind.' I'd be happy to give it a go. Have you been able to find anything out at this end? But, first things first—I'd like to get my gear back. The deputy said you had it secured on site."

"I've got it for you right here," Det. Townsend said, handing her the evidence bag containing her Glock and other personal belongings as they walked. "I do want to go over it all with you. But, right now, we're checking out something that your boys found. I've got it here. I'd like to have you take a look at it, and see what you think."

Kate loved being in the middle of an investigation. She'd grabbed a black coffee from the hospital lobby before she left. She held it up with a smile for Det. Townsend's benefit, and said, "As you can see, I'm all set with my coffee. Shall we go in the house to talk?"

"I've not checked the house out, yet," Det. Townsend said. "It's still closed and locked. Appears not to have been violated. Maybe we can take a sit-down over here at the picnic table and I can get your thoughts on a coin the boys found. It appears to be some sort of Chinese coin, we think."

"Yeah, Aunt Kate," Robby said. "Red thinks it's a Chinese coin too. Actually, we're pretty sure it's a Chinese coin—we looked it up. But, we've really got no idea about what it might mean, or what it was doing by your car. Red remembered seeing one like it on Henry's computer back in the camper. Earlier, though. Not today. And we also checked out some books on coins. We think—"

"Boys," Det. Townsend interrupted. "Please let Kate take a look before we start talking about what we think it is, or might be."

"Sure," Kate said. "I'd like to take a look at what you found out about it. But, I think that Det. Townsend still has the real thing right here. Right, Detective?"

Det. Townsend nodded and unzipped a leather satchel that he used for case documents, and to transport some of the evidence. He removed a sealed plastic evidence collection bag, and handed it to her.

"What do you think about this?" he asked.

She looked at it from both sides, and said, "This is very interesting. Where did you find it, exactly?"

"About fifteen feet from your Tahoe—driver's side," Det. Townsend said. "Does it mean anything at all to you?"

She examined it again through the plastic.

"Did you fellows touch it at all?" she asked the boys. "I mean, at all. Did your fingers even come in contact with it?"

"No," Robby said. "We know what you always told us. 'Never touch evidence,' you say. We saw it on the ground, and we immediately told the detective about it. We did not touch it."

She then looked Det. Townsend in the eye, and said, "I know you understand how to handle evidence—you're obviously protecting it properly. But, are you also convinced that no one has done anything to corrupt this coin? I'm sure you exercised proper precautions and procedures. Right?"

Det. Townsend did not appreciate being cross-examined in the field by someone totally outside the jurisdiction. However, he responded in a dignified and respectful fashion: "We exercised all proper precautions. But, I'm wondering what prompts your comments. Is there something about this coin that sparks your curiosity? I know, you've got my attention. Do you care to share with me what you're thinking, or might suspect?"

"Absolutely," Kate replied. "But, if you don't need the boys for a bit, is it okay if I have them run over to the camper? Are you finished with them for now?"

"That would be fine," the detective said. "Just don't send them out fishing or anything, at least not right away."

"Great," Kate said. "Guys, wait for me in the trailer—or the camper. I'll look you up when I'm finished here. Okay?"

"No problem," Robby said, as he gave her one more hug. "Buddy. Come on, let's go get you some water."

"Should I go with them?" Dep. Fisher asked. "Or should I stay here?"

"They should be fine," Det. Townsend replied. "Why don't you check with Conners and see if he could use a hand. He's going to be checking out the house."

"Right," Dep. Fisher replied, as he turned and headed toward the house.

With that, the two boys and Buddy broke into a full-blown race toward the camper—which, of course, Buddy easily won.

"Okay, Lieutenant Handler, share with this veteran cop what this mystery is all about," Det. Townsend said. "Please."

"Sure," she said. "I'd be happy to. But, is it okay with you if we step into the house first? My knees are still feeling just a little shaky, and I could use a softer chair."

"I can certainly appreciate that," Det. Townsend said. "Let's go. I'm more than a little surprised that they'd release you so soon after an experience like that. They didn't think you should take a little more time to recuperate?"

She immediately turned and began walking toward the main house door.

"No," she said. "I explained how well I was feeling and they had no problem letting me check out."

Dep. Fisher, who was walking a half a step behind her, overheard what she had said. He looked back and over at Det. Townsend with a bit of a grimaced grin, and rolled his eyes.

"Any evidence that the house might have been broken into?" she asked. "Anything at all to suggest that?"

"We did a perimeter," Det. Townsend said, "We saw nothing to suggest a B&E, but we have not entered the house yet. So, if you would unlock the door, and allow the deputy and me to look around a little, that would be nice. Det. Conners is around here somewhere as well—he's probably doing a thorough perimeter."

"Sure," she said. "Would you like me to turn the alarm off? I had armed it last night before I set up in the Tahoe."

"Right," the detective agreed. "You go in and disarm it, and then we'll enter."

Kate unlocked and opened the door, and then waited to hear the entrance tone. But none went off.

"That's not right," she said as she stepped in and looked around. "I clearly recall having set it last evening. I should have heard the entrance tone. I need to take a look at the keypad—see what it has to tell me."

The alarm control keypad was located just inside a coat closet across the hall from the entry door. The second her eyes fell on the open closet door, she growled in anguish, "I don't believe this! I know I closed that door after I armed it up." She took the three short steps over to it, and complained even more vociferously when she saw that the alarm system had been turned off.

"Damn it all!" she barked. "Someone's turned it off! I've got to call the alarm company to see who's been in here!"

"I think I recall the boys saying that they were just in here as well—they were checking on some of Jack's books, regarding the coin. They must have turned it off. Deputy, would you run over to the camper and check with the boys? Find out if they turned it off."

"Will do," Dep. Fisher responded. "I'll check with them, and come right back to let you know."

He immediately turned and left the house.

Kate took a look down the hall behind her and had a thought.

"I'd like to do a brief prelim on this level," she said. "Have you checked it out yet?"

"No," Det. Townsend replied. "Go look around and see what you can find."

She had proceeded only about fifteen feet when she heard the muffled sound of a police radio. But she could not make out the gist of the conversation. So, she turned back and again approached Det. Townsend.

"Was that your deputy?" she asked.

"Yes, Deputy Fisher did talk to the boys about it."

"Great," she said. "They could have been in the house looking at Dad's books. Were they? And had they shut the alarm down?"

The boys told Dep. Fisher that they had entered the house and looked in some books about coins. "Yes and no," Det. Townsend said. "They say they were in the house earlier, but they found the alarm already off when they entered."

"Really," Kate responded. "Then I really do need to call the alarm company and find out what's going on here.

"Dad still has a hardwired phone in here. And, do you mind. I have no intention of giving out his security password. Just a little privacy, please. I need to get to the bottom of this right now. I'll fill you in on what I discover. Okay?"

"Sure," Det. Townsend said. "You do what you have to do, but I do want to know how it got disarmed. So, go for it."

By that time Det. Conners had rejoined Dep. Fisher just outside the door. Det. Townsend stepped out with them to provide Kate a little privacy.

She dialed the number and waited. On the second ring a voice answered, "This is United Protection Services Central Station. My name is Todd Russer. How may I help you?"

"My name is Kate Handler," she said, "account number 513542. I just entered my father's house on Sugar Island. And I found that someone had disarmed the alarm. I am positive that I armed it up just after ten last evening. So, somehow the alarm was disarmed, by someone, between ten and now. Would you tell me when it was disarmed, and by whom, please?"

"Sure, just give me a moment. And, did you tell me your name was Kate Handler?"

"That's right. K-A-T-E H-A-N-D-L-E-R. I am Jack Handler's daughter. I should be listed as one of his authorized users for that account. I know I'm on the account, because I've called in on it before."

"Yes," he said. "I've got you here."

"Good, then please let me know what happened with the system between ten last night, and just now. I walked in a few minutes ago, and the system was disarmed. I'd like to know who turned it off, and when."

The dispatcher realized that he might very well be dealing with a serious problem. So, rather than trying to help Kate, he told her, "I'm going to get my supervisor and have her help you. She'll be right with you, just stay on the phone."

Kate knew what was going on, and so she tried to interrupt, but he had already placed her on hold.

Twenty seconds later a new voice addressed her: "Hello, Ms. Handler, this is Jessica Spencer, Dispatch Supervisor. Mr. Russer indicates that you have some questions with regard to your alarm system during the past twenty-four hours. Maybe I can be of assistance."

She's trying to cover her ass, Kate thought to herself. Something not so good is up.

Kate took a deep breath to compose herself, and then said, "I armed the system up between ten and eleven last evening. I just now walked through the door, and the system was disarmed. I'm wondering who turned it off, and at what time. Can you help me figure that out?"

"Yes, be happy too," the supervisor said. "At 2232 last evening—that would be ten thirty-two P.M.—the system was armed using Kate Handler's code. And then, at 2350, we show that one Jack Handler called in with the proper name and password, and requested that the alarm be disarmed from our central station. He said that his keypad was not working properly, and that he needed help from this end. And, he then requested service when he got back from his trip. We have service scheduled for tomorrow. Before 1700 hours tomorrow, in fact."

"So," Kate said slowly. "My father came in at around eleven-fifty last night, and he had you disarm it for him. Is that right?"

"Yes, Ms. Handler, that's what happened. If he's there, just please check with him."

"Okay," Kate said, "If I'm understanding you correctly, at eleven-fifty last night, you did a disarm of this system. But, you do not show any alarms having been tripped. Is that correct?"

"That's correct."

"You do show that it was armed at or before eleven P.M. last evening," Kate said. "Is that right?"

"We show that the system was armed at 2230. Which would be ten-thirty. And Jack Handler requested that we turn the system off for him at around eleven-fifty. That's it. Does all that make sense to you?"

"Well, the part about it being armed at ten-thirty," Kate said, "That works. That was me arming it up. That's correct. But, the part about my father requesting that it be disarmed at eleven-fifty last night—that part is impossible. My father was not here at that time. And the part about his requesting service on the system, you can cancel that service call. There's nothing wrong with the system."

"Then," the supervisor said, "You do not wish to have our technician come out. Is that correct?"

"That would be correct," Kate replied. "No one on our end requested service. So, please do cancel it."

"Okay," the supervisor said, "I will call the service department right now. Is there anything else I can help you with?"

"There is one thing," Kate said. "I assume that all conversations to your central station are recorded. Is that not true?"

"Yes, all calls are recorded."

"I would like to hear the one from last night," Kate said. "The one from my father. May I hear that one?"

"We can produce it only upon a court order, or at the request of law enforcement," the supervisor said.

"I am a lieutenant in homicide," Kate replied.

"Is that Chippewa County?" she asked. "Are you with the Chippewa County Sheriff's Office?"

"New York City. But, I have one of my associates here right beside me. He is a sheriff's detective right here in Michigan, Sault Ste. Marie—Chippewa County. Hang on, I'll put him on while you bring it up."

"Okay," the supervisor said haltingly. "I'll get it ready, and you get him."

Kate walked over to the door and asked Det. Townsend to come in and listen to the recording. "They said my dad called them at eleven-fifty and asked them to turn the system off, and they're going to play the recording for us, but they insist that there be a local law enforcement officer requesting it. I'd like you to hear it."

"They don't need a law enforcement officer. They frequently provide recordings to end users. Let me talk to them."

"Hello!" Det. Townsend said in a disgusted tone. "Anybody there? Hello."

"Yes, may I help you?" the supervisor said.

"I certainly hope so," he said. "My name is Det. Greggory Townsend. My colleague here, Lieutenant Kate Handler, would like to hear the recording from last evening. Will you please play it for us? We're having an issue here at the Jack Handler residence— Jack's her father. That tape just might answer some of our questions, and concerns. Please run it by us ASAP."

"Absolutely," the dispatcher said. "Stand by. Okay, here it is."

Another few seconds passed, and then the recording:

"This is United Protection Services Central Station. My name is Tom Payne. How may I help you?"

"My name is Jack Handler," the voice said, "account number 513542. I was just about to enter my house here on Sugar Island. But, before I did, I looked in the window, and I see that my dog has ripped my keypad off the wall and destroyed it. I'm not going to be able to turn my alarm off. But I must go in. Could you get online with it, and turn the system off for me? You've done this for me before. So, I know you can do it."

"I'll have to get my supervisor, anyway," the dispatcher said. "Just please hold on." The dispatcher did not put the call on hold, so Kate and Det. Townsend could both overhear his conversation with his supervisor.

"Jan," Tom could be heard saying, "I have one of our subscribers on the line—a man named Jack Handler. He says his dog ruined his keypad and he wants us to disarm it from here. Should I do it?"

"I know Mr. Handler," the supervisor said. "He can be one miserable SOB. Did he have the correct password?"

"Yes."

"Then don't screw around with him. If he had the password, just disarm the damn system, and say thank you. Get rid of him as quickly as you can. Okay?"

A few seconds later the dispatcher, Tom Payne, came back to the caller.

"Mr. Handler. Are you still there?"

"Yes," the caller said. "You gonna take care of this for me?"

"It's done, sir," Tom Payne said. "I've disarmed the system for you. Shall I write you up for service? To fix that keypad?"

"Yes," the caller responded, after having taken a moment to consider what that might entail. "Write it up. Not tonight or tomorrow, however. I'm leaving again. Maybe come out in a couple days."

"How about the day after tomorrow?"

"That works. In the afternoon before five."

"Do you want a call before we head out?"

"No need. Thanks."

A few seconds later, the supervisor came back online with Kate and Det. Townsend, and said, "That's the call you requested. As you can see, Mr. Handler provided all the correct information to warrant having some help to get in his house."

"Yes," Det. Townsend said, "Mr. Handler's daughter is standing right beside me here. But, and we both agree on this, the voice of the man who identified himself as Jack Handler, was definitely not Jack Handler. Now, please send us a copy of that call as soon as you can. Send it to my attention, Detective Greggory Townsend, care of the Chippewa County Sheriff's Department, here in Sault Ste. Marie, Michigan. Got all that?"

The supervisor took a moment to weigh what she had just been ordered to do, and then she said, "I would like to do what you're requesting, but, I am sorry, that request will require a court order. We can't just send out recorded conversations without a request by a judge, not even to the Sheriff's Department."

Kate then began shaking her head and hand, indicating that the detective should not pursue it further. So he thanked the supervisor for her help and disconnected from the call.

"We've got a recording," Kate told him after he had hung up. "Everything that comes in on this land line is automatically recorded. Might be slightly illegal, but it will save us a little time in this case. Do you have a problem using it? At least for a preliminary analysis? We should probably initiate a formal request, in case we go to court. But for now, this will do just fine. Do you agree?"

Det. Townsend did not need to think that one over. He was happy to do anything that he thought might make Kate's dad the least antagonistic. He was totally aware that when Jack found out what had happened the previous night, he was not going to be very understanding of the whole matter. And, the last thing the detective wanted to do was to give Jack the idea that he, Det. Townsend, did anything that might have made the situation worse, or was in any way contrary to what his daughter wanted.

"Yeah," he said. "Make us a copy as well. I'll submit it to forensics and see what they come up with. Okay. I'd say we need to see what they were after here. We did a thorough perimeter, and it appeared as though everything was in place and undisturbed. We found no obvious signs of forced entry—not through windows or doors. Not on the main level at least."

"It looks like they prepared well," Kate said. "Even when it came to dealing with me."

As she finished her thought, Kate's eyes shot over to a blank space on the hall wall and fixed on nothing.

"Hold on, Detective," she said. "What sort of hose did they use in their attempt to gas me? I assume you collected it for evidence—fingerprints, and such. What kind of hose was it?"

"A vacuum cleaner hose," Det. Townsend replied.

"Really?" Kate said. "That's unusual, to say the least. They would have had no reasonable clue that I'd be sitting in a Tahoe surveilling the house. That's a strange item to bring along on a job like this. Was it a newer one, or an old one?"

"Brand new," the detective said. "We thought it a bit strange as well. But it still had a warning taped on it. Something like that usually gets torn off and discarded right away."

"No kidding," Kate said, moving in closer to the detective. "Describe to me how they did it—logistically. How did they run the hose—attach it, and so forth? I've investigated several deaths involving the use of carbon monoxide, mostly suicides. Just tell me exactly how you found it."

"By the time officers were on the scene," Det. Townsend described, "your boys had already turned the engine off on the Tahoe, and had you stretched out on the ground. My officer said that the red-haired boy was monitoring your breathing, and that he was checking for a pulse. My officer took over as soon as he arrived, and he said that you appeared to be breathing on your own, just a little erratically. And that you had a weak pulse. But, you were not responsive. He said that the ambulance was on the same ferry as he, so the medical personnel took over almost immediately. They checked you and gave you oxygen. And then brought you into the hospital."

"I understand that part," Kate said. "But, describe how they set the hose up to gas me. Tell me about that one more time. In greater detail, if you can."

"You had cracked the rear windows. Right?" Det. Townsend asked. "About an inch or so. Do you recall that?"

"Sounds about right," she replied.

"Well," the detective went on, "He, they, they squeezed the hose a bit and forced it into the crack, rear passenger, and then used duct tape to hold it in the crack. They'd cut both ends off the hose, so it would squash into the crack. They also attached a strip of the tape over the opening in the window. But, they only did that on the passenger side. And then they taped the other end of the hose over the exhaust pipe. We figured that they didn't attempt to tape up the crack on the other three windows for fear that you might see them doing it."

"They might have gotten away with doing it," Kate quipped. "That was basically my third night without any real sleep. I suspect I might have drifted off a bit."

"Anyway, Detective," Kate said, "what are the chances that a professional criminal would have a vacuum cleaner hose with him on a job? What are the odds about that?"

The detective didn't have to think about it.

"I don't investigate many murders up here in Chippewa County," the detective said. "But I would say that it, a vacuum cleaner hose, would be about the last thing a professional killer would carry with him on a job."

"So," Kate went on, "that would strongly suggest that they were somehow able to come up with one out here. Either they stole one from Dad's house, or that they are staying out here—probably someplace nearby."

"That's what we figured," the detective said. "We intended to check the main house here to see if there's a vacuum missing a hose, or—"

"Dad's got a central vac system," she said. "He detests the canister vacuum cleaners. He has a couple battery-powered uprights in the house, but nothing with a hose except for the central system. And, the way you described it, the hose they used would not be from a central system—hoses on those systems are much too large. You can check, but I'm quite confident about that. Even in his shop, all he uses is a central vac system. And it's also one with a very large diameter hose, with a metal grid, or spring, running inside it to keep it from collapsing. That's not what you described. I'm sure that there are canister vacs in the units, just not at this house.

"I have an idea," Kate continued. "Why don't you fellows start looking around inside, while I visit the ladies' room. Sound like a plan?"

"Great idea," Det. Townsend said in a slightly uncomfortable tone. "Let me take a peek in the bath right here, and then it's all yours."

"Sure," Kate replied. "Go for it. I can wait that long."

"Whoa, Nellie," Detective Townsend blurted out so Kate and Conners could easily hear. Less than twenty seconds later he emerged from the restroom.

"Kate," he said. "What are the chances one of your boys would take a leak in the toilet, and not flush? Might they be guilty of that?"

"No chance!" Kate replied. "Dad does not tolerate that. The boys would never fail to flush. I take it you found something?"

"Yes. Somebody was in here recently and it looks like they emptied a very full bladder."

"I'm going to hit the other bathroom on this level," Kate said. "But, you can trust me. I'll make sure first that no one beat me to it."

Det. Townsend smiled, and then told Det. Conners, "Put the gloves on, and then set the tank lid on the seat so no one uses it. Take a sample for the lab, even though urine is beyond difficult to work with for usable DNA—still worth a shot. There could be other helpful hitchhikers riding around in it. I'm gonna do a quick once-through. Then let's get a full crew to go over the whole house."

Det. Townsend slipped on his booties and gloves, and headed to the upper level.

As soon as he heard the toilet flush below, he walked back to the top of the steps and beckoned Kate, who was already heading in that direction.

"Kate, here's some booties and gloves. I'd like you to slip them on and come up. I've got something I'd like you to take a look at."

"That sounds a bit ominous," she said as she caught the sealed packet the detective tossed down. "I'll be right up. Whatcha got?"

"Not sure," he said. "I'm gonna need you to take a look and tell me what you make of it."

Kate proceeded to sit down on the bottom step and donned the gear.

"Okay," she said. "What's happening up here? This is Dad's private office. He never leaves the door open. I take it that you found it that way. Right?"

"Wide open," he said. "But, there were no signs of forced entry. They must have had a key. I assume that your father keeps it locked?"

"All the time. Even when he's working in there. The boys do come in on occasion, but only when Dad's with them."

Kate stood at the door for nearly a full minute, and then she made a beeline for the closet.

"Let's take a look in here," she said as she opened the closet door. She took a single step into the walk-in, surveyed the little room, then stepped out and away from the door before she addressed the detective.

"Detective Townsend," she said. "I know this is not standard procedure, but would you please step into the hall and close the door behind you. I need to check out something in here, and it would be best for everyone if you didn't observe me while I do it. Would you please do that for me?"

Under any ordinary circumstances, the detective would have strongly objected to the request. But then, Det. Townsend pictured Jack Handler getting very angry at him for not honoring his daughter's request.

"Sure," he said. "You've got gloves on, and you're a professional. Can I count on you sharing with me whatever you find? No matter what? Even if you think it wouldn't be helpful to the case?"

"Yes I will," she said. "I just know that this is how my father would like to have this handled. And I want to be able to tell him how cooperative you were in dealing with this whole unfortunate incident."

With that, the detective stepped outside the office and Kate closed the door behind him. As she did, she thanked him again, and checked the door for any sign of its ever having been forced. She found nothing, and she did not lock it.

The detective, she reasoned, *will hear me locking him out and that will make him even more suspicious.*

But, instead of walking back into the closet, she proceeded to a large framed oil painting of the East Channel lighthouse on Grand

Island hanging behind her father's desk. She lifted and removed it from the wall, exposing a counter-sunk keypad. There was a small red LED on the top of it, and it was still on.

Must be they didn't know about this, she concluded. *Had they, they would not have rearmed it once finished.*

After having examined the keypad thoroughly, she disarmed it and rehung the picture over it.

She then returned to the closet and entered. At the rear of the walk-in was a small chest, some drawers of which remained slightly opened, indicating to her that they had been searched.

She then lifted up on the front of the chest and found, as she anticipated, that she could not budge it.

"That's good too," she said to herself.

Next, she returned to the light switch and turned it off. While this switch did turn the light off, it also controlled a powerful array of electro-magnets that held the chest of drawers in place—one magnet under each of the four legs, and two behind the piece of furniture.

The way it worked is like this: with the keypad disarmed, it was still required that the light switch be turned off in order to disable the magnets. Once she turned the light off, she was able to quite easily slide the chest out from the wall.

Once the chest was about a foot out into the closet, she peeked behind it. There was located a three-foot high, and two-foot wide, safe.

"Great!" she exclaimed out loud. "This safe does not appear to have been tampered with. I wonder what they were after? Whatever it was, it wasn't in Dad's office."

She then lifted and slid the chest back into position, turned the light switch on, went back out to rearm the keypad, and then to invite the detective back into the office.

"Thanks for humoring me on this one," she said to him. "It's just that I'm going to be the one explaining all this to Dad, and I want to get it right the first time. Dad does have a private area in this office, and it is not obvious to someone who does not know about it in advance. I am happy to tell you that it was not compromised. And, I can promise you that I will be even happier when I can assure Dad about that same thing. It looks to me like someone did rifle through the chest of drawers in the closet, but nothing of significance is ever kept in his desk up here, or in that chest. So, I'd say that we fared well in Dad's office. But, there is an area that is much more significant to Dad than this office."

"Really?" Det. Townsend questioned. "And where might that be? And what, exactly, are you talking about? What does your father keep in the house that is so important? Are we talking weapons? I know your father carries. Is there something else I need to know about?"

"He does have a few firearms in the house," Kate explained. "But there would be nothing—nothing exotic, at least—stored on this level. He might have a Glock in the desk, but that would be about it. I'm not sure what to look for, not entirely, so we can be certain that he will inventory this office when he gets back. Specialty items, they would be in his basement office. Plus, he stores some of his private papers there as well. We should probably take a look down in the pit—that's what I call it—to see if that area is what they targeted. My guess is, if they know anything at all about my Dad, and the layout of this house, that would have been the logical area to have targeted. Depending, of course, on what they were hoping to find."

Det. Townsend flashed Kate a smirky smile and said, "Well, your father had me do a sit-down with him in this office, but I've never been down in the 'pit,' as you call it. Should we have a look?"

Kate did not respond verbally. In fact, she did not even look at the detective. She just put on a slightly affected smile, turned, and began walking out of room. She was not comfortable taking anyone into her father's inner sanctum. Even though she felt that Det. Townsend was a bright, upstanding officer of the law, it still made her a bit nervous. She played in her mind the task of breaking the news to her father: "You did what!" Those would be the first words out of his mouth upon learning of it. "Did he force you? Or in any way try to intimidate you into allowing him down there to inspect? What all did you show him?"

While Kate was not frightened of her father, she understood that he felt strongly about protecting his privacy, both as it related to his person, but also with regard to the identity of those with whom he associated. Then, there was the unusual nature of his business.

Kate and the detective had barely reached the halfway point on the stairs when Kate stopped and turned to address him. "This is how we are going to have to do this," she explained, "or else my dad is going to raise holy hell with both of us."

She knew that Det. Townsend was uncommonly intimidated by Jack—she could sense that whenever the subject of her father came up—and she felt that by grouping herself into the lot of those who were frightened of her father, she could win over his cooperation in this matter.

"This is how we'll have to do this. When we reach the pit, I will open the door. It's a combination lock, with a separate alarm keypad inside the door. Most likely, that alarm system was also turned off by the alarm company. It operates under a totally different account number. But, I won't know if it's been disarmed until I open the door.

"Anyway, once I am inside the pit, we will be able to see if there has been substantial damage. Hopefully there will be none, but I won't know until I actually open the door. If the damage is minimal, I would like you to again wait outside that door while I spend a minute or two surveying the room. If I in any way deem that I need your help, or, I determine that the damage is significant, or presents any sort of hazard, I will immediately let you know. And you may then enter and gather evidence. Can we do it that way? Pretty much like we handled it upstairs. Will that work for you?"

It was clear by Det. Townsend's facial expression that he was not pleased by Kate's words, but he did seem to be reluctantly accepting of them.

"Okay," he agreed, "but this time we will leave the door open, and you will remain in sight the whole time. Right?"

"Exactly," she said. "Neither one of us has any idea as to what we're going to find down there. I just want to be able to paint the least objectionable picture to my dad when I explain it all to him. You understand, I'm sure."

"Any issues up there?" Det. Conners said as they passed him where he stood waiting on the main level.

"All's well in Jack's office," Det. Townsend assured him. "There was some evidence that the perps did go up there, but we found nothing damaged. No doors, or desks, forced. We're going to check out Jack's other office now. That one downstairs. Kate suspects that the break-in probably targeted the lower-level office. So, we will soon see about that."

"Shall I come down with you?" Det. Conners asked. "Or should I just hang in right here unless you give me a shout?"

"For now, wait up here. Maybe it'd be a good idea if you checked out the rest of the main level. See if you spot anything else up here that looks out of place. Okay?"

"Sure," Det. Conners said. "Sounds good to me."

Kate had continued walking while the two men talked. By the time Det. Townsend reached the top of the stairs, she was checking out the opened door to Jack's headquarters.

"Alarm turned off to that office?" Det. Townsend asked.

"Sure was," she answered. "From what I can see standing here, there does not appear to be anything damaged. At least nothing from what I can determine to this point. I'm going to walk around and inspect it more closely. You're going to wait at the open door as we agreed. Right?"

"Yup," he replied, clearly not pleased to be relegated to backup. "Shouldn't the alarm company have said something about that being turned off? When we talked to them earlier?"

"No," Kate replied. "This system is under a different account number, so we would have had to have asked about it specifically. I will follow up on that, but I'm pretty sure we're going to hear the same story. Or not. Perhaps they had the combo for this secondary system. It sort of looks that way. We'll see."

Kate slowly made her way through the office.

"It would be great," she said loudly enough for Det. Townsend to hear, "if I could tell my dad that there was no evidence of intrusion into the pit, and that there was nothing that required my permitting entry into his office by law enforcement. That just might placate some of his anxiety, when I have to tell him about it."

"Yeah, right," Det. Townsend muttered so as not to be heard.

Kate's first point of interest was the vault. Standing by the bar on the other side of the room, she inspected the section of the bookcase that covered the vault door. "Certainly does not appear to have been violated," she said, again loudly enough for the detective to hear.

And then she said to herself, *I'm not positive yet, but nothing on those shelves looks to have been disturbed. Highly unlikely that anyone broke into the vault. Doesn't even look to have been violated in any fashion. But I'll look at it more closely tonight, after everyone's gone.*

What she had not shared with the detective was that there was a separate camera system monitoring the lower-level office, and the headend for that system was located in the vault itself. To her father, the security of that secret vault was of special concern to him. He had earlier explained to her that all the cameras monitoring the vault and the lower-level office were hardwired, which meant that they were not subject to the type of radio interference that can jam Wi-Fi cameras, or other varieties of wireless equipment. Her intentions were that later—once she was totally by herself—she would enter the vault, inspect it closely, and take a look at the video. That, she believed, would categorically allow her to determine the extent of, and possibly the reason for, the attack.

She then turned and checked out the bar.

"What's this?" she said audibly, but only to herself. "That bar looks a lot more empty than the way Dad usually keeps it. Not sure at all what that suggests. Have to determine that tonight when I take a look at the video."

"Looks all clear to me," she announced to the detective.

"You mean to tell me that someone went to all the trouble to break into this place," Det. Townsend said in virtual disbelief, "and during the break-in, they almost killed you? And, they didn't take a damn thing? What the hell kind of crooks must these assholes be? Doesn't make any sense to me. None whatsoever."

It was clear to Kate that the detective was not calling her a liar, but neither was he buying the line she was selling.

"I don't disagree with you about that," she said. "But, look around. You can't point out anything that is out of place. Someone did get in here alright, but they didn't break anything up, nor does it appear that they took anything.

"Take a look for yourself," she said, standing in front of him at the door and motioning across the room with her hand. "Can you see anything at all that appears to have been disturbed? Well, neither can I."

She thought about the strange liquor situation, with some of the bottles possibly missing, but she did not bring it up with the detective.

"The one thing I still can't figure out is why they got in," Kate continued. "Do you have any theories about that? We know that they were in the house, and that they even came down here, disarmed this keypad, and opened the door. But I can't see where they touched a damn thing. Very weird, to say the least, don't you think? Is it okay if I secure the pit? We're done here, aren't we?"

"Shit!" he complained. "I suppose we are, if you're one hundred percent sure that nothing is missing, or disturbed."

Kate did not respond to his comment. She just smiled and sort of pushed him back, leaned into him and gave him a fast kiss right on the mouth. She then closed the door and latched it.

"I'll turn this alarm on later," she said. "That should be good for now."

Must have been the result of my lack of oxygen, she thought. *At least it did throw him off his game a bit.*

Trapped between shock and confusion, the detective turned and followed her up the steps. "I suppose I should check with Detective Conners. He was going to see if he could figure out how they got in. Whether they broke in, or had keys and codes for these physical locks. They're definitely good ones, and none of them appear to have been forced. Why don't you walk with me and we'll do a perimeter? Or, maybe I should ask you if you're up to doing it."

"I'm good to go," she replied with a wink. "Feeling better all the time."

"Then let's catch up with Conners and see what he's learned."

Kate and Det. Townsend then went out the entry door. The detective looked in both directions before determining that the logical route would be counter-clockwise, covering the front of the house first. By the time they reached the first corner, they spotted Det. Conners down on his knees. He was inspecting the earth in front of a lower-level window—one that looked into the hall where Kate and Det. Townsend had just been.

"Find something?" Det. Townsend asked.

"I think I might have," Det. Conners replied. "Looks like someone used this window to gain entrance."

"Really," Det. Townsend said. "Kate, doesn't this lead into the downstairs hall?"

"Yes," she said. "If that's how they entered, it's strange that we didn't see some of this soil tracked in down there. How about I run in and check it out and see what it looks like from the inside."

"Call the security company while you're in there," Det. Townsend said. "Find out if they show anything happening with this window. They would be able to tell you if it was involved."

"Right," Kate said. "But I actually did that before. The alarm company showed no violations—only the request to have them disarm it. I think that if entry were gained at the window, it would have been after the company disarmed it. I've encountered that type of entry before. It suggests that the key they had made didn't work, and they did not want to destroy the door."

Det. Townsend understood that what she was suggesting was probably right, and passed on pursuing the matter.

Before she re-entered the house, Kate put on a fresh pair of booties.

Kate then went downstairs and checked out the floor beneath the window in question. It appeared to be as clean as the rest of the floor—perhaps even a little cleaner. She considered checking further by using a piece of paper towel. However, she thought better of it because there could be fingerprints on the ceramic tiles, and a paper towel could destroy evidence.

When Kate went back outside, Det. Townsend asked her, "Find any dirt under the window?"

"None," she replied. "But, it was almost too clean. Like maybe somebody tidied up after getting in. Figured I'd leave that for you to determine. I'd have to say that it appears that the intruders had contacted the alarm company requesting them to disarm the system before they entered."

"What you were thinking makes sense," Det. Townsend said. "Calling the security company for help turning it off before it had been tripped, if you think about it. Makes total sense—uncharacteristically clever, actually."

Dets. Townsend and Conners spent another hour poking around the house, while Kate walked over to the camper to spend a little time with the boys.

They explained to Kate that they had been trying to "hide out" from the detectives, for fear that the "cops" might find some reason to remove them from the house. Kate understood completely what they were thinking.

Finally, Det. Townsend knocked on the camper door. When Kate opened it he said, "We're finished for the day. As far as we can see, we've gathered all the evidence that has been left for us. If you come up with anything, let us know in the morning."

Kate asked him if it would be okay for the three of them to have dinner at the house, and if she would be able to spend the night in it. The detective had no issue with that. "Just keep your eyes and ears open for anything that seems suspicious, or even just unusual. If you find something moved or missing, or even if you run across something that seems slightly out of the ordinary. Such info might be helpful if you make a note of it and pass it on to us."

"Definitely—I will most certainly do that," Kate said, flashing him the biggest flirty smile she could muster. "But, do you think you could do me a little favor?"

"Will try," Det. Townsend said. "What would you like me to do for you?"

"I would like to find out as soon as possible if you are able to lift any prints from that hose they stuck in my window. And, I would like to see whatever else you can find out about it. Like, if you could send me a picture of the hose. That would be great."

"We can do that for sure," the detective said. "In fact, I've got one on my cell. I can text it to you."

"Terrific," she said as she pulled out her burner phone. "I'll text you right now, then you'll have my number. I'll let you know if I don't get it. I'm thinking of taking the boys into town and buy them a burger. I'll be looking for it. Thanks!"

Kate was very happy that Det. Townsend was winding up at the house for the day.

And so, after the detectives had gone, Kate did have the boys prepare to run out for the burger, while she headed back to the house to arm the system. Then, the three of them did jump into the resort's RAM 2500 Twin Cab that Jack kept in the garage for emergencies.

While they were sitting in the truck at Clyde's enjoying a delicious to-go burger, Kate showed the boys the image of the hose that was used in the attempt on her life.

"Ever see a hose that looks like this?" she asked.

Red and Robby both enthusiastically nodded their heads.

"Looks like a plain old vacuum cleaner hose," Robby said. "Is that the one they stuck in your window?"

"Yes," she said. "It does look pretty generic. And also pretty new, don't you think? But, does it strike a note with either one of you? Like, do you recall ever having seen one exactly like it? Or even similar? Like, maybe around Dad's resort—perhaps at one of the other units? Or, at one of your friends' houses? You see, it would appear that these guys discovered that they would need a hose like that only after they were on scene at the resort. I'm reasonably sure that they would not just have one with them during the course of a regular burglary. That would have been highly unlikely. That means that one of them would have to have bolted out to pick one up. Or, maybe they discovered me on the first night, and they came back the next night with a hose in hand. That makes me think that they are living, or at least staying, nearby. On that basis, do either of you have a thought?"

Red pulled a pen out of his pocket and grabbed a scrap of paper that was lying on the seat. He wrote: "Looks brand new. Right?"

"Pretty much," Kate said. "Looks new to me too. Does that suggest something to you?"

Robby smiled brightly. He pointed at Red and said, "Are you thinking about the new cottage downstream from the resort?"

Red nodded convincingly.

"Uncle Jack just bought a small house by the resort," Robby explained. "It's located on the property just north of the main house. It's on the St. Marys, too. But you can't see it from the main house—even in the winter. There's that hill, and all those pine trees. It just came up for sale a few months ago. Uncle Jack had it fixed up a little, and one of the things he bought was a new vacuum cleaner. We haven't been over there helping him after he ordered the vacuum, so we haven't actually seen the hose. But, it is possible. And it's new. We know that."

"Is it rented out?" Kate asked.

"Everything is," Robby said, while Red was nodding his head in agreement.

"Did either one of you get a look at the people who rented it?" Kate asked.

"No," Robby said. "I don't think either one of us saw anybody.

We've been totally busy looking out for Henry's aunt."

Robby looked over at Red, and he was nodding his head slowly in agreement.

Kate, for the next five minutes, concentrated on her thoughts, and on devouring her delicious burger and a chocolate shake and swirling her fries through the ketchup.

"When we go back," she finally said. "I'll check out that unit. See if it might be the source of the hose."

Once they had all finished eating, Kate and the boys took the ferry and headed back to the resort. The boys retired immediately to the camper to watch over Henry's aunt.

Kate, however, did not run immediately over to the unit up-river from the main house. Instead, she took the opportunity to go downstairs at the main house. She went back into the pit and removed the one book in the bookcase that hid a fingerprint reader. She placed her right index finger over the sensor and activated the powerful hydraulic mechanism that allowed the bookcase to hinge out from the wall.

Behind it was a vault that looked mighty enough to protect the average bank's cash reserves. She placed her right hand on a sensor near the center of its door, and it automatically swung open revealing an expensive vault. She took a long moment to look around inside, and was pleased to note that initially it looked totally intact.

"That's good news!" she exclaimed audibly. "Now, to take a look at that video of the pit."

She had been dying to get a chance to check that out.

She played back the motion-activated video from the previous evening. And it shocked her. While she saw no one immediately approaching the bookcase that hid the vault door, she did observe two men, dressed in all-black, walk directly over to the bar. There they gathered up what looked to be about a half a dozen opened bottles of liquor. They put the bottles in a box that they had brought with them, and then taped the box shut.

"Well I'll be damned!" she muttered several times. "I was right, all they took were a few bottles of booze. What the hell could all that have been about? How could that possibly be worth killing me over? And I had to come all the way from Manhattan to witness this kind of crazy. I'm sure we could beat that in that borough alone. I can't wait until my dad hears about this."

It was right at that time the unexpected happened again. She watched the two men walk out of the main door to the pit. And just before she shut the video player down, thinking that the intrusion episode had completed, the two men-in-black walked back into the pit, and over to the bookcase at the vault door. She then observed one of them shooting a picture with his cell phone of the bookcase. He then removed the book that blocked the keypad, and, using his cell phone, somehow opened the vault door.

"Damn it!" she groaned disgustedly, "They *did* get in the vault! And they had the combination for it! Or, somehow used their cell. Not sure what that was all about."

Right next to the fingerprint sensor was located a keypad, allowing for entry other than by the print reader.

She then observed the two men-in-black, who were still wearing gloves, enter the vault. They immediately walked over to the security mechanism that mechanically protected the firearms. The taller of the men had a key, and he unlocked the securing device on her father's sniper rifles.

"That bastard had a key! I don't believe that could happen. The bastard had a key!"

Memory told Kate that her dad had at least one sniper piece—a Barrett M82. That was the only one she could picture in her mind. She did not initially realize that the display was absent a second sniper rifle. That was the Finnish SAKO-TRG42. "Why didn't I spot that one missing right off?" she asked herself. "I guess I was trying to mitigate the gravity of this whole damn mess."

As she earnestly studied the video, she observed the shorter of the intruders fitting the SAKO into one of the strapped camouflage rifle cases from the drawer below the display. The same man then removed some ammo; it looked to her like he took only a few rounds for the SAKO from that same drawer, and then he slid them into the zippered pocket on the side of the case.

"Why the SAKO and not the Barrett?" she asked herself. "They're both fine pieces, I'm sure. Dad wouldn't have them if they weren't. Or, why not both? If these assholes are planning to sell them, why not take them all? There's a lot of black market cash in this room."

"That's it!" she said aloud, and loudly. "They're *not* gonna be selling them! They're gonna use that SAKO to kill somebody! That's why they're taking only two or three rounds of ammo! The whole point behind this break-in was not to make money."

"There's an assassination in the works!" she announced loudly.

She then replayed the end of the recording several times as she stood there. Each time she looked for more clues into the crooks' thinking.

And why the SAKO and not the Barrett? she asked herself again. *The principal difference between the two is that the Barrett represents a much heavier piece of equipment—not only in weight, but possibly more importantly, in the size of the bullet it delivers. The Barrett is a bona fide fifty-cal rifle. It can take out the block of a large vehicle. But the SAKO TRG-42 is much smaller. Dad's SAKO is chambered for a .300 Winchester Magnum. It's designed to kill a man at 1,500 meters. Dad said it would be his choice if he wanted to take a target out at a good distance. That's what this is all about. They're going to be using Dad's SAKO to kill somebody! That's gotta be what's in the works!*

After the fifth time through the video, Kate finally switched it from *play* to *record*. But she didn't yet budge from her station for another ten minutes. Instead, she simply stared unfocused at the white wall above the monitor, and thought. *Can't report this to Det. Townsend,* Kate said to herself. *After all, that was a sniper rifle that just went missing. I can't report that to law enforcement. They'd have Dad's ass. He'd have to be on the run. Maybe forever. How the hell could he explain away an unregistered piece like that? Or, it might be properly papered. Damn! I wish he were here. He'd want to know about this. He absolutely needs to know what's goin' on.*

She thought about the situation more, and concluded that she was going to have to try to find a solution without her father's help. "I have no idea where Dad is," she mumbled aloud to herself. "And there is no way to reach him. Can't talk about this to Detective Townsend either. Face it, girl, you're on your own with this one."

She then carefully closed the vault back up and secured it. But she didn't go to bed.

Chapter 28 —

Kate was still stewing in her anger when she went up and fingered through the resort's log her father kept on a desk adjacent to the main entry door. She did not know how Jack might have referred to the new unit, but when she found an entry by that exact name, "The New Unit," she was quite confident that would refer to the cottage Red and Robby were suggesting.

"Yes," she said as she checked it out. "It was rented out six days ago—through today, to be more precise. I'm going to have to check that out right now. Can't wait on this one."

Before setting out, she physically confirmed that the Glock 10mm that Jack kept in his office was good to go—along with a second fully-loaded magazine. Her thinking was that if she were forced to shoot someone, it would be best not to involve a piece issued to her by the NYPD.

She slid it under her belt. And then, based on what the boys had told her, she walked down to the riverfront, turned right, and then proceeded to the newly restored cabin.

As she approached she quickly observed that there were multiple lights on inside. She checked her watch and found it to be 10:10. She removed the Glock from her belt and carried it in her right hand, which was extended downward and slightly behind her. Walking straight up to the front door, she stood listening for nearly a minute. Hearing nothing, she then knocked loudly.

No one came to the door.

She tried the door knob, but found it latched.

So she walked along the wrap-around porch and cautiously looked in the living room window.

It was as her eyes surveyed the room that she saw the most unsettling sight since leaving the hospital. She immediately ran back to the locked door and put her shoulder in to it. On her fourth attempt, she shoved the door in, ripping the Schlage triple faceplate from the jamb and casting it halfway across the living room floor. With the Glock 10 now raised to shoulder height and pointed upward, she stepped fully into the room and stopped.

Chapter 29 —

To say that Henry was distraught would be an understatement. Even though his mind was racing in ways he'd never before experienced, his heart was locked in deepest anguish. He asked himself some of the most difficult questions he could imagine: *what do I tell Red and Robby? What could I possibly say that would help? I'm sure this mission is totally classified—where do I go with it? I can't even explain anything about it to Kate; or tell her that her dad was a genuine hero.*

And then he caught his eyes fixated on the diver's wristwatch. Henry was staring, and he could not pull his eyes off it. Finally it came to him. It was not a wristwatch—it wasn't even a typical diver's watch. *That SEAL diver is wearing a very expensive Dive Computer!* Henry exclaimed in silence. *It's a Garmin Descent MK1! It's got gyroscope, for God's sake—GPS and GLONASS—all built in. Those puppies cost a grand or more! I know that for a fact because Jack bought one just like it for missions like this. And I'm positive that they're not standard government issue, even for a SEAL. Holy shit! What's happening here? Did that SEAL steal Jack's equipment? Shit like that just doesn't happen—not with an elite group like the SEALs. I'm sure of that.*

Henry then reached down and pulled the diving mask off

the dead man crumpled up on the floor at his feet—the man he'd thought was Jack. His discovery snapped his head up and threw him into a shocked stare at the standing SEAL.

Damn it! he moaned, again in forced silence. *Is that? Could that be Jack standing beside me? Is it possible that Jack's not dead?*

Henry immediately stood to his feet. He grabbed the diver by the shoulder and spun him around.

He leaned in and took a close-up look at the diver's eyes through his twin lens dive mask. *It is Jack!* Henry barked without making a sound. *It is my friend! Oh my God! Jack is alive!*

Jack was nearly in shock. *What the hell's goin' on!?* he wondered in astonishment. *What's got into Henry?! He gonna kiss me, or what? What the hell's he got in mind?*

Needless to say, kissing Jack was the farthest thing from Henry's mind. He was happy enough to hug his friend, but resisted even that urge. Instead, Henry looked and pointed down at the dead man. Jack's eyes followed. Then, looking back at Jack, Henry turned both hands palms upward as if to ask, "What the hell happened? Why's Agent One dead?"

Jack just looked puzzled and pointed toward his Garmin.

Henry correctly understood that to mean that they would talk about it later.

Slowly the pressure in the chamber dropped. Both Jack and Henry were well aware that leaving the wet room too quickly could be dangerous if not fatal, even with a rebreather. So they remained patient.

While communicating verbally via the Underwater Wireless Network (UWN) was possible, it was not plausible, as they both understood that the code of silence still prevailed. They would both wait.

Twenty minutes left, Jack thought to himself as he looked at his Garmin.

He sensed that the mini-sub had begun to rise slowly. *I wonder just how deep we were? Must have been substantially over one eighty. Probably as much as two hundred. Maybe more! We're lucky to still be alive. I guess you could say this little fish is put together pretty good.*

He then turned to the digital communication pad and entered: "How the hell deep did we get before we got it turned around?"

The pilot read his message and responded: "Deep. Too deep. We hit 222 before you freed us up. That could be the first for this little guy. We're damned fortunate to not be shark bait in the middle of the Yellow Sea."

"Shit!" Jack entered. "Let's not do that again." He thought for a moment, and then wrote: "How long before we can drain this bathtub? I'm really anxious to get the hell outta here."

"Another twenty minutes. Don't want to rush it."

Both ends of the communication were totally the product of strokes made on keypads.

Damn, Jack was thinking.

"It's taking a little longer because we are inching toward the surface," the pilot wrote. "I'd like to hang out at about 150. I'd say twenty more minutes would be just about perfect. Can you hang in that long?"

"Yeah," Jack wrote. 'You know we lost Agent One. Right?"

"We see that. Caught it as Henry pulled him in. Thought it was you, at first. You were the one with the tether. At first. Realized it was our buddy when we spotted the hardware on your wrist.

Glad you were able to retrieve his body. What happened to him, anyway?"

"Assume he got clipped by the sinking fishing boat. He took quite a knock on the side of his head. Knocked his rebreather off. Broke it. Probably knocked him out. I found him hooked up on the railing. I could see that he was gone. Moved the rope from my ankle to his and had Henry bring him in. Shitty way to end this mission. He was a good man."

"Don't be too sure about this mission ending," the pilot wrote.

Henry and Jack were both reading the lines of communication. When that sentence appeared they looked at each other in surprise.

"What does that mean?" Jack asked.

"Right now we have something above us," the pilot responded. "A vessel of some sort. We assume it is a Nork patrol boat. Probably the one that took out the fishing boat. It's just hanging out up there. Maybe it's looking for us. Or anything of interest that might float to the surface."

"Hell. You sure about that?"

"We're sure it's there. But, not so much sure what he has in mind. Not sure he even knows that we're down here."

"Might have had agents on the fishing boat."

"Possibly. But no one but the captain should've known about this. That's why we made the connection from here."

"But they might have figured out that something was up. Are you sure it's North Korean, and not Chinese?" Jack wrote.

"We're hoping it's a Nork. Chinese patrols have better sensing capability. We're watching it carefully. They might be sitting up there waiting for bodies to come up to the surface from the fishing boat. Doubt they have divers. But it wouldn't surprise us if they dropped a few charges before they go home. Nork patrol boats are practiced at that. A good reason to lay low. And as quiet as possible. At least for a time."

"How are we for air and battery?" Jack asked.

"Good on air. That'll not be an issue. Battery's another question. We're okay as long as we stay put. Not ready to make a run without help."

"Are we still taking water?" Jack asked. "From where the fishing boat clipped us?"

"A little," the pilot wrote. "It wasn't exactly a pin hole. But this little fish has a self-repair mechanism. For minor breaches, of course. And that's what we got. We've been able to pump it out. The 'stop-a-leak' is doing the job for now. If it starts up again, it could be a big problem. It would help to stay above 150. Cuts down on the pressure."

"Should I see what I can do from the outside?" Jack asked.

He knew before he wrote those words that there was nothing he could do from the outside that would work any better to stop the water than the classified system that their UOES3 already employed. Earlier prototypes were equipped with a virtual second hull, or smaller chambers that would be sealed off in the event of a leak. When it became apparent that, in a mini-sub, any sort of an inner hull would add too much weight, engineers began developing a system of miniature jets that would eject a sealant in the direction of a small leak. It was thought that if the vessel remained static in the water, the rapid flow into the hull of the mini-sub would draw the sealant into a small hole, and if it hardened quickly enough, it would serve to seal the breach until the sub could be serviced, or junked.

Of course, if the hole was too large, or became larger from the rapid flow of water through it, then flooding was sure to occur. This would require secondary countermeasures, or evacuation.

While Jack was not privy to any specifics as to the technical data on the stop-a-leak, his research indicated that it would work on any small hole in the mini-sub's hull, and that it would work better than anything that human intervention could achieve.

Besides, Jack was exhausted, and he was not overly excited about doing more work outside their little boat—especially if it were not totally warranted.

"There's nothing you can do out there that the new system can't accomplish on its own," the pilot said. "We've triggered it, and it seems to be working. It would be nice if you could do something about that damn Nork up top. Do you got a solution for that?"

At first Jack thought that the pilot was making a joke, and so he did not take him seriously. However, as soon as he and Henry had completed their decompression and drained the wet room, he was immediately confronted by Agent Two as he passed through the chamber door.

"We're gonna have to do something about that patrol boat up top," Agent Two had scribbled on his message pad. "Any ideas? We really cannot just sit down here and wait. Not forever."

Jack grabbed the pad from him and wrote, "Hell if I know. What would you suggest?"

"Maybe take it out with a Thermite grenade."

Even though Jack had never used Thermite before, he knew what it was and what it could do.

"What? How would we deploy it?" Jack wrote.

"It likely has a steel hull," Agent Two wrote. "That patrol boat. We have two Thermite grenades that are magnetic. I think they're actually *Thermate*—not Thermite. Very powerful incendiary devices. One of us would have to swim up, stick it to the bottom of the boat, and then activate the timer."

"Swim up," Jack said in a near whisper. "Or could we take the mini-sub up?"

"Wouldn't want to do that." Agent Two, taking his lead from Jack, said it in a near whisper. "We think, we *hope*, that they don't know we're down here. But if we move the SDV, it will give our position away. If we're gonna attempt it, we'll have to do it by hand."

"Are they directly above us?" Jack asked.

"Pretty much. Perhaps ten meters to the north."

"So, what's our depth?" Jack asked.

"One hundred and fifty. That's feet."

"We need to get this shit resolved and get the hell outta here," Jack said. "They might be on their own right now, but they're gonna have backup before long. We gotta do whatever it is we're gonna do, and then head south about as quickly as this little fish can swim. Do you agree?"

"That's what I'm thinkin'," Agent Two agreed, getting a little louder with every exchange.

"What's our options on the timer?" Jack asked, also above his original whisper. "Could we deploy the ... I'll call it a mine, for lack of a better word. Could we place the mine on the bottom of the patrol boat, return to our mini-sub, and then prepare to move out as soon as the device ignites? Could that be done?"

"I've never used the device in a real theater," Agent Two said, making it a point to keep his decibels to a minimum. "For me, it's always been in a training exercise. But, from what I recall, the timing mechanism is quite flexible."

"All right," Jack replied. "Let's do it like this. I'll set the timer. Here, while still in this boat. We'll fasten a nylon cord to it—if you've got one. We'll rise slowly to a hundred feet. I will gear up, go out and drag it until it is directly beneath the patrol boat. I will float the device up to the bottom of the patrol boat. Attach it with the magnet. Then I'll return to our boat, and we'll wait for it to ignite. As soon as it does, we'll head south. Does that sound like it would work?"

"Almost," Agent Two said. "We'll actually have to hook up the spare battery pack that the Jimmy Carter dropped off. It's actually only about thirty minutes from here. But we can't run forever on this battery. Not without another tow."

Jack was already pulling out his diving gear as he was laying out the plan.

"I'm damn glad this gear is all black," Jack said in a serious tone. "It matches the murky waters of this incredibly turbid sea."

"It's as good a plan as anything I could come up with," Agent Two replied. "Probably offers us our best chance to survive. Worth a shot, I'd say."

"Great," Jack said. "Get me what I'm gonna need to do it. Don't forget, I'll need a floating device to take it up to the patrol boat."

"They come with one," Agent Two said. "The ones we got are equipped with attaching magnets and have a small inflating mechanism built into them. Exactly for that purpose. A two-hundred-foot cord as well."

"Ten minutes?" Jack asked. "Can you get it ready for me in ten?"

The SEAL nodded, turned, and began to make his way toward the small ordinance compartment.

Jack stopped him, and quietly asked, "Do you have body bags onboard? Henry and I would like to take care of Agent One."

Agent Two did not verbally respond. Instead he simply diverted his attention one bin to the left of where he was originally headed. He opened it and pulled out a carefully folded black bag with three handles on each side, and he handed it to Jack without a word.

Jack and Henry entered the tight quarters of the wet room. They would have liked to close the door behind them to protect the sensitivities of the North Korean couple, but decided against that because the floor space of the room was so small. Instead Jack stretched the bag out in front of the door, and opened it fully. He then reached under the body's arms and hoisted the torso over the raised threshold, while Henry guided it through the doorway. Once the bulk of the body's upper torso was stretched out on the bag outside the chamber, Henry picked up the lower portion of the body at the knees and the two men slid it onto the bag until it was totally outside the chamber. They then squared it around until properly placed on the bag.

After Jack had removed every imaginable means of identification, they zipped the body up.

"Where do you want to put him?" Henry asked.

"Just hang on," Jack said. "And no more questions on that."

Jack disappeared for a couple minutes as he made his way over to his storage bin. When he returned he was carrying what looked to be a very heavy canvas bag.

"What the hell's that?" Henry asked.

"A little bit of water pollution," Jack replied as he slid the canvas bag in with the body, "forty pounds of it, along with a little fish deterrent."

"Looks like lead pellets to me," Henry said. "Where did you find that?"

"Special order," Jack replied. "It'll give us a little more time before Agent One floats to the surface."

After Jack had strapped the bag to the dead man's ankle, he zipped up the body bag and sealed it. He then connected a small vacuum pump to it and sucked out all the air. The bag soon conformed in shape to the body inside it, making for an eerie, unsettling sight for the North Korean couple.

Jack saw their reaction, and even though he was not sure that they fully understood what was taking place, or what he was about to say, he smiled at them and explained, "Sorry about this unfortunate accident. I'll take care of it shortly."

They each flashed an affected brief smile at him.

What Jack had in mind was to perform a 'burial at sea.' The canvas bag he had inserted into the body bag did contain forty pounds of lead pellets, along with two water-soluble capsules. The lead was intended to keep the body at the bottom of the sea for a few extra days, and the capsules contained a compound intended to make the body less likely to attract fish as it decomposed.

The body bag itself was special. It was designed specifically for burials at sea. The material from which it was constructed had some unique qualities. For one, the fabric was designed to seal up totally within twenty-four hours after coming in contact with water, at which point it became both totally water and airproof. But, even more significantly, it was also designed to react to water by hardening into a very stiff, almost brittle plastic-like composite. It became a virtually impenetrable burial vault.

Of course, the lead pellets were intended to hold the body bag at the bottom for a longer period of time than it would were it not for the additional weight.

For instance, while under any ordinary circumstance, a typical lean body will sink to the bottom of a body of water upon drowning. It will then likely remain at the bottom of the water for two to three days. That's when major decomposition sets in. Gases are created at that time, and the body will begin to float to the surface.

But, as already mentioned, the stiff nature of the body bag helps maintain its initial shape, so as not to become like a balloon as the body decomposes. The valve allows the gases and liquids to escape as they are produced, and the two capsules included with the lead ballast dissolve into the liquids produced by decomposition, producing a chemical that even the most undiscriminating of sea creatures find disgusting.

And, finally, even though at some point, the body-bag device will undoubtedly give way to aggressive carnivores. When that happens, rather than having what might remain of a human body floating to the surface, the weight attached to the body's ankle would hold it down at least a little longer.

Bottom line, a body buried in this fashion would most likely remain submerged for several days, or likely even longer. *Long enough*, Jack hoped, *for the survivors to make their escape.*

Henry had not been aware that such a 'burial at sea' was even possible. And, in fact, Jack had not heard of it either. Not until he had done his research, in his spare time on the day before setting out on this most dangerous of missions.

"Here you go, Jack," Agent Two quietly said as he handed Jack the anti-ship package. It contained a magnetic Thermate mine, and two hundred feet of what looked to Jack like large fishline. "Here's what I've got for you. This is the magnetic incendiary device we discussed, and the cord to use to deploy it from a distance. As you can see, it is not exactly what you were asking for. You'd requested a nylon cord, but we're instructed to use this under this type of circumstance. It's more like a heavy-duty fishline—I think it's rated for seventy-five pounds. The engineers thought that a white nylon cord might be spotted from the surface. And this black fishline would be virtually invisible. It's already attached to the device, so all you have to do is let it unwind from the reel that it comes with. You can see the markings on the side of the spool. They let you know approximately how much you've spun off.

"I checked the field manual for submarine deployment of this device on a surface vessel, and it states that we should avoid depths of less than one hundred thirty feet. Unless, of course, we do not have that much water to work with. So—"

"So," Jack interrupted, "You're saying that I should go out and deploy it right from the depth we're at right now. Is that about right?"

"Exactly. We're at one hundred fifty—give or take. Ideally we shouldn't be diving unprotected at that depth. So, I'll take it up a bit, and you can go after it."

"That works for me," Jack said. "But, tell me if I'm wrong—I think you called it a Thermate mine. I thought it was Thermite. Are we talking about the same thing? I'm somewhat familiar with Thermite. Do I need to understand the difference?"

"Same thing, basically," Agent Two replied. "Thermate is the name now used for the compound. It's a refined version of Thermite. Still burns under water at four thousand degrees. It's effective to cut through half-inch steel. I think we're assuming that the patrol boat in question fits that description. I think it should. But, this is North Korea, so all bets are off."

"I get it," Jack said. "Let's get this job done. Longer we wait, the more apt things are going to keep going wrong."

"Right," Agent Two said. "I take it you're ready."

"I am," Jack replied. "I'm going to have Henry come out into the wet room to give me a hand. We'll take care of Agent One while we're out there. But I couldn't be more ready. How about you, Henry? Is it time to rock and roll? And it looks like you're becoming an expert with the rebreather."

"Let's get it done," Henry replied, without offering a response to Jack's additional comment.

The two men began gearing up for yet another trip out into the murky waters.

As they checked out their rebreathers, Jack asked, "How about Agents Three and Four. Do they know what we're up to?"

"Totally," Agent Two replied. "I've gone over this with them. We've all trained for this sort of eventuality. They're going to continue remaining in place, and to monitor the situation. There will be no electronic communication attempted with you except in extreme emergency. And then only if you initiate it. We're expecting you to deploy the device, and then to immediately return to the mini-sub. If you return within the time allotted, we'll be waiting. And as soon as it ignites, we will leave the area. Immediately after it's triggered. Whether or not you've made it back."

"The time allotted," Jack said. "What does that mean, exactly?"

"From the time you leave home base," Agent Two said. "Which in this case is this mini-sub, you have a total of twenty minutes, unless you communicate otherwise. That's standard protocol."

"Understood," Jack replied. "That ought to put me back in the wet room, I take it. That's when it'll trigger? Sound right? How does that work, anyway? You mentioned a timer. How can we know in advance just when I'll have my part done?"

"It is on a timer," Agent Two replied. "But there's more involved. The timer merely establishes a time after which, if you're deploying the device, it protects you. When we're ready to trigger it, we do that remotely."

"From our boat?" Jack questioned. "How's that possible? I thought wireless transmissions were blocked underwater? Is that fishline I'm looking at? Can that conduct a signal?"

"You're right—traditional wireless does not work down here," Agent Two replied. "But we will use something that does work underwater—TARF. That's Translational Acoustic-RF Communication. It's basically a sonar setup. It uses transducers to convert vibrations into an electronic signal. Complicated as hell. I can tell you for a fact that I couldn't explain it well enough so that I could even understand it. But, I just know it works. Actually, we've all trained for and with it. I'm not supposed to discuss it. Shit! I can't discuss it because I don't understand it well enough to discuss it. But I've personally used it, and I've seen it blow shit up. And do it very well."

"I'd bet that it's expensive as hell," Jack said.

"I'm sure you're right about that—it's like lighting a cigarette with a thousand dollar bill. You have to keep in mind that this is the US military. That's how we do things here."

"As long as it works," Jack said. "That would be capitalism at its best. I just don't want this sparkler to light up while it's in my pocket. And, you should hold off on it until after the rocket launch. At least until after it's scheduled to launch. You've deployed that wired antenna to the surface? Monitoring Chinese radio? We ought not to initiate the timer until the Nork missile has launched. Right?"

"Imminent. We're almost at that point now," Agent Two said. "But, yes, we are monitoring Chinese communiqués. We'll know when the missile is launched. I'm going to set the timer right now. We can adjust it as need be when they launch. If they should hit us with something, I would not want to miss this opportunity to inflict some pain. And destroy evidence. How long do you expect it to take you to get it ready to go?"

"Give me that twenty minutes," Jack said, "start it from the time I leave the wet room. That should do it. If nothing else, I should have it on the bottom of the boat by that time."

Agent Two continued his work in the preparation of the device for activation. As soon as he was finished he handed it over to Jack with these words: "Better get moving, my friend. I'll start the 20 when you close the hatch."

Jack and Henry checked their equipment, and performed a quick visual of each other's rebreather, and then stepped into the wet room chamber. They closed and secured the door behind them and began the filling process.

Before the water had reached their upper torsos, Jack pulled out his closed-circuit mouthpiece and said to Henry, "We'll take care of our friend, here. Then I'll head out with the device. If I don't get back in time, do not delay anything for me. Just get the hell outta here."

"Even if it's *without* you?"

"Absolutely," Jack said. "But, it won't come to that."

Henry smiled broadly and said, "Aren't you gonna tie a ribbon around your ankle. Like you did before?"

Jack had only a second to respond before the rising water eclipsed his breathing gear, but he did manage a few words. "Yeah," he said. "It didn't work so well last time, did it?" With that he made himself comfortable with the rebreather and prepared to pop the hatch when the pressure was right.

Three more minutes passed before the green "OK to Open Hatch" came on. That meant that the pressure in the chamber had been built up to equal the pressure outside of the mini-sub. Jack quickly opened the equalization valve, and then swung the hatch up and fully open. Wasting no time, he stepped up the ladder and passed through the opening.

Henry marveled to see the "OK to Open Hatch" LED. He'd missed it earlier. As soon as Jack had set himself to receive the body, Henry lifted Agent One up and out. Jack gracefully patted the SEAL on his back, and allowed him to slide toward the bottom.

At the precise moment that Jack started to climb back through the hatch, Henry read a message that was flashing on the screen. It said, "Rocket launched. Timer set. Jack can move out."

Henry grabbed Jack's ankle to get his attention. When Jack turned his head to see what was going on, Henry gave him a thumbs up and signaled that he should be on his way.

Jack returned the thumbs up and raised his body back through the hatch and kept going.

With the sun beginning to set, the darkness above made it

even more difficult for Jack to determine exactly where the patrol boat was. *Have they moved?* he wondered.

The waters in the Yellow Sea are not very clear to begin with. In fact, it derives its name from the huge volume of sediments washed down by the two principal rivers that run out from the Chinese mainland—the Yangtze and the Huang He rivers. Even though most of the silt-laden river water had deposited its mud closer to the Chinese land mass, there remained enough soil suspended in the water to make vision of surface objects difficult even with the aid of a bright sun.

Now, however, with the sun preparing to yield altogether, Jack found it nearly impossible to determine the position of the targeted patrol boat.

"Damn it," he complained to himself. "I can't see anything up there! What the hell am I supposed to do?"

Not wishing to waste any time lamenting his latest misfortune, Jack said to himself, "at least I don't have to worry much about decompression, not with this rebreather. I'm gonna have to go way up to get a closer look. And I sure as hell better do it soon, 'cause it's not going to get any brighter up top before morning."

He immediately began swimming toward the surface. As he grew near the light he took a quick glance over at his Garmin. "Damn it! I'm going to be running out of time if I don't get my ass in gear! And quickly!"

The last two feet before his head popped above the surface, he looked around again to see if he could make out the boat's location. But it didn't happen.

At this point Jack put all thoughts for his safety out of his mind. *The completion of this mission trumps my safety,* he reasoned. *I al-*

ways knew this was eventually going to happen. Hell, happen again. This is not the first time I've been in a situation like this. How many times have I been shot? What is it? Seven times came immediately to his mind. *And I survived them all. So no big deal. I make it, or I don't. The job still has to be done. Or at least I have to give it my best effort.*

It is what it is, he muttered silently just before his head neared the surface of the water. *It is what it is,* he complained silently again after pausing. *Who the hell was it that used to say that: "It is what it is?"*

And then he remembered—*Sparky Anderson. Michigan's Hall of Fame Baseball Manager. That's who it was. ... No! It wasn't Sparky. It was Jim Leyland. Camel Smoking Jimbo. He'd always grumble that when a reporter asked him a question he didn't like. Anyways, I've always admired that sonofabitch's grit. He didn't take shit. Ever.*

Just then Jack's head slowly rose above the water's surface, and he looked around.

What the bloody hell! He suffered silently. *How'd that damn boat get clear over there?*

Jack had spotted the patrol boat. It was not now moving, but for some reason it had slid over to the east nearly two hundred feet.

"What the hell!" he growled quasi-audibly, "Gone too far to give up now." So he got his bearings as best he could, dropped below the surface, and began swimming in the direction of his target.

At this point, he said to himself, *I have no real idea where my boat is—besides down there 130. I can have a hunch. But I really don't know. Not to worry, though. My only concern right now has to be taking out that patrol boat. Find it, and take it out. Or it takes us out! That's it! One damn thing at a time.*

Jack was not a great swimmer. But he did not regard himself as a particularly poor one either. For him, this mission represented the first time he'd ever been forced to don diving equipment and go deep. The operative word being *forced.* Jack had dove many times on shipwrecks in Michigan's Lake Superior—some deeper than this. But, in those instances, the dive was driven by desire, not total necessity. And, during those earlier dives, he had always suited up and used the conventional oxygen tank—not the new rebreathing apparatus.

Yes, Mr. Leyland, Jack muttered inaudibly. You're exactly right: it is whatever the hell it is.

Jack swam about five to seven feet beneath the surface in the direction he surmised would eventually bring him into the vicinity of the patrol boat.

He counted off the seconds: 1-2-3-4-5 … From his dives in fresh water he had it pretty much down as far as the distance he could cover every ten seconds.

But this is salt water, he thought to himself. *All of my dives were in fresh. Wonder if that makes much of a difference. And, I'm in a rebreather. Wonder what sort of a difference that would make. I'm sure it would have to make some impact on my speed, but not sure how it would affect it. What the hell. Guess I'm going to have to have another look.*

When his count had reached thirty, he stopped and very deliberately swam to the surface. He immediately spotted the boat and, this time, it was precisely where he thought it would be.

Well, at least I'm headed in the right direction, he reasoned silently. *I'm three-quarters of the way there.*

Slowly he slid out of sight, dropping this time to a pretty consistent ten feet beneath the surface.

He began counting again. This time, however, he stopped at one twenty-five. But, instead of poking his head above the water, he remained at the desired depth. He righted himself in the water—now ten feet below the gentle waves—and studied his surroundings.

I see the boat, he told himself. *Dead ahead. Maybe only another ten feet away. For the rest of this journey, I'm going deeper—much deeper.*

Carefully he spun over so that his head was pointed at an angle that would take him to a depth of about twenty feet by the time he was directly beneath the patrol boat, and he headed in that direction.

Once he reached his target he stopped and looked up. *There it is!* he gleaned silently. While the water was so filthy that he could not see it clearly, he was still able to determine the boat's outline.

He maintained a near static position by using his fins, and an occasional arm motion. He broke out the incendiary device, and activated the small flotation ring. And then he proceeded to allow it to unwind from the reel until it neared the bottom of the boat's hull. At that point he stopped the reel, and gently swam upward until he sensed the tension drop from the attached line.

It's there and attached, he, with a sense of relief, declared silently. *Must obviously have a steel hull. All good.*

He then took his knife out of its sheath and cut the fishline.

He then set his dive downward, even though he did not know

where the mini-sub was. *One thing I do know for sure,* he reasoned, *the sub is down there someplace. And very soon life is not going to be safe anywhere near the surface.*

He took another look at his Garmin.

Damn! he barked in silence. *This marvelous little jewel provides GPS Timelines. I can retrace my route. And I'd damn well better get a move on. That mine is already past the time he set it for. I sure as hell hope that they don't get carried away and trigger that little devil. Cuz, when it ignites, everybody on board that little Norky shit-boat is going to be dead or dying, or at least mad as hell.*

After he had found his bearings on his Garmin he twisted it around on his wrist so that it would be easier for him to read as he swam back to the mini-sub. And he then began the lengthy jaunt.

But, after only a few strokes, there was an enormous flash of light slightly above him and to his right.

"Damn!" he growled inside his closed-circuit mouthpiece. "What the hell's goin' on?!"

Chapter 30 —

Twenty minutes earlier, former President Bob Fulbright was pouring two shots of Pappy Van Winkle's Bourbon. He was seated with Jack's friend, Roger Minsk, at a small table on an enclosed penthouse deck in a DC suburb.

"What the hell did you just pour me?" Roger asked. "Let me take a closer look at that label. Isn't that the same stuff we were drinking on Sugar Island with Jack? Wasn't that it? That was that bourbon whiskey that was actually bottled in the previous century? Hell, the previous millennium! Right? You trying to poison me? I'm wondering. And what, exactly, are we doing tipping glasses at this time of the morning?"

"That, my friend, is a very special drink I just poured for you," Bob declared. "It didn't kill you before—it won't kill you now. I promise you that. Even though it seems a strange time of the day to be drinking anything except orange juice. Just keep in mind that time is relative. And we feel like celebrating. So, that makes it okay to tip a glass of Pappy's. In fact, like I've said before, I doubt that you will ever have the opportunity to treat your taste buds to a better Kentucky Straight. No one's making you violate your drinking habits—least of all me. Do what you want. But, if you don't drink with me, you'll have to watch."

"Really?" Roger said, as he lifted his hand-crafted Waterford Lismore Crystal to his lips. "I do think I recall having heard you say something like that before."

Roger's accusation was completely in jest—he knew that Bob was not trying to get him drunk, much less poison him. And Bob not only recognized the nature of what his old friend was up to, but he also knew why. He saw that Roger had observed that he was serving up something unusual, and that the manner in which Bob was doing it suggested that he was seeking to drive home the point that what was flowing into the glasses was very special.

What Roger was after from his friend was an adequate explanation. He knew that Bob had a very specific purpose for switching to a different brand of alcohol. Up to this point Bob had been serving a corner-store variety of Kentucky whiskey—and that original bottle remained over half full. Bob's intention became very clear to Roger when the host set the new bottle practically in front of Roger, and then turned it to face his guest.

This is by design, Roger thought to himself. *I'm supposed to say or do something that will draw Bob out for an explanation. That's what he's after.*

So, he turned his full attention toward Bob, but he did not say a word. He just stared into Bob's eyes.

"My friend," Bob said, after he'd caught the lead, "this one bottle of Kentucky whiskey most likely cost as much as you and I paid for our first cars—over four thousand dollars. In fact, I haven't cracked open one of my own bottles of Pappy since I retired from the White House. That night I was by myself—totally alone. I started out with a couple glasses of Four Roses Single Barrel Bourbon. I was halfway through my second glass when it came to me: what the hell am I doing here? This Four Roses is a fine enough bourbon, but tonight is special. It calls for a special drink. It calls for a glass or two of Pappy's.

"I knew I had a few bottles of Pappy's hidden away somewhere. They were gifts from wealthy friends—more than likely rich friends seeking favors. Anyway, I found a bottle and popped it open."

"I get that," Roger said. "I can see why you considered your last night in the White House special. That makes total sense. But today, right now, this little talk we're having, what makes this so special? Tell me what you're thinking."

"Roger," Bob said. "This whole mission that we've got the boys on—Jack, Henry, and our SEAL team. This task we've sent them on is more than special. It is monumental. And I think you know why."

"That big a deal, is it?" Roger came back with as he lifted his glass of Pappy's.

"You're damned right it is!" Bob said slowly, gently chastising his friend. "And I'm sure you know it is as much as I do. I haven't felt this pathetically useless in decades. Not since I lost in the primary on my unsuccessful run for the White House. If I would have had a bottle of Pappy's back then, I'd have finished it off by myself. Hell, I'd probably have drunk two of them. After my concession speech, I felt just like a pile of steaming shit. Frankly, I wanted to die. I got so drunk that night I was puking the whole next day. Maybe longer. Don't remember."

"I've never seen you like that," Roger said, "at least not in all the years I've known you. In fact, I don't ever recall having witnessed you even getting drunk."

"That's because I've never lost again," Bob said. "Chances are you'll never see me get drunk, either. Unless this mission fails in a big way. Then I promise you, I'll drink myself sick again. Guarantee it."

"So," Roger said, "It's really that big a deal, is it?"

"Hell yes it is! I would not have had you put those men, our good friends, in that untenable of a position. Or me either—there is no part of this crazy mission that I'm pleased with. It just feels bad for all of us. You were there when I explained to them that the odds were that they'd never make it back home. You remember that, don't you?"

"Yeah," Roger said, staring unfocused at a blank section of wall. "It's never been quite like that before. With other missions. They knew you and I both meant it. So, they were under no delusions. But, we've been in tough situations before—"

"No we have not!" Bob interrupted. "We've never been in any situation quite like this one. I swear to you, my friend, if they are unable to complete any part of that mission, we could be at war with China—possibly within hours. That's all that the leadership over there has on its mind. And that's what the North Koreans are working toward—destroying America. That is the sum total of the whole backstory to this crazy exercise.

"Worse yet, even if they manage to pull the mission off just like our people have designed it. And, I do mean the whole damn thing—if our boys are one hundred percent successful, lucky, and do everything we are asking, odds are, I'm afraid, we will still go to war with China. It's damned near inevitable. Maybe not today, or next week, but soon—perhaps even that soon. War is what the CCP is planning for. They would like it to be as bloodless as possible, but they are on a path to make it happen no matter what it takes. The best that we can hope for with this mission, is that we can put it off for a while, until we can prepare the American people for it."

"When will we know if we're successful?" Roger asked, as he gulped down the rest of his first glass. "What do you see as the best case scenario? As far as the mission's success. What would be a desired, or an acceptable level of success? Were we being totally candid with Jack?"

Bob took a moment to pour two more glasses of Pappy's, looked at his watch, and then said, "Yes, we were entirely straight with Jack. And to answer your question, we'll know how they did within a few minutes—two minutes, actually. That's when the Norks are scheduled to launch. If they get it off on time, and they usually do, then we will know in short order whether or not the team was able to pull off at least the first part as planned. If that happens, it should set the CCP back at least a few months. But probably not much more than that though. I would be happy with that. In fact, at this point, two or three months would really be something."

"And that's the best case?" Roger incredulously asked.

"Perhaps, my friend, that would be, if not the best case, at least an acceptable scenario. What that would accomplish for us, according to our generals, is that would give the Chinese leadership cause to doubt the effectiveness of their new system. And Schwarzkopf, he's the general in charge of this mission, he is of the opinion that it would take another few months for them to restage this test, and attempt to pull it off successfully—from their standpoint."

"Schwarzkopf?" Roger said in disbelief. "You gotta be shittin' me! Didn't he die several years ago? Like in 2012?"

"Yes, of course," Bob explained. "That's our guy's code name. Everyone's familiar with the name—Norman Schwarzkopf. Without a doubt he was the most famous American general in the modern age. Much like Eisenhower was deemed the genius during World War II, Schwarzkopf was the genius behind Desert Storm. Even more than that, he was credited with developing the first major test of modern warfare tactics. His Desert Storm combined air attacks with artillery, armored vehicles, and troops. He was brilliant. I think we lost under two hundred fighters in destroying one of the largest and best-equipped armies in the world. And he accomplished the whole thing without nukes.

"So, my guy leading our effort here, behind the scene, has appropriated the name of General Schwarzkopf. Don't get me wrong. Our guy is no military slouch. But that is all I can tell you about him. This whole mission has to be conducted in total secrecy. And, it has to stay that way, forever. This 'Deep State' shit runs very deep. Damn near pervades the whole military. Damn near."

"Does that mean that in a few hours we will be hearing from Jack?" Roger asked.

"I told you before we ever talked to him—to Jack," Bob said. "I explained to both of you that the odds are good that this crew of ours, for this mission, will never be heard from again. That's why we did not spend a lot of time working that part out. It just ain't gonna happen. Practically speaking, the plans for extraction are on the table, but that's just about all I will say about it. If they manage to get back to Hawaii, we'll all be shocked. Jack knows that. And I'm sure he made it clear to Henry. Did I not make that abundantly clear in the basement of Jack's house?"

"Yeah," Roger said, holding his glass up for another hit. "That's exactly how you put it. It's true—that's how we all understood it. Sort of like a kamikaze in World War II."

"I prefer to look at it differently," Bob objected. "Kamikaze pilots were not even issued parachutes. There is a plan in place to extract our brave soldiers—a parachute, if you will. But there must be no delusions. If these men ever get back to the States, it will be the result of their individual intelligence and resolve. We don't give a shit how closely they follow our directives once they have successfully affected the missile launch. We've provided a road map, and a vehicle to ride in. But we do not regard them as kamikaze pilots—not by any stretch."

"Holy shit!" Roger swore. "This Pappy's bourbon goes down about as smoothly as anything, but it's knocking me loopy. It must be a hundred proof."

"Yeah, I'm sure it's that. At least," Bob agreed. "I'm feeling it too."

Bob took a moment and looked down at his watch.

"I'm gonna give the Bear a call," he said. "You know, old Stormin' Norman. See if he's got any news for us."

Chapter 31 —

The blast spawned a shockwave that not only stunned Jack, it practically dislodged his rebreathing equipment. More significantly, the impulse wave launched a piece of the explosive's casing in his direction. Had it struck him a mere inch more directly, it would undoubtedly have caused a serious, if not totally incapacitating, injury to his person. As it was, the damage that it did do was not minor. It smashed across the face of his Garmin rendering it inoperable, and ripping a sizable gash in his wrist.

As soon as he was able to recover his senses, he glanced over at the wrist computer to check the map, but it was not working.

I just cannot believe all this bullshit, he said to himself. *How the hell do I get back without my map?*

He immediately stopped dead, and considered his position on the basis of his pre-blast memory.

He recalled that the patrol boat was virtually directly above him. *And the GPS map told me that my boat looked to be toward the bow, he was calculating, maybe fourteen degrees starboard.*

He was not as certain as he would like to have been with regard to the mini-sub's position, but he knew that he needed to vacate the vicinity as quickly as he could, because he had no doubt that the blast that nearly killed him was not the result of the incendiary he had just attached to the patrol boat's hull. Rather, he figured it was actually some sort of anti-personnel depth charge. *Someone on that patrol boat had spotted me, estimated my depth, and dropped it down to kill me,* he declared to himself. *Got to get the hell outta here, even if I go in the wrong direction. ... Hopefully I'm headed right, but just need to move quickly.*

If he didn't already have his plate full, his situation got even more complicated.

Back at the mini-sub Agent Two, having detected the explosion of the depth charge, activated the Thermate device for immediate detonation. While Jack was able to detect the flash when the Thermate ignited, he was by that time far enough away so that the primary detonation did not in any way endanger him. But, such was not the case when the secondary explosion occurred.

As it turned out, this patrol boat was carrying enough high explosive materials to sink any ship in the sea. Not only did it have onboard nearly one hundred small anti-personnel depth charges, but it also carried as many Russian-made submarine depth charges as could be jammed into it—both above and below deck.

So, as soon as the Thermate device was able to burn a hole through the hull, which was only about a minute, it was able to bring to bear its four-thousand-degree torch right into a cluster of stored submarine depth charges.

That explosion was enormous.

Fortunately for Jack he had been swimming in the right direction. But not so fortunate for him was that he had not yet reached the team's mini-sub, much less managed to board it.

Because most of the force of the blast was directed above water, only a small percentage of the shockwave was thrust downward. Yet, it still exerted enough force to render Jack's mind and body temporarily inoperative. He did manage to keep his mouthpiece in place, but as for his eye protection, the force of the explosion totally ripped his diving mask from his face and deposited it somewhere on the floor of the Yellow Sea. The loss of that piece of equipment rendered him virtually blind. He was unable to even check his tank to confirm that his rebreather was working properly, or even if the oxygen still flowed.

Many thoughts raced through his mind: *this mission is now officially finished—at least for me. Henry is smart enough to pull the plug on it, and get the hell outta here. He's got to take care of that young couple, and those dedicated SEALs. I've trained him well. And, he needs to get himself back to Sugar Island and take care of my boys. Kate will help, but she's much too busy to do a lot. She'll make sure that they're receiving proper care, but she's got her own demanding career. Damn, I've had a good life. Hell, it's been much more than that. I've had a great life. Couldn't ask for more. Unbelievable kids—Kate, Red, Robby. Only an absolute fool would dare ask for more. And friends. No human being I've ever met had more loyal friends than I do: Henry, Roger and Bob. Closer than brothers, we are. God, am I thankful for all of them. And Beth—a fantastic woman. What she ever saw in me I'll never know. Babe, it looks like I'm gonna be spending the rest of the day with you. Beth, my darling—you were the best woman God ever placed on this earth. Damn, I sure hope you still like me. I've become an old man—more wrinkles, less hair, and a lot less energy. But you still are the love of my life. What a girl you were. And what a crazy mess we were. Thank you, babe, for all those good times.*

Those were Jack's last thoughts while still conscious. He noticed that he was losing his sense of awareness and realized that, this time, there was truly nothing he could do about it. He took a deep but trembling breath, and surrendered blindly to the cold waters of the Yellow Sea.

Chapter 32 —

There Kate stood—her right arm bent at the elbow, and her hand now holding the Glock 10 beside her right cheek.

The object that had gripped her so powerfully when she spotted it through the window was now lying right in front of her—a bright red Bissell Canister vacuum cleaner lying on its side near the closet door—with its hose appearing to have been unceremoniously hacked off at both ends. She spent another few moments scouring the cottage with her eyes for the hose, but determined that most likely it had been removed, and then used in the unsuccessful attempt to kill her.

She had recalled the picture of the hose that Det. Townsend had showed her, and it looked exactly like the short remnant left on the canister. "This is *definitely* where those two worthless slugs were staying," she said to herself aloud. "Can be little doubt about that at this point."

She pulled out her burner phone and called the sheriff's office. "This is Kate Handler," she informed the officer taking calls. "I'd like to leave a message for Detective Townsend. Please inform him that the hose in the picture he sent me was taken from the cottage just upstream from the resort. I'm inside that cottage right now, and there appears to be no one in the unit at this time."

"And what is your name again?" the officer asked.

Kate did not respond. She just disconnected from the call by turning her phone off and slid it into her jacket.

"That tells him all he needs to know," she told herself. "I'm surprised that they didn't figure it out. Chalk that one up to Red and Robby."

She still had not taken another step after having entered through the broken door. Instead she continued to allow her trained eyes to do the walking—at least for the moment.

"Nothing I can see from here to suggest that anyone is currently hanging out in this cottage," she said to herself. "No clothes visible. Dirty dishes on the table. So they may have stayed here for more than a couple of days. But probably not much more, as they didn't take the time to do their dishes, or to shove that vacuum back out of the way. Had they been here for longer than a few days, they'd more than likely have taken the time to at least wash up their dishes. Unless they were just pigs. I'd say the odds are still good that they're gone."

Keeping the Glock raised and ready, she shouted out loudly, "Anyone here? This is the police. Is there anyone in this cottage right now? If so, announce yourself, and come out with hands raised."

She was not comfortable declaring herself to be law enforcement, because she had no authority in Michigan. Nevertheless, she was eager to get this part of the job done, so she was not greatly troubled about her misleading proclamation.

It was a small building. It looked to Kate like there were two bedrooms, and a bathroom. The kitchen and eating area were openly connected to the living room. That meant that someone could still be in either of the bedrooms, or in the bath. She would have to inspect.

"Second entry door totally visible from here," she said to herself. "Probably not going to be more than two entries into a building this small. Ought to check that other door out to see if it's locked. If not, possibly could indicate that there might be someone still in here."

So, she carefully made her way over to the other door. She was relieved to find it locked.

Next she approached the southernmost bedroom. She tried the door handle. It was not locked. Using the wall as a shield, she twisted the door knob and pushed the door inward. Again she announced her presence. When no one answered, she assumed an isosceles stance, which is a double straight-arm firing position, and stepped into the empty bedroom. She could see almost everything from the doorway because there were no closets. Except, she concluded that it would have been possible that someone could be hiding under the bed. So, she walked over, dropped to her knees, and looked beneath it. "Nothing here," she said aloud to herself. "Not even a suitcase. If anyone were here, they would have left something under their bed—they always do. Must be no one around."

Next she inspected the bathroom. It was located between the bedrooms, and was accessible from both, as well as having an entrance from the living room. *This is one huge bathroom for such a tiny cottage,* she was thinking. She checked it out thoroughly, including the bathtub, but again found no one.

The only room remaining was the northern bedroom. At first she was going to enter it from the bathroom, but thought better of it, because that would have offered her no good place to stand when she swung the door open. So, she walked out of the bathroom door leading into the living room.

However, just as she stepped out, she was greeted by a barrage of bullets fired by an unmasked man who had just entered the same door she had broken open.

He was obviously as surprised by her as she was by him, because every one of his shots missed her.

The first round that he fired struck the door frame less than six inches from her head. She leapt forward to the floor immediately, all the while squeezing off four rounds from her Glock.

The attacker managed to spray a total of six slugs into various parts of the cottage. These included two rounds in the living room ceiling, two more in the wall behind Kate, and one somewhere in the cottage. That last round was never found.

None of them, however, struck Kate.

She, on the other hand, did a much better job.

Her first round struck her attacker two inches above the heart. While that 10mm slug would not have been immediately fatal, it served nicely to knock the man off balance. Two of her next three struck him in the lower abdomen, and the fourth caught him in the left eye. With her last shot, the man was dead before his face found the floor.

Kate watched all four of her rounds find the target. And she saw her attacker go down—it was like slow motion from her perspective. "The first was a great shot," she later told herself. "The other three the result of instinct and pure luck."

So, even though she knew she had dispatched him, she was also aware that there had been two perps, at the very least. That meant that there was at least one more thug still out there who obviously would like to see her dead.

She was flat on her belly, and there she intended to stay until she felt comfortable to change positions.

At least two minutes passed, and Kate remained glued to the floor, with the Glock pointed at the door. "Can't stay here all night," she finally said to herself. "I don't know where that other piece of shit is, but I've got to finish what I started."

To her right was a large recliner, and there was nothing between her and that chair. So, keeping the Glock fixed on the door, she rolled over twice and then rose to her knees behind the massive recliner.

Finally, she stood and retrieved her phone from her pocket. But, just as she entered her password, a second gunman bolted through the door, pointed his semi-automatic in her direction and prepared to shoot. However, as fate would have it, he had inadvertently left the safety on, and so was unable to get his first shot off. Kate, who had holstered her weapon in order to call the sheriff's office, was a trifle slow in getting off her first round.

Fortunately for her, Red and Robby had heard the earlier gunshots, and figured it out that Kate had run into a little trouble. The two of them, with Buddy leading the way, had burst out of the camper and had headed toward the cottage.

Naturally, Buddy won the foot race handily. He bolted, teeth-first, into the gunman's backside like a bat outta hell. The force of his strike knocked the man down squarely on top of the first shooter, and his QSZ-92 flew all the way into the bathroom—with the safety still engaged.

Buddy was not satisfied with his initial score. He began to bark and growl, and moved his attack to the back of the gunman's neck. Just then Red burst through the open door to check on Kate. Robby was right behind him.

"You okay?" Robby passionately inquired.

"Yeah," Kate said. "Thanks to your friend Buddy. I thought I loved him before, but from now on, he's gonna be my special pal— my personal *buddy.*"

Meanwhile, with Buddy still attacking ferociously, the second man-in-black cried out in pain and fear.

"I'm just fine," she said. "Couldn't be better. I think we've got both of these jerks now. But, I don't have cuffs—I'm on vacation, you know."

The man remained screaming in great pain and fear as Buddy wrenched and tore at his neck muscles.

"Should I call Buddy off?" Robby asked.

"No," Kate answered as she walked over to kick the first man's handgun further out of reach. "Not yet. If he tries to get up, I'll have to shoot him. And I've got some questions I'd like to ask him first. Give me a minute and I'll find something to tie his hands with."

After using a bath towel to pick up her last attacker's pistol, she looked around for a piece of rope. Finally she said, laughing through a big smile, "This is perfect. I'll cut the cord off of the vacuum cleaner. That ought to work just fine."

So, that's what Kate did. She walked over to the kitchen drawers and found a sharp, serrated paring knife, cut the cord off at the canister, and securely tied the man's hands behind him. Then, as he still lay on the body of his friend, she called Buddy off, grabbed the man by the collar of his jacket and slid him off to the floor, turned him flat onto his belly, drew his feet up behind him, and tied the cord around them as well.

"Glad that rope was long enough to do the job," she said in a very satisfied tone, "otherwise we wouldn't have been able to call Buddy off before he chewed all the way through this guy's neck."

She did not know how well Buddy's downed man could understand English, but Kate had watched his reaction to her words, and it was clear to her that he at least got the gist of what she had been saying. "While he might not have understood all of my words," she said to herself, "I'm quite certain that he could have got some of them, and correctly read the tenor of my tone."

"Okay, Buddy," Kate said. "Good boy. Back off, now."

Robby recognized that Kate was wanting Buddy to let up on his victim, so he told Buddy the same thing, but in different words: "Good job, Buddy. Come here." And then Red slapped his thigh, which was the signal Buddy best understood.

Buddy obeyed and backed off, but still stood guard over the badly bleeding body of the second "man-in-black" to fall that day while trying to kill Kate.

•

Chapter 33 —

"Holy shit!" Roger blurted out. "Bob, did you see that?" Three seconds later, he yelled again, "And did you see that?! … I don't believe it! What the hell's goin' on over there?"

Out of the corner of his eye Roger had been monitoring satellite imaging which was being transmitted live from US orbiters positioned directly over the area of the mission in North Korea. "I assume that first flash was the rocket launch that we've been waiting on. But that second one—I have no idea what that could have been. All I can say is that it was huge. Nuclear, or non-nuclear—can't tell. But it was colossal."

Bob had stood momentarily to stretch out his stiffening leg muscles, and at the same time he was pouring the two of them another round of Pappy's Kentucky Straight. By that time Bob recognized that they had both drunk way too much bourbon, so he filled the glasses only one-quarter full. About an hour earlier Roger had begun diluting his drink by mixing a little water with it, because he knew that he must remain at least somewhat in control of his faculties. He was, after all, still technically leading the Secret Service team charged with protecting Bob's estranged wife,

Former First Lady Allison Fulbright.

"What the living hell!" Bob let out. "That was our missile, alright—the first flash. But that other shit. I don't have any idea what caused that. What would you say? It would look to be a hundred miles or so south and west of the launch site. That sound about right? Where was that in relation to the 38th? Maybe just south of it? Or maybe a little north. Could that be? That's how it would look to me. Could that have somehow been our guys? H-o-l-y s-h-i-t!

"Can't tell from that angle. Let me see if I can toss that over to a different satellite. And maybe zoom in a bit."

Bob did his best to rein in the monitor and controller to improve the image they were wanting to look at more closely, but his hands were not speedily implementing the signals his brain was trying to send.

"Too damn much expensive booze," Roger said, laughing. "Here, let me have a go at it. I'm not doing much better, I'm sure, but I do screw around with video shit a bit more than you, I'm sure."

After only about fifty seconds Roger had tuned into the right satellite and enlarged the image.

"Where the hell did it go?" Bob queried. "All I'm seeing is a few little pieces of debris. Nothing bigger than a threaded life jacket, or an empty can of some sort of flammable shit."

"What the hell was that all about?" Roger asked.

"I don't have any idea," Bob observed. "At least about what it is, or was. But there is one thing I can tell you. And you can take this to the bank. The explosion that we just witnessed—the one right after the launch, I'd be willing to bet that it was Jack who lit the damn fuse on it. That much you can be pretty sure about."

By the time he'd let those words pass between his lips he was on his way across the room to make a call on the secure phone.

"Who you callin'?" Roger asked.

"Norm," Bob replied, not looking at his friend. "Gotta see what the Bear makes of it. See if he's had a better look at it than we did. I doubt that he did, though, because that was pretty much out in the middle of nowhere. No reason to be monitoring that area, I should think. Whatever it was. But, that's just my take on it. We'll see what—"

Just then Bob's call went through and interrupted him.

"Norm. Bob here. You watchin' what we're watchin'? Besides that missile launch, I mean. I assume that you saw the explosion just south of there—south of the launch. Any idea what that was all about? Just a second. I got Roger here with me. I'd like to put you on speaker. That okay?"

Schwarzkopf responded in the affirmative, and Bob triggered the speaker.

"There," Bob said. "I got you on speaker. Would you please repeat what you just told me?"

"Roger," Schwarzkopf said, "nice to be talking with you. Hope you're not offended that I don't introduce myself further. I'm sure that Bob explained all the secrecy. You are okay with that. Right?"

"We're fine from my end, Mr. Schwarzkopf," Roger said. "We just want to find out what you think is going on."

"Good. Good," the new 'Stormin' Norman' said. "Well, I have to admit, we were watching the launch, just as I presume you boys were, and then all of a sudden, something blows up just south and west of the launch. We did go back after the fact and zeroed in on those coordinates, and it appears like some sort of what must have been a North Korean patrol boat just blew up. Granted, it was almost too large to be considered a patrol boat, but I have to think that it still would fit into that class, largely because that appears to have been its assignment. It was probably patrolling for submarines, and that's apparently what they had onboard—a whole shitload of anti-sub charges of one sort or another."

Bob started laughing.

Norman heard the laughter and interrupted himself. "Did I say something funny?" he asked, sounding a little put-off.

"Sorry, Norm," Bob said. "It wasn't what you said that made me chuckle. It's what I know it means."

"And, what would that be, Bob?"

"I don't think you've ever met him," Bob said, still with a huge grin, but no longer articulating the humor. "About the only thing I know for certain is that this explosion involved one of my other good friends—Jack Handler."

"The name's familiar," Norm said after a short pause. "But, you're right—I don't think I've ever met him personally. What makes you think he was involved?"

"I really can't talk about it," Bob said. "Not at this time. Maybe later. But Handler was taking care of some things for me over in that area. And, it just seems that wherever he goes, something big happens. We'll talk more later. But, for right now, I suggest that you keep your eye on that North Korean missile. See where it goes. It might prove interesting. Just saying, we should all watch that missile carefully."

"Hell," the General said, "You know that is all that's on our mind right now. We've got two carriers just south of the launch, and half the rest of our Pacific fleet in the area as well. This is pretty significant shit that's goin' down right now. We are on high alert across the board. Need I say more?"

"What the hell!" Roger said as he stood to his feet. "Bob! You never mentioned that the damn missile was going to reverse course! Tell me if I'm wrong, but doesn't it look to you like it's now headed for the Chinese mainland? You didn't tell me that was going to happen. Damn crazy, if you ask me. And isn't that thing loaded with—"

"Shut the hell up!" Bob blurted out. At the same time he hung up the phone.

Bob then slid over and stood beside Roger. They both just stood watching in disbelief as the missile continued to head to the northwest, which was directly toward China.

"What are we watching here?" Roger asked. "Is this what I think it is?"

"It sure as hell looks like it to me," Bob geeked out. "And, yes, that missile is fully armed. Holy shit! This could be the start of World War III. Do not share with anyone, except me, what you know about this. This could get us both a firing squad. And that goes for Norm, too. Do not talk to him, or anyone—not about this. This is just terrible! What the hell did that man do?"

"I thought you told me that Jack was going to arm the missile," Roger said, "and then reprogram it to drop a couple small US nukes harmlessly out in the Pacific—north and east of the launch. You said that was why the Navy was pulling everything that floats out of that specific area. What is it here that I'm missing? Isn't that how you explained it?"

"Roger," Bob said. "That was exactly what my directives were as far as Jack was concerned. That was how we set it up. I, we, there were several of us who planned this out—Norm was one of them. That's how I explained it to Jack, too. How the hell is this happening? I haven't a clue. That's all I can say. I don't know what's goin' on!"

Bob then grabbed the nearly-empty Pappy's bottle and threw it at the TV monitor. It missed the screen altogether, smashing harmlessly against the wall without breaking. It did, however, shatter into a hundred pieces when it hit the marble floor.

"That sonofabitch," Bob growled. "How the hell did he figure out how to change the targets? We never went over that. He was merely supposed to enter the program my guys had already set up for him in the programmer. It was preset to drop the minimum load at two nondescript locations in the Pacific. That's it. Period. Damn that sonofabitch! Damn him to hell!"

"If the new targeting involves China," Roger asked, "what's gonna happen when the Chinese technicians determine that the nukes were from the US? Will they reciprocate? And if so, how? What would they do? Don't we need to prepare? Looks to me like that missile continues to head deeper onto the Chinese mainland. This could get very nasty."

Just then the phone rang. For several seconds the two men stared into one another's eyes. Bob finally answered it. It was Norman Schwarzkopf. Bob listened for nearly one straight minute. This time it was not on speaker-phone, and he made sure that Roger had picked up on his gesture to him to shut up.

Finally, Bob said, "Yes, General. I know we've got a big problem. I am completely aware that this is not what I discussed with you and the other generals. And it's not how I left it with my guys on the ground. This was not supposed to happen. This could all—"

"Oh hell!" Norman barked. "That missile has just released its package. At least one of them. And it looks like it knows where it wants to go. And it sure as hell ain't out in the Pacific!"

"Have the Chinese tried to intercept?" Bob asked.

"They haven't done a damn thing to stop it," Norman said. "Not one damn thing, as far as I can determine. The package looks to be headed directly for … Oh shit! I could be wrong, but it appears to be headed for Wuhan. That's where that bio-chemical lab is located. Right? The one that developed and tested that Covid-19 virus. Is there anything else there? Anything else that is of importance? Who the hell is behind this? Did you have anything at all to do with this, Bob? And who the hell is this guy—the one you sent over there? Did he do this? Because this is no accident. It's not some kinda mistake, either. This is all intentional. Has to be. Someone's going to go down for all this shit. And I do not want it to be me. So you'd better start explaining!"

Bob was not used to being talked to like that.

"Back off and shut up!" Bob told him. "You'll not be addressing me in those tones."

"Hang on," Norman said, this time in a more respectful voice. "The second payload has been released as well. We hadn't seen it at first. It looks to be circling around toward the big dam—the Three Gorges Dam. … Holy shit! The first one did hit in Wuhan! It looks to be devastating. Incredibly devastating. Wherever it might have struck in Wuhan, it had to have done a whole lot of damage. I'm looking at 30.53629, and 114.35077—give or take. That looks to be in the center of that damn Wuhan campus—the heart of the lab.

"And now, now the second warhead has struck. Unreal! Holy shit! It looks like it has taken out the big dam—the whole damn thing! It struck right at that Three Gorges Dam. Right in the middle of that dam, I think. That huge, new dam. Trillion dollar project, give or take. Unbelievable! These are the numbers—30.82350, 111.00373. And that is dead on—right in the center!

"And, Bob, I apologize for the attitude. But, this whole thing has caught me by surprise—unbelievable surprise."

"I totally get it," Bob said. "This is certainly not what we were anticipating either."

Bob expected the General to immediately jump down his throat again. But, when that did not instantly take place, he thought he should take this opportunity to reiterate what his intentions had been for the mission.

"These payloads," he said, "they were supposed to be the minimum, and we intended them to strike harmlessly out in the Pacific—not on the Chinese mainland. General, you know that's what we were planning—you were there. Intelligence had told us that the test shots were intended by the Chinese Communist Party to demonstrate that North Korea possessed long-range missile technology capable of striking at least two targets located several hundred miles apart. That's what the Chinese military thought they were testing. And both of their presumed targets were located out in the Pacific. Plus, they were shooting blanks—dummy warheads.

"They'd warned the whole area as what to expect. And the eyes of all the world were on them. While this missile originally was not to carry any nuclear payload, or any real payload at all, for that matter, our defense department had the job of treating it like it was a genuine threat. That was the whole point of it in the first place. All the Chinese were interested in was to track and record exactly how the US would defend against it, had it been a real threat. It was nothing more than a training mission for them."

"Well, that's not the case anymore, is it?" the General said.

Again, Bob was not pleased with the General's tone. But, this time, he let it pass.

"We created some serious casualties on the ground with all this bullshit," Roger commented, wishing to take some of the pressure off of his friend. "Any idea as to the explosive power of those bombs? As I understand it, they were programmable to go up to a hundred and fifty megatons. I imagine that if Jack managed to change the programming with regard to target, he probably figured out how to change the programing as to the strength of the payload as well. So, can we determine yet just how powerful those blasts were?"

"Well, I can't give you specifics," the General said. "While I can't state unequivocally what is the precise power of either of the explosions, I am quite certain that the destructive power of the one used to take out the dam was at least equal to, and possibly far greater than, first one—the one that knocked the hell out of the lab where the Covid-19 was developed. In fact, it looks to me like all your guy intended to accomplish there, at the lab, was to put the university lab out of business. Forever!

"But, in the case of the one that took out the huge dam, I can't help but think that he set that one for maximum devastation. It looked to me like it could have been programmed as high as one hundred fifty megatons. My guess is that's where he set it—at the max. The damage done to that dam was significant. Beyond devastating. I would estimate that Jack cranked that one all the way up.

"And, how about distance from the ground?" the General continued. "This one, the one that took out the Three Gorges Dam, it looks to have been triggered virtually on impact—apparently a total surface blast. While the first one, the bomb that blew up Wuhan, it was an air blast. I think it was likely detonated at a thousand feet—maybe more. Apparently your guy figured out how to program that part as well.

"In the case of the dam, it's apparent that he wanted to destroy the foundation of that dam—to take out the bedrock beneath it. And to create the maximum amount of nuclear fallout. And that's what a powerful surface blast will accomplish. Because of the nature of that bomb, the Three Gorges Dam will never be reconstructed—not at that location. It simply could not be rebuilt, I should think. And not just for the foreseeable future. There can never be another dam built on that site. Period. It wouldn't matter if you waited a thousand years—it could never be replicated. There'd be no solid foundation to build it on!

"What the hell did he have in mind with that? Whatever possessed him? Do you have any idea?"

Bob knew he'd do well to weigh his words, so he thought for a few moments as to how he should address the General's questions.

"All I can tell you is this," Bob finally said. "Jack is a unique person. He has a way of completing a mission like this, or any project, for that matter, by providing an outcome greater than what was anticipated. He's always done a fine job for me—in that, and every other respect. But, I'd have to say that over the past few years he has taken his performance to a new level. It's as though the real Jack has been unleashed. Roger and I have discussed this over the last year, and we've concluded that his newfound vigor seems to be somehow related to his new life in Michigan's Upper Peninsula."

Bob was concerned that he might be opening up a bit too much to the General, but he was also looking for any way to deflect some of "Schwarzkopf's" animus, and he sensed that this angle just might serve that purpose—deflection with a hint of confusion.

"Roger says that the people up there, in Michigan's UP, just seem to have a unique way about them. He describes it like this. He says that up there, in the UP, there's a thing called 'Problem Solving UP Style.' And that it's simply viewed as smart, decisive, and resolute. Roger believes that in Jack's mind, what he accomplished in China actually might just solve the Chinese and the North Korean problems for more than a month, or even a year. I'm not exactly sure what Roger is getting at, nor am I totally convinced that he's correctly sized up the UP influence, but I have a hunch that he just might be onto something."

All three of them took a moment to reflect on Bob's words. This was particularly the case with the General.

A lot of people do not know what the Three Gorges Dam is, that it was quite recently completed—2006 or 2008, depending on who you ask. In a certain respect, it represents the largest dam of its type in the world. In megawatt capacity, for instance, it is capable of producing over 22K megawatts, while the world's second largest hydroelectric dam is just about one-half as productive.

Another interesting aspect about the Three Gorges Dam is its location. The dam was built on the famous Yangtze River, in the Hubei province, just one hundred miles upstream from Wuhan, the home of the now-infamous Wuhan Institute of Virology. After passing through the Wuhan province the Yangtze flows eastward toward Shanghai, the largest city in China. From Shanghai it empties into the East China Sea in the neighborhood of Japan and

South Korea.

Since completion, the dam has been blamed for numerous ecological problems throughout the whole of China, both above and below the construction. Neighboring countries have also reported suffering significant ecological changes brought about by the dam.

In China, nearby provinces have not only reported numerous landslides and devastating floods directly caused by the very weight of the waters backed up by the dam, but of late the existence of all that additional pressure has even brought about hundreds of tremors. The depth of the lake formed by the dam is extraordinarily great—in some places it measures over five hundred feet in depth.

Furthermore, because the Three Gorges Dam is built directly over two major fault lines, scientists fear that eventually the very existence of that huge construction, and the enormous weight of the waters behind it, will result in a single giant earthquake that will not only take out the dam itself, but its sudden removal will result in a catastrophic flood which will inundate major downstream Chinese municipal centers such as Wuhan and Shanghai.

"I'm not lookin' to insult you two gentlemen, or anything like that, but I wonder if you men are totally aware of just what sort of havoc this shit-ass North Korean missile threatens to wreak on Communist China. I respect both of you immensely, so don't be slighted if I toss a couple thoughts your way. Deal?"

Roger was not sure just how he ought to respond, so Bob stepped in.

"Go for it, Norm," Bob said. "We both want to hear what you have to say."

"Okay, then," Stormin' Norman said. "Whoever came up with this idea is a military genius. Might create some temporary political problems for ones holding offices right now; but from a military standpoint, it was flat out brilliant.

"So, Bob, if it was you, then that's just you being Bob Fulbright again. Here's what has just happened— from a geopolitical/military standpoint. China has just been ruined. Simple as that. Devastated might be a better word to describe it. They are not just a wounded serpent—they are literally destroyed. All that shit about the enormous cost they shoved down our throats—you know, with that Covid attack. That's what it was. It was an attack. One of those so-called 'non-warfare' military actions. They call it part of their Unrestricted Warfare strategy. They've even written books about it. In fact, that's the official title of the best of those books— Unrestricted Warfare. They think they are so damn smart. Well, it looks like it's coming back to bite them in their haughty asses."

While neither of them commented aloud about this, Bob and Roger exchanged a long glance they each interpreted as the other saying something like, "I do believe the General has been hitting the bar too." Roger even feigned downing a shot, and Bob nodded in a smile of agreement.

"Anyway, Bob, that's enough of my ranting," the Bear added. "If you don't know what I'm talking about, just buy the book. It's all there in black and white. And, it's in their own damn words! Just—"

"Hell," Bob, seeing that Stormin' Norman was lightening up a bit, interrupted, "Norm, I didn't know you even liked to read."

"Go to hell, you asshole," the General threw back at his friend, "You got no idea just how much guys like me go through just to keep you priggish bastards safe under your fluffy blankets. I'm damn proud to be a jarhead. And, as you sure as hell know, I do read!"

With that comment, Bob thought for sure that he had dulled the axe Stormin' Norman initially seemed to have been sharpening. However, he quickly learned differently.

"Now," the General continued, "When I'm done here, you'll have to think long and hard about just how you decide to go about publicizing what you've just orchestrated. And, if and when this whole episode becomes attributed to you, you'll be in deep shit. No matter what the final outcome turns out to be, the history books are going to look for someone, or something, to attach it all to—whether it's good or bad. And, in my mind, if you're not very careful, it will be your face that always pops up when reminded of this."

And then he paused for a long moment as though carefully choosing his next words.

"In my opinion," the General finally continued, "you and anyone you might know, ought to carve out for themselves that portion of memory history that includes any of this shit. And then destroy it. Because, if it ever—and I do mean ever—if it ever becomes personally associated with you, in the mind of the CCP, and they get their bloody mitts on you, you're dead! Forget about prison. You'd never see the inside of a prison. You will be interrogated as only a member of the CCP interrogates. And then, once they've got what they want, you'll be dead. Not only you. Members of your family. Close friends.

"Now, you'd damn well better take me serious on this. I'm very familiar with CCP tactics. ... I will repeat what I just said, in case you didn't hear me. If they ever associate you with what just went down, you will regret the day you were born. If you think having Novichok on your door handle might be bad, you've no notion the pain and suffering that actually awaits you.

"And your buddy there with you, Roger, he would do very well to disappear from sight. You too, Bob. And you damn well better never connect me with this. Never! It would mean more than just the end of my career, it would be the end of my life. Same damn thing, in my book. Hell, if I ever get the notion up my ass that either of you might spill the beans, and name me, I'll do you myself. Now, I'm not shittin' you. Tell me right now if you understand what I'm saying. I want to hear it come from each of your mouths. Do you get what I'm telling you?!"

"Yes," Bob said.

"How about you, Roger. Do you understand what I'm sayin'?"

"I do, General. At least I think I do."

"Not good enough! You damn well better know what it's all about!"

The General took a moment to gather his thoughts, and then continued, "Okay, then. If you do not totally understand what has transpired in the last hour, let me explain. Even if you know, listen to me and just shut up."

Bob, as a former President of the United States, was not used to being ordered around, nor had he been so talked down to since he was caught cheating on a history test in high school. However, he made and held eye contact with Roger, and then took a seat and kept his mouth shut.

"This is what we have just witnessed," the General said, "And I will tell you what it means. What it means to you and me. What it means to the Chinese—to the CCP, actually. And what it means on the entire geo-political stage.

"I think I've already laid out how significant it is for us front line grunts to keep totally silent about it. So, I'm not going to belabor that again.

"But, if you can appreciate just what this means to us, and to our families, just think about what this will mean for the Chinese leadership. This, my friends, could bring about a civil war in China. Hell, I'd say odds are it will do just that. Civil war.

"Now, boys, I do not know how familiar you are with the story behind this project, so I will summarize for you the history of the Three Gorges Dam. If this is old news to you, humor me. This project dates all the way back to the time of World War I—1918. That's when President Sun Yat-sen first got the idea.

"Nothing much happened at that time because there was no money to tackle it. And, actually no one believed it could be done. In 1944, Chiang Kai-shek invited US experts to review the possible project. Still, nothing came of it. But, starting in 1949, Chairman Mao began pushing the construction forward. However, it again produced nothing substantial.

"It was not until 1986 that a committee consisting of over 400 experts produced a comprehensive report on the feasibility of building the dam. In 1987, a group of appointed political leaders declared the project was not feasible. But they did not give up. In 1992, the Chinese parliament narrowly approved the project, and ground was broken in 1997.

"So, you can see that this dam did not just happen in a vacuum, or without objection. It was, after all, the single largest construction project in China since the building of the Great Wall of

China.

"And, here we are today. You boys, me, and a few of my old military friends. What we have just witnessed here is the destruction of the Second Great Wall of China. And, with this national catastrophe, we are not just talking about the total annihilation of a great monument, we are watching the obliteration of the principal power source for most of Chinese manufacturing, the flooding of the entire Yangtze River bed, and the destruction of China's largest city.

"I cannot really say how many will die as a result from what has just taken place. But, I am sure it will be in the millions—certainly more than the three million they killed with their Covid pandemic. In this case some will die as a direct result of the flood, others indirectly from disease, starvation, and radiation. Horrible things like that.

"You can be sure that the Chinese leadership will change. And it will likely be gradual and unceremonious. You can also be pretty sure of that, in my opinion.

"And, Bob, you haughty sonofabitch, I guess you can see now that this old stupid general has read a few books. Right? Can you see that now? Don't answer me. Just listen.

"The first thing that the Chinese are going to look for, after the dust and smoke settles down a bit, maybe even before, but, likely sooner than later, they're going to look for someone to blame. They have to find a fall guy—most likely quite soon. Otherwise they're considered weak, and they can't stand for that. They will want justice to be swiftly meted out. Now, I don't pretend to be some kind of scientific genius. So, correct me if I'm wrong. But, I do understand that nuclear materials are as distinctive as fingerprints. And that by testing after the fact, technicians will be able to tell where a bomb was built. Is that not true?"

Bob did not want to interject himself into the discussion, but at this point he felt constrained to do just that.

"We anticipated something like this years ago," Bob replied, "even before my presidency. And what I'm about to tell you is highly classified—it's even above your pay grade, General. So, I will not get into great detail. Suffice it to say, those before me worked with Big Tech to set up a significant facility to manufacture certain pieces of ordinance—all off the record. And that was one of the considerations we, they, took into account here. Not only did the pieces made reflect the latest scientific advancements, but they are untraceable. That's where we procured materials for this mission. We knew that even given that the devices were supposed to have been detonated at innocuous locations in the Pacific, we also knew there would be enormous scrutiny surrounding this whole project. So, that's what we did. We obtained the devices and the nuclear materials from this secret depot—bottom line, nothing can be traced back to us. Simple as that. We're safe there. Absolutely safe. At least in this regard."

"That's damned good to know," the General said. "Then, who are they most likely to blame? If we keep our mouths zipped, in your opinion, who will they think did it?"

Bob carefully considered his answer, and then he said, "I would be lying to you if I told you that they will never tie it to us—the United States. That has to be their first thought. But, the big question is, can they prove it? In fact, will they have any evidence whatsoever that will point to the US? If so, I don't know what it would be. Now, we're talking about real evidence.

"Because, if they are to strike out, militarily, they are going to have to present something substantial. And I'm pretty damned sure that we've not given them anything they could use."

"Except for your buddy—Jack and his crew," the General followed. "And I'd bet that they are using a US mini-sub right now as we speak. Right?"

"Right," Bob replied.

"How do you intend to deal with that vessel when this is done?" the General asked. "That is, if they don't get their asses captured or scorched first—or just blown out of the water."

"After the mission was over," Bob answered, "the plan did not include the disposal of the mini-sub. So I can't give you an answer about that."

"We can't just dispose of that boat," the General replied. "It's on the official registry. We can't just draw a line through something that we wish to make go away. Doesn't work that way. We're going to have to quietly move it to the other side, and bring it out for regular maintenance. We'll adjust the manifest to show that the SEALs were using it for training in the Atlantic. Whatever they're up to is secret anyway. That should work. They might build up a case against India. They hate them almost as much as they hate us.

"Guess we can't worry about all that hypothetical shit. Our biggest job is to do everything possible to deflect blame from us— both as individuals, and as agents of the US Government."

"We agree," Bob replied. At that point, he was satisfied with the General's assertion that the actions they had taken "could work." Bob never dreamed that he would be so engaged with an active-duty military general, or that such a conversation would be as emotionally packed. Bob saw this as his opportunity to move on, and get sobered up. He immediately walked over to the refrigerator, grabbed two bottled waters, and handed one to Roger.

Roger got the message.

"So," Bob quickly added, "Roger and I will wait to hear from our guys in the field. Pleasure talking with you, General. Appreciate all your good advice, and help."

"Yeah," the General said. "It could be worse, I suppose. And, perhaps it will be. But, right now, it looks like you've got a lot of it covered. Would be nice to pull your buddy out of that damn Yellow Sea. It's too small a body of water to hide in for very long. We'll be watching, too. By the way, what in hell ever possessed that sonofabitch to take out those two Chinese landmarks? Had you ever talked about it with him before? Where'd he get that idea?"

"That's just the way Jack Handler works," Bob replied. "He doesn't always stick to the book. He's his own man. I hope you someday get a chance to meet him."

"Hell no!" the General barked. "You can just keep him as far away from me as possible. I don't ever want to run into that bastard. Not for the rest of my life. He is one dangerous piece of shit, and I can assure you that I intend to do everything I can to avoid him. I just want to get to the other side of this mess as fast as I possibly can—if there even is another side to it. I think I need to retire ASAP. And don't expect me to ever cover up your mistakes again."

Bob was at a loss for words. He felt that the General was mischaracterizing his role in the mission, but he recognized the fact that there was nothing he could say to change the man's mind, especially given that the old man was drunker than he and Roger were.

And then, just as Bob opened his mouth to sign off, the General spoke out again: "That Jack Handler fellow is either a genius, or the most stupid man I've ever had to deal with. It's like he's been cursed with some kind of unique audacity. Perhaps it's ruthlessness. Having never met him, all I can say for sure is this, your Jack Handler guy must have a set of cojones the size of harvest-ready pumpkins. If I stop and think about it, it's quite possible that his actions today just might have prevented a military clash between the world's superpowers. At the least, I think it will likely put it off—perhaps indefinitely."

With that, the General paused to think. And then he said, again through a perceivable whiskey-generated grin, "In a very real sense, I suppose that this Jack fellow carried out a little bit of his own style of Unrestricted Warfare. You boys need to buy that book and read it."

For several seconds none of the men spoke a word. Finally, the General said, "Anyway, Bob, I wish you well. And you, Roger, the same. And you can tell your buddy Jack, if he manages to emerge alive from this whole disaster, that I hope I never get the opportunity to meet him. We'll all be better off if he disappears, at least as far as I'm concerned. And you should tell him that. Don't mince words. I don't ever want to hear about him again. Period."

Bob was finished with this conversation. Neither he nor Roger desired it to continue. So, Bob simply thanked the General again for his help, and signed off.

Then he and Roger sat back in their chairs, and took a few deep breaths. After only a long minute, Bob checked the bottle on the table and found it empty. So, he stood up, walked over to the bar, and found a fresh bottle of Pappy. He unscrewed the cork out of it on his way back to the table, and poured them another glass.

When he'd given each of them a healthy pour, he took the bottle over to the sink and dumped the remainder of it down the drain—a pour that symbolically ended their night.

The two men just sat silently for the next twenty-plus minutes, slowly tipping their drinks.

"Ready to call it a night?" Bob asked as he slid out and prepared to stagger to his feet.

Roger did not verbally respond immediately. Instead, he tipped the empty bottle upside down and balanced it. He looked up at Bob and smiled. He then pushed his chair back with his legs and stood up. He shook his head and said, "That one hundred proof shit sure goes down nicely. Remind me again, how much do you pay for a bottle?"

Bob firmly kicked the leg of the table, toppling the empty bottle. "Roger," he said. "I don't think you really want to know the answer to that question. Actually, my friend, I think I did tell you already. It's just that you've had too much of it to drink."

Chapter 34 —

Kate looked around the kitchen searching for something like a Ziploc bag. She didn't find one out in the open, so she opted for a couple plastic grocery bags which were lying on the table.

"These will do just fine I'm sure," she said.

She grabbed the bags and took a step toward the first man's handgun. But she then had a thought. Stopping in her tracks, she mumbled, "I wonder ..."

She plunged her right hand into her front jean pocket, but did not find what she was looking for.

Kate then felt the outside of her right rear pocket, and smiled. She reached into that pocket and pulled out the latex gloves she had worn earlier. After slipping them on, she reached down and picked up the shooter's QSZ-92. "I'm not familiar with these at all," she mumbled after spending a moment examining the man's pistol.

So, keeping her finger off the trigger, Kate looked around until she found the lever that released the magazine. She removed it and placed it in one of the plastic bags. She then slid the action open and ejected the round in the chamber. This effectively rendered the pistol harmless.

Kate slipped the firearm into the grocery bag, along with the magazine and the unfired cartridge. Then, using a permanent marker she'd found on the cupboard, labeled the bag: "Shooter One."

She then scoured the floor for as many of the spent cartridges as she could readily locate. She found only two. She also dropped them into the grocery bag.

From there, she went into the bathroom and retrieved the other pistol. She disarmed it as well, and put it in the other bag, labeling it: "Shooter Two."

All the while the two boys just stood inside the door watching her. Buddy, of course, stood guard over the fallen fighter.

While she would have liked to have the use of some good packing tape, she found none. So, she satisfied herself by rolling each of the bags up and securing them with some rubber bands that she found in an evolving junk drawer directly beneath where she'd discovered the marker.

"Are you gonna call the sheriff now?" Robby asked. "Uncle Jack did not want us to use our cell phones. But, you're the police, I'm sure he'd want you to use yours for that."

"Good thinking, Robby," she said. "It's okay to use this burner cell, anyway. It's not my regular phone, so no one would know that it was me using it. I will call Detective Townsend, but not right yet. I still haven't checked out that second bedroom. Once I do that, I'll begin reeling this whole thing in. You boys just hang in here for another minute or two. I'll be right back."

With that, Kate checked on the living gunman one more time, and said, "Move a muscle, and I'll have my dog snap your sorry neck. Do you understand me?"

The man did not react, so she said, "Look, you stupid sonofabitch, I know damn well you can understand what I say to you. So don't act like you can't. I asked you if you understood me. Either tell me you do, or nod your sorry head. Now do it!"

With that, he nodded, and with a substantial Chinese accent said, "I understand."

It was obviously difficult for the man to talk, because Buddy had ripped a small hole in his left cheek, and blood was running both into his mouth and directly onto the floor.

"That's better," Kate said. "Now, if you don't want Buddy to have you for his evening snack, do not move another muscle."

The man did not acknowledge her verbally, but he didn't move, either.

Kate did check one more time to be certain that his hands and feet were secure, and then she headed for the second bedroom.

Again she had the Glock positioned in her right hand beside her cheek.

The second Kate's eyes focused in the darkened bedroom, she let out an angry groan, and then muttered, "Oh hell no! Not this!"

There on the bed she found a fiftyish woman, hands and feet tied in much the same fashion as she had secured the second gunman's. But the woman on the bed was gagged, and had her throat slit.

Even though Kate knew the woman was dead, protocol dictated she check for a pulse. Of course, she found none. She returned to the kitchen and prepared to call Det. Townsend.

The two boys had heard her reaction to what she had seen, but they knew better than to seek explanation. Instead, they locked their eyes into one another's and exchanged an extended period of probing as to what might have prompted Kate's ominous reaction.

Their silent conclusion was to take a seat at the small dinner table, and to wait until Kate either volunteered an explanation, sought their aid, or simply opted to keep it her business. Whatever it was.

The two boys soon concluded that whatever it was that had so captivated her attention, she was not about to seek their advice on how to deal with it. Instead, she totally ignored them as she removed her burner cell from her pocket and just stared at it. The boys remained seated at the table and silently monitored Buddy as he stood guard over Kate's fallen foe.

"Who would she be calling, if not Detective Townsend?" Red asked himself. Both boys managed to maintain their silence, but they did listen intently, Red especially. He tuned his ears and eyes solely to what was going on between Kate and her cell phone.

At first she did prepare to call Det. Townsend to alert him regarding the latest development, but she halted before hitting the call button. Instead, with one dead and one injured, and with significant questions owning her entire thought process, Kate had decided the time had come to touch base with Roger.

He was surprised to hear from her. She started right off by asking him if he knew what firearms Jack had and kept at the Sugar Island Resort. But, she found his answer disappointing. Roger told her that he didn't know for certain. "Jack is always changing things up," he told her. "And he doesn't consult with me about that."

She then told him that the main house at the resort had been broken into, and that there appeared to have been at least one long firearm rifle missing. "A sniper rifle, I believe," she said. Roger suggested that odds were good that if a long weapon were to be stolen, it would likely be a sniper rifle.

"I do know that Jack has, or at least had, two rifles that fit that description," he said. "Perhaps he has others that I haven't seen, but I do know that he had kept two at his house there on the island. Not long ago, in fact. He showed me his Barrett M82, which is a Swedish big boy, a 50 caliber. And, I know he's also got a SAKO TRG 42. I think the SAKO is a Winchester .300 Magnum. But, they are both bona fide sniper weapons. The SAKO is a particularly fine one from Finland."

"I found only one sniper weapon in the case," she said. "And that one was a 50 cal. So, that would suggest to me, that the Finish 300 rifle is missing. What do you think? It is a demonstrable fact that there was a break-in, and that the arms vault was violated during that break-in. I've got it on video. I'd say that, until we learn differently, we have to assume that there is a .300 on the street. And that it's one that was locked up until yesterday."

"You're right," Roger said. "If you only found one there, Kate, then that would most likely indicate that at least one of your father's sniper rifles was removed by the intruders."

"Now, Kate," Roger continued, "I am more troubled that you found only a single weapon missing, and that the weapon stolen was a long piece like that. I find that very curious. If their intentions were to sell the weapons they're stealing, why, I wonder, would these fellows take only one weapon? Jack has a virtual arsenal there at the house. Why only a single sniper?"

Roger then excused himself so that he could talk to Bob about Kate's news. When he returned he informed Kate that they had decided that he, Roger, should immediately fly out and take custody of the case. "That missing .300 has us both troubled."

After he had fully explained to her what he intended to do, she told him that she was very pleased that he would be flying in, but that there was more to her story than she had initially revealed to him.

"Roger," she said, "I am greatly relieved that you will be taking this over, but you should also know that I have apprehended two of these guys. Plus, when I was forced to return fire with one of them, I killed him. The other one is alive and in pretty good shape. Buddy, the boys' Golden Retriever, nicked up his face and neck a bit. But he is not damaged much beyond that."

Kate then told Roger that she would hold the survivor separately from the dead one, and then she could call Det. Townsend. "I really need to touch base with local authorities, especially given that I was forced to kill one of them. Why don't we do it like this? If you would call Detective Townsend. Local sheriff's department. Let him know that the Feds are taking the case over. That would help get me off the hook. Then, he could decide how he wants to handle the dead guy. I'm sure he will want to have his people at least take charge of the body."

"That's reasonable," Roger agreed. "I know him, not well, but I met him once when I was visiting Jack. I will tell him I'm on my way. He can take care of the body. And I will inform him that I have authorized you to hold the second man until I get there. That should work just fine. Can we do it like that? Separate the two of them, and direct the locals to the dead one? I don't see why we can't. That Detective Townsend is a pretty reasonable fellow. Right?"

"He is," Kate agreed. And then she thought to ask Roger about the missing bottles of booze. He said that he had no clue, at the moment, as to what that could mean. When she told him what the bottles looked like, he responded that it sounded a lot like the expensive whiskey that he and Bob had been sharing with Jack only a few nights ago when they were there.

"I'm not getting *that* business at all," Roger added.

"That's what I figured," she said. "Doesn't make much sense to me, either. Oh, there is one more thing I need to tell you. I just found another body here in the house where they were staying. There was a women in one of the bedrooms. Her hands and feet tied, and her throat slit. I figured that she would have been the one who originally rented the cottage, and that these "men-in-black" killed her, and moved themselves into it. Haven't had a chance to confirm my theory by checking the log book, but that's my theory. I'm sure the detectives will figure that out quickly."

"My God, Kate," Roger moaned. "What the hell is goin' on there? Men-in-black. Dead women laying all over the place. This all sounds incredibly insane to me."

"There's more," she said. "One night ago there was an attempt on my life. But, as you can tell, it didn't succeed. Our boys ended up saving me, actually. I assume you want me to leave that part of the case with Detective Townsend as well. Right?"

Roger paused for several seconds, and then said, "Yeah. You do it that way. And try not to kill anybody else until I get there. See you in a few hours. And be sure to watch your back. That place is beginning to sound like a bad Agatha Christie movie. I'll make sure and give you a call when I get there. I'm sure you've got a few more rounds in your Glock. I wouldn't want you to use them on me."

After disconnecting the call, Kate checked the cord securing the captured man, to be sure the knots remained intact.

And then she looked over at Red and Robby. "You boys take Buddy and head back to the camper," she said. "This place is gonna be crawling with uniforms in a very short time. The less they see of you guys, the better."

With that the two boys jumped to their feet and bolted toward the door.

"Come on, Buddy," Robby commanded. "Let's go home."

Red slapped his thigh and grunted in such a fashion that only Buddy could understand, and the three of them ran full speed toward Henry's camper.

Kate wasted no time either. She untied the cord from around the injured man's feet, and forced him to stand up. She then wrapped the length of cord that she had freed up around the man's midsection, making it impossible for him use his arms or hands to struggle with her.

"We're going to take a little hike," she told him. "Give me any trouble whatsoever, and I will shoot you in the gut. It will hurt like hell, but you will live long enough to tell me whatever I want to know. And then, after a day to two, you will die a horrible death. I know you can understand me, so don't pretend you don't. Just walk in a straight line over to my car. And don't fall down. If you do, I'll shoot you right where you lie. And I'll leave you to die right there. You got what I'm tellin' you?" she said as she gripped him firmly by his bicep and shook him. "I'm talkin' to you! Do you understand me?"

The man did not verbally respond, but he did nod his head indicating that he knew what she was saying. Easily perceptible were a stream of tears running down each cheek.

Just as I figured, she thought to herself, *this guy's plenty good with English. And, he's not as tough as he'd like me to think.*

Kate dragged him out of the cottage, and wrestled him onto the small porch facing the river. "Walk toward my truck," she told him.

She shoved him on ahead of her a few feet, and then carefully observed his next move. She wanted to see if he would be able to find the most direct way to where she'd parked at the main house. And also to see if he would know which vehicle was hers. *If he can do that,* she calculated, *it will probably tell me whether or not this fellow could have been one of the men who tried to kill me.*

It took him only seconds to gain his bearings and step off toward the main house.

Just as she had promised, Kate allowed the bleeding man to lead the way. Instead of following the river back toward the main house, and her Tahoe, which was the route she had taken earlier, he set out on a far more direct, fairly well-worn path through the woods. Within a minute they emerged onto the lawn that surrounded the main house.

Well, she said to herself, *that was a very interesting little test. He's obviously walked that before. Now, let's see if he finds my Tahoe just as easily.*

The man-in-black continued to lead the way. As he neared the house, he veered left and proceeded to move around the garage end of the house, and from there he headed directly toward her Tahoe. As soon as it became clear to her that this fellow was a viable candidate in the assault on her, she grabbed his arm and said, "Hold on! I gotta get something out of the garage. I'll lead the way from here."

As they approached the garage service door, she seized his arm yet again, stopped him dead still, and turned him around. "That'll do for now," she barked at him. "You just keep an eye on my truck over there, and don't move a muscle."

With the man facing away from her, Kate entered the code on the digital dead bolt, and opened the door.

"Okay, you can drag your sorry carcass in here," she said to him. "I need to find something better to tie you up with."

The man just stood there for a short moment, so Kate continued, "I mean it. Get in here or I'll shoot you right where you stand. Your choice."

With that admonition, the man-in-black nearly jumped through the doorway.

He sure as hell understood the shooting part, she observed. *Maybe this guy does have a bit of a problem with English. But he seems to have that shooting shit down pat.*

She pulled out a stool and told him, "Here. Sit down and keep your mouth shut."

She looked around Jack's work area until she found a couple of soiled red shop rags. "These could be useful," she said as she snatched up two of the cleaner ones.

She continued looking in tool drawers until she found some heavy-duty zip ties. "And these oughta do the trick just fine," she declared, after scooping up a handful.

She grabbed him by the upper arm again and pulled him up off of the stool. As she turned him toward the door she had a further thought. "Hang on, I gotta get one more thing." She returned to the tool drawer and removed a pair of small wire cutters.

"Okay," Kate said. "Let's go find my truck again." And with that, they headed over toward the parking area.

When they reached her Tahoe, Kate opened the driver's side door and started to hoist the man up into the seat. But then she had another idea.

"Here we go, you idiot," she said. "I never searched you properly. Step back, spread your legs and lean your chest on the truck. I gotta take a better look at what you're carrying."

Even though she had searched him earlier, Kate wanted to see if he might have accumulated anything of interest since.

She slid her hands into a fresh pair of latex gloves, and then reached her right hand into the man's right pants pocket, but she found nothing. She repeated the process for his left pocket. But, again she came up empty. She then took half a step backward and checked to see what other pockets she might search. Finding none, she completed the process by frisking him. Again, her search turned up nothing except for a second magazine for his pistol.

"You're quite the odd duck, aren't you," she commented aloud. "No personal items of any sort. Weird. You couldn't even buy yourself a cup of coffee, or a Snickers."

She then used the wire cutters to cut the cord she'd used initially to tie him up.

"Get up in the seat and wrap your arm around the steering wheel," she said," and then cross your wrists over the wheel." He crossed his wrists but she had to place them over the steering wheel. She secured his hands together over the wheel.

After Kate had securely fastened his wrists together using two of Jack's monstrous zip ties, she ordered him to "open your mouth as wide as you can." He didn't object. She promptly stuffed one of the red rags into it, and then attached one of the zip ties to a second one, and placed them around his neck, tightening them firmly enough to make sure he would not be able to force the rag out of his mouth with his tongue.

"Now," she told him, "sit back in the seat and hold still."

Again, he obeyed.

With his head pressed firmly against the headrest, she connected another set of two zip ties, end to end, and wrapped the strap around the headrest support bars, and then attached it around his neck. She then tested to be sure it was not squeezing too tightly around his neck.

"There," she said, "I think that should do the job just fine. Now, if you're quiet, and don't try to get away, I won't have to come back and shoot you. Do you understand what I'm telling you?"

When the man-in-black failed to respond, Kate pushed the barrel of her Glock firmly against the bottom of his chin.

With that, he muttered through the rags what Kate understood to convey his compliance once again.

"Are you saying that you will be good if I go away for a little while?" she asked, as she squeezed the index finger on her left hand between the zip tie and the headrest, and drew it very tightly around the man-in-black's neck.

In considerable pain he struggled to nod his head in the affirmative.

"Very well," Kate said, pulling her finger out and removing the Glock from his chin. "We'll just have to see how you do, won't we? I have a little business to take care of, so you behave yourself. I'll be back in a flash."

She then hurried back down into the pit to review the original video of the burglary. After carefully studying it, she firmly determined that neither of the men on the recording looked at all like the two she'd run into at the cottage. That led her to assume that the first pair, the two on the video, had already left with the bottles of alcohol, Jack's SAKO sniper rifle, and whatever else they might have stolen.

And, even though that assumption turned out to be accurate, Kate remained a long way from figuring out what it all meant, at least at that time.

Chapter 35 —

Three hours and forty-nine minutes later Roger's military flight landed in Sault Ste. Marie. And, using a rental, he arrived at the resort almost exactly five hours after Kate's original call.

The first thing Roger wanted to do was to inspect the status of the captured man. After assuring himself that there might be much to be learned from the bound man, he replaced the zip tie that secured the man's hands with a pair of bona fide handcuffs. He then cut the straps that secured the man's head, and escorted him into the main house. There he secured him to a cold water pipe that Jack had installed and left exposed during construction for that specific purpose.

He then turned to Kate and said, "He looks to me like he isn't going to be getting away anytime soon. I will want to interrogate him later. But, for right now, I'd like to have you take me through the place where they'd been staying. Can we do that? I believe you referred to it as the cottage. Right? Is the body still over there? Or has the county removed it already?"

"It's still there," Kate replied. "In fact, both bodies are still over there, the man-in-black, the one I was forced to shoot, and the woman. After you called the locals, they decided that they did not want to tamper with the scene here until after you'd had a chance to go through it. As long as you wanted to take over part of the case. Shall we head over there now?"

"If we could," Roger replied.

"Definitely," Kate said. "I haven't been back to the cottage either, not since we talked on the phone. And I actually still have some unfinished business to take care of over there."

"What does that mean?" Roger asked.

"The second bedroom," Kate said. "I wanted to remove the witness from the cottage as soon as I possibly could, largely because I knew you were going to want to question him first. And I've not thoroughly searched that second bedroom yet. That's what I was about to do when the second man burst in with gun drawn.

"After Buddy put him down, I did enter that bedroom. That's when I discovered the second body. I do know that the body is that of a woman, as I told you earlier. I suspect she was the one renting that cottage when these bad boys-in-black—that would be all these fellows who always wore black came in. I surmise the dead woman was renting it when they invaded. I did not choose to do a thorough examination of that room at that time because my prisoner was still in the cottage at that time.

"So, if you're ready, we can head over there now and we can both check out that bedroom. No need to drive. It's like a hundred and fifty yards from here—just over a hill and through a small growth of trees."

"Lead the way," Roger said, as he unsnapped his Glock 10. "Do your local detectives know about the woman?"

"No," Kate said, "Unless you filled them in on it. I haven't told them yet."

When they arrived at the cottage, Kate and Roger found the front door open, just as Kate had left it. As they approached, she assumed a position on the left of the door, Roger on the right.

With his Glock raised to chest height, Roger carefully peered in.

"Well, your dead friend is still there in the middle of the floor," he said. "I assume that's where you left him."

"Right," she replied. "The bedroom on the right—I have already been through it pretty thoroughly. Same with the bathroom in the middle. It's the bedroom on the left that is the one in question. That's the one I was about to check out when I was so rudely interrupted. That's where the dead woman is. On the bed—all tied up. And with her throat slashed, as I said before. I did not disturb anything after I found her, because I assumed either you or Detective Townsend would want to start fresh."

"Well," he said. "I'd like to take a quick look at it now? You ready?"

"Let's go," Kate said. "I'll follow you. You're in charge from here on."

They both then headed for that second bedroom, Roger leading the way.

He announced his presence, opened the door, and peered in.

The room was dark, so he reached in and switched the light on. But he didn't immediately step in.

"Watch my back for a minute," he said. "I'll go in and check it out."

Kate did not respond verbally, but she did as requested. She raised the Glock to cheek level, pressed her back to the wall beside the bedroom door, and watched the still-open entry to the cottage.

After a long two minutes, Roger approached where she was standing and said, "Come on in, Kate. Something here that you're gonna want to take a look at."

Kate stared blankly at him for a moment as if to say, "I've seen dead bodies before." She then took a deep breath and proceeded to follow him into the bedroom. The second Kate reached the bed, she muttered out of exhaustion and frustration, "That's the body I was talking about. Is that what you wanted to show me?"

"No," he said. "Take a closer look at the table beside the bed. Is that one of the bottles you were talking about? The ones missing from Jack's basement office. It is, right?"

There on the night stand, beside a small lamp, was what appeared to be one of the empty Pappy bottles she'd earlier witnessed the theft of on video.

"What the hell!" she muttered. "Why's that here? I'm sure this dead chick wasn't draining it."

"If I'm not mistaken, Kate," Roger said, "that is the one bottle that neither Bob nor I touched. Only Jack handled it. He emptied that one when he was pouring our first round. Take a closer look. Looks like they washed it off, but there is a distinct residue of graphite power. They've dusted it for prints. Somethin' crazy sinister is up here. Not at all sure what it is yet, but I'd bet it somehow involves Bob and me. Toss in that damn SAKO TRG-42, and it makes for a very dicey set of possibilities."

Kate looked worn out. She just stared down blankly at the floor as she contemplated Roger's words. When she looked back up at him, she said, "I've got to find a chair and sit down. This is getting way too heavy."

Roger then led the way out into the dining area, and said, "Have a seat at the table, I'll get the front door."

After he'd closed the door, he tried to engage a lock, but there was none.

"The lock is busted," Kate said. "I had to do that to get in earlier."

"No problem," he said as he slid a chair from the table over in front of the door and propped it up under the door knob.

And then, sitting down across from her, he said, "You are, of course, aware that our current president is going through a very rough patch—primarily due to his accumulation of years, and apparent diminished mental capacity. The poor fellow is just getting old."

"I've heard talk goin' round, that his problems run deeper than that," Kate replied.

"Really?" Roger said. "What sort of talk?"

"That he's not just old and a bit senile," Kate said, "but that he is as corrupt a man as has ever occupied the White House."

"They say that about every president," Roger retorted. "Don't they? Isn't that what the opposition always claims?"

"True," Kate replied. "But with this one, there is evidence, at least that's what I've heard, that he and his family have accepted tens of millions from the Chinese government. I'm sure you've heard about that too."

"Don't they all do it for the money?" Roger asked rhetorically.

"One way or another. My biggest concern is not so much that this guy is corrupt, as much as it is that he has made a close bond with the Deep State. That's where the really big problem lies, I'm afraid."

"What do you mean by that?" Kate asked.

"It's pervaded the whole government—Republicans, Democrats and Independents. Even the military, if you can believe that. All the way up to the Joint Chiefs of Staff. It's gotten to the point where there has become a shadow military, one that answers more to the Deep State than it does to the President of the United States."

"Really?" Kate asked in disbelief. "How does that work?"

"Believe me," Roger replied. "It doesn't. I do not know how we could adequately respond anymore, should a true national emergency arise. I would not really know what to expect from some of them should we need to act quickly, and decisively. It is a big problem."

"Okay," Kate said. "I am a little confused here. How does this relate to our present situation?"

"Not sure," Roger said, after taking a long moment to respond. "I am thinking that this is all part of a larger picture. And, I still do not have a clear enough view of that larger picture. So, I can't seriously answer your question. I don't know definitively what all this means."

"Roger," Kate said, "You've got me a little worried here. Are you suggesting that this president has something sinister up his sleeve? And, if so, I still can't see how it might relate to our current situation—here at the resort."

"No," Roger said. "Not at all. I really don't think that the president is the big problem—at least not the one I think, I fear, that we're about to experience here. What we in the Secret Service are concerned about is those in the Deep State community, the ones responsible for getting him elected in the first place, just how they might opt to implement the transition."

"The *transition?*" Kate queried. "What transition are you referring to?"

Now she was sitting straight up in her chair and leaning forward. All signs of her fatigue had dissipated.

"Bob put it like this," Roger explained. "There is no glory in forcing the leader of the free world out so unceremoniously. That is, forcing him out through impeachment, or the 25th Amendment of the Constitution. The embarrassment, and all. Bob does not see that happening."

"What other way are you thinking?" Kate asked.

"Well, it seemed to Bob that the poor guy would make one hell of a martyr."

Kate then just leveled a blank stare in Roger's direction, but she didn't say a word for over a minute.

Finally, she said, "One hell of a martyr! Are you suggesting that Deep State might have him assassinated? The sitting President of the United States? Are they actually capable of that?"

"Certain elements of Deep State are, we think—hell, we don't just think, we know they would do it in a nano-second, if it satisfied their purpose. And if they thought they could get away with it," Roger said. "Hell, like I said, they are the ones that got him elected in the first place, and Bob believes that they would at least seriously consider using such an event simply for the political advantage that they might leverage from it. We've got mid-terms coming up. And, like they say, in politics, nothing trumps a sympathetic martyr."

"Well," Kate said. "I'll be damned. That thought never entered my mind. Never. And, you're thinking that this whole load of bullshit somehow relates to your little story? How? I see something in the missing SAKO sniper rifle. That, I'll admit, is more than a bit strange. But, why the nearly empty whiskey bottles? That's how they looked to me on the video. All three or four of them were only part full. They looked to me on the video like they were virtually empty. What's with them? According to the plot you two worked up."

"Bob and I struggled with that bottle business as well," Roger said. "But, we both came up with the same theory, at virtually the same time. I'll start with the ammunition that was stolen from Jack's arsenal—only two or three rounds, I think you said. If Bob and I were right about them, it helps explain the booze bottles.

"Both of them, the rounds of ammo, they will be from the same lot as the rest of the .300 Winchester Magnum ammo Jack has in his vault. If they are used in an assassination, the spent rounds will likely be left at the scene along with the SAKO. Because, they can all easily be tied back to Jack by their history, plus they will most likely have his prints on them."

"Well I'll be damned!" Kate blurted out. "You mean, they're gonna blame my dad for the assassination—the assassination of the President of the United States! That's what all this means. Right? Isn't that what you're saying?"

Roger, not reacting immediately, finally did respond: "We're afraid it might. It certainly looks like that could be the plan. But, not just Jack. The bottles they took, not only do they have your dad's fingerprints on them, but the ones they took, they also have Bob's and my prints on them as well. If this turns out to be what's going down, if we're right, then the three of us—Bob, your dad, and me—we all just might be the scapegoats for the assassination—"

"And the creation of a *sympathetic martyr*," Kate added, interrupting.

"It is a fact," Roger replied, "Deep State certainly has an agenda against Bob and me, and your father figures into that equation as well. Even though your dad is not a politically motivated figure, if the hit on the President is as imminent as we suspect, and if it can be tied to the three of us, it could take all of us out—permanently. And that would go a long way toward accomplishing their ultimate goal. Just keep in mind, Deep State owns the press. They can spin anything their way—truth or fiction. Your dad once said that the media is so skewed, they can make night look like day."

"I've heard him say that too," Kate countered. "But I think all that sounds too Orwellian to be taken seriously. I just am not ready to buy into such a farfetched plot as that. These guys, the men-in-black, as the boys and I like to call them, they were not nearly sophisticated enough to come up with a plan like you've just outlined. I have a—"

"You're right about that," Roger interrupted, "These men-in-black would have been only the lowly field operatives. They would not have been the ones doing the planning. They would simply be the expendable guys who steal guns and murder women. But, there are others. They're the ones we refer to as the Deep State. They are neither Republicans, nor Democrats. However, many of them are former senators, Representatives, and the retired heads of various governmental departments. But none of them are ever up for re-election, not anymore. Now they are in it for the power and the money. And they are very good at it. They understand how it all works, and they have learned all the tricks.

"Also, you must keep in mind that many of them are paid handsomely by foreign governments. The Chinese government, for instance, they are well practiced at making good use of these Deep Staters. And the family members of elected officials.

"But, there is one thing that they all have in common. And that is this, every last one of them is in it for their own advancement—and they don't care what they have to break to achieve it. Or who they have to kill, for that matter. They will do whatever they think they have to in order to retain power, and to fill their own pockets."

"If this thing is as real as you seem to think it is," Kate said, beginning to take Roger seriously, "is there not something you can do to prevent it? It's not right that my father might get blamed for something this terrible. That is, of course, if you turn out to be correct in all of this."

"Good question," Roger replied. "Before I left Bob, we discussed that at some length. We decided that unless we were able to acquire some sound evidence, demonstrable proof that it was real, there was not much we could do. At least not yet. Bob and I agreed that I should notify some of my fellow Secret Service agents, particularly those assigned to the President, advising them to exercise maximum caution. Not that they don't do that all the time anyway, but they need to be aware that there just might be an additional demand to exercise maximum caution right now. In fact, we, Bob and I, have a real concern that this could even involve some of my friends in the Secret Service—the Deep State, that is. Now, I do have to be very careful as to what I—"

Just then Roger's phone vibrated.

"Excuse me," he said, looking at his phone. "It's Bob, I have to take this."

He stood up from the table and walked away a few steps to gain some privacy.

"Yessir," he said. "Roger here."

Roger did not utter another word for over a minute. And then he finally said, "Has that information been confirmed? … I see. Yessir. I will be flying back immediately. Should land within five hours or so, depending on whether they've got my plane fueled and ready to go. In any case, I will leave here ASAP. I intend to bring the surviving intruder back on my flight. We can interrogate him there. … Yessir."

And then he disconnected.

"That was Bob," he said to Kate as he turned to face her. "He just informed me that the President of the United States has just been shot. And, according to all reports on the ground, he did not survive the attack. The shot was taken from some distance, with what would have had to have been a sniper rifle—a good one of some sort. We will eventually know. If it turns out to be a SAKO .300 Winchester Mag., excellent chance that it will all lead back to Jack."

Kate, immediately seized by a blank stare, within a few seconds stood up and screamed loudly, "Oh my God! No! This cannot be happening!"

And then, still standing at the table, she leveled this agonized challenge at Roger: "But, isn't Dad working for you right now? Can't you vouch for him? I have no idea where he is, or what he's doing. But you do. Right?"

"Your father is on a secret mission, and I can't talk about it. Not now, or ever, for that matter."

"Don't be playing games with me about this!" Kate complained. "His life depends on your clearing his name. You've got to!"

"Sorry," Roger apologized. "Can never do that. Only Bob could clear it all up. And, I can promise you, Bob will be very slow to relent on this matter. There's just too much at stake. If this all moves in the direction that we fear it might, we, Bob and I, our heads will be on the block as well. Of course, it might all take a different turn. It's possible that this is all a coincidence. It's just that I think it more likely, much more likely, to follow the course I just laid out. In any event, it will almost certainly not lead back to your dad until after he returns. And, while that has not yet happened. It should be very soon."

"Then, can I assume that he is fine right now?" Kate asked, still terribly shaken. "And that he is on his way home?"

"My best guess is, that would be correct," Roger replied. "But, when will the next shoe fall? That, I don't know. I have not yet filled your dad in on any of this. He's totally in the dark about it. This whole thing is a developing situation. But, one thing is for sure. I do have to get going. Bob ordered me back immediately."

"What should I do about the dead body?" Kate asked. "Bodies. There are two bodies in this cottage right now. What do you want me to do with them?"

"Call your detective friend back," Roger said. "Townsend. Call him and tell him that I have placed the prisoner in Federal custody, and have taken him with me to... Just say that I was here and that I took custody of the single prisoner, and that he should deal with the rest of it. I doubt that there will be any commercial flights going in or out of DC for a while. I may just take him to our New York office. Your detective is going to have to deal with the bodies. He can call me, if he wants to. But I've got to get going right now."

Kate was so shaken she did not know what to do or which way to turn. Roger did not spend any additional time excusing himself. He simply made his way out of the door. When Kate later went back to check on the prisoner, he was gone. And so was Roger's rental vehicle.

Kate assumed that Roger simply gathered up the prisoner, put him in his car and drove him to the plane waiting to return him to New York, or wherever.

She turned out to be correct in her assumptions. Once it was determined that Roger and his prisoner had cleared the scene, she called Det. Townsend. And, as was always the case when he became convinced that he would not be having to butt heads with the Federal Government, he headed immediately over to the resort with a full complement of detectives, along with medical and forensic workers.

The detectives had barely been able to set up shop at the resort when the surprise of all surprises began to cascade down upon all of them.

Chapter 36 —

Back in the mini-sub, approximately one hundred and twenty feet beneath the surface of the Yellow Sea, Agent Two fired off an order in Henry's direction: "Close the hatch, Henry, and prepare for us to get the hell outta here."

"What are you talkin' about?!" Henry barked back. "We ain't movin' without Jack. He's still out there. We ain't leavin' here without him. Don't you dare move a thing until I get him back in here. You'll be dealin' with me if you do anything before I find him."

Agent Two remembered what Jack hăd told him before he went after the North Korean patrol boat—that if he did not make it back after blowing it up, they should get on the move as fast as possible.

"What the hell," Agent Two mumbled to himself. "There Henry goes again. He thinks he's running the show, now that Jack's gone. I'll give him ten minutes to find his friend's body, and then

I'm splitting. We're outta here whether or not he makes it back in. Hell, he can't possibly pull this off. It would be difficult even for a trained SEAL. This arrogant bastard's gonna die today—right here in the Yellow Sea."

And he meant it. He checked his watch, as he viewed Henry squeeze through the hatch and swim upwards.

Agent Two realized that it would not be long before North Korea would dispatch everything they had to go after them, as soon as they had time to process what had just happened to their patrol boat.

Henry headed up in search of his best friend.

I have no idea where he might be, Henry said to himself. *And I've got to do this quickly, or we will both be left here to die.*

Henry looked in every direction, but saw nothing but filthy water.

He repeated his search a second time, turning slowly in the murky waters of the Yellow Sea. Still nothing.

And then Henry stopped and thought about it for a second. *When that explosion occurred, it impacted our sub from the port side. So,* he deduced, *it figures that Jack would probably be somewhere left of our bow.*

Henry took another look at their mini-sub to get a fix, and then started moving to its port side.

If he was unconscious, Henry calculated, the dead weight of his equipment would likely take him downward, not up.

So, he reasoned, *I'd best not head up. I'll just move over to where I think that patrol boat was, and check there. I wonder how deep this shitty water is here. Can't tell because it's too damn polluted.*

He continued to move in the direction of where he'd concluded the patrol boat must have been. And then he got lucky.

Even though the water was unbelievably filthy, he started to spot larger pieces of debris drifting downward past him.

Damn! he said to himself. *Take a look at the shit that's coming down. That's not pollution—that's parts of that Norko patrol boat. This is where Jack would have been when he blew it up. Except, if he was knocked out, he would probably be deeper. I've gotta go lower and check.*

He guessed that he'd already been out of the sub for over ten minutes. It was with resolve and not panic that he scoured the surrounding waters, but his eyes landed on nothing.

Forget them, he said to himself as he glanced around looking for the mini-sub. *Looks like they took off without us. So be it. I ain't gonna stop until I find Jack. What difference would it make anyway? They're gone.*

You're supposed to be able to dive very deep with these rebreathers, he was thinking as he went further and further toward the bottom. *I don't think anybody really knows how deep you can go. It ain't like the old type of system. Don't get the bends like you used to. At least not the same. What the hell difference does it make, anyway?*

He looked down to check his watch, and then recalled that it was broken. *Seems like twenty-five minutes,* he said to himself. *Jack, you crazy sonofabitch! Where you hidin'? Oh, what the hell. Might as well see just how deep it goes here. Since I'm gonna be spending the rest of my life down here, might as well take a closer look.*

Henry had no idea as to how deep he had gone. Only that it was getting much darker, and he could sense a lot more water pressure on his whole body.

Don't think I can do this much longer, he muttered in his mind. *This just might be about all there is for me on this day. Can't see a damned thing. My ears feel like they're busted. Might as well just let the water take me down as well.*

He stopped dead in the water, and quit trying to swim. When he did, he did notice that he was very slowly sinking. The water was so dark and dirty at that point that he could not see more than inches in front of his mask. Just seconds after he had given up, his left fin struck an object below him. It caught him by such surprise, he flipped in the water so that he could feel it out with his hand.

It was Jack!

He twisted his fingers in Jack's hair and pulled his friend up so they were face to face.

He was shocked to see that Jack was still breathing, and that he was still partially conscious. He could tell, however, that he was unable to open his eyes, much less use them.

Hell, Henry said to himself, *I'm goin' up and see if the sub is still there. Nothin' to lose by trying.*

Slowly, Henry began making his way toward the surface. It began to become a little more light, but he knew that he was nowhere near the surface. He considered looking for the mini-sub, but was totally confused about the direction. All he knew for certain was up and down. So, he continued to rise slowly in the murky waters.

And then, his second miracle of the day occurred. Looking directly above him he spotted the hazy form of the mini-sub. It had stopped directly beneath the spot where the ill-fated patrol boat had met its demise.

How the hell could that be?! he wondered in disbelief. *And they're stopped dead. Like they're waiting for us! I thought they'd be halfway back to Japan by now. Thank you, God!*

Henry pulled Jack, still by the hair, up to the top of the sub, and then over to the still-open hatch.

As he did this, he made sure that he passed directly in front of the camera.

Gotta make sure those SEALs see we're out here, he said to himself.

Within another five minutes Henry had slid Jack through the hatch, and had himself squeezed through the small opening. After another sixty seconds, he had secured the hatch and was attending to his still-blind buddy.

Both men were, at that point, again hopeful of a successful ending to this most dangerous of missions.

What they could not have known or imagined, at that point, was what awaited them on their return to the United States.

Chapter 37 —

For the first time since leaving Sugar Island, the mission began to go as planned. While there were no further efforts to hitch up with another South Korean fishing boat, upon closing the hatch after Jack and Henry were safely inside, the SEAL pilot plugged in these coordinates: 37.40043, 123.99782.

They had anticipated that it would take around a half an hour to maneuver to that location, but it was closer to an hour before they'd reached it. And it was just in time. That was where the USS Jimmy Carter had deposited the backup battery pack for the SDV. By the time they were able to adequately tether the battery to the mini-sub, and make the connection, they had drained the onboard battery pack to the level of less than 2 percent, which was well below operational level for the vessel. However, once the necessary connections were made on the fresh battery pack, they knew that they were in a good enough position, with regard to power, to successfully reach and hitch up to the USS Jimmy Carter.

Once the mini-sub was safely secured in the DDC on the USS Jimmy Carter, and the seven passengers moved from the SDV into the nuclear sub, the captain made haste to leave the area.

Initially, the plans were to drop off Jack, Henry and the defectors in Tokyo. But, on the basis of Bob's meeting with "the General," it was thought wiser to transfer the four passengers to a US medical ship which was stationed with a contingent positioned well off Japan, and then have the USS Jimmy Carter head directly toward the Atlantic.

Another reason for such a change in plans was that it was felt that Jack's underwater ordeal warranted his receiving medical attention as soon as possible, even though he adamantly protested that proposition. So, that's what they did.

Fortunately, that particular medical ship was equipped with a specialized portal designed to facilitate the transfer of patients or other personnel between that ship and a submerged submarine.

Once aboard the medical ship, it took Jack only moments to convince the staff that he did not require further medical attention, and so he and Henry were quickly transferred to a helicopter and whisked away to Guam. From there a B-52 flew the two men to Chicago, and then a private charter returned them to Sault Ste. Marie. They were back in their Tahoe and headed for the Sugar Island Ferry in less than twenty-four hours after blowing up the North Korean patrol boat near the 38th.

Needless to say, both men caught up on their sleep en route at 40,000 feet.

Chapter 38 —

You'll have to talk to Det. Townsend," the uniformed officer told Jack. "He's the lead investigator. He's inside. But, *you* can't go inside. I'll announce that you're here. What's your name?"

"I'm Jack Handler, the owner of this whole damn resort!" Jack barked as he pushed past the officer and stepped inside the door.

"But," the uniformed officer started to say.

"But nothing!" Jack barked again, as he forcibly closed and locked the door behind him. He listened intently as he stood just inside. Soon he heard the detectives talking down in his lower level office.

"Greg," Jack belted out at maximum decibels. "Detective Greggory Townsend. This is Handler. What the hell are you doing down in my office?"

"Jack?" the detective shouted back. "Yes. We're all down in your office. We've had a significant incident here at your house.

Hell, the whole damn resort is a crime scene. I'm surprised they let you in. Forensics are still working in your office. I would appreciate it if you would not come down here yet. I am on my way up right now. We can talk there. Okay?"

Jack never slowed down after he'd heard Det. Townsend's voice. For the first time ever he took the stairs three at a time, reaching the entry into his office at the same time Det. Townsend was exiting through it.

"If you don't mind, please," the detective pleaded, "I would like you to wait out here and give them a chance to complete their work."

"Bullshit!" Jack barked, shoving the detective aside with a heavy forearm. "What the hell's goin' on down here? I need to take a look for myself!"

"Handler!" Det. Townsend complained while trying to catch his balance. "You stop right there or I will have you arrested and locked up. Not one more damn step."

Out of the corner of his eye Jack spotted the detective keying his radio, and so he stopped and turned around. "What the hell is going on? Who did this? You got a fix on that yet?"

"That's what we're trying to determine," Det. Townsend replied. "And that is exactly why you must leave. Now! All you're doin' down here is screwing around with my guys. I mean it when I tell you I will have you restrained and locked up, if you do not leave immediately. And I do mean right now. You're already the victim here. Don't make it worse than it already is. Okay?"

By that time Jack was already standing nearly in front of the bar. From there he could do a visual of the table where he, Roger and Bob had earlier shared a couple glasses of whiskey. Plus, he could look into the open door of his arms vault.

"What the hell are you doing in my vault?" he growled, taking three steps in the direction toward it. But, before he was able to enter, two armed deputies stepped in front of him and reached out to restrain him.

Det. Townsend, seeking to prevent a physical confrontation that would culminate in Jack's arrest, or worse, jumped between the deputies and Jack.

"Enough!" Townsend voiced with everything within him. "Back off, Jack! I won't be able to warn you again."

"I hope you and your boys know that I am video recording everything that goes on here," Jack warned him. "They need to behave themselves in there. I won't be putting up with any shit. None whatsoever."

The detective then reached around Jack's forearms and locked his own hands.

"I'll go over everything we've got, Jack," Townsend said. "But we've got to leave here right now. Right now! Just take a look in there, but from here. I can assure you that there is only one fire-arm missing—it was your SAKO sniper rifle. It was taken, along with what looks to be two rounds of ammunition. That's it from here. Now go with me. We will go upstairs, sit down, and talk. I'll fill you in on everything we know. And I have some questions for you. But, you have to understand, this is a real crime scene. And we all have to respect it as such. We've seen an attempted homicide perpetrated upon your daughter. Tried to asphyxiate her in her own vehicle. Almost succeeded. Put her in the hospital. They were apparently the same burglars who hit your office and vault—at least that's how it appears at this point. One of them has been shot dead by your daughter. And a second burglar is, as we speak, on your friend's plane and headed back to New York or DC, or wherever the hell he plans to take that asshole. So, I'm sure you can appreciate the seriousness of what has gone down here. Can we leave now? Will you go with me? Peaceably? Will you walk with me upstairs? Now?"

"My friend?" Jack queried. "Who you talking about?"

"Roger," Det. Townsend answered. "He's in charge of virtually everything that's going on here today. You should talk to him."

Jack had accomplished what he set out to do. He had satisfied himself as to the scope and magnitude of the intrusion. "This was perpetrated by professionals," he said to himself while Det. Townsend maintained the tight grip on his shoulder. "These guys knew what they were after, and they had all the tools to get it done."

"Sure," Jack said to the detective, after taking one more survey of his office and vault. "Let's go up. I want to talk to you as well. And, you said they tried to kill Kate. She okay?"

"She's just fine," Townsend said. "I think she's over with the boys right now. In the camper. We asked her to vacate this area as well, so forensics could do their job uninhibited. I would like to talk with you first. Upstairs. And then you can look her up and she can tell you what she knows as well. But, right now, I'm sure her major intention is to comfort the boys. They actually were instrumental in bringing the second shooter down. That was actually more about Buddy. But they were with him. They should be the ones to fill you in on that."

By that time they were already halfway up the stairs leading to the main living area. Jack stopped dead when told about the boys' role in the apprehension.

"You've got to be shittin' me!" he said. "Are you saying that my two boys were involved in bringing one of those sons-a-bitches down? Is that what you're telling me?"

"Let's keep moving up," the detective said. "Those deputies are nervous enough about your being here. Let's not push them into something that won't be good for any of us. Shall we just keep moving along? That's what I'd really like to see us do."

Jack did not respond verbally. He just checked his cell, then turned his body around and headed upwards.

Once they reached the dining area, Jack just walked in and took a seat facing the entry door. He motioned for Det. Townsend to take a seat directly across from him.

"Okay, Detective," Jack said in his most commanding voice. "I want you to tell me everything you know, or suspect, about what has transpired on my property since I've been gone. Let's hear it. All of it. Keep in mind, I'll be getting Kate's side of it as well. After I've talked to you."

"Sure," Det. Townsend replied, clearly relieved that Jack had not physically engaged any of them directly. He then did as Jack had requested, and sat down across from him.

"Okay," Jack growled, both hands displaying tightly clenched fists. "I just this minute got a text from Roger. He says that I've had a burglary here at the house. And that the only items they, you, I guess, the only things you've determined to be missing are my SAKO TRG-42, and two or three nearly empty bottles of very expensive whiskey. Does that sound about right to you?"

"According to Kate your daughter, those items looked to be the only items missing—those, and the two SAKO .300 rounds. You might check with her later and see if that's still her story."

"Kate doesn't lie, you sonofabitch!" Jack had risen to a half-standing position at the detective's comment. From that posture he could reach Det. Townsend's jacket. And he did more than reach it. He grabbed a fistful of the detective's jacket and yanked him nearly off his chair.

"Don't you ever accuse my daughter of lying, unless you're ready to invest heavily in dental surgery. Do you got that!"

"Mr. Handler," Det. Townsend said in a quasi-apologetic tone. "That's not what I was intending to convey. Sorry if that's how it sounded. You see, my department was investigating the case, when suddenly it was wrested away from us by the Federal Government. That's all I was getting at. Kate and that fellow named Roger—your good friend—he's an investigator with the FBI, or the Secret Service, not sure which. But, he made it clear to me that we were off the case. And then, he had Kate call me back and tell me that he wanted me to run this part of the investigation. He whisked the surviving suspect off to New York, and he wanted me to pick up and process the deceased fellow—the one Kate said that she had shot dead. This whole mess has been a bit of a circus for me and my team. First I'm running it. Next, I'm off. And then, I'm back on it—at least for two murders. I truthfully was not insinuating that your daughter had been untruthful about anything."

Jack then released his grip and sat back down. But he did not apologize. "I'll talk to Kate after we finish here. Now, am I to understand that Kate spent some time in the emergency room? Is that right? Apparently, these assholes had attempted to asphyxiate my daughter with exhaust fumes … from her own damn vehicle. Is that how you understand it?"

"Exactly," Det. Townsend said. "About that, I'm quite certain.

Kate had positioned herself in her vehicle to watch. She had repositioned it by parking it out on the outer drive—almost a hundred yards away from the house. That's where she was when they connected a hose from a vacuum cleaner onto the exhaust, and stuck the other end through the rear window—Kate had left it cracked an inch or so."

"Damn those bastards!" Jack muttered. "Was that the one that she killed?"

"We don't know if he was directly involved in the attack on her. In fact, Kate believes that there were a total of four of them here pulling the job off."

"Four!" Jack said. "And you can account for only two of them? Where are the other two right now? Do you have any idea whatsoever?"

"Kate concluded that the two who actually perpetrated the break-in had already left the area," Det. Townsend said. "She had made that call after viewing the video from your office. She said the two on the recording were both smaller than the ones that accosted her in the cottage—"

"In what cottage?" Jack interrupted.

"It would be your cottage, the resort's cottage, just up the river. She found the vacuum cleaner with a missing hose. Which suggests that the men were staying in that cottage."

"Men? A woman from Vermont had rented that cottage," Jack said. "I showed it to her myself."

"Oh," Det. Townsend said, "I understand that she is still there, at least her body is. I forgot to mention that murder. She's next on the list for my forensic team."

"They *murdered* the lady?" Jack asked. "Then she's the second murder you're talking about?"

"Right," the detective said. "That's also where Kate shot one of those men, and apprehended the second. Busy place, it sounds like to me."

Jack pulled out his cell phone and said, "I need to give her a call. She's with the boys in the camper right now? That's what you said, right?"

"Haven't seen her for a bit," the detective answered, "but I think that's a safe assumption. But, I doubt that you will be able to call her on her phone. She's got that turned off. Said that's how you wanted it. She's got a burner. I can give you that number. I've got it on my phone. Would you like it? Here, let me find it for you."

Det. Townsend was very happy to perform that little task for Jack, because he reasoned that by so doing, he might be able to relieve some of the extreme pressure he felt oozing from Jack's psyche. As soon as he located it, he asked Jack if he should ring her up, or did he just want the number.

"Here," Jack said, "let me see it. I'll enter it into my phone."

Ten seconds later Kate had picked up his call.

"Where are you?" Kate asked.

"I'm sitting here at the house talking with your Detective Townsend. I'd like you to come over if you could. You're with the boys. Right? And they are okay. Right?"

"They are," she said, "but you're not. You need to get off Sugar Island as quickly as you can."

"Wait!" Jack blurted out. "What the hell are you suggesting?"

"I just talked to one of Roger's buddies in New York—a Secret Service agent," Kate explained. "Roger had him call me, so that I could tell you to get outta Dodge immediately. Rex, Roger's associate, said that the FBI just picked him up—Roger, that is. And that Bob was on their list as well. And, of course, as always, you are on the top of that list. Roger wanted no further record of communication between you and him."

"You gotta be shittin' me! What the hell is this all about?" Jack asked.

"Just do it," Kate said. "We can talk later. I think it has to do with the shooting of the current President. Apparently it was your rifle that was used to kill the President. Not only is that SAKO traceable to you, so is an empty shell casing found at the scene, because they found your fingerprints all over it and the rifle. And, they found your prints on the booze bottles, along with those of Roger and Bob. That ties all three of you into this whole mess."

"They want me for the killing of the President?! Who the hell are these fools, anyway? You're talking about the FBI? My God, how is all this shit possible?"

Just then the house was hit from three directions with tear-gas grenades, and from all four sides with floodlights. And then, from a large PA speaker outside, an authoritative voice burst forth: "This is the FBI. This building is totally surrounded with heavily armed Federal agents. Immediately lay down all weapons of any sort, and come out with your hands raised, and fingers locked behind your heads. Do this immediately. This is for everyone inside that building. Law enforcement officers as well. Everyone come out immediately with your hands raised, and fingers interlocked behind your heads. Leave your weapons behind."

"Shit!" Jack complained to Det. Townsend. "You'd better do what they're saying, or they'll shoot you too. I know I'm the one they're here for, but they're not going to mess around. Leave whatever you're carrying, and get out of here. Make sure your guys downstairs don't mess around. I'll head out first, and that might take some of the edge off. No use anyone getting hurt here today."

Det. Townsend did start to head downstairs to round up his men, but they were already heading up the steps. He did a quick head count to be certain all were accounted for, and then he told them to make sure they removed from their persons anything that could be defined as a weapon.

Jack peeled off his Glock 10, and his Smith & Wesson calf holster, and headed for the door—hands raised and fingers locked.

An unaffected smile crept across his face.

"Shit," he said aloud but to himself, "my heart rate's steady. Blood pressure down. Even though I'm gonna be staring into the barrels of a few dozen automatic weapons. At least they're in the hands of the FBI, and not the CCP. I guess there's always a bright side to every situation."

As one would expect, Jack's sardonic smile survived throughout his apprehension, and beyond.

Chapter 39 —

To many of his friends and associates, Jack made an uncharacteristic mistake by laying down his Glock and S&W, and surrendering to the Feds that fateful day on Sugar Island: "It's just not like Jack to quit so easily," they were saying. "We were just not ready for anything like this."

It was the consensus of opinion that Jack did not actually fear the forces that had gathered outside his door. In fact, to a person, those who knew Jack best were quite certain that the term fear, or any of its derivatives, did not even play a part in his decision. "He's just not that kind of guy," they would say. "We're not about to put words in his mouth here, but we believe it would be safe to say that the thinking behind his *raising of the hands* was based solely on a sound rationale—not on emotions of any sort. While he never opened up to discuss his motivations, we would bet that he reasoned it out something like this:

1. Most of these agents out there were not my enemy. They're

Americans who were simply obeying an order. Nothing to be gained by killing a few of them.

2.   My daughter, my boys, and my best friend Henry would all come to my defense would I have called upon them, and they all would likely have died with me. Hell, I'm sure that even Buddy would have jumped into that fray.

3.   The assholes pulling the strings from backstage were not clear-thinking patriotic Americans—they were Deep Staters. And there is simply nothing they would like to have seen happen more than for someone to have put an end to me.

4.   I don't have any idea as to how they will go about it, but Roger and Bob will find a way to prove that I was not around DC at the time of the assassination, and therefore could not possibly have participated.

5.   There can be no doubt that this assassination of a sitting President accurately represents what is intended by the term "the elephant in the room." Next to that elephant, nothing else warrants concern.

6.   And, finally, I have no doubt that the plan in place by the Deep State was to surround my house, and force me into a situation where they could kill me for 'resisting.' That has to have been the case. Therefore, the best bet for me to beat this whole thing was to survive and prove who it actually was behind the assassination. I am sure to lose some credibility for the short term, but will be exonerated in the long. That is, if they don't come after me and successfully put an end to my life. But, I can't allow myself to get distracted by those unfortunate possibilities.

And, that is exactly what Jack set about doing.

While I will not go into a great deal of the details, I would like to explain to my readers how Jack, Bob and Roger did manage to beat the charges against themselves, and eventually were successful in pointing the finger of guilt back at the ones actually responsible for the death of the President—the treacherous Deep Staters.

First, I will explain what happened to Jack immediately following his arrest.

He was not put in a typical, run-of-the-mill lockup. Instead, he was securely shackled, placed on a plane, and flown directly to Washington, DC. From the airport there he was transported by a sizable motorcade of armored vehicles to 935 Pennsylvania Avenue NW, where he was held in solitary confinement and was subjected to numerous indignities, some of which were very painful, both on the physical and the emotional levels. But Jack refused to answer any questions, or even to open his mouth beyond the old standby: name, rank and serial number.

He spent exactly seven days there at FBI Headquarters. While he had no way of knowing what was going on outside his cell, he knew he could count on his friends and family. And he was right in so trusting.

The initial reports were wrong about Roger having been apprehended. Rather, he cleverly managed to elude capture. In fact, he squirreled not only himself away, but he took his "prisoner" with him.

This is how Roger did it: he had a friend who owned a small log cabin located on the Potomac just north of Fort Hunt Park in Virginia. In the past he had used this same small home when he needed to get away from New York and DC—more specifically, to escape the rampages of Allison Fulbright. But, there were very few others who even knew the cabin existed. That is to say, it was not a "party house" in any sense. And so, for the sake of propriety, and to preserve a certain level of anonymity, I will not describe that house in any further detail.

Now, while we will probably never know much about the sort of methods Roger might have used to squeeze information out of his prisoner, it is very safe to say that he did his to-be-expected exemplary job. When Jack asked him later what he actually did to get the man to talk, Roger would not even tell him. His answer was, "Look, Jack, just know that I was one highly motivated so-nofabitch. That's all you need to know. All anyone needs to know. And it doesn't really matter how I convinced him to talk to me. In the end, I managed to squeeze out of him everything I needed in order to clear us from prosecution. And the dirty little bastard survived. ... End of story."

Jack asked him about it only that one time, and then he dropped it—forever.

What follows is a brief summary (written in quasi-acceptable English by Roger) of what Mr. Lin Song had told him:

Approximately six weeks ago, Mr. Lin Song related this to me (I am Secret Service Agent Roger Minsk). He said: "One month ago I was contacted by a [senior] agent [Agent 2013] of the CCP [Chinese Communist Party]. He told me that I must aid him in an effort that was headed up by his superiors [at the CCP]. He told me that they [the CCP] were engaging in the mission at the request of certain large business/financial entities headquartered in the US and abroad, but he did not indicate precisely who or what these powerful organizations represented. In the past, and in connection with earlier similar missions, he had described them as being part of the "American Deep State," and various international political organizations. As my part of the mission, I was ordered to break into a private home and steal some of the items from that home. The ultimate goal of the mission, according to the agent, was to assassinate the sitting President of the United States, and to do it in such a way so as to make it look like it was done by domestic terrorist parties who were politically at odds with the policies supported by that President.

I should tell you in advance that I have performed other tasks for Agent 2013 and the CCP, both inside and outside the US. I can also tell you that I am never given a choice—I must do what he said, or I would be replaced and eliminated.

Jack Handler was the one hand-picked by the CCP to serve as the fall guy. Not only did the home targeted for the burglary belong to Mr. Handler, but the items we were supposed to steal also belonged to Mr. Handler. The items on the list we were supposed to steal included one Finnish TRG-42 Sniper rifle, two rounds of .300 ammunition for that firearm, and three specific bottles of whiskey. We were guaranteed that all of these items were in Mr. Handler's house on Sugar Island. An image of each targeted item was included with the packet provided to us. I must say that I have no idea how the images of the targeted items were procured. But I was commanded not to allow my hand to come into direct contact with any of the items we were sent to steal. Furthermore, I was ordered to destroy the images once procured. And so I did.

We were told that "while it was widely known that Jack Handler was not into politics, it was also common knowledge by other agents and associates, that not only did Mr. Handler not have a high opinion of the President, he let his feelings be known. That's why the CCP chose to make Mr. Handler the fall guy."

I [Roger Minsk] then inquired as to whether agents of the CCP normally shared such intimate knowledge with field operatives [such as Mr. Song] regarding the nature of a mission. In response to that question, he said: "Normally I would not be briefed with details not directly involved with the task at hand. It's just a fact that, on the particular night that Agent 2013 chose to give me this assignment, Agent 2013 was more than slightly intoxicated."

That, I [Roger Minsk] have to say, Mr. Lin Song told me a lot about this operation.

Mr. Song went on to tell me this: "I [Mr. Lin Song] was told to send to New York, two of the men who had been helping me, along with the items stolen, and he [Agent 2013] would have a private charter jet waiting at the airport in Sault Ste. Marie, and that it would fly them directly to JFK Airport. There they would be met by Agent 2013 himself, and that he would collect the items we had been assigned to steal.

"We did exactly as he had ordered. I gathered up the two men who had broken into the resort, and I sent them to New York with the items just as he had ordered me to do. Unfortunately, my friend who stayed on Sugar Island with me, he was shot and killed in the cottage that we had appropriated.

"And then, Minsk, you showed me proof that my two friends that I sent to New York, that they had been killed at the airport after delivering the specified items we had procured. Now, that leaves only me surviving—the other three are all dead."

Mr. Song then provided me with all the notes contained in the original mission   packet of orders that he had received from Agent 2013 [They were in the form of a chip hidden in his shoe. This aspect alone is very significant, because Mr. Song had been ordered to destroy this packet, but he failed to do so.]. I have included a copy of this information with Mr. Song's note.

I [Roger Minsk] am also sending a separate packet of information that not only proves that Jack Handler was not in possession of that SAKO rifle at the time of the assassination, but it also outlines the source and history of all of the evidence supplied by the CCP to frame Mr. Handler. There also can be no doubt that what we are here supplying proves beyond any doubt that former President Bob Fulbright, Jack Handler, and I [Roger Minsk], could not possibly have had any involvement in that assassination. It was totally the work of various Deep State operatives, in conjunction with the CCP.

Almost immediately, the so-called *shit hit the fan*. Jack had to reveal where he was and what he had been up to—that is, he had to admit being in the vicinity of the virtual destruction of the Chinese nation and economy. All the secrecy he had striven to maintain regarding the diversion and redirection of the North Korean missile, the destruction of the lab responsible for developing and dispersing the deadly Covid-19 virus, and the absolute devastation of the Three Gorges Dam, while not directly admitted to by Jack, little doubt was left in the mind of the CCP that it was they, Jack, Roger and Bob, who had perpetrated the whole event.

While the mission remained on the official list of "Top Secret Missions," no one in DC possessing an ounce of smarts, or any connections whatsoever, could have had any doubt about the role played in it by Jack and his two friends. True, while the trio could never be prosecuted for it, the three of them were left without any cover. And, sadly, that was to be their lot in life from that point forward.

Henry, on the other hand, basically emerged from the whole matter with a clean record. His name appeared on no lists of any kind—except, of course, as one of Jack Handler's good friends.

Never discussed by anyone outside the team of three, and top-level operatives in the CIA, was the culmination of that ominous Covid-22 threat. Even before Jack blew up the "Second Great Wall of China," the Chinese national that the CIA had been watching the most closely, made his move. At the hands of the FBI, he was nabbed leaving the campus of an unnamed Ivy League bastion. In a hidden compartment of his satchel was found fourteen sealed glass vials containing that deadly Covid-22 virus.

Fortunately, now laboratories in this country, and in friendly labs abroad, scientists are busy at work developing an effective vaccine to fight it. While the project seems not to be fast-tracked, as was previously the case with "Operation Warp Speed" (OWS), scientists are equally optimistic as to outcome—their thinking: since the Chinese were able to develop an effective vaccine, the free world will most certainly come through as well.

Regarding the destruction of the Chinese economy—there is no doubt about that either. The Three Gorges Dam, described by contemporary scholars as the new "Great Wall of China," was now gone. All the industry that was dependent upon the power supplied by the dam, it was all gone as well. While it was a fact that hundreds of thousands, perhaps totals even reaching over a million, of Chinese souls did immediately perish with the floods that cascaded down the Yangtze River, through the industrial city of Wuhan, and all the way down to Shanghai. However, curious as it might seem, many world leaders breathed a huge sigh of relief that this evil threat was so soundly put to rest.

And, just as the new 'Stormin' Norman' predicted, not only was the Chinese economy totally destroyed, but its collapse also brought down the Communist regime that most informed world leaders correctly blamed for the whole Covid-19 worldwide pandemic.

When asked for his opinion, Jack simply denied any knowledge of how it all happened. And then, he would sometimes add with a smile, "Even though I don't have any personal knowledge about it, there is that old saying, you know, that 'One good deed deserves another.'" While never seeking to explain that comment, still sporting a slight smile, he would take his patented glance over his left shoulder, and then walk away.

Jack was also asked to explain the meaning of a sizable strip of aluminum found by CCP inspectors about fifteen kilometers from the destroyed Wuhan laboratory. While it was largely destroyed by its collision with Earth, a message in English (written with a broad-tipped marker) was still substantially discernible. It read: "To China with Love." Jack simply replied when asked, "I have no knowledge about that."

Oh, I would not want to forget about Henry's aunt—Aunt Halona. The moment that Henry reached the resort, he immediately went to the front door of the tastefully decorated cottage that Jack had provided for the little lady. Not knowing what to expect, and not wishing to disturb the sweet old lady in case she were sleeping, he gently knocked on the door.

He was expecting a long-faced nurse to walk softly up to the door, and break some sort of bad news.

But, was Henry ever in for a surprise.

The door was answered not by a nurse at all. Instead, Kate walked up and gave him a big hug. And then, sporting the biggest smile she could muster, she grabbed him by the sleeve and pulled him through the door toward Aunt Halona's bedroom.

"Come on in, Henry," she said, not releasing his sleeve, "Am I ever happy to see you. And, I've got something pretty special to show you." Still leading him by the arm, she turned and walked him swiftly into the cottage.

As Henry entered his aunt's bedroom, he was not greeted by a pale, bedridden old lady. Instead, Aunt Halona was sitting at the breakfast table (which the nurses had brought into the bedroom at her request). Seated with her at the large round table were two nurses, Red, and Robby. Kate's chair was located between the two boys. And in the middle of the table was Aunt Halona's new favorite board game—*Trekking the National Parks—2nd Edition*.

"Surprised to see her looking so well?" Kate offered up enthusiastically. "Two days ago the doctor declared your aunt totally out of danger. And, not only is her Covid no longer transmissible, but she is well on the road to recovery. Go ahead, you can give her a big kiss, if you want."

They were all wearing masks, but Henry still placed a kiss on the top of Aunt Halona's head as she sat at the game table. He then dropped to his knees at her feet and laid his head on her lap. Henry neither moved nor said a word for an extended length of time. Because of the curve of the table, his head was not fully visible to any of those seated at the game. Only Kate, who still remained standing, and the little old lady could see the tears streaming down his face and into his less than pristine surgical mask.

No one made a sound as the lovely Halona stroked her fingers through her beloved nephew's splendidly long and clearly unmanaged Native American coiffure. She struggled mightily, but she managed to hold her emotions in check.

"One of us has to be strong right now," she said to herself, "and on this glorious day, it's obviously not my precious Henry's turn."

Kate looked around until she found another chair, and she made everyone make room so that Henry could sit beside his aunt. And they continued playing Halona's now favorite game.

However, a new round had barely kicked in when Kate's phone vibrated. She checked it, stood up, and with a sincere smile said, "'That was Dad. He has something he needs me to do for him ...'"

Chapter 40 —

I t had been nearly one hundred and fifty days since Jack and Henry had successfully taken out China's Three Gorges Dam, along with their bio-warfare lab at Wuhan. It was eleven P.M. on a Thursday night. Normally, the boys would be in bed early, but school had been canceled for Friday due to a furnace issue, so Red, Robby and two of their friends had just engaged in a "life-and-death" marathon to see who was the Sugar Island champion of their favorite game—Azul Summer Pavilion. Even though the boys lost to Kendal and Mackenzie, when Kendal's dad appeared at the appointed hour to pick the girls up, neither of the boys were at all disheartened at having been stymied by the young ladies.

"So," Henry asked them when they walked into the big room downstairs, "So, tell me, did you win or did you lose?"

Both boys were sporting full-face smiles.

"The girls had higher scores than we did," Robby replied. "At least, overall. But, we don't really think we lost, because we didn't actually finish the game—they're both coming back next Friday night to finish the game."

"You mean you fellows have dates for next Friday night?" Henry asked, as he looked over at Jack and winked at him.

"No!" Robby protested. "It's nothing like that. No date. They're just comin' over so we can complete the game. That's all."

"Right," Jack said. "It's not a date. You boys are fourteen. That's too young to be dating. We get it. … But, Henry and I've been talking, and he's pretty sure that they're having a walleye tournament over on Gogebic Lake this weekend. Do you fellows think you'd be interested in going there and dropping in a line with us?"

The fishing trip was all Henry's idea at first. At least the part of the plans that would be taking him, Jack, and the two boys to Lake Gogebic which, at over thirteen thousand acres, represented the largest inland lake in Michigan's Upper Peninsula. Located near the western border of the state, Lake Gogebic had become one of the favorite four-season fishing spots for residents of Michigan, Wisconsin, and beyond.

The two boys gazed at each other with eyes so big they looked like they might fall out. "Would we ever!" Robby exclaimed. "Can we really do that? We thought that Uncle Roger would be flying in to check out his new camper? Isn't that the plan?"

"Sure," Jack said. "We already called Roger to let him know it's here. My guess is right now that he might be interested in flying in to check it out, but then to drive it to the lake with us. It does sleep ten, and I know that he loves to fish. And so does Bob. I'll just run it past them, and see if they have an interest in going with us."

Jack pulled his cell out and called Roger. It took his friend only seconds to think it over, and he said, "I think that sounds like a great idea. Let me give Bob a call, and then I'll let you know."

"How about Legend?" Henry asked. "We haven't seen him in a while. Want me to see if he's doin' anything this weekend?"

"Yeah," Jack said. "Give him a call and see if he can make it. It's a long drive for him, but I'd promised him we'd invite him on our next fishing trip. The boys really like that guy."

Three minutes later Roger called Jack back and said, "Bob's just about as excited as you guys are. He said that he and I could fly into Houghton County Memorial, and rent a car. It's only an hour and a half drive from the lake. So we're on."

"Actually," Jack said, after thinking about what Roger said, "I'll have Henry drive your new motor home over and meet you at Houghton Airport. That should work, don't you think?"

Roger was good with Jack's plan, and he even suggested that Jack give Kate a call to see if she might even fly in, "if she can get away."

And so that's what Jack did.

"Your Aunt Kate is interested in joining us at the lake," Jack told the boys after talking to her. "She's going to check into it."

The boys were ecstatic.

"If it all works out, we'll bring both campers," Jack added. "So, there can be plenty of room."

When Jack said that each of these monster motor homes could sleep ten, he was telling the truth. They weren't the type of camper that mom and pop could pull behind their SUV. Jack had put his order in to an Australian manufacturer for a forty-foot double deck motorhome. It was unique in that at the push of a button, the second story automatically lifted into position, providing a fully enclosed 6'5" high sleeping quarters capable of accommodating comfortable beds for up to ten adults. It's called the SLRV

8x8 Commander. Built on a heavy-duty military chassis, it was originally designed to serve the purposes of those interested in exploring the most remote of the backwoods wilds, such as the Australian bush.

Jack had ordered his several months before being recruited for his notorious North Korean exploit, and it had arrived shortly before that mission had even kicked off. Jack had told Roger early on that he was thinking about buying a large motor home in order to take some trips with the boys, and so Roger and Bob were able to check it out on their Sugar Island visit just before the mission.

Upon inspecting it quite thoroughly from the outside, Bob advised Roger to order one as well. "Something like this would be very good for you to have," he told him. "When this mission is done, it is not going to be safe for you to stay in any public hotel. You, Jack and I will have targets painted indelibly on our backs for the rest of our lives. A large, durable machine like this, just might save your neck. Get one, I'll pay for it, and you can store it with Jack and Henry on Sugar Island. I might use it occasionally as well. And, hell, I might even get one for myself."

Roger followed Bob's advice and placed his order for virtually an identical Australian monster motorhome.

And now, on that very Thursday evening, while Jack and Henry talked, and the boys played games with their cute "not girlfriends," the second monster motor home arrived.

"The reason we're dropping it off so late in the evening," the delivery crew told them, "was because we had a hard time getting it on the Sugar Island Ferry. While we were waiting to board the boat, we decided to grab a couple hotdogs from Clyde's. While I was picking up the food, Jimmy, my helper here, "accidentally" hit the button that lifted up the roof on the motor home, and we couldn't get it back down. They wouldn't let us on the ferry with it up, so we had to pull out of the line. We read the manuals, but nothing worked. We ended up calling the manufacturer in Australia. And, because they're sixteen hours ahead of us, we had to wait until it was six before we got through. It was a simple mistake at our end. We got the upper level down, loaded it on the ferry, and here we are."

As soon as all the papers had been signed for the delivery, Henry and Jack immediately began planning the fishing trip. They called Roger to let him know his motorhome had arrived.

When Roger announced his plans to Bob, he even suggested that Jack should ask Det. Greggory Townsend to join them, if he were available, because he (Bob) had some questions he wanted to ask the detective. Jack at first hesitated to invite Townsend along, but Kate also thought it would be a good idea, so he called him as well.

When Jack called Townsend, the detective was a bit apprehensive about going with them, until Jack explained that his presence on the trip was personally requested by Bob Fulbright, a former President of the United States. Townsend then knew that his invitation truly constituted more than a fulfilled courtesy on Jack's behalf, and so he accepted the offer. To that point, Townsend had remained a little fearful of Jack's role in the mess that had just transpired in the Far East, and even still felt a little intimidated by that surprise kiss Kate had planted on his mouth during the early stage of his investigation. *But, if a former president is requesting me specifically,* he reasoned, *how can I refuse?*

By the time the girls left, Jack and Henry had assembled a

good-sized crew to fish for walleyes in Gogebic Lake over the weekend. They had Jack, Henry, Red, Robby (Buddy, of course), Roger, Bob, Kate and Det. Townsend. Plus, Henry had reached out to Legend as well. And, as is always the case, Bob, as a former president, was required to travel with at least two Secret Service agents. That meant that there would be a total of ten pairs of shoes goin' on this trip, along with one four-footed shoeless K-9.

Jack's motorhome began its trip to the US about two weeks before Jack and Henry left on their mission, arriving on Sugar Island two days before they shoved off for North Korea. By the time Jack was released from Federal custody and allowed to return to the resort, Kate, Henry and the boys had totally familiarized themselves with the monster and had it ready for christening.

Jack, however, was also eager to take to the road. Almost as soon as Henry's fishing suggestion had escaped from his lips, the gears in Jack's brain started spinning. He found that Roger was not only eager to see and test his new motorhome, but he was equally motivated to have a sit-down with Jack and Henry.

It took Jack no more than twelve minutes to nail down Roger's and Bob's acceptance, and another five to confirm Kate's participation. Of course, Jack knew before asking the boys that Robby and Red would be good for it. So, the deal was made in less time than it takes to prepare a ham and eggs breakfast.

It was quite understandable why the adults involved were quickly convinced of the trip's merits. The notoriety associated with all of them regarding the recent North Korean mission made any recreational exposure virtually impossible. Kate and Henry were, to a large degree, exempt from the dangers facing Jack, Roger and Bob, but just being in proximity to the toxic three posed a significant threat to their well-being as well.

So, the idea of traveling to one of the more remote areas in the US, and doing such by bringing their own home-on-wheels with them, seemed to all of them a very safe way to get together.

And then to further seal the deal, they would all get a big kick out of spending time on one of the best fishing lakes in the country, in the big boat Jack always rented—it all made it seem like an opportunity not to be passed up.

Kate's call informed them that not only would she be able to get away for the fishing trip, but that she would be able to get an express flight out first thing in the morning which would land her at Chippewa International, which is near Sault Ste. Marie, just about the time Jack and the boys would be hitting the road to Gogebic Lake. While the route to the lake did not exactly take them across the airport's landing approach, it was not excessively out of the way—not perfect, but close enough.

Morning came to the Handler house in an electrified fashion. Normally on a Friday morning Jack would be the first one up, and it would take him two trips to the boys' bedroom to get them motivated for breakfast. The first trip he would wake them up. He would already have taken Buddy out for his morning run, and so the boys' best friend would be totally wound up and breathing steam. While Buddy would not jump up on the beds, he was plenty tall enough to bury his nose under their blankets and pillows and to lay a big wet lick on each of their faces. While they would protest energetically, truth be known, they loved his attention. Jack would then leave Buddy in their room, close the door, and he would go back downstairs and prepare breakfast.

If the boys were not showered and dressed for school in twenty minutes, he would return to their bedroom and raise a little hell with them.

Today, however, was a different sort of day.

The night before, Jack announced to the boys that they would be eating breakfast at 6:30, and that they would make every effort to get packed and on the road by 8:30. He told them that they would most likely fish all day Saturday and Sunday; and, if everyone was having a good time, they might consider fishing Lake Gogebic for another two days. They would, however, give it at least two full days before electing to return to Sugar Island, or to move on to an alternative location.

This Friday morning, however, produced a different scenario from that pictured by Jack the night before.

By 5:30 both boys were dressed, packed for four days, and downstairs eating a bowl of cereal and a piece of peanut butter toast. And Buddy, who was now standing over his bowl and devouring his morning meal, had already gone for his brisk morning run.

Jack smiled when he heard them trying to be quiet. "Looks like somebody is awfully damned eager to go fishing," he said to himself. "Wonder if they put on a pot of coffee for Henry and me?"

"What time are you getting in?" he said to Kate after dialing her number. "The boys are already up and at 'em. I can tell you right now they are going to have a great time this weekend."

"I'm belted up and ready for takeoff," she replied. "I never knew that they had flights this early. They just told us to turn our cell phones off, so I guess I'd better comply. We're scheduled to arrive at seven-thirty—Chippewa International. How's everything at your end?"

"We'll be filling up both motorhomes, looks like," Jack said. "Like I said, the boys are ready to go fishing. Roger and Bob are both planning to meet us over there. Henry is driving the other monster. He'll be picking those guys up. Of course, Bob is bringing some Secret Service. Don't know how many yet, but I'd suspect it will be two. And we're stopping to pick up Greg Townsend— hope that works for you. Bob wanted to talk to him about what he found at the resort. Not sure exactly what that's all about."

"Gotta go, Dad," Kate said in a near whisper. "They're starting to give me the evil eye. See you shortly."

The first part of the fishing trip went as planned. Even though the whole Sugar Island crew were ready shove off at 7:30, Jack had everyone double-check their gear because he did not want to leave the resort before the scheduled time: 8:30.

First stop was to pick up Det. Townsend. He was waiting in his parked car adjacent to the ferry approach on the mainland side. Henry was following directly behind Jack as they drove onto the ferry.

"How do we handle Townsend?" Henry asked Jack over his cell. "Do you want him to ride with me, or should he go with you?"

"Doesn't really matter to me," Jack replied. "Except that Bob had some questions for him. Since you're the one who is going to pick up Roger and Bob, maybe Greggory ought to ride with you. That would give Bob a bit more privacy."

"I thought he was going to rent a couple cars at the airport," Henry said.

"I talked with him again," Jack said, "and he is going to have a single car waiting for him at Houghton. But we decided that you should pick Roger up at the airport, along with one of the Secret

Service Agents, and drive them back in the monster. And Bob will ride with the other agent. Greggory can ride with them. They can follow you and Roger."

"Sounds good to me," Henry said. "I do know that area pretty well."

Jack's reasoning was sound. Bob had originally offered to find his own way to Gogebic Lake from Houghton Airport. But Jack thought better of it, because he knew that neither Roger nor Bob were as familiar with the area as he and Henry were. At least once a year he and the boys, sometimes taking Henry with them, would go fishing on Gogebic Lake. No point in getting the former president lost in the Northern Michigan woods, Jack was thinking. And besides, this will give Bob a chance to download all the information Detective Townsend might have regarding the Chinese agents who had tried to kill Kate.

"You grab Greggory when we get off the ferry," Jack said. "And the boys and I will beat it to the airport and pick up Kate. Let's do it that way."

What nearly escaped the attention of both Jack and Henry was the Toyota rental parked at the far southern end of the Ferry Dock parking lot. It was facing outward, and it contained two very fit-looking men. The occupants of the Toyota appeared to be Chinese. They watched intently as Jack drove off the ferry, and then proceeded to pull to the left, stopping nearly in front of them, followed by Henry, who pulled in directly behind Jack. Their eyes also scrutinized Det. Townsend as he locked up his vehicle, was greeted personally by Jack, and then was walked back over and into Henry's monster motorhome.

Jack and Henry then signed off, and Jack, with his visibly excited boys safely belted in, headed off to pick Kate up.

The two men in the Toyota waited until both motorhomes had turned right onto Riverside Drive, and then they carefully pulled out to follow behind them. While neither Jack nor Henry made too much of it as a threat, both of them did take note of the mysterious vehicle.

Jack and Henry made their way west on Portage past the locks, under the approach to the International Bridge, and up to Easterday, where they merged onto I-75 south.

The best route to Gogebic Lake and most points west was M-28, which was only about eight miles south of the International Bridge. The plan was for Henry and the detective to exit I-75 and head west on M-28, while Jack and the boys were to proceed on down on I-75 until they picked Kate up, and then they would jump back on I-75 to M-28. If they did not have to wait long for Kate, the whole operation would set them back less than an hour—perhaps even forty minutes or less.

However, Jack could not get out of his mind that car parked at the Ferry Dock when they were picking up Det. Townsend.

"Hey, buddy," Jack said to Henry right after he and the detective had turned off on M-28, "what did you think about that car with those two fellows in it? They seemed to be paying a lot of attention to us, don't you think? You didn't recognize them, did you?"

"No," Henry replied, "but I did pick up on them. What do you think about 'em?"

"I think they turned in behind you when you exited," Jack said. "Did you see them following you?"

"They did lay back a ways, but pretty sure it was still them. Not sure they were tailing me, but it did look like it."

Det. Townsend overheard the conversation, and so he tried to look back through the monster, but the rear window was not visible to him. And when he leaned forward to use the rearview mirror, Henry grabbed him by the arm and pointed to a screen on the dash. While he remained on the phone to Jack, he adjusted the rear-mounted camera to throw a close-up image of the vehicle in question on the screen.

"Have you picked up Kate yet?" Henry asked.

"Not yet," Jack said. "But she just called me. She got in about ten minutes ago, and she has no check-ins, so she should be waiting outside when I get there. ... And, I can see her now."

"So, how many minutes ahead of you are we?"

"I should be less than forty minutes behind—at the usual speeds," Jack replied. "What are you thinking?"

"Oh, I don't know," Henry said. "Our friends are now only one car behind us. How do you want me to handle this?"

"You hold your speed at about fifty," Jack said, as he pulled in to pick up his daughter. "I'm just about to pick Kate up. Let me see what she thinks and I'll get right back to you."

"Roger that," Henry said. "Traffic's moving at sixty-three. I'll drop down to fifty or so, and hold it there. And we'll see what our friends do."

"Yeah," Jack said. "Let 'em get on your tail and see if they pass you. If they hold back and don't go around for five, take your speed back up a bit so they don't get suspicious. Take it up gradual, though. I'll be back on the road in just a few. Keep me appraised."

"Will do," Henry affirmed.

"Hey, Kate," Jack said, as he jumped out to grab her one small bag. "I'll stow this for you, and you say 'hi' to the boys, and then come up front. We've got a bit of a thing goin' on. Make sure the boys stay belted up back there."

"Yeah, Dad," Kate replied. "What's up?"

"Probably nothing," he said. "I'll explain it to you after you greet the boys."

"I'll be back up in a flash."

"Are they still back there?" Jack asked Henry.

"They are," Henry said. "Only now they are right behind me. The other car passed me."

"See if you can coax them up fairly close," Jack directed, "and hit them with the camera. Send it to me and I'll have Kate run it on Facial Recognition. Bob's got me tied into the Federal database. We'll see if they can be ID'd."

Just then Kate slid into the front passenger seat and said, "Whatcha got going here, Dad? Another Federal conspiracy?"

"I sure as hell hope not," Jack answered without a smile.

Kate saw that her dad was not picking up on her effort to make light of whatever it was that was going on. She then glanced down at the image that had just appeared on the monitor.

"Run them through Facial Recognition," he said. "And we'll see what pops up. Probably nothing, like I said. But that car was parked at the far end of the parking area at the Ferry Dock, and they pulled in behind Henry and followed him even after he turned west on M-28. They're riding on his tail right now. Probably nothing, but worth checking out."

"This looks like pretty standard equipment here," Kate said. "Did you get it from Bob?"

"Exactly. Should be just like what you're used to."

"Holy shit!" Kate blurted out. "They look a lot like the jerks who burgled your office at the resort! Do you suppose they could be?"

The setup Bob had provided for Jack allowed him to run facial images through DHS's ABI (Automated Biometric Identification) system as well as the FBI's FACE (Facial Comparison and Evaluation service). Kate, very familiar with both, had earlier entered the images of the Sugar Island burglars into both systems.

Within minutes Kate's initial observations were confirmed—a ninety-five percent positive confirmation that the driver of the vehicle following Henry was one of the resort's intruders, and an eighty-five percent match that the other man in the car was also one of Kate's burglars.

"Well, Dad," Kate observed, "Looks like you guys pegged those fellows right on the nose. They are a couple of very bad dudes. … And, the report we initially received was that the CCP had them both killed. Shows you that no one in DC tells us the truth."

"I'll bet you didn't buy that story that they'd been killed," Jack offered, now through his patented Jack Handler smile. "Even though it was sourced through the FBI."

"You're right," she replied. "I had no way to confirm or reject their version, so I just logged it and moved on. … But, this is nice information to have, even now at this late stage in the game."

"Might not be that," Jack added. "Might just be the early chapters of a new book."

Kate stared at him for a number of seconds, but did not respond to his comment.

"Hey, Henry," Jack said after calling his friend again. "You've got a couple non-friendlies behind you, so exercise caution."

"How unfriendly?" Henry asked.

"They appear to be a couple of the CCP agents who broke into the resort while you and I were out of town on vacation," Jack replied. "At least according to Facial Recognition—one of them registered at ninety-five percent. If one of them is positive, then they both are. So, they should be considered *very* problematic characters. Dangerous."

"How do you want me to handle this?" Henry asked.

Jack hit the accelerator and sped down the access road and headed back to I-75.

"This should work out fine," Jack said. "I will push it hard. Be hitting 28 in six or seven minutes. Should be able to come up behind you on the other side of the Chippewa County Line—possibly about ten miles east of Newberry. We'll be talking, so we can narrow it down. Townsend works out of Chippewa. And we don't want to create any jurisdictional conflicts for him. If we can get fifteen miles past the Paradise exit, which is the eastern leg of 123, then we will be outside Chippewa. If you can hold it at around fifty-five, I should be able to catch up right where we would like. There's a decent straight stretch there, and that'll be where we make our move."

"Got it," Henry responded.

Fifty-five minutes later Jack called Henry and asked him where he was and how it was going:

"What's your 10-20? And how's it all looking to you?"

"Just crossed over into Luce County," Henry replied. "Nothing's changed. They're still on my tail."

"How's Greggory handling it? Think he suspects anything?"

"All's well," Henry replied. "Greggory's aware of what's going on. That we've got a tail on us. He commented that we are no longer his problem, as we crossed the county line."

"I can see you ahead of me," Jack said. "I suspected that was going to be you. I now can see the Toyota clearly as well. When I get up behind him, you hit the gas, and I will slide up and get between you."

"Just let me know when you're ready to make your move," Henry said.

"Oh," Jack retorted, "you'll know. I'll block their moves and cut them off. You just hit the gas when the time comes."

Jack came up behind the Toyota like that proverbial "bat outta hell." Jack quickly figured out that he'd been spotted, and so altered his plan. Instead of attempting to immediately pass, he simply pulled in behind the Toyota and pinned it between the two monsters.

As soon as his front bumper made contact with the car, he hit a switch on the dash that was labeled "MAG." And then he began braking gradually. At the same time Henry sped away.

The button he hit activated a powerful magnet that was connected to the monster by a half-inch rope cable that was mounted on a monstrous hydraulic cylinder. That meant that no matter how hard the driver of the Toyota tried to escape, it wasn't going to happen. Jack maintained his speed at 50 MPH until Henry was well down the road, and then searched for approaching vehicles. Convinced that there were none close by, he began to slow down.

"Get ready!" he told Kate. "There are two tasers in the compartment. Put your gloves on, then take one and give me one. If they bolt, shoot the one on your side. I'll get mine."

"These the 35 footers?" Kate asked, knowing that the wires

used in police issued tasers was limited to that length.

"Specially set up for me," Jack replied. "Wires are fifty plus feet. Cartridges loaded to the max. Just make sure you hit the bastard."

"Maybe they won't run," Kate said, checking out the gun.

"Maybe, but don't count on that," Jack countered. "Put your window down and get ready. I'm gonna attempt to box these bastards in from in front. I'm passing them." With that he switched the MAG off and accelerated, allowing him to shoot past the Toyota.

Once ahead of them, which turned out to be easier than he expected as they seemed to make no effort to thwart his effort, he began to slowly decelerate until the monster was moving between 10 and 15 miles-per-hour.

"To hell with this shit," he finally hollered, as he slammed on the brakes and shoved the shifter into park. The car behind them continued to slow, until it harmlessly bumped into the rear of the monster.

Jack and Kate both bolted out of the monster and hurried back to the Toyota. They were surprised, however, that neither of the men had tried to run. Just before Jack arrived at the driver's door, he pulled out his Glock 10mm with his right hand, and a handkerchief with his left.

Kate saw that her dad had drawn his pistol, so she followed suit.

Still, as they approached, they could spot no activity in the car.

Jack quickly opened the Toyota's door and shouted for the men to get their hands up. Kate did the same after opening the passenger's door.

But, neither of the men moved a muscle.

The smell of spent gunpowder rolled out of both doors. It was obvious to Jack and Kate that the two men in the car were both dead. The driver had apparently shot the passenger, and then taken his own life. A pistol was lying on his lap, and he had slumped forward onto the steering wheel.

"Holster your weapon and lock their door," Jack shouted, as he shoved the shifter into park and locked the driver's door. "Wipe for prints and get back in the monster as quick as you can. We gotta get the hell outta here."

As they slid into their seats, Jack handed Kate his taser and said, "Stash the tasers. … Do you have an untraceable?"

"Yeah," Kate said. "I have a burner."

"Let me see it for a minute," he said, as he accelerated.

Jack then used her burner to call the Luce County Sheriff's Office. He told the dispatcher, "I'm on my way to Wisconsin, and there is a tan Toyota stopped in the middle of M-28, just west of Newberry. Looks like a road hazard to me. You might want to check it out."

Jack immediately turned the cell off and told Kate, "This burner is burned—it could be traced back to you. Must be destroyed."

"Buckle up," he told Kate. "We gotta get the hell outta here before someone else stops."

As Jack pulled away, both boys made their way to the front out of curiosity.

"What's happening?" Robby asked.

"Car stopped in the road," Jack said. "Everything's fine. We just gotta get to the lake. You guys go back and buckle up. Okay?"

The boys stood silently for a few seconds, and then complied.

After they had gone back to their seats, Kate asked her dad,

"Did you see those glass vials on the floor in front of my guy? Any idea what they were?"

"I didn't," Jack said. "What did they look like? … And you said *vials*. How many were there? More than a couple?"

"I didn't get a close up," Kate replied. "But there were maybe a dozen—give or take. They looked to be about the diameter of a pencil, maybe a little smaller. And probably an inch and a quarter long. Clear glass. Not sure how they were sealed."

"Any writing you could see?" Jack asked.

"All I could see for sure was that it appeared like each of them had a small white label with some Chinese writing on it. And, something was also written in English. Looked like 'C-22.' … Any idea what that might have meant?"

Jack did not verbally respond to her question. Instead, using his own cell, he called Bob's number.

Jack was a little surprised when the former president quickly answered, "Jack, I see you've had your coffee this morning."

"Bob," Jack replied, "are you already on the ground?"

"About an hour and a half out," Bob replied. "What's up?"

"We ran into a bit of a situation down here. We discovered we were being tailed by two of the assholes who burgled my office. We know that by Facial Recognition. So it's most likely legit. They are both dead now—at their own hands. I've got the Luce County Sheriff on the way to deal with them. … But, the real problem is that Kate just told me she had spotted some glass vials in the car, and they sound to me to possibly be that Covid-22 shit."

"Damn!" Bob said, more than a little shocked at the news. "We can't have the local authorities dealing with that! What makes you think that it was Covid-22?"

"They were labeled C-22," Jack replied. "Chinese writing on them too. What else could it mean?"

"I've got to get a team out there immediately," Bob said, after pausing a few seconds. "Luce County, you say?"

"Right," Jack answered. "Westbound on M-28 just west of Newberry."

"Damn it all!" Bob growled. "You know, I thought I had rounded up all those vials. Wasn't expecting this. ... Maybe I should have. Anyway, gotta go." With that, Bob disconnected the call.

Jack then said to himself, "On a scale of absurdity, this whole mess measures off the chart. How in hell did they even know about my weapons vault? Or that I kept sniper rifles in it? And, how did they discover that I'd be out of my house in the first place? So they could break in. Someone had to have told them about the liquor bottles, and that there would be prints on them. Do I have a rat? Must have. Or some damned sophisticated electronics. ... I am going to have to rebuild my entire security system, and my operational protocol. Have I been careless? Maybe I just took it for granted that I was staying ahead of the game. ... I'll get started with the upgrade after we finish this trip. Right now I have to show these boys a good time, and help them get back to normal."

Roger had helped Jack clear out all remaining weapons and other critical materials, securing it in a bank vault just outside Washington D.C. But, that solved only the immediate problem for him. Jack still had a lot of questions seeking answers, and even more doubts regarding the safety of his family.

Kate sat there silently staring straight forward through the windshield. Finally, she spoke: "What is this Covid-22 you are talking about? Is it like that Covid-19?"

"Bob describes it as a relative to Covid-19," Jack answered. "And, it was developed in that same Chinese Wuhan Virology Lab—the one that recently blew up. ... But, according to Bob, there are a few big differences. He says that the information he has states that the new one does not respond to the vaccines developed for Covid-19. HCQ doesn't work on it either. Plus, it is far more communicable, and usually fatal."

"Bio-weaponry at its worst," Kate declared, after weighing his words.

"That appears to be the case."

"Well then," Kate said. "Let's take these boys out and let them catch a few fish ... while we still can."

Epilogue —

Some of Jack's Private Notes During the Mission

These are the private notes that I, Jack Handler, compiled while aboard the USS Jimmy Carter navigating on the Yellow Sea off the coast of South Korea. I read Michael's book after the mission was completed, and I determined that there remained certain aspects about it that required further consideration. So, I discussed it with him. I explained that I had taken some fairly extensive notes during the early stages of the mission, and after he'd read them, he suggested that I might include some of them at the end of his book. What follows are a selection of what Michael and I thought the readers might enjoy reading:

I observed that the captain had the big sub running with basically everything turned off that could generate unnecessary noise. We were, at that time, deep beneath the surface of the Yellow Sea approximately sixty miles south and west of Incheon, which is about thirty miles west of Seoul.

The reactor's cooling system on the USS Jimmy Carter was turned off at that time in order to allow it to run even quieter, using only the recycling of water to cool the reactor. Secrecy over speed was the name of this game.

The plan was to slide slowly north up the Yellow Sea to a point close to the 38th parallel. We would follow a course that would keep us in the deeper waters of that pond, which, in reality was not actually very deep at all—not for a nuclear submarine. In general terms, that body of murky water averaged only 144 feet in depth, which was not nearly what the Navy sought for the big subs.

There was one line, however, which would allow us to be submerged at a depth of around 260 feet. It followed a northern course from Jeju-Do, an island just south and west of Busan, to a point not far from the desired location to the north. It was at that point just south of the 38th that the captain would ascend to a depth of 190 feet so the UOES3 could be successfully launched. After releasing the mini-sub, he would take the big one back down once again to the maximum depth permitted by the geography, and then proceed south several miles. There he would shut it down, and wait.

During these hours I spent on the USS Jimmy Carter I was in communication with Roger on a regular basis. He informed me that while he and Bob did have a lot to get done in a relatively short amount of time, they were still able to lay the proper groundwork to make this mission successful.

Roger explained to me that even though the US always had several spy satellites locked in geosynchronous orbits looking at various portions of North Korea, Bob was able to sneak one of them over slightly to give him a near perfect view of the Yellow Sea in the vicinity of the Sohae Satellite Launching Site. One of the great advantages of this particular satellite was that it was equipped to detect and virtually identify not only surface ships that might threaten the USS Jimmy Carter, but also Chinese submarines on the hunt for US mini-subs. In general terms, this class of satellite allowed our military to know the whereabouts of every major piece of equipment assigned to the Chinese Navy. But even more significant, this satellite spelled out in detail not only what their location was, but also, to a large extent, could actually predict their intentions.

I did, during this time, go over the details of the various legs of the mission with Henry and the Navy SEAL team—not just once or twice, but several times, and in a pretty extensive fashion. Even though each of the SEALs had thoroughly practiced his individual role in the mission, they all realized that there would be one or several occasions which would require improvising. It's just always that way—they all knew it. And, to a man, they all sought to be ready for when surprises struck.

"Once we successfully make it over into North Korean waters," I repeated to the group several times, "and become secured to the friendly North Korean fishing boat, we will be towed in as close as possible to the targeted landing area. This will be near Oma-Do, which is a small island just off the North Korean coast, and only a few miles east of the Sohae Satellite Launching Station."

After the hookup, the plan was for the crew of the North Korean fishing boat to continue deploying their nets just as they normally would. And, eventually, they would get us in to an appropriate drop-off point, near Oma-Do, and there disconnect us. The fishing boat would then work itself out from the shore, continuing to fish, while we pushed in on the mini-sub. At the appropriate point, our mini-sub would be shut down, and we would make our way on in with the torpedo modules, and two additional sets of scuba diving gear. Once we had appropriately stowed the diving gear on shore, we would set about completing the rest of our mission.

That, in general terms, is how Bob and Roger had laid out the logistics involved in getting our team to the launch site.

After completing the work at Sohae, we were to basically reverse the process we used to get there.

We would retrieve the diving equipment, suit up ourselves and the defectors, swim back out to and board the SDV, and then head back toward the 38th.

Hopefully, we would be able to find that same (or a similar) North Korean fishing boat, and connect with it. Were the connection not to happen, we would be forced to run on battery as best we could. If that were to be the case, we should be able to make it back to where the USS Jimmy Carter left the backup battery pack, but not much beyond that. And to make it even that far, we would, of course, be forced to conserve as much power as possible.

When I addressed the whole team, this is how I framed it. I said, "If all goes as planned, we will have aboard the mini-sub at that time, the four SEALs, the North Korean defectors, Henry and me. It might be difficult, but, somehow, we will squeeze the North Koreans in. It'll be tight, but doable. And, as I said, if need be, we will switch out the battery module with a totally fresh one.

"Both Bob and Roger believe that we will have conserved enough battery by being towed by the North Korean vessel into the initial drop-off location near Oma-Do, so that we could successfully run on our own power south all the way back over the 38th, to either the battery pack we have hidden there, or to hook up with another South Korean fishing boat.

"If, however, we are able to hook up with the North Korean fishing boat on our trip back out of harm's way, and then hook up with a South Korean fishing vessel as planned, we will not have to be concerned at all about having sufficient battery.

"I should point out that, even though the USS Jimmy Carter will be waiting near the 38th in reserve for the unforeseen, if all goes as planned, we will not attempt to hook up with it again until we have rounded Busan.

"That is the plan, unless using Jimmy Carter should become absolutely necessary. The concern is that to engage again with the USS Jimmy Carter could create too large a footprint.

"If we are able to hook up with the South Korean fishing boat on the return, it will tow us back well into South Korean waters, to an area south of Busan, and it will be there that we will hook up again to the Jimmy Carter. And, from there, our mission will likely carry us to safer waters in Tokyo, or Guam. That's the plan.

"The way the mini-sub has been set up for this mission, we cannot jettison the onboard battery pack if we don't think it will be adequate to get us back. But, we can bypass it. And then, using an umbilical cord sent with us for that purpose, we can attach the fresh battery to the outside of our SDV, and connect to it.

"And, here's the kicker. Roger told me that on the day of the proposed launch Bob is having the military set up a major military exercise—a major exercise. The strategic point of this exercise is to draw attention away from our part of the mission.

"He said that the US Air Force confirmed that its B-1B Lancer bombers will be conducting extensive training in the East China Sea. He said that he had an announcement spelling all that out in a recent Pacific Air Forces Public Affairs press release. I'll read selections of it to you.

"It reads in part:

'The North Korean launch is scheduled to take place on Tuesday morning at approximately ten A.M. North Korean time. ... and a 9th Expeditionary Bomb Squadron B-1B Lancer will land at Andersen Air Force Base, Guam, Tuesday afternoon, after completing a training mission in the East China Sea. ...

'The squadron is deployed to Guam as part of a Bomber Task Force deployment. ...'

"It goes on to say:

'... the Bomber Task Forces support the National Defense game plan of being strategically predictable and operationally unpredictable. ... Four bombers and approximately 200 Airmen from the 9th Bomb Squadron, 7th Bomb Wing, Dyess Air Force Base, Texas, deployed to support Pacific Air Forces' training efforts with allies, partners and joint forces; and strategic deterrence missions to reinforce the rules-based international order in the Indo-Pacific region.'

"The reason for the B-1B training mission," I explained to my team members, "in this specified location, and at this time, should be clear. First of all, China has been behaving in an aggressive fashion throughout the area—particularly with regard to their Navy.

"Of course, China is well aware of the impact of a weapon system such as is exemplified by a squadron of B-1Bs, especially when it comes to a ship-to-air confrontation. I'm sure you all are already aware of the capabilities possessed by such a group of B-1Bs, but here is what the Defense Department's blog spells out regarding what it could do in a theater of war:

'The B-1 is able to carry a larger payload of Joint Air-to-Surface Standoff Missiles and a larger payload of 2,000-pound class Joint Direct Attack Munitions. ... the B-1B is able to carry the LRASM (Long-Range Anti-Ship Missile), giving it an advanced stand-off, counter-ship capability. It also has an advanced self-protection suite and is able to transit at supersonic speeds to enhance offensive and defensive capabilities.

'The last time the B-1Bs were deployed to the region was in 2017. Bombers from the 9th Expeditionary Bomb Squadron supported missions from Andersen AFB in Guam, conducting multiple sequenced bilateral missions with the Republic of Korea Air Force and the Japan Air Self Defense Force.'"

While there were only the four SEALs chosen for the mission, plus Henry, physically sitting in on my pep talk, there were the rest of the platoon—another twelve SEALs—listening in via a sound system on the USS Jimmy Carter. They were out of Pearl Harbor, Hawaii, and formally designated as SDVT-1—SEAL Delivery Vehicle Team One.

The Platoon was divided into two squads, each consisting of eight SEALs. Each of those squads was further divided into two elements: Primary and Backup. The Primary element consisted of four SEALs—One through Four. The remaining four members of that squad were designated as the Backup element, also consisting of One through Four.

By design, Henry and I went by our real names—howbeit, only our given names. That was because Bob thought it best if we all remained as anonymous as was practicable. Therefore, the SEALs were granted even greater anonymity than were we. Neither Henry nor I knew any of SEALs by anything other than a number. As for last names on this mission, all of the SEALs shared a common last name: Anonymous. So, each squad was composed of two groups of four, and they were Primary-One through Primary-Four, and Backup-One through Backup-Four.

In all cases, Agent One and Agent Two were the ones who were to work in the field with Henry and me, while Agent Three was the driver, or pilot, of UOES3, and Agent Four worked as navigator.

They all were issued name-tags: AP (A=Squad-1, P=Primary Element) followed by a number 1, 2, 3, or 4. AB stood for Squad-1, Backup Element. BP stood for Squad-2 Primary. And BB stood for Squad-2 Backup Element. If either a One, Two, Three or Four on a squad's Primary Element somehow became ineligible or disabled, the corresponding member of the Backup element would step in and assume the duties of the member leaving the mission.

"Yes, Jack, I have a question," one of the SEALs announced.

"Identify yourself before you speak, please," I requested.

"SEAL AP Two," the SEAL said. "We've been briefed by Lieutenant Commander Grady as to what is expected of us on this mission, individually. But he did not fill us in on what would be the ultimate objective. Such as, what we are intending to accomplish with it. Are you prepared to paint that picture for us? Or is that not for us to know just yet?"

"I would imagine that your commander told you everything

you were supposed to know," I replied. "At least enough so that you can adequately perform your jobs. You're all aware that we are delivering a package that Washington wants installed in the missile that the North Koreans are about to launch. Your job is to help Henry and me deliver that package to the right people, at the right time. The right people would be that North Korean couple there who wish to defect to the West. They will accept the package we deliver, they will take care of the associated details, and then they will hitch a ride back with us. And, hopefully, we will all get the hell out of Korea Bay in record-breaking speed."

"My question is," the same SEAL said. "Oh, excuse me. This is SEAL AP Two again. My question is just how far are we going to have to carry that tube—I think, because of its shape, it's been referred to as the torpedo. I'm talking about the larger one. I hefted it back at the base. It's pretty damn heavy—even for the four of us. Is there going to be a vehicle or something that we're going use to move this thing? Or are we just going to carry it?"

"Yes," I replied. "The male defector will meet us only a short distance from where we come on land. We will carry it up the beach and load it in his truck. It weighs only about four hundred pounds. Heavy, but not insurmountably so. Four of us can handle it. After we get that on the truck, as you know, there is a second separate package. It's much lighter. We will get that loaded on as well. The five of us will ride in the truck a couple miles. Hidden there he will have a tracked all-terrain vehicle to take it the rest of the way.

"But, before we send the torpedo on its way, we will first slide the second package into that torpedo—we will do that after it has been loaded on his truck. Once he delivers it to his fiancée, she, with the help of her technical crew, will see to it that it is properly installed inside the missile. The four of us—two SEALs, Henry and me—will wait in the woods until we receive a signal that the task has been completed. The job is finished once the fully-activated torpedo has been successfully mounted inside the missile, and they have signaled us to that effect. At that time we will go back to where we left the truck. And then the four of us will use the truck to head back to the beach.

"When they can get away, the couple will return to the all-terrain vehicle, and use it to transport themselves to where we are waiting for them on the beach. When they arrive, we will all put on our diving gear, re-board the mini-sub, and prepare to head back to friendly waters.

"We will wait at the beach a maximum of thirty minutes for the defecting couple to take care of their business, and to reconnect with us. If they do not reappear and join us within that time, we will be forced to leave without them. Those are our orders. And that's what we will do."

"Jack, this is Number Three speaking—AP-3: I drive the UOES3. That is, as you know, the mini-sub. Tell me, how long do we wait? That is if none of you make it back, what do we do back in the UOES3?"

"The clock starts when we hit the beach," I said. "That would be at 39.647N, 124.738E. That's our Landing Target. Fixed point of reference is an island called Oma-Do. After we all off, take the UOES3 out five hundred feet from shore. To approximately 39.648N, 124.741E, and there wait. The water in that area is quite shallow, but you will find it to be one hundred feet or deeper once you're five hundred feet off shore. I've affixed all of these coordinates on your control panel. Anyway, after we've gone ashore, if we are not back in four hours, then pull out. As we've discussed, do not use your radio under any condition. Just head out to deep water.

"And then, if all hell breaks loose, remember that no one should be taken alive. Period. We've talked about that before. And that goes for every last one of us. As for you especially, you must not let our equipment be captured. You have each received a small L-pill. That stands for 'lethal pill.' You know what that's all about. If you are forced to take one, you will be dead within a few minutes. I repeat, if capture becomes imminent, we should all terminate our lives. Being captured is not an option. The L-pill is virtually painless, irreversible, and very fast.

"It should be very clear that we are going to have to move along swiftly. Not wasting any time at all. We've a lot to do, and we must get it all done. Take too long, and we're going to be left. And, again, there can be no survivors. No one understands torture better than the North Koreans. It would be far better for us to die quickly than to undergo the sort of treatment that awaits capture.

"I have preprogrammed these coordinates in each of our GPS modules. If you sense you are about to be captured, trigger the destruct button on the top of your module. It's a failsafe switch above the pilot's seat. And there's a second such switch located in the main compartment. But, before you activate that button, instruct everyone on board to take their L-pill. That will effectively destroy the device and make all stored information unusable, if not totally irretrievable. It, also, must not be captured.

"Under any normal circumstances, the members of a SEAL team would be training for this mission at the base in Pearl Harbor, Hawaii. And, only after the team's captain was totally comfortable that his men were prepared for every contingency that might be demanded of them, would he clear them to move into range of the attack.

"But the high level of urgency, which was the case this time, did not allow for the standard level of training. This mission was to be thought of as a 'One-Off Endeavor.' I have been told that every single member of this team was fully aware of the extreme pressure this mission was under.

"The North Korean Hwasong-21 missile launch is scheduled to take place during a four-hour window starting in forty-two hours. For our mission to succeed, training needed to be carried out in a hurry. So, that's what this meeting is all about—urgency, coupled with at least a degree of sound preparation."

When I shared with the men the dire warning against being captured alive, the captain of the team, which happened to be AP-1, cringed at my words. While he did not open his mouth, I could tell that he was steaming. "We don't need this son-of-a-bitch comin' in here and lecturing us on protocol," I could just tell he was thinking. "Every one of these men know what those crazy Norks are capable of. So this asshole had just better shut the hell up about that shit."

I caught his fixed glare of chagrin, and I made eye contact with him. Perhaps I misinterpreted his state of mind. And he remained silent, so I moved on.

Shortly after this one of the SEALs said, "I have a question. As a member BB-3, I am wondering if we will be receiving any additional training? Other than what we are just now experiencing on this ship? Will there be any further hands-on training? Or is this pretty much it?"

"As I explained earlier," I replied, "this is it. Far from ideal, I know. The time constraints we're faced with here mean that there are no further training options open to us."

"Fair enough," BB-3 replied. "We're very good at improvising. I do have one more question—if it's okay. As part of B backup, where will I be when the A Team goes in? Will the backups even be close enough to jump in, should we be needed? Will there be more than one than one SDV? And if so, what does that mean for members of the second team backups?"

"We are deploying a second SDV," I replied. "It will contain Squad Number 1's backup team. That second SDV will remain in the second DDS mounted on the top of the USS Jimmy Carter. If something goes amiss with the first group—while it is still in proximity to the USS Jimmy Carter—then and only then will the backup element be called upon.

"Once Squad Number 1 crosses the 38th parallel, the backup team will stand down and re-enter the USS Jimmy Carter.

"Any more questions?"

All sixteen SEALs remained silent for several seconds. Finally one of them spoke up.

"AP-1 speaking. I'm sure everyone here today would agree— SEALs take a lot of pride in what they do. We all like to think that we make a difference. With this mission, when it's over, will we know if we've succeeded or failed? And if so, how will we know it?"

I thought about his question for a long moment, and then I spoke:

"This mission is unique in that there will be several angles from which to view it. Some of those angles will only be discernible in the future. If it succeeds totally, you will have no difficulty seeing what you've accomplished. Quite literally, it could save thousands of American lives—perhaps even many, many more than that. That is, if it is overwhelmingly successful. Of course, you dare not ever talk about it. But, you will be able to recognize its benefit, and take pride in it. I know the SEALs to be the best there is. So, I trust you will have no problem keeping everything about this mission to yourselves. And that means forever. You never get to talk about it.

"If, through this mission, we simply manage to survive, and if we help the couple defect from the clutches of the Democratic People's Republic of Korea, and relocate to the West, and nothing more, the mission will still have been marginally successful. Their lives spared—that alone, would be significant.

"But, if all, or even some of us, make it back to Pearl Harbor or Guam alive, with the UOES3 intact, then that will still afford the mission a high level of success, and you can feel good about that. In fact, to view the merits of the mission ex post facto, given the dearth of training that we are giving you, there is not a way in which this mission could possibly fail due to your efforts. Any and all lack of success will clearly rest solely on me. That's how I see it."

I paused for a moment, seeking out and making eye contact with nearly all of the SEALs as I waited for additional questions. While they were well-trained fighting men, I knew that they were very young, and that in only a few years I could be looking at my Red and Robby. Each of these men represented the best America had to offer—so courageous, and with such a bright future ahead. Yet, they were still very young.

Hearing nothing but silence, I grew satisfied that there were no more questions. I picked up a stack of sealed envelopes and passed them through the group. Each of the envelopes had a name on it: AP-1, AP-2, AP-3, etc.

"Each of you should remove and open the set of instructions that bears your name," I told them. "Study it until you're comfortable with your role in the mission. And then run your sheet through the shredder by the entry door. I've had it placed there for that very purpose."

At that time all of the SEALs opened and read the single sheet that each envelope contained. They then stood to their feet, in virtual accord, and one by one they destroyed the evidence.

That was the end of the meeting.

Henry and I were finished as well. I was tired of talking, and it was obvious that Henry had tired of listening to me talk. It was just as obvious that the rest of the team did not want to discuss it further either—not with me, nor with the other team members. We had all simply reconciled ourselves to the fact that the mission had little chance of going totally as planned—there were just too many major loose ends. We all realized that it would take an amazing amount of luck for the SDV to even make it intact to the North Korean shore. After all, there was probably no better-guarded strip of real estate in the world than was the territory of North Korea.

But, even if some of us were to make it ashore alive, the danger of the mission was only just beginning. Next we had to hook up with a defecting North Korean technician, then infiltrate the terrain all the way to the principal, super secretive launch pad for the testing of North Korean Intercontinental Ballistic Missiles. And on, and on, and on. Each small part of the overall plan provided its own steep precipice to climb.

What we were about to undertake reminded me of one of my favorite documentaries. It was that of the two young mountain climbers who determined in their hearts to attack the impossibly steep cliff—the infamous "Dawn Wall"—of El Capitan in Yosemite National Park. From the beginning of time, until January 14, 2015, no human being had ever accomplished it as an authentic free climb. Day after day, through storms and high winds, the two climbers worked and worked, trying one route, and then another. Always they seemed to fail, but they never gave up. Finally, against all odds, after nineteen long days, hands bleeding and relationships destroyed—finally, they made it.

One of the reasons I so appreciated this story was that both of the climbers were totally aware of the fact that all it would take was one angry crosswind, one failed spike, or one blinding ray of sun at an inappropriate time or angle, and they would both be dead. It was abundantly clear that the climbers had determined before they set out on their adventure that they would either reach the peak, or their bodies would someday be scraped up off the bottom—that is, if they were ever to be found at all.

Henry and I had watched the chronicle of the climb together more than once. Both climbers knew what they were up against—climbing the steepest part of El Capitan's face in a snowstorm.

The major difference for us was this: if we failed, some of us would most likely not be so lucky as to have the luxury of a swift death—if captured, our death would come slowly and with great pain, at the hands of the most practiced torture specialists in the world.

Disclaimer

To China with love is not a true story. It is a work of fiction. All US characters, locations, names, situations, and occurrences are purely the product of my imagination. Any resemblance to actual US events or persons (living or dead) is unintentional and coincidental.

Cast of Main Characters in the earlier "Jack Handler" books

(Characters are listed in a quasi-chronological order.)

This book, *To China with Love,* is the fifteenth book in the evolving Jack Handler Saga, and the first book in the third Jack Handler series—*Jack Unchained.* The first series was the *Getting to Know Jack* series, and the second was called *Jack's Justice.* It is intended that each series will contain seven Jack Handler books when complete.

While many of the characters encountered in this book have already made appearances in one or more of the previous Jack

Handler books, if you want a deeper understanding how a character thinks, you can refer to *The Cast* to answer additional backstory questions.

Main characters include:

Jack Handler:

Jack is a good man, in his way. While it is true that he occasionally kills people, it can be argued that most (if not all) of his targets needed killing. Occasionally a somewhat sympathetic figure comes between Jack and his goal. When that happens, Jack's goal comes first. I think the word that best sums up Jack's persona might be "expeditor." He is outcome driven—he makes things turn out the way he wants them to turn out.

For instance, if you were a single mom and a bully were stealing your kid's lunch money, you could send "Uncle Jack" to school with little Billy. Uncle Jack would have a "talk" with the teachers and the principal. With Jack's help, the problem would be solved. But I would not recommend that you ask him how he accomplished it. You might not like what he tells you—if he even responds.

Jack is faithful to his friends and a great father to his daughter. He is also a dangerous and tenacious adversary when situations require it.

Jack Handler began his career as a law enforcement officer. He married a beautiful woman (Beth) of Greek descent while working as a police officer in Chicago. She was a concert violinist and the love of his life. If you were to ask Jack about it, he would quickly tell you he married above himself. So, when bullets intended for him killed her, he admittedly grew bitter. Kate, their daughter, was just learning to walk when her mother was gunned down.

As a single father, Jack soon found that he needed to make more money than his job as a police officer paid. So he went back to college and obtained a degree in criminal justice. Soon he was promoted to the level of sergeant in the Chicago Police Homicide Division.

With the help of a friend, he then discovered that there was much more money to be earned in the private sector. At first he began moonlighting on private security jobs. Immediate success led him to take an early retirement and obtain his private investigator license.

Because of his special talents (obtained as a former army ranger) and his intense dedication to problem solving, Jack's services became highly sought after. While he did take on some of the more sketchy clients, he never accepted a project simply on the basis of financial gain—he always sought out the moral high ground. Unfortunately, sometimes that moral high ground morphed into quicksand.

Jack is now pushing sixty (from the downward side) and he has all the physical ailments common to a man of that age. While it is true that he remains in amazing physical condition, of late he has begun to sense his limitations.

His biggest concern recently has been an impending IRS audit. While he isn't totally confident that it will turn out okay, he remains optimistic.

His problems stem from the purchase of half-interest in a bar in Chicago two decades earlier. His partner was one of his oldest and most trusted friends—Conrad (Connie) O'Donnell.

The principal reason he considered the investment in the first place was to create a cover for his private security business.

Many, if not most, of his clients insisted on paying him in cash or with some other untraceable commodity. At first he tried getting rid of the cash by paying all of his bills with it. But even though he meticulously avoided credit cards and checks, the cash continued to accumulate.

It wasn't that he was in any sense averse to paying his fair share of taxes. The problem was that if he did deposit the cash into a checking account, and subsequently included it in his filings, he would then at some point be required to explain where it had come from.

He needed an acceptable method of laundering, and his buddy's bar seemed perfect.

But it did not work out exactly as planned. Four years ago the IRS decided to audit the bar, which consequently exposed his records to scrutiny.

Jack consulted with one of his old customers, a disbarred attorney/CPA, to see if this shady character could get the books straightened out enough for Jack to survive the audit and avoid federal prison.

The accountant knew exactly how Jack earned his money and that the sale of a few bottles of Jack Daniels had little to do with it.

Even though his business partner and the CPA talked a good game about legitimacy, Jack still agonized when thoughts of the audit stormed through his mind. This problem was further complicated when Conrad was murdered in what was thought a botched robbery. Connie's lazy son, Conrad Jr., inherited his father's share of the bar.

A year earlier Jack had been convicted and sentenced for attacking a veteran detective, Calvin Brandt. The day that his conviction was overturned, an attempt was made on his life inside a federal prison camp (*Assualt on Sugar Island*). He believed at the time, and still does, that Calvin Brandt had been responsible for contracting the Aryan Alliance to carry out the hit.

Fortunately for Jack, Chuchip (Henry) Kalyesveh a Native American of the Hopi tribe, who was also an inmate at the prison camp, came to his rescue.

Kate Handler:

Kate, Jack's daughter and a New York homicide detective, is introduced early and appears often in this series. Kate is beautiful. She has her mother's olive complexion and green eyes. Her trim five-foot-eight frame, with her long auburn hair falling nicely on her broad shoulders, would seem more at home on the runway than in an interrogation room. But Kate is a seasoned New York homicide detective. In fact, she is thought by many to be on the fast track to the top—thanks, in part, to the unwavering support of her soon-to-retire boss, Captain Spencer.

Of course, her career was not hindered by her background in law. Graduating Summa Cum Laude from Notre Dame at the age of twenty-one, she went on to Notre Dame Law School. She passed the Illinois Bar Exam immediately upon receiving her JD, and accepted a position at one of Chicago's most prestigious criminal law firms. While her future looked bright as a courtroom attorney, she hated defending "sleazebags."

One Saturday morning she called her father and invited him to meet her at what she knew to be the coffee house he most fancied. It was there, over a couple espressos, that she asked him what he thought about her taking a position with the New York Police Department. She was shocked when he immediately gave his blessing. "Kitty," he said, "you're a smart girl. I totally trust your judgment. You have to go where your heart leads. Just promise me one thing. Guarantee me that you will put me up whenever I want to visit. After all, you are my favorite daughter."

To this Kate replied with a chuckle, "Dad, I'm your only daughter. And you will always be welcome."

In *Murder on Sugar Island (Sugar)*, Jack and Kate team up to solve the murder of Alex Garos, Jack's brother-in-law. This book takes place on Sugar Island, which is located in the northern part of Michigan's Upper Peninsula (just east of Sault Ste. Marie, MI).

Because Kate was Garos's only blood relative living in the United States, he named her in his will to inherit all of his estate. This included one of the most prestigious pieces of real estate on the island—the Sugar Island Resort.

Reg:

In *Jack and the New York Death Mask (Death Mask)*, Jack is recruited by his best friend, Reg (Reginald Black), to do a job without either man having any knowledge as to what that job might entail. Jack, out of loyalty to his friend, accepted the offer. The contract was ostensibly to assassinate a sitting president. However, instead of assisting the plot, Jack and Reg worked to thwart it. Most of this story takes place in New York City, but there are scenes in DC, Chicago, and Upstate New York. Reg is frequently mentioned throughout the series, as are Pam Black and Allison Fulbright. Pam Black is Reg's wife (he was shot at the end of *Death Mask*), and Allison is a former first lady. It was Allison who contracted Reg and Jack to assassinate the sitting president.

Allison:

Allison is a former first lady (with presidential aspirations of her own), and Jack's primary antagonist throughout the series. Usually she fears him enough not to do him or his family physical harm, but she and Jack are not friends. She seems to poke her nose into Jack's business just enough to be a major annoyance.

On a few occasions, however, Allison's anger at Jack reaches a boiling point, and she strikes out against him. To this date, she has been unsuccessful.

Over a year ago Allison suffered a severely debilitating stroke, so her current activities have been dramatically limited, a situation which has provided Jack a bit of a reprieve in his having to worry about what she might be up to vis-à-vis his well-being.

Roger Minsk:

Roger is a member of the Secret Service, and a very good friend to Jack. Roger is also friendly with Bob Fulbright, Allison's husband, and a former president.

Red:

This main character is introduced in *Sugar*. Red is a redheaded fourteen-year-old boy who, besides being orphaned, cannot speak. It turned out that Red was actually the love child of Alex (Jack's brother-in-law) and his office manager. So, Alex not only leaves his Sugar Island resort to Kate, he also leaves his Sugar Island son for her to care for.

Red has a number of outstanding characteristics, first and foremost among them, his innate ability to take care of himself in all situations. When his mother and her husband were killed in a fire, Red chose to live on his own instead of submitting to placement in foster care.

During the warmer months, he lived in a hut he had pieced together from parts of abandoned homes, barns, and cottages, and he worked at Garos's resort on Sugar Island. In the winter, he would take up residence in empty fishing cottages along the river.

Red's second outstanding characteristic is his loyalty. When put to the test, Red would rather sacrifice his life than see his friends hurt. In *Sugar*, Red works together with Jack and Kate to solve the mystery behind the killing of Jack's brother-in-law (and Red's biological father), Alex Garos.

The third thing about Red that makes him stand out is his inability to speak. As the result of a traumatic event in his life, his voice box was damaged, resulting in his disability. Before Jack and Kate entered his life, Red communicated only through an improvised sign system and various grunts.

When Kate introduced him to a cell phone and texting, Red's life changed dramatically.

Robby:

Robby is Red's best friend. When his parents are murdered, Robby moves into the Handler home and becomes a "brother" to Red. Robby and Red are now virtually inseparable.

Buddy:

Buddy is Red's golden retriever.

Bill Green:

One other character of significance introduced in *Sugar* is Bill Green, the knowledgeable police officer who first appears in Joey's coffee shop. He also assumes a major role in subsequent books of the series, after he becomes sheriff of Chippewa County.

Captain Spencer:

Captain Spencer is Kate's boss in New York. The captain has been planning his retirement for a long time, but has not yet been able to pull the trigger. Kate is his protégée, and he almost seems to fear leaving the department until her career is fully developed.

Paul Martin and Jill Talbot:

Two new characters do emerge in *Sugar Island Girl, Missing in Paris (Missing)*. They are Paul Martin and Jill Talbot. They do not appear in subsequent stories.

Legend:

Legend is one of the main characters in the sixth book of the series, *Wealthy Street Murders (Wealthy)*. In this story, Jack and Kate work with Red, Robby, and Legend to solve a series of murders. Wrapped up in a rug and left for dead at the end of *Wealthy*, with Buddy's help he lives to play an important role in *Ghosts*, and in this *Sault*.

Mrs. Fletcher:

Mrs. Fletcher, one of the caretakers at Kate's resort on Sugar Island, progressively plays a more prominent role as an occasional care-provider for the two boys. And, of course, she becomes embroiled in the intrigue.

Unfortunately, Fletcher and her husband are murdered in an earlier segment of this series: *Dogfight*.

Sheriff Griffen:

The sheriff first appears in *Murders in Strangmoor Bog (Strangmoor)*. He is sheriff of Schoolcraft County, which includes Strangmoor Bog, and Seney Wildlife Preserve.

Angel and her mother Millie:

In *Strangmoor*, the seventh and last book in the "Getting to know Jack" series, two new main characters are introduced: Angel and Millie Star.

Angel, a precocious fun-loving redhead (with a penchant for quick thinking and the use of big words), immediately melts the hearts of Red and Robby and becomes an integral part of the Handler saga. In *Deadwood*, everything changed for Millie and Angel.

Lindsay Hildebrandt and Calvin Brandt:

These two significant new characters are introduced in *Ghosts of Cherry Street (and the Cumberbatch Oubliette)*. Lindsay, a rookie detective in the Grand Rapids Police Department, quickly becomes a special person in Jack's life. If you were to ask her if she is dating Jack, Lindsay (who is about two decades younger than Jack) would immediately inform you that people their age don't *date*. But she does admit that they are good friends and occasionally see each other socially.

They have in common the fact that they both lost their spouses in a violent fashion. Lindsay's husband, also a Grand Rapids detective, was shot and killed several years earlier. This crime has not yet been solved.

Calvin Brandt, a veteran Grand Rapids detective, does not get along with anyone. And that is especially true of Jack Handler. Jack would be the first to admit that he was not an innocent party with regard to this ongoing conflict.

Chuchip Kalyesveh:

Chuchip generally goes by the name of Henry because he has found most people butcher his Native American first name.

Jack first met Henry in a federal prison camp where both were serving time. They became good friends when Henry saved Jack's life by beating up four other inmates who had been contracted to kill him. Jack says he has never met another man as physically imposing as his friend Henry.

Now that both are free men, Henry works for Jack at the Sugar Island Resort. And, sometimes, he partners with Jack (unofficially, of course) to help out with some of his tougher private security cases. And, of course, he has absorbed more than a couple rounds intended for Jack. Expect to learn more about Henry as subsequent Jack Handler books roll off the press.

Emma:

Emma (Legs) is a very attractive thirty-something-ish contract killer. Prior to this book, Emma makes her first powerful appearance in *Dogfight*. You should expect to see her again?

Here are the Amazon links to all my Jack Handler books to date:

Jack and the New York Death Mask:	http://amzn.to/MVpAEd
Murder on Sugar Island:	http://amzn.to/1u66DBG
Superior Peril:	http://amzn.to/LAQnEU
Superior Intrigue:	http://amzn.to/1jvjNSi
Sugar Island Girl Missing in Paris:	http://amzn.to/1g5c66e
Wealthy Street Murders:	http://amzn.to/1mb6NQy
Murders in Strangmoor Bog:	http://amzn.to/1osAjJ8
Ghosts of Cherry Street:	http://amzn.to/1PvWfJd
Assault on Sugar Island:	http://amzn.to/2n3vcyL
Dogfight:	http://amzn.to/2F7OkoM
Murder at Whitefish Point:	http://amzn.to/2CxlAmC
Superior Shoal:	https://amzn.to/2pbM89v
From Deadwood to Deep State:	https://amzn.to/330eElx
Sault:	https://amzn.to/3gq21Dj
To China with Love: